This book is part of Stockholm Text's
Scandinavian Crime Series.
To find more titles in the series, make
sure to regularly visit
www.stockholmtext.com.

STRANGE BIRD

"One of the best [Swedish] mystery novels of all time…
Well-written, well-reasoned and credible in a very scary way."

— **Dagens Nyheter,** Sweden's largest and most
influential daily paper

STRANGE BIRD

ANNA JANSSON

First Published in the United States in 2013 by
Stockholm Text
Stockholm, Sweden

stockholm@stockholmtext.com
www.stockholmtext.com

Copyright © Anna Jansson 2012, by agreement with Grand Agency

TRANSLATION BY Paul Norlén
COVER DESIGN BY Ermir Peci

Printed in the United States of America

1 3 5 7 9 8 6 4 2

ISBN 978-91-87173-95-0

Chapter 1

Ruben Nilsson stepped into the summer twilight to tap his pipe out against the railing of the porch. If he had known how few hours he had left to live, perhaps his priorities would have been different. The wind had died down, the trees cast long shadows across the well-tended lawn, and he stood there feeling melancholy. Perhaps it was the scent that made him think of Angela, the sweet scent of mock orange that came in bursts with the evening breeze. The blossoms hung in large clusters over the stone wall, shining strangely white in the dim light. When Ruben reached for the branch, petals fell like snowflakes across the ground. Too late. The mock orange must have just been in full bloom. He had not noticed; in fact, the scent was a bit stale, the leaves already wrinkled with age and brown at the edges. He was too late, just like when he loved Angela Stern but couldn't find the right words. It still hurt to think about it.

At the Midsummer party at the Jakobssons' house in Eksta, she had sat down beside him, straightened his shirt collar, and slipped her arm under his as they left the table.

They strolled in the garden in a silence that felt increasingly awkward. He was walking arm-in-arm under the lindens with the most beautiful woman on the island of Gotland, but all he could think of to say was that the price of wool didn't look too good but the potatoes were doing fine. She listened patiently and then pointed toward the bower. He would never forget the look she gave him right then. Hidden from the others in the green grotto of leaves, he took her in his arms. There had been an understanding between them all evening—glances that could not be mistaken, her light touch when she approached him. The scent of wild strawberries was intoxicating. The thin fabric of her dress stretched across her breasts and over the soft rounding of her hips—it embarrassed him and made him mute and very aware of the reactions in his own body. Not long ago they were children; she was a girl he played with. Angela with her angelic hair like spun gold in a cloud over her shoulders, the blue-green eyes and slightly protruding upper lip he was compelled to kiss. In the leafy grotto he summoned up his courage and did it. It was a somewhat unsuccessful kiss, their teeth scraping together, and they both pulled back in embarrassment. He tried again more carefully and noticed that she softened. Her hands caressed his back, slowly gliding along his muscles and in under his shirt. He felt a light shudder throughout his body as her nails lightly scratched his skin and her breathing became more rapid. His hand felt its way into her panties and she caught it in mid-motion and held it in hers.

"How much do you love me, Ruben?" She looked him right in the eyes without turning away, waiting for him to say the impossible password. How much do you want me? How much do you love me? And he answered by pressing his throbbing member against her stomach. She recoiled and he guided her hand where he wanted, so that she would feel his hardness and understand how much he wanted her, how much he longed for and thought about her. Stop! Her body turned rigid. He tried to touch her but she turned aside. The smile on her face was gone. When he still did not say anything, she pushed him away and ran over to the others. He caught up with her, tried to embrace her from behind. Say something you stupid idiot; whisper the words she wants to hear. But the words never came, not then and barely even now, fifty years later, when he thought about what he should have said to change the course of history. How much do you love me? How do you answer that? Can love be weighed and measured? She'd torn out of his grasp with a fury he could not understand and did not look at him the rest of that Midsummer night. And then—it was too late.

Ruben turned his pale blue eyes toward the evening sky, tears running down his face. These days he often felt paralyzed. As a child you cry because you're sad or you've hurt yourself; when you're old you cry because you're moved when you hear "In the Good Old Summertime" or recall a long-ago love. He adjusted the crotch of his pants and smiled to himself. The body remembers too.

High above the dovecote a flock of pigeons was circling. Ruben stood quietly and watched as they landed on the sheet metal roof, cooing and strutting back and forth before they went in for the night. He knew them by appearance and name. General von Schneider, Mr. Pomoroy, Sir Toby, Mr. Winterbottom, Panic, Cocoa, and Sven Dufva crowded and pecked at each other as they went through the opening to see their females and chicks and then get supper. Always the same routine.

Farthest out on the roof ridge sat a new pigeon who must have followed the flock home. A sturdy, light brown speckled bird with a white head. Probably a male. He would have to take a closer look at it. Ruben crouched through the low door to the out-building and slipped up the creaking wooden stairs to the dovecote in the loft and over to the sack of hemp seed. Goodies that ought to entice the new pigeon. He adjusted the opening and the grate so the birds could go into the dovecote but not out, and waited in the darkness while the setting sun painted the sky and sea reddish orange in a glowing river of light.

The birds were fighting over food. Von Schneider pecked Winterbottom on the head and got a wing in return. Anyone who thinks a dove is a believable symbol of peace is mistaken. Ruben had said so on many occasions. No bird is more aggressive and domineering than a dove, but they serve well as a symbol of love and fidelity. The best flyers are males whose females are sitting on eggs or have chicks. They give their all to get home quickly, something to keep in mind when you select homing pigeons for a competition. Ruben had already started to pick out the pigeons he would enter in the club's race over the weekend. The pigeons would be released from Gotska Sandön early Saturday morning. Before that, the pigeon owners' clocks would be calibrated so that they were synchronized according to official time. That way you avoided rancorous discussions afterward when the average time in kilometers per hour was being calculated. There were those who cheated, of course. Petter Cederroth had drilled a barely visible hole in the O on the manufacturer's name in the glass. Then he used a pin to stop the clock at a point when he could record a winning time. To keep from being discovered, right before the clock opening he pushed the hands forward so the time would tally. Smart, if his wife hadn't spilled the beans when she'd had a few drinks. Offhand, Ruben could not think of anyone as communicative as Sonja Cederroth under the influence of alcohol.

If this had concerned big money, like in the national competitions, and not just the "Silver Dove" traveling trophy,

Cederroth would have been kicked out of the homing pigeon association. But the club hushed it up. He was usually so darned nice, and good at brewing Gotland ale too. That must be said in his defense.

The newly arrived male pigeon lingered out on the roof and was in no hurry, even if he looked in with curiosity now and then. Ruben picked up the binoculars and studied him. A truly powerful bird, although a bit worn out after the flight. Marked with a metal ring around the foot. A foreigner—in Sweden, the pigeons have plastic rings. A flying tourist on a visit? He ought to be more hungry than suspicious and come in. It was annoying to have to fetch him from the sheet-metal roof.

Ruben crept out onto the roof with a cage. The pigeon fluttered up in the air and then sat on the far end of the roof by the gutter and watched as the cage was set. A stick with a nylon line held up the hatch and inside the net cage were appetizing hemp seeds on top of the feed, like gravy on mashed potatoes. Come now! Come closer! Ruben crept back and stood motionless behind the wall with the nylon line tense in his hand. Come now! A little more. There now, you're hungry after all. The pigeon looked at the cage with eyelids half-closed and smiled teasingly. Ruben thought it looked scornful as it twitched its neck. What kind of bird are you and where do you come from? It was exciting to think about how far the pigeon might have flown.

Cederroth had bragged all spring that he had taken in a pigeon from Poland, but no one saw it before it flew away, and Jönsson said he'd had a bird from Denmark last summer and recently one from Skåne. There now. Go in now. No. The pigeon turned abruptly in front of the cage and marched like a straight-backed general in the opposite direction. Then turned completely around at the gutter. Now he was coming back. Ruben was prepared. He held his breath. Not a sound was allowed to frighten the bird.

Anna Jansson

The pigeon took the decisive steps; he could no longer resist the goodies. The hatch closed. Yes, there it was.

Ruben carried the cage with the pigeon across the roof and did not open it until he was in the dovecote. It was truly a splendid bird, even if its plumage was somewhat battered after the long journey. Ruben spread out the wings, one by one, in his hand and studied them carefully. Two quills were missing on the right and on the left one quill was short but growing. To see the marking on the ring more closely he had to put on his glasses. He found them on the wooden molding above the transport cages, wiped off the white dust, and inspected the ring. The letters looked Russian. This was really interesting. Ruben gave the pigeons clean water and fed them a corn mixture. Then he went into the house to call Cederroth. But he was at his brother's in Martebo and was not expected home until late that evening, said Sonja.

A glance at the free ICA store calendar made Ruben realize that it was already the end of June. He sank down on a chair and looked out the window at the sunset's magnificent play of color as the red disk slowly slipped down into the sea. He found it to be a great blessing and solace for the soul to live where he could see the sun go down into the sea. He got up to pour a cup of coffee and cut a slice of rye bread, which he layered with Falu sausage—two thick pieces on a sturdy base of butter, no plastic balls of artificial margarine for him. The sea was breathtakingly beautiful to look at this evening. It almost made him devout and tenderhearted— full of thoughts about what exists beyond time.

He thought of the word reconciliation and he thought about Angela. Is there a more beautiful word than reconciliation? Making peace with what has happened, not forgetting it or belittling it, but remembering it without pain. Being reconciled to the fact that it didn't turn out the way

10

you'd thought and hoped for in your heart. Getting to the point where you can reconcile yourself with your fate.

It was Angela's father who had started raising pigeons. When he got tired of them and started playing golf instead, Ruben and his little brother Erik took over the pigeons and moved the operation to their place on Södra Kustvägen in Klinte. But Erik lost interest, too, and acquired a motorcycle instead. And then everything went wrong.

Chapter 2

In the first light of dawn Angela came walking across the sea toward him. The train of her thin dress merged with the foam on the waves and her long hair was spun by morning light. In her emerald eyes, the sea was glistening. She was holding a white dove in her hands and released it up toward the sky. Come. She extended her arms toward him. Come along now. Her smile was just as alluring as he remembered it from that fateful Midsummer Eve. Come, you too can walk on water. But he turned his back to the sea and no longer saw her. And she came like darkness, like a storm over land. The trees bent down. The clumps of reeds were pressed against the ground; the birds fell silent and lightning crackled like fireworks between the clouds. But he refused to listen to her, closed his eyes and covered his ears. Then she came as a scent. How do you defend yourself against a scent that recreates memories?

When Ruben woke up he realized he had been crying. He felt a longing for Angela all over his body; he felt it as an ache in his belly. Angela. Angela. How can regret suddenly become so strong? In his dream she was holding a white dove.

He could still remember how her hands with their short, blunt thumbs had held the injured pigeon that the hawk attacked, back in a different time when everything was still possible. It was one of the first times they met.

Her small hands stroked the pigeon's back. "You poor thing. We'll take care of you."

While Angela tried to feed the pigeon porridge and made a bed for it in the softest nest, Ruben loaded his shotgun and waited for the hawk, which was circling high above the dovecote. His finger rested on the trigger, waiting until the bird of prey settled in the pine tree next to the outbuilding. Then he fired. The hawk fell dead to the ground. In triumph he carried the bird by its legs and threw it onto the kitchen table so that Angela could see that the guilty party had been punished. He did not expect her to start crying. But she did.

"How could you? How could you just shoot it?"

He stood there in the kitchen with his arms hanging by his side, unable to say a word in his defense. The only sound was the buzzing of a fly caught in the sticky strip of tape hanging from the kitchen lamp, and it droned on until his head was empty of thoughts.

Ruben went to the library as soon as it opened. Once he was back home, he had his morning coffee while he listened to the weather report. Then he went out to the dovecote to take a look at the new pigeon. The bird had seemed tired and worn out after the flight. Its eyes were a little dull. Not surprising given how far it had flown. But with its powerful physique, the pigeon should have been in good form today. As a breeding pigeon it was a really fine specimen. Cederroth would be green with envy. The pigeon had come all the way from Biaroza in Belarus, imagine that. The librarian had helped Ruben search on the Internet to find a list of country codes and designations of homing pigeon clubs in various countries, and finally found where the pigeon belonged. A Belarusian. He had reported it as found. If no owner got in touch he could keep it. He was hoping for that.

With these thoughts Ruben Nilsson went up the stairs to his dovecote, and came out again even more thoughtful. The foreign bird was lying dead on the stone floor below the window. In the overcast daylight the pigeon's plumage looked almost gray. It was not injured, as far as he could see. The other birds might have attacked him in competition for food and females. But there were no such signs. When he picked up the limp body he saw the heap of pigeon droppings on the floor, loose. Perhaps it had eaten something bad. Or was it sick? He caressed its wings thoughtfully. It was truly a beautiful, well-built pigeon.

At first Ruben thought he would bury the White Russian next to the garden wall, where he had made a bird cemetery and interred other bird bodies one by one, but it felt like a nuisance to go for the spade in the outbuilding. The aches in his hips were worse than usual. He could just as well bury it later; there was no rush. On his way into the house he caught sight of his neighbor Berit Hoas, who was hanging laundry behind her house. It was a source of constant conflict that Ruben's pigeons circled over her sheets, dropping calling cards on the clean laundry. As if he could stop them. Pigeons drop their load as they climb toward the sky. It's a law of nature. She could just as well hang her darned laundry in front of the house instead, but she didn't want to. What would people say? Yes, what *would* they say? So you're keeping yourself clean? If they have so little to worry about they could at least grant her that, he thought. Berit was of a different opinion.

"Are you home already?" he asked to be polite.

"Yes, the children have had their breakfast and I don't

need to fix the noon meal because they're taking a sack lunch. They're playing a match against Dalhem today. My goodness. This soccer camp goes on for three weeks and then I'll be off. I'm thinking about visiting my sister on Fårö. The job doesn't pay all that much, but it's fun—they're hungry and appreciate the food. By the way, I have some creamed morels that I took out of the freezer. Last year's. I need to clear things out to make room for this year's mushrooms, so it will be good to finish them up. You're welcome to come over for a bite if it suits you. If you hadn't planned anything else, I mean."

"Thank you. I was going to fry up a piece of sausage, but that can wait till tomorrow. Give me a call when it's time."

Ruben limped over to the tool shed to get a spade, but as he was standing with his hand on the catch he changed his mind. Cederroth would never believe him if he didn't see the pigeon with his own eyes. It was almost better if it stayed in the galvanized tub on the ground floor of the outbuilding until Petter had time to stop by. He was out driving his taxi a lot, that Petter Cederroth. Although maybe with a wife like his it was safest to flee the house so his ears didn't wear out.

Instead of burying the pigeon, Ruben rode his bicycle down toward the harbor to see about getting a couple of smoked flounders. At the newsstand he stopped and read the headlines on the placard. "Tips for Better Vacation Sex." Ruben laughed. If the plague or civil war had broken out in Sweden the headline couldn't have been bigger. Swedes had to be told the most basic things, such as how to perpetuate the species, when animals like rabbits with a much smaller brain manage all on their own. Vacation sex sounded like some kind of hunting season requiring a permit. Do it this way.

Uninvited thoughts of Angela appeared again, although he tried to push them aside with more important things. It was time to order more wood and the packing on the faucet in the kitchen needed to be changed and he had to drive in to the Central Association in town and get feed for the pigeons. Angela, what do you want from me? It was getting impossible for him to defend himself against the memories that kept crowding in.

Angela tore herself from his embrace and ran off to the others who were gathered around Erik and his new Harley-Davidson.

"Will you take me for a spin?" she said and Erik nodded. Ruben watched her climb up on the pillion and take hold of Erik's new leather jacket. In a cloud of dust they took off down the gravel road.

Damn it, now it really got bad! In a weak moment Ruben wished his brother bad luck and misfortune on the ride; he was willing to admit that afterward. Not to anyone else, but to himself. But he truly never wished for what happened next. As a child you have ideas that you can control the world with mental power. As an adult you sometimes have relapses to that magical way of thinking. When Angela came running back all out of breath with scratches on her face, Ruben felt guilt like a hand squeezing his throat.

"Help! I think Erik's dead! He's not moving. He doesn't answer. He's bleeding! I think he hit his head on a rock. We drove off the road. Come!" Her tense voice broke and she started sobbing. Ruben had not meant that he wanted to see his brother dead. He wanted to see him less arrogant and a little chastened, that was all.

They ran in the direction Angela pointed. Ruben arrived first at the scene of the accident, his eyes blurry from sweat or perhaps it was tears.

"Erik!" My dear little brother! He didn't answer. He

didn't move from under the motorcycle, his body at a strange angle. There was blood on the stone alongside his head and blood stained the white shirtfront alarmingly red.

"Erik!" Ruben bent over to lift the motorcycle and got help from several arms. Please let him be alive! He shook his brother's shoulders and held his hand over his face to feel whether he was breathing. The others had gathered behind him.

"How is he? Does he have a pulse?" Ruben found the inside of Erik's wrist. Did he feel a pulse? Perhaps it was his own. He couldn't tell.

"Feel the carotid artery," said Gerd Jakobsson, who often helped out with the district nurse. Then everything got very quiet. A hollow, impatient waiting. And everyone's eyes were turned toward Ruben, as if he could perform miracles and raise his brother from the dead by will. He noticed that in his terror his fingers were pressing too hard and he eased his grip. Yes, there on the neck he felt a pulse. Now he felt it clearly. And now Erik was moving and opening his eyes, and a murmur of voices broke through the silence.

"He needs to go to the hospital; he probably has a concussion," someone said.

"No way!" Erik sat halfway up and then sank back against the ground and held his head. His face was very pale; he tore open his shirt and looked at his stomach. There was a sizeable scratch, but nothing deeper. "What happened to the motorcycle?" he moaned.

Yes, Ruben remembered it as if it happened yesterday. What happened to the motorcycle? was the first thing his brother asked when he regained consciousness. He didn't ask about Angela. She was sitting in the ditch, crying. Erik didn't see her. She could easily have been dead or seriously injured.

There was no trip to the hospital in town. Erik had consumed more than a quart of moonshine and did not want to lose his driver's license. So Ruben got the transport moped and drove him back to the Jakobsson place and then led him to the bed in the maid's chamber beyond the living room.

"We can't leave him alone," said Gerd. "He mustn't fall asleep. That can be dangerous. Svea says so," she added quickly, so that no one would question the assertion. If District Nurse Svea had expressed that opinion, it was gospel. An indisputable truth.

Angela pushed the hair from her face.

"I can stay with him." She slipped past Ruben in the doorway without so much as looking at him. "I'll stay here," she said. "Go on, Erik needs peace and quiet. I'll keep an eye on him."

Ruben bought his flounder from the fisherman where he usually shopped. That would be his contribution to lunch. Berit had promised to make an omelet with the creamed morels. That could easily be a little tasteless. He didn't think she would say no to a couple of fresh-smoked flounders. Perhaps he should bring a bunch of flowers, too. Over the years he had discovered that women like that sort of thing. They didn't have to be expensive store-bought flowers. It was just as good to stop by the side of the road and pick blueweed and daisies and lady's bedstraw, red clover and columbine, and then edge the bouquet with ferns that grew on the north side by the corner of the house. It may seem a little sad that it took fifty long years to passably understand women, but better late than never. Women like to be surprised.

Angela had a half-withered wreath of meadow flowers around her head when they met at the ballast wharf on the afternoon of Midsummer Day. She sat dangling her legs in the water in an irritated way, like when a cat bats its tail, and pretended not to notice him. Her hair was disheveled. She looked tired.

"Want to swim?" he finally asked, after a long time had passed and neither of them had said anything. There was relief in being able to tear off their clothes and jump in the water. It was cold and Angela screamed, but seemed to come alive in the chill. A quick dip. He reached for her towel to dry her off and she let him do that. Her skin was almost pale blue and goose pimply with cold and her nipples were clearly visible through the fabric of her white bathing suit. He dried her hair, which had darkened several shades from the water, rubbed and rubbed so that it would regain its proper color. He wanted her to look like usual, be like usual. When she tried to free herself he kissed her on the tip of her nose, all that was sticking out of the beach towel.

"How's Erik doing?" she asked.

"Good, I think. He left on the boat for the mainland. There was nothing seriously wrong with him. Not with him or the motorcycle, miraculously enough."

Suddenly Angela threw her arms around Ruben, tripped him, and wrestled him down onto the ground. They rolled around like kids in the grass and she tried to get him to eat dandelions like a rabbit.

"I'm not a vegetarian, I want meat," he growled, biting her on the arm. She laughed as only Angela could, a rippling giggle. Then she straddled his stomach. He had nibbled her arm from the elbow up to the shoulder and was now in a sitting position. Then she suddenly got serious.

"Will you ever grow up, Ruben?"

He laughed out loud and continued to pretend to eat her other arm up too, without understanding that the game was over, that she expected something else.

19

"I mean, what do you think about the future? What do you want with your life?" she clarified.

"Want with my life?" he asked stupidly. "I think it's good the way it is. I'm a carpenter. I can do a little masonry—I can support myself that way." He showed her his big, sinewy hands.

"Don't you want to study, like Erik, and be somebody?"

"I am somebody. I'm Ruben." He placed his cheek against her soft, soft skin and drew in her scent of salt and summer heat. Sought her mouth and got an unexpected response.

"Do you love me?" she asked when he opened his eyes and saw the aurora of hair shining again around her face, like he wanted it to, like it always did later when he remembered her.

He nodded in reply.

"How do you know that? How do you know that you really love someone? You don't know me. The real me." And then she burrowed her head next to his neck. "You can't even be sure you know yourself, Ruben. Don't you understand that?"

Chapter 3

Later that afternoon Ruben took the car up to Klinte cemetery to put flowers on the graves. Usually he rode his bike, but his body ached. Perhaps there was a change in the weather.

J. N. Donner, of a ship-owning family and owner of Klinteby's, had been buried up under the wall. But he found no peace in the soil of the cemetery and Klinteby's horses refused to go past, so the body was moved home to the lovely park that belonged to the farm. On the dark north side of the cemetery second-class citizens were buried: suicides and religious dissenters. State-church members and true believers who died of old age and sickness were given a place on the south side. On the north side were his grandfather and grandmother, who belonged to the Baptist congregation. Ruben usually took the opportunity to say a few words to Grandfather Rune. Grandmother had always been a bit more reserved, but the conversations with Grandfather Rune did not need to end just because he found himself on the other side of the line. He had always been a good listener.

"The price of gas has gone up again. You'd turn in your

grave if you knew what it costs now—and yet we fill up our cars anyway. You have to. I really need to buy a new pair of pants, but I can't afford it. You know, Grandfather, all of a sudden there I'll be, filling up bare-assed, 'cause I've got to have gas." The eloquent silence was answer enough. Ruben placed a bunch of blueweed in the tapered vase and limped across the road to the other part of the cemetery below Klinteberget. It was sunnier here, yet Ruben felt raw and cold. Here was his mother, Siv Nilsson, and little Emelie who died the year after Erik was born. Ruben could vaguely remember her as a shrieking bundle in a basket dressed in layers of thin pink cloth. A pair of tiny kicking feet and a cap with lace that almost completely concealed the little face.

His father was still alive—at the old folks' home in his own world, where Siv was within earshot in the kitchen with the coffee pot simmering on the stove. At five o'clock he always wanted to get up and milk the cows, but fell back asleep gratefully when the night staff promised to take care of it. And when he got coffee in bed, even though it wasn't his birthday, he thought it was as if he'd gone to heaven. Well, not really, but well on the way.

"Listen, Mom, do you remember when you wanted to talk with me about Angela?" he said, resting his hand heavily on the gravestone. "That's fifty years ago now and it was the worst day of my life." Ruben sat down on the grass by the grave and leaned his head against the stone. He suddenly felt so weak. He was definitely coming down with a cold; he felt it in his throat. Presumably he had a fever. That was bad, considering the homing pigeon competition over the weekend. With the fast young pigeons he had picked out he should have a reasonable chance of winning the traveling trophy. He closed his eyes, and the memory of Angela returned with full force. The muscles in his stomach tightened in defense. There was an ache behind his eyes and he let the thoughts and tears come. It was the fever that made him so miserable and sentimental, he was sure of it. Otherwise, he would not be sitting there snuffling and making a fool of himself where people could see him.

Angela had changed somehow since that Midsummer Eve. Ruben had a hard time explaining how. She often brooded about life and death and the meaning of it all, but after the accident with the motorcycle it was worse than ever.

"You only have one life and there are so many possibilities. How do you know you're choosing the right one? I mean, so you don't change your mind later when it's too late." He didn't know, he had never thought along those lines. Everything was just fine the way it was. You got up in the morning, you did your work, and that was all there was to it.

Angela got a job at Klinteby's canning factory. In the evenings, when Ruben came to visit on his bicycle, she just wanted to sleep. But on weekends when she was off they might bicycle to Björkhaga or Tofta to swim. She no longer invited kisses and hugging. It seemed as if the magic had been lost after that playful moment on the ballast wharf, and he did not know what to do to get it back.

"We could have died, Erik and I," she said again and again. "What if we had . . . if we actually died . . . and this life isn't real, but just something we keep on pretending because death is so awful? Not existing scares me. Do you understand that, Ruben? Do you understand what I'm saying? But maybe we can live parallel lives; do you believe that? I like that idea, because then you don't need to choose and then you can't go wrong. Many parallel lives, the way a tree branches out, do you understand?"

"Well, not really, but I'm happy to listen anyway," he answered in an attempt to be truthful and still try to please her.

They spent time together more as friends or siblings than

as lovers. So it surprised him when one evening she invited him to go with her up to her room. There was something in her eyes. It was not like usual that evening.

"Nobody's home," she said. "They're not coming back until tomorrow afternoon." With astonishing casualness she started to undress in front of him. As if petrified he stood there watching her. When she pulled her sweater over her head and had no bra on underneath, he didn't know where to look. Then she stepped out of her skirt and panties and looked at him seriously. She had never been more beautiful and never looked more sorrowful than at that moment. He hardly dared breathe, much less move. Then she took him by the hand. Come. As in a dream he followed her to the bed. He fumbled with the buttons on his shirt and she helped him. When the paralysis went away they made love frantically. All the playfulness was gone. There was a hunger in her, as if she were possessed, as though she were making love to keep death away.

"How much do you love me?"

He kissed her and caressed her so that she would understand that he loved her more than life itself, more than anything or anyone else. He had never had the words; his language was in his hands. He hoped that would be enough.

The tears came unexpectedly. She cried, and he consoled her without words. Is it something I did? He could not ask the question and got no answer—not then.

Toward morning he finally fell asleep and discovered when he woke up that she was no longer lying next to him in the bed. Her scent was in the sheets. It was light outside, but it was not even six. The door to the bathroom was locked and he heard her sobbing between fits of retching.

"Don't you feel well, Angela?" She laughed shrilly, and then sobbed. "What is it? Can I do anything? Angela, open up!"

"Go home, I want to be alone." And he still did not

understand a thing until later that evening, when his mother Siv took him aside to say what had to be said. She pushed the hair from her face, smoothed her apron, and straightened her back the way she always did when she had to collect herself before a difficult task. Her face was so serious that he got scared and her voice was as brittle and dry as last year's twigs.

"I've spoken with Angela's mother."

"Yes?" Something in her gaze made him lower his eyes in shame.

"As I'm sure you know, Angela is pregnant."

"What?" The thought was dizzying. It wasn't possible, they had just . . .

"Angela is going to the mainland on the evening boat. To be with Erik. Erik is the child's father. It happened accidentally on Midsummer Eve. Even so, Erik has to take responsibility for what he's done and take care of them."

"What the hell!" Ruben leaped out of the chair so that it turned over. "That bastard." His concussion had just been a way to go after Angela . . . "I'll kill him. I'm going to kill—"

"Calm down, Ruben. Angela has agreed to it and she has chosen to go to him on the mainland. I've sensed that you had different hopes, but things don't always turn out the way you want in life. You'll meet another nice girl. . . ."

He couldn't hear anymore. He rushed from the room so that he would not break down in front of her. He had to be alone. Had to get away from her sympathetic eyes—they made the pain even worse. He ran through the village and past the church, not stopping until he got lost on a path in the Buttle forest. There he collapsed on the moss and pulled his knees up to ease the cramp in his belly. He tried to think clearly. Angela was leaving on the evening boat. He could still stop her. Maybe he could convince her to stay. Did he want her to stay after what she'd done? Yes, if she regretted it and didn't go to Erik on the mainland he would forgive her and take care of her and the child. But only if she chose to stay behind and never see Erik again. He must have time to talk with her before the boat left. Must.

But the Buttle forest is not like other forests. Once she has caught someone in her green embrace, she does not let go that easily. He did not know how long he wandered around, trying to get his bearings. When he came out on the road at Alskog a few hours later, it was already starting to get dark and hope was lost. All that was left was the anger and, after a while, the bitterness.

There had never been anyone but Angela. And there would never be another nice girl, as his mother said in her clumsy attempt to console him. He had had one brief conversation with his brother during the fifty years that passed.

"If you come home I'll kill you, Erik. You should know that."

Word was that Erik opened his own law firm and that things went well for him. Siv travelled to the mainland a few times a year and visited them and her little granddaughter Mikaela. There were also rumors that Angela was in a sanitarium for her nerves, that she had been given electric shock treatments and refused to talk. It was Sonja Cederroth who said that. Whether it was true or not was uncertain. Ruben had made it very clear that he did not want to hear one more word about Angela and then she had the good sense to remain silent. There was plenty of talk as it was. Ruben withdrew, as if the shame were his alone. If he'd been worth having, Angela wouldn't have taken off, wasn't that so?

"Sure I missed Erik, Mom. Of course I did. I lost both of them. But if I let them come to the island as if nothing had happened, I would have lost my mind. Would that have been better?"

Ruben parked the car under the oak tree, but as he was getting out he felt as though his strength was gone. He remained sitting a while with the car door open and must have dozed off with his face against the steering wheel—he was wakened by a loud car horn. When he looked up still half-asleep he saw Berit Hoas waving on the other side of the fence. She probably thought he was honking at her. She could just as well believe that. Ruben shivered as he walked toward the outbuilding to see to the pigeons for the night. It was a little early, but he should probably think about going to bed. The stairs up to the dovecote were an exertion. One step at a time; he kept firm hold of the handrail. On the top step he had to stand a long time and catch his breath. His chest ached. The scoop for the feed was gone. It should have been in the sack but it wasn't. Ruben cupped his hands, filled them with grain and then went to the first nest, where he had made a bed for the Belarusian. There was the scoop. He had discovered the dead pigeon there below the window and dropped the scoop and carried the bird down. That was it.

With his hands full he approached Sir Toby and saw immediately that the pigeon was not healthy. His eyes were dull and his feathers untidy and ruffled. And it was the same with Panic. He didn't look well either, and he had diarrhea too. Ruben took his wrinkled handkerchief out of his pocket and blew his nose. This was not good. The biggest young pigeon race of the year and he had illness in his flock. Yet they had been vaccinated, although for what he couldn't say right offhand. It was Cederroth who brought the bottle with him. The syringes and the needles were still in the drawer in the cupboard next to the cages. This was really too bad. If he called the veterinarian the rumor would spread to the other guys in the club and he would mercilessly be denied entry into the competition with his pigeons.

It must be resolved some other way. With discretion. Ruben sat down on a stool by the window and leaned his head against the wall while he thought. Out in the garden Berit Hoas was taking in laundry. Under the kitchen towels she had hung up her salmon-pink unmentionables, so no one would see she had washed them. What a god-awful color—salmon-pink. Ruben chuckled to himself. Berit had never married either. No wonder, with such solid underclothing. There was no place for levity and shameless display. He had seen the slips and corsets swaying in the wind from his outlook in the dovecote and they were at least as terrifying as the salmon-pink underpants with legs.

But, undergarments aside, Berit had her good sides, of course. She was not one to run around gossiping and she was helpful. Perhaps he could ask Berit for advice. Ruben took out his cell phone. He did not use it very often. The buttons still felt unfamiliar. He had it mostly because the other old guys in the homing pigeon club had cell phones.

"Berit Hoas," she said, and Ruben said his name and explained his predicament.

"I think they need medicine, but it's awkward to talk to the vet. You don't have anything at home? Something strong?"

"Penicillin, you mean. I think I have a little left in a bottle from when my sister had tonsillitis. She can't swallow tablets so she got liquid medicine, but it tasted so disgusting she stopped after half the round when she was feeling better. I got the rest in case she infected me while I was there. Although I never needed it."

Ruben smiled and his spirits rose immediately from the good news, despite the fever. "If you can spare those few drops I'll be eternally grateful to you."

"Are you sure it's a good thing to give penicillin to the pigeons? I mean—can you give animals and humans the same medicine?" Her voice had become astringent, the teacher's voice he had never liked and which demanded an answer.

"Absolutely. It'll work out fine. Do you think you can bring the medicine over to me? I'm up in the dovecote."

If he were to draw the medicine up in a syringe and then remove the needle he could feed it right into the beak, just like Angela did when she fed the pigeon the hawk had attacked. Angela, Angela, Angela. This wasn't working. He had to stop this foolishness now and think about something else. Ruben scratched his beard stubble. He had definitely forgotten to shave.

"There was a painting salesman here yesterday," said Berit while she puffed up the steps. "Was he at your place too?"

"No." Ruben had not seen anyone the whole day yesterday. In the morning he had gone down to the harbor and bought fish. But after that he stayed home. "I don't like people wandering around here. Maybe we should be more careful about locking up."

"I thought it was so sad," said Berit. "He didn't know any Swedish, but he had a piece of paper where it said in English that he needed money because his son needs a new kidney."

"I don't know. I don't like them begging for money. Didn't he have a job?" Ruben muttered a long string of oaths to himself while he waited for her to come up the steps.

"He paints pictures. Really beautiful pictures with the sea and reeds and boats and—"

"Did you buy a painting from him? Then we're going to have them swarming around here, you can bet on that."

"I felt sorry for him. Imagine if you had a boy who was sick and needed a new kidney. Imagine that, Ruben. Then you would probably do anything at all to get the money."

Chapter 4

The next day Ruben did not wake up until eleven o'clock. A persistent fly was wandering over the bridge of his nose. He did not have the energy to swat it. The sheets were sour with sweat and were wrapped around his legs. It was thirst that drove him out of bed. His tongue felt like a chunk of wood in his mouth and the dizziness made him grab the bookcase, which swayed alarmingly and almost fell on top of him. When he had drunk from the faucet he realized that he would not have the strength to make it up the steps to the outbuilding to give the pigeons feed. The fact was he barely had the strength to go back to bed. The last stretch he crawled on his knees while his chest heaved like a bellows. He didn't feel like he was getting enough air. Every breath hurt and his muscles ached. As he pulled himself up over the edge of the bed he was like a drowning man taking hold of the railing of the boat. Only by summoning his last ounce of strength could he heave himself up.

He would have to ask Berit to look after the pigeons. Maybe, if a miracle occurred and he got better, he would still make the deployment of the homing pigeons tomorrow. Ruben decided not to call Cederroth until he was absolutely compelled to drop out. Berit he would call right away. But as soon as he put his head on the pillow, he felt himself gliding away. Berit, he was going to call Berit. Soon. Just wanted to wait a little and rest. Close his eyes a little, just a little while and then he'd call . . .

When he woke up it was three o'clock in the afternoon. Ruben sat up with a jerk and then fell back on the pillow. His head felt like it was bursting when he coughed and his chest rattled. Berit. He had to call that very minute. Someone had to look after the pigeons. His arm felt heavy as lead as he raised it to reach the cell phone. It was a great relief when she answered at the first ring. Of course she could give them water and feed. Not right now, but a little later in the evening. If he would just tell her what he wanted done. Neighbors should help out. As luck would have it, he had left the outbuilding unlocked and didn't need to get up again to give her the key. Now that it was arranged, he could go back to sleep a little. Release his hold and go with the wave out toward rest.

And she came to see him over the sea as he had hoped. Angela the angelic. She cupped her hands and filled them with water. Drink. And he leaned forward to drink from her hands, but just as his lips reached the surface of the water she pulled them back. His thirst was excruciating, but the answer to the riddle she had asked was the requirement for him to satisfy his thirst and she vanished in the waves when he hesitated. The fear of losing her again made him beside himself. The sea was endless. Would he ever see her again? He sank down and searched the seabed. His mouth was dry and he tried to drink the water where he was lying, but it was salty and brown from rotten seaweed. Angela! He never should have let her go. Then he felt her hand against his cheek. He heard her, but was unable to open his eyes and could not understand everything she was saying. But the voice was Angela's.

"I came," she said. "At last I came. Are you still angry with me?" He took hold of her hands and pulled her to him. He breathed in her scent. It was just like then, sweet and full of summer.

"You came." And everything he wanted to say and ask about her sickness and about the little girl whose name was Mikaela and about the time that had passed became a wordless stream of mutual understanding.

"I'm thirsty." When she handed him the glass he drank until it was empty. With this toast, everything was reconciled and forgotten, and only the present was left and her soft skin against his bare arm. Angela. She was running over the meadow with outstretched arms, just like then. He struggled to keep her there but the dreams were leading him farther away and suddenly he was sitting on Grandfather Rune's lap in the good, warm silence where all dreams were allowed, everything was understood, and nothing had to be explained.

"I'm thirsty."

Angela was standing over him again and her face was like the sun and he smiled back. I never want to be apart from you again. As he raised his hand to caress her cheek she was transformed before his eyes and the face was rubbed out and assumed the graying form of Berit Hoas.

"How are you feeling, Ruben? You don't look healthy at all."

"I was on the bottom. I couldn't get air, but it's better now. A dove came, a present. Did you see her? She was here."

"You know, Ruben, I think you're delirious. You must have a high fever. I think you should go to the hospital. It's too bad I don't have a driver's license; otherwise I would wrap you in a blanket and drive you into town. Perhaps we could call Cederroth?"

"Never. Then she won't find me when she comes back. I have to stay here."

Berit shook her head at his foolishness. "Would you like a little something to drink? I set a pitcher here on the night table and then I brought a twig of mock orange for you so you would notice the scent when you woke up. I know how much you like that. I've seen you standing there sniffing at it sometimes. Have you eaten anything at all today? No, I doubt it. There's a little of the omelet left."

"I don't have the energy and my throat hurts when I swallow. It will have to wait until tomorrow."

"I think you should go to the doctor. I definitely think so." Berit looked at his feverish eyes and the damp sheets. "You may have pneumonia. That's not something to play around with at your age, Ruben."

"No. I'll take a couple of Tylenol and I'll be better tomorrow. It will be fine. I'm okay."

Without convincing him to get help, Berit Hoas went over to the outbuilding to look after the pigeons. People always said that Ruben Nilsson was contrary and headstrong, and they were quite right. It would be hard another man so bullheaded. He never let anyone get close to him, seldom left his house even to go to the store, and did not associate with anyone except the old men in the homing pigeon club and his dead ancestors. He was often up there at the cemetery, and a number of people told her they had heard him talking out loud to himself as he walked around raking the graves.

How peculiar do you have to be to be considered sick? It was if he lived in the borderland and did not have strength enough to choose a side. He should go to the hospital. Perhaps they could do something about his head too while he was there. What a strange old curmudgeon he was! Maybe she should have called Cederroth anyway and asked him to try to take Ruben into town with him. Berit opened the door to the outbuilding and listened to the cooing sound from the nests. There was a dead pigeon in a galvanized tub by the door. She went up the stairs with effort. The first thing she noticed were the binoculars sitting by the window that faced her garden. Had he been sitting here spying on her, that old coot? She was about to get really angry when it occurred to her that naturally he was watching the pigeons. Of course, to think anything else was unfair to him. He would stand with his binoculars and watch as they circled over the roofs. From a distance he could see which pigeon it was and identify it by name. Panic, Sir Toby, or whatever their names were.

There was a dead pigeon right above the steps and another one between the cages, and the two who had been given penicillin the day before were dead too. He should have listened to her. It's not a certainty that animals and people do well from taking the same medicine. When Berit found three more dead pigeons she started to think seriously about what had happened. Did the hawk get in, or a polecat? She had heard stories about henhouses where a polecat got in and then all the hens were found dead. Polecats kill for sport. Kill until all life is extinguished, without needing to do so to feed themselves, not so different from humans in that respect. She looked around with a shudder. Or was there perhaps something in the water that was making the animals sick? Ruben had a separate well he took water from for the garden. As far as she knew it was not approved as drinking water. But he also had municipal water. Could he have given the pigeons bad water? Seven dead pigeons besides the one lying down there in the galvanized tub, that was not good at all. Should she tell Ruben or should she leave it until he felt better? Right now he didn't have the strength to do anything about it anyway. She decided to spare him the bad news for the moment.

Berit Hoas sat down in front of the TV with her knitting. She was used to solitude, yet it felt silent and empty in the house. She was actually retired, but when she got the invitation to serve food at the soccer camp she could not refuse the offer. She missed her work in the cafeteria at Klinte School. She liked the children and they liked her. Even though there were so many of them she got to know them quickly and prided herself on knowing which foods they liked and didn't like. If Pelle ate poorly a couple of days in a row she tried to change the menu a little so he got something he liked, and when Sofia poked at her food three days running Berit cautiously asked how things were going and Sofia told her that her mom and dad were planning to separate. It was the same with Gabriel. He sat on a stool in the kitchen with Berit after school and said that his whole tummy was sad because his rabbit was dead. It got a cold and was given penicillin and then it got diarrhea from the penicillin and then it got an overbite and then it died. He brought the dead rabbit with him to school in a shoebox and together they buried it under a tree by the creek, and Gabriel played "Three Blind Mice" on his recorder in farewell.

It felt cold and raw in the old stone house. Berit went to get a cardigan and put on a cup of tea. But the chill in her body would not go away. She was not feeling well. Her muscles felt stiff and strange. She wasn't getting sick, was she? She had a job to do. The children needed food. The TV news was on. She must have fallen asleep for a while and missed part of the program. She couldn't understand how it was all connected: was it the present or the past or a film she had seen . . . there was a stock report. It used to be that ordinary people didn't pay any attention to the stock exchange, and now the numbers took up more and more of the TV screen. She must have fallen sound asleep in her chair. Toward dawn she woke up, sweaty and cold at the same time. She took a detour to the kitchen and drank some water before she set the clock for six and went to bed.

It was difficult to wake up a few hours later. She almost struck her head on the kitchen table when she nodded off over the news in the morning paper about the annual gathering of politicians in Almedalen. Was it that time again? Berit washed herself quickly in the sink instead of taking a shower as she had intended. If she was just able to get lunch for the children she free for the day. In the evening they would grill hot dogs down on the beach and play Kubb. She could manage the morning hours even if she was feverish and coming down with a cold. She shouldn't have sat out in the wind peeling potatoes. You have to be careful not to get cold.

If on this morning Berit Hoas had followed her initial instinct to check on Ruben Nilsson, several lives might have been saved. But she didn't have the energy. Not then. Not later either, when she came home after serving lunch at the soccer camp. As soon as she was inside the walls of her house she collapsed on the bed. The headache made her nauseated and she couldn't stop coughing. When she had to rush to the toilet to avoid an accident, she started wondering about the creamed morels she had shared with Ruben. Could it be that through her good intentions she had poisoned them both? She knew they were morels and she had parboiled them exactly the way it said in the cookbook. Could she have misunderstood something or mixed in an inedible mushroom? She had to call Ruben. If she could just rest for a little while she would call him later.

It didn't turn out that way. Instead she was wakened an hour later by a hard knocking on the door and Cederroth's deep bellowing out on the porch.

"Open up, Berit! Open up! Something terrible has happened! You're not going to believe it unless you see it yourself. It's too awful! Damn it, it's worse than awful! I can't even say how awful it is!"

Chapter 5

"Calm down, Petter, and tell me what it is." Berit Hoas was holding onto the doorframe; everything was swimming before her eyes. All she wanted to do was crawl back into bed. Her whole body ached and her eyes were stinging and now she was standing in a draft in the doorway. Cederroth was gesturing and whimpering like a dog. He was usually fairly wound up when he was telling stories, but this was going to extremes. She couldn't deal with him right now and was about to shut the door when he said, "Ruben's pigeons are dead. Every single one. Do you get what I'm saying, Berit? Every single damn bird has its legs in the air! What is going on? I banged on the kitchen door but the old man doesn't answer. Do you think he may have had a fit and killed them? You know how he is."

"I don't know, Petter."

"He has pigeons that are worth five thousand kronor apiece or more. The lunatic could have sold them or given them away. What has he done? Gassed them, given them arsenic? I don't get it! He didn't come to the pigeon deployment, even though he has every chance of winning the competition. Of course you wonder. He could have phoned anyway. Someone must have said something that put his nose out of joint."

"Are you sure they're *all* dead? It's not just the pigeons in the galvanized tub by the door?" Berit asked feebly. Now she had to sit down. She felt like she was going to faint. A high, ringing tone cut through her head and the sound of Petter's voice came and went in waves.

"Come in, Petter, and don't stand outside."

"Every single pigeon! I counted them. There was even one too many. Sometimes I just can't figure him out. What is it with him?"

"Have you tried calling his cell phone?" Berit rubbed her eyes and adjusted her bathrobe. It was annoying that she was running around half-undressed when people came.

"I'd gone to bed. Feeling a little under the weather," she excused herself and tied the sash even tighter around her stomach. "Ruben wasn't feeling well either when I was there yesterday. He'd gone to bed. I had to take care of the pigeons for him. Could I have done something wrong, do you think? Given them the wrong feed? It would be terrible if I did something to make a mess. What would people say?"

"I've called his cell phone at least twenty times. Could something have happened to him? Maybe he fell and broke something? What if he killed himself! First he kills off the pigeons and then himself. Is that possible? I hope I'm wrong, but we ought to take a look."

"I don't know if I'm able. I'm not feeling well at all. It must be the flu or something. Or else it's the creamed morels we ate. Ruben had some too. You're right, we must see what's going on." Berit staggered out to the hall again and opened the outside door. The daylight cut into her eyes and she felt weak and dizzy. "May I hold your arm, Petter? I hope no one sees that. Because what would people say? But it's probably necessary if I'm going to make it all the way over there."

"But Berit, I thought you'd never ask." Petter let out one of his famous laughs and placed his arm around her. "I've gotten worse offers, my dear."

They banged on the kitchen door, but nothing happened. It was locked. The formal entry with the little glassed-in porch was never used and it was locked too. They would not have expected anything else. Berit was getting more and more anxious and self-accusing. If she had poisoned Ruben Nilsson she would not be able to live with the shame. Not as a cook.

"We'll probably have to break in," said Petter Cederroth. "The question is where it will do the least damage. It will have to be a window. We'll have to knock out a window-pane."

"No, we can't do that, can we? What if someone sees that and wonders. What would they say then?"

"I don't care. Necessity knows no law. If we take one of the cellar windows that will be cheapest. Although I'll never make it through that little hole," he said, putting his hands on his imposing beer belly. "Would you consider—"

"Absolutely not!" Berit gasped for air. She was neither willing nor able to do such a thing. "Never, ever!" True, she was slightly less expansive than Cederroth, but not by much, and the mere thought of disgracing herself made her choke.

"Then it will have to be one of the kitchen windows." Where Petter Cederroth was concerned, words always quickly led to action. Before Berit had closed her mouth he had taken his clog and knocked out the kitchen window by the steps and started removing shards of glass from the molding. "I see the key, it's in the lock on the inside of the door. I'll open for you in a moment," he said, heaving himself up into the window with surprising agility.

"Be careful you don't hurt yourself when you jump down on the glass."

"Ouch, dagnabbit." Cederroth staggered and put his foot down alongside his clog. He cut a big gash in his heel. "It's bleeding like hell. I'll have to wrap something around it before I open the door for you," he shouted from the darkness. "It will have to be the kitchen towel. It's dark as the grave in here. I can't see a thing, dagnabbit. I really cut myself."

"He hasn't touched the food I brought," Berit noted when she had come in and opened the refrigerator. The creamed morels were still in their little serving dish and the omelet was on the plate. Limping, with a flowery piece of cloth around one foot, Petter made his way upstairs to Ruben's bedroom. Berit sat at the kitchen table with her hands feebly in her lap. She could not bear to take another step. Her legs would not hold her. After a little while Cederroth came down again with a strange expression on his face. He was holding onto the handrail with both hands with such a firm grip that his knuckles were white as he sought her eyes. It looked as if he was about to start laughing or crying or both at the same time. He looked really horrid, thought Berit, and his voice would barely obey him.

"What is it, Petter? Why do you look so strange?"

"He's dead. Dead as a doornail. Completely cold. I touched him with my hand and patted his cheek. Like this." Petter stroked his big fist over the handrail. "Ice cold."

"Good Lord, what are we going to do? What if it's the mushrooms!" Berit put her hands to her mouth and closed her eyes. All she wanted was to get away from here, far away to a safe place where everything was as usual. Her dizziness was increasing and she felt like she was going to vomit. She got up quickly and fumbled her way over to Ruben's toilet. His bridge was in a water glass on the edge of the sink. That was enough to trigger the reflex. Berit got on her knees and held onto the seat as her stomach churned inside out.

"I'll drive you to the hospital," said Petter. "Yes, I'm going to. No more protests now. This may be serious. I guess they'll have to send out a doctor who knows what to do with . . . the body. Or do you call the police? You probably call 911. But I'll do that on the way to the hospital. If it's the mushrooms this may be urgent."

"But Ruben . . . we can't just leave, can we?"

"Well, he's not going to run away. He'll stay where he is. Your stomach may have to be pumped." Cederroth took hold of Berit's arm and helped her to her feet.

"Are you sure he's really dead? It can't be that it looks like—that he's asleep?" Berit wrung her hands in despair and hoped for a miracle.

"Dead as a doornail—and now you're going outside with me, so I can drive the car up."

"I don't even have any clothes on. This is terrible. I have to put regular clothes on. This can't be happening. If he died from the mushrooms I might as well stay home and die too. What will people say? There's going to be talk. I won't be able to go to the store, won't be able to look anyone in the eye—"

"It's not certain that he died from the mushrooms. He may have had a heart attack or a stroke or what do I know. Now let's take it easy and then we'll see what happens. There now, sit in the front seat. I have plastic bags here that you can use if you feel sick," said Petter, placing the roll between Berit's knees. He had been driving a taxi his entire adult life and knew not to take any chances.

At the emergency room they had to wait. At first a misunderstanding arose when the intake nurse thought the visit was about Petter Cederroth's foot, which was conspicuously wrapped in a flowery cotton rag. She was busy and had a hard time making sense of the story. The wound on the foot was rather deep and it had bled profusely. Berit fainted the moment when the flap of skin was turned to the side so that the periosteum came into view. This was taken as a shock reaction. Petter Cederroth's talk of stomach pumping, homing pigeons, and a deceased neighbor was taken as "crazy talk." There must be some reason why he had an escort. He was apparently not properly oriented.

When the woman did not revive at once, a doctor was summoned and it was quickly determined that her condition was serious. Oxygen saturation was down to 79 percent and blood pressure immeasurable. She was lifted up onto a stretcher and taken into a treatment room. Left behind in the waiting room was Cederroth. He watched the little lamp by the door change from green to red and wondered what that might mean. A little boy was driving his plastic tractor on the floor and rolled right over Cederroth's foot. It hurt so much that he screamed in pain and the boy started crying. To show that he was not offended Petter offered the mother and the little boy each a piece of candy and then it was his turn to go into a room to get stitches.

"When was the last time you had a tetanus shot?" the doctor asked. He looked young and inexperienced, but he appeared confident enough as he injected the syringe of anesthetic.

"I can't remember. Well, if I think about it I got a rusty nail in my butt when we were tearing down a shed one time. There must have been four years ago, I think." Petter grimaced. The stitches still hurt quite a bit despite the anesthetic. The doctor could have waited a little longer before he picked up the needle. On the other hand it was over quickly. It was a nice-looking white bandage too. Petter was about to tell the doctor about Ruben when the man heard an alarm and rushed off. Through the open door Ruben saw Berit's bed being taken toward the elevators at great speed. He really wanted to ask how she was doing. The oxygen mask she had on her face and the activity around the gurney were alarming. Was it that serious?

No one came into the room for a long time. They seemed to have forgotten him. Half an hour passed and Petter sat up again on the edge of the cot. Perhaps he should just say thanks and go home. He couldn't lie here waiting. The nurse in reception was occupied with a young mother with a screaming baby in her arms and Petter did not care to speak with her. He had to go home and try to sleep a couple of hours before the night shift started.

Chapter 6

On Thursday the twenty-ninth of June, the day after Ruben Nilsson found a new pigeon in his dovecote, Mats Eklund left the apartment on Donnersgatan in Klintehamn in great haste. He did not even bother to tie his shoelaces, much less pull on a jacket despite the chill in the air.

He hardly suspected that the worries that occupied him at the moment would take on new proportions before the evening was over. As he closed the door behind him he doubted that there was any way back. It had finally been voiced. There was no way around it. His jogging session was only a temporary respite before his security was smashed to bits forever. He knew it was cowardice to just take off and he wished he could have approached it in a better way, but he needed time to think.

"Do you want a divorce?" Jenny had asked the question flat out and without the slightest trace of anxiety. She should be just as scared and shaky inside as he was, but she didn't show it. Her face was strangely expressionless. Her neck twitched a little when she saw his surprised look, as if with a nod of her head she could help him along. But nothing came out. No dead certain yes. Not a "no, I love you,

you know that" either. Not a "Why are you saying such a silly thing, darling?" They were in a borderland. In meaningless, and in every way unarousing trench warfare, about whose fault it was that the garbage didn't get taken out and the stove wiped off. In the midst of their togetherness he felt so infinitely alone and unhappy and tired of it all. Was this life? Daycare, cloth diapers, organic carrots, and Jenny who had lost the desire for making love when she got the children she wanted. No, tonight I'm too tired. No, the children might wake up! But do the kids have to sleep in here with us? Yes, because Henrik is afraid of the dark and Stina threw up this morning. Was life supposed to be this monotonous? Sleep, work, pick up the kids, put the kids to bed, sleep, work . . . in a perpetuum mobile that was only interrupted by weekend shopping and visits from the in-laws. If they had a better sexual relationship presumably the other problems of life would have been first-degree equations to solve. Then there would have been warmth and intimacy that might have lifted them over the mountain of laundry and the mountain of ironing and the abyss of nighttime screaming. But that's not how it was. I'm suffocating, he thought, and started to jog as he crossed the road to Klinte Church and continued up toward Värsände. He thought he would take the embankment home and quickened his pace to shake off the uneasiness. But his thoughts followed him like a swarm of sweat-loving flies.

Next week Jenny would be the coach at a soccer camp in Klinte School and spend the night there, and the children would be with their grandparents. It would be good if they could wait on a decision until after that. Then they would have time to think over what they should do, each one separately.

How could it get this way? They had loved each other so much. Where did the love go? The caresses, the words, the passion? Fear came over him with a force he was not prepared for. Abandonment like a dizzying abyss. The adrenaline was rushing in his blood and he felt nauseated.

Until now he had only thought about himself, about his own dreams about how life together with Jenny should have been, and deep down he had accused her of not fulfilling all his needs, as if he were a little child with the right to unconditional love. He had no idea what Jenny thought about their life together. He had never dared ask. What if she was the one who wanted a divorce and that was why she was asking him? No, this can't happen. They needed to take it calmly and think it over before rushing off and doing something they couldn't fix. They had to think about the children.

Mats Eklund was rounding the corner at the outhouse at the old abandoned farm in Värsände, when he caught sight of the tent. A small, dirty gray pup tent. He'd had one like it himself as a boy, with old-fashioned wooden pegs and a front flap tied with cord instead of a zipper. He couldn't keep from peeking in. It took a little while for his eyes to get accustomed to the darkness. Gradually a figure emerged from the gray. The sight of blood, black as pitch, could be discerned in the darkness. And white skin. A person. The sight made him gasp for air. He staggered backward and sat on the ground, got up again, and ran out toward the road to get as far away as possible from what he had just witnessed. He fumbled in his pocket for his cell phone to call the police, but didn't dare rely on his senses without checking that he'd really seen what he thought he saw. This time he tied back the flap and took a proper look. The view paralyzed him and he just stood there, unable to do anything. A man a few years older than himself was lying on a tarp on the ground. His eyes were staring vacantly and his mouth was open. A large, black, shiny bloodstain had spread over the light-colored shirt.

The police officer who questioned Mats Eklund was a woman. She introduced herself as Maria Wern, Detective Inspector. With her long blonde hair and brown eyes she resembled Jenny so much that it made him even more shaky and nervous. And the warmth and calmness in her voice caused him succumb to the tension and completely lose self-control.

"How are you feeling? Is it all right if I ask you a few questions?" He started shaking beyond all control. She waited for him and then very carefully asked question after question while she noted the incoherent answers. While they were talking he could not help glancing in the direction where the police technicians were working. A barricade had been set up. The body was carried out and covered. If he had looked in a different direction at just that moment perhaps he would have avoided the nightmares that would plague him, but his gaze was drawn there as if by a magnet. There was dried blood everywhere. When the men in uniform carried the body to the waiting black sack one of them stumbled on an uneven spot in the ground. For a moment he lost his hold and the dead man's head was slung sharply backward, showing a large gap in the neck.

When Detective Inspector Maria Wern drove Mats Eklund home after he refused to go to the hospital, she was relieved to see that his wife was at home. She would have felt uneasy leaving him alone. When the murder victim was lifted into the black sack Mats fainted, simply collapsed in front of her. She didn't think he struck his head, although she was not able to cushion the sudden fall. He was very pale and affected and his hands were shaking terribly. The wife's name was Jenny. Maria had met her earlier in the week at an informational meeting about the soccer camp Emil had signed up for. Jenny was one of the coaches. She seemed confident and considerate and helped Mats sit down. She made sure he got something hot to drink and a blanket around his shoulders.

Back at the scene of the murder Maria wrote down the questions she had not had time to ask. She would have to return later that evening, when Mats Eklund was more composed. Maria went up to the barricade that surrounded the old farm buildings, the house and smithy and barn. Mårtenson was just rolling up the tarp the body had been lying on. He tried to avoid getting blood on his clothes. The victim had apparently bled profusely.

"He had no identity papers on him. It looks like he's been sleeping right on the tarp, without a mattress. It must have been freezing." Mårtenson shuddered at the thought. "And hard as stone. Something occurred to me. His clothes seem to be homemade, there are no labels on them, size, manufacturer, you know."

"How did he get here? Did he walk?" Maria looked around for a vehicle. A car or a bicycle that might explain how he got there with his luggage.

"Hartman found a car, parked up on a gravel road in the bushes a little way up. He's still there." Mårtenson gestured in the direction and Maria headed toward it, after asking a few more questions for which the technician had no answers. A few hundred meters farther down the road Maria could hear Hartman's voice from behind the shrubbery. Soon he became visible and alongside him was a rusty car of a make unknown to Maria, without wheel rims, and with the trunk jerry-rigged shut with twine. The car even lacked license plates, she noted after looking it over.

"Is this his car?" she asked.

"I think we can assume that." Hartman opened the door to the driver's seat with a gloved hand and held up a bag for a tent and a couple of wooden tent pegs. "But what was he doing here? Why was the car hidden? There's a birdcage in the backseat. Did you see it? I think it's made of willow, homemade. And there are some paintings wrapped in worn-out sheets. Nice oil paintings and the occasional watercolor. In the glove compartment there is a pack of cigarettes with Cyrillic writing, but no identification whatsoever."

"The neighbors didn't see anything?" Maria had talked to several of those who had gathered outside the barricade and taken names and telephone numbers.

Hartman shook his head. "Nothing so far. No one seems to have noticed the tent either, so we'll have to assume it hasn't been there for long. The technicians are looking at the grass—it turns yellow fast if it's covered for any length of time."

Maria turned quickly around when she heard a rustling coming from the bushes. It was their colleague Ek. Pensively and without the slightest embarrassment he pulled up his fly and adjusted his pant legs.

"Well, you'd think the farmers around here or someone from the historical society would have seen that someone was camping. This isn't exactly a regular campsite. Maybe he didn't quite have the hang of the right to access, it can be a little tricky. Although in a way it seems well-planned. He wasn't far from the restroom."

After a couple of hours at the station, Maria's son, Emil, called wondering where she was. "You said you were going to come home early!"

Bad conscience again. The children. She had promised to drive them to the shore to take part in a sand sculpture competition in Tofta. She had completely forgotten and now it was too late. On her way home it occurred to Maria that she had to shop. The fridge was almost empty and she had not thought about what they would have for dinner. Anything at all except Mamma Scan's meatballs, they'd already had that twice this week. Who are those mothers who can whip out a home-cooked meal after a day at work? It would have to be quick, too, before the kids got too tired and impatient. The day before Maria had been at the recently opened Vigoris shopping center and was instructed in how to shop according to the new system where you scan in the price of the product yourself and put it right in your bag, and then simply present the scanner at the register. Quick and efficient if you know what you want. Salmon fillets, maybe. Maria saw the long line for counter service, where there were fresh fillets at a sale price, and grabbed a package from the freezer instead. Not without bad conscience. Maybe that isn't a time saver when you have to thaw the fish first before cooking it, but the thought of standing in line was a deterrent.

In the line at the front counter Maria noticed a mannequin-thin woman with short dark hair who was playing with her scanner while she waited. She must have been bored. She scanned in goods and changed her mind, double-clicked, and clicked again. Presumably she had been oriented in the Quick Shop system that same day. According to the advertisements, all goods were followed from producer to customer, the whole transport route, through a little chip placed in each label. No unnecessary warehousing, which in the end is paid for by the customer. The woman continued playing with her scanner and dragged the handgrip along her upper arm and clicked. When she saw Maria's amused expression she stopped abruptly. Suddenly, as if she had forgotten something important, she left her place in line and rushed toward the exit. The basket was left behind with her groceries and her wallet. Perhaps the parking meter had run out or else she happened to think of something more urgent. A meeting? Maria ran after her and called that she had left her wallet, but the woman did not stop although she must have heard.

"Hello, you forgot your wallet! Wait!" Maria saw her get onto a bicycle and disappear around the corner. Maria opened the wallet before turning it in to the cashier. The woman's name was Sandra Hägg, according to the driver's license.

When Maria was in the car on her way toward Klinte, her thoughts returned to the murdered man in the tent. It was nasty. The murder scene was only a few hundred meters from the house where Maria lived with her children.

Chapter 7

Sunday morning the second of July arrived with over-cast skies and rain showers. The wind was blowing hard in the harbor in Klinte. Shiny gray waves, like molten lead, reflected the dark sky overhead, and white-foaming masses of water heaved against the pier where several sloops were tied. The trip to Stora Karlsö was canceled. Maria Wern was disappointed, but as she was inclined to get seasick, maybe that was just as well. Summer has only just started. There would be other boats, and the moments you remember later and long to return to are perhaps not the days of major outings but moments of rest. Earlier in the week Maria had gone down to Kettlevik's stone works at Hoburgen—there she sat on a bench and let her eyes rest on the sea. With her back leaning against a sun-warmed plank wall she listened to the sound of a one-cylinder ignition bulb engine, like a thumping heart, while her daughter, Linda, concentrated on making her own rock carvings in the limestone. Meditative and soothing.

It was later that Sunday morning, when Maria was going to drop off a flashlight to her son at the soccer camp in Klinte School, that she found out that the cook had not arrived that morning, and did not leave a message either. Berit Hoas was reliability itself. The coach, Jenny Eklund thought it was strange. All morning she had tried to phone the woman, but no one answered, which was why she asked whether Maria could possibly drive past Berit's house on Södra Kustvägen and see what might have happened. Perhaps the cook had misunderstood her schedule and was out in her strawberry patch or whatever it might be. Maria had no objection. She had no definite plans for the day, other than the cancelled trip to Stora Karlsö, and now she had nothing in particular to do. The weather forecast on the radio promised no improvement for the next few days, so that would mean staying inside and cleaning house.

Yet another summer on Gotland and this time Maria had come to stay, if possible. During the past winter the house in Kronviken had been rented out. It was a relief to move to a new place of her own after the divorce. The joint decisions and compromises were built into the walls of the old yellow wooden house. The kitchen that was too cramped because Krister wanted room for a bar and his jukebox. The bathroom that never got renovated because Krister spent the remodeling loan on a classic car, which never passed inspection. And the floor of the porch that was never redone because the money they should have used to buy lumber was gone before they even talked to the contractor. Even if both the house and Krister had their charms, they were a closed chapter now. There was a new freedom in this, but sometimes also worry and sorrow at not having succeeded in their life together. Especially now when Krister and his buddy Mayonnaise had taken Linda with them on a camper vacation and Emil was at soccer camp. It was so empty. Lonely, meaningless, and empty.

Maria was not entirely happy to have made Mayonnaise's

acquaintance. There was nothing bad about him exactly—it was mostly that he was so impulsive and disorganized that you couldn't put up with him for long. It did not feel secure putting responsibility for Linda into the hands of these two gentlemen on Friday evening. But there was no choice. Krister had the right to every other weekend and how he spent it was his own business. The last Maria saw of them when they left on Friday was Mayonnaise reaching for a soda can he was keeping cool in a holder attached to the outside rearview mirror and handing it to Linda, who was standing up between the seats.

"Seat belt!" Maria had run after them and gestured, but Mayonnaise only waved happily back and turned up the volume on the stereo so that the lyrics of the dance band music drowned out her voice. "Seat belt!"

Later that evening Krister phoned because Linda had forgotten her stuffed frog, Helmer Bryd. They hadn't made it any farther than the Tofta campsite, and then they'd had a little too much beer for them to continue, so if Maria would be nice and bring that damned-piece-of-cloth Helmer so the kid could fall asleep, Krister would be grateful. On the way to Tofta Maria thought about whether there was really any difference between being married to Krister and being divorced from him. This was exactly how tiresome it used to be when he took care of the kids on his own, and that was one of the reasons she had left him.

When Maria stopped at the house where Berit Hoas lived she saw the police car parked beside Ruben Nilsson's hedge. She was not on duty and did not really want to get involved in anything on her weekend off. To keep going you have to distinguish between work time and personal life, especially as a single mother. Energy is not an unlimited commodity. How many times this weekend did she push away the thought of the murdered man who was found at Värsände. No one knew how he got there. None of the neighbors had heard or seen anything unusual, and a preliminary run-through of the registry of missing persons in Sweden produced nothing at all. The man was most likely in his fifties. Short, muscular, and dark, with an old scar on the right side just below the rib cage. Without identifying the victim, it's hard to get an effective investigation under way. Witness accounts were limited. There were other unresolved cases—assault, robbery, and car break-ins—that would be put on hold while the murder investigation was going on.

But when an ambulance arrived at Ruben Nilsson's house and Detective Inspector Jesper Ek opened the door to the porch to meet the ambulance personnel, curiosity triumphed over good sense, and Maria couldn't help going over to the house and asking what happened. Ek gestured for her to wait and then answered her after showing the ambulance personnel into the house.

"We don't know. I really don't think there's any indication of a crime. We got a call from a taxi driver this morning, Petter Cederroth, who said he'd found this old man dead already yesterday evening, but that he drove the neighbor lady to the emergency room and clearly a number of misunderstandings arose there. He thought they were going to inform the police, but that didn't happen."

"Neighbor lady? Berit Hoas? That's who I'm looking for. Is she in the hospital?" asked Maria. They would sometimes run into each other in the store in Klinte and make small talk about everyday things. Maria hoped it was nothing serious.

"Unfortunately it seems to be pretty bad. We've called to try to speak with her. According to the taxi driver she was the last one to see Ruben Nilsson alive. But she was in no shape for a conversation. Unconscious, they said when I asked the nurse a while ago. Her condition appears critical. The taxi driver said something about creamed morels. The dead man in there"—Ek pointed toward the upper floor of the house—"and the neighbor lady shared some creamed morels. Morels apparently have to be parboiled before you eat them. I've never tried."

"Poor Berit, if she accidentally killed someone she'd never get over it. This is just awful." Maria unconsciously backed up a few steps. "The taxi driver, did he eat the mushrooms, too?"

"No, I don't think so. I was thinking we should talk with him a little. But he's sleeping right now, according to his wife. He's been driving a taxi all night and will probably sleep until two or three, she thought."

Maria got in her car again, took her cell phone and phoned Jenny Eklund, who was quite dismayed.

"It's not easy to get hold of a substitute in the middle of the summer. Today I guess we'll have to serve packaged meatballs and pasta but the rest of the week something has to be worked out. You don't fix food for fifty kids with the wave of a hand. The milk alone, you know!" Maria agreed and offered to go and shop if that would be of any help, but Jenny had already sent another parent out to organize that. "Maybe we'll call you later, if we don't get hold of anyone who can work in the kitchen. But you're probably working next week?"

"Yes, that is if Krister, Emil's dad . . ." Maria broke off the sentence before she got to the point. On second thought, that was not a good idea, not if he intended to bring Mayonnaise along. She wanted to spare her son that experience. She decided to go home, but first she stopped at the newsstand and bought a couple of paperbacks and a big package of candy. On a rainy summer day that was probably the best you could do with your time.

Detective Inspector Tomas Hartman pushed his lawn mower back and forth over the lawn. His much-too-short shorts fluttered in the wind and made his skinny white legs look even narrower. His shirt was buttoned up to his neck, but he had taken off the tie he always wore on duty and stuffed it in his pocket. It peeked out of the cloth gap like a dog's tongue. When Maria parked outside the garage he did not look up right away, but instead continued straight across the lot in the direction he had started in, not stopping until he turned around and was once again on the drive.

"I'm taking the opportunity to cut the grass now that the weather has cleared up. Looks like there'll be more rain." He squinted and looked up toward the sky.

"Yes, probably will be," said Maria, continuing toward the house. "Is the door locked? I bought a book Marianne wanted since I was in town anyway."

"She's going to water aerobics so she's in the kitchen waiting for her ride."

Maria had actually wanted to buy a house by the sea, but the prices were even higher than she'd expected. Without a sizeable down payment and on a normal police salary it was impossible to find even a small shed with a sea view. True, she had been offered a place in Eksta by Olov Jakobsson, but somehow she had the feeling that he expected more than rent for such a contract. Olov was all right, that wasn't it. But Maria didn't have the energy for even modest expectations after the divorce. It takes time to gather up your skirts and move on. Renting the top floor from Tomas and Marianne Hartman felt more neutral. They were very low-key; they all might have a cup of coffee together if they happened to be outside at the same time in the yard, but otherwise they respected Maria's privacy when she went up to her apartment. Marianne was on disability after undergoing a lung transplant due to emphysema. She was very happy to have children in the house and immediately offered to watch them if that was needed. She could not exactly kick a soccer ball with them in the yard, but she could be available to watch them. Tomas took care of the yard; that was his major hobby and Maria had nothing against having access to a green oasis without having to take responsibility for it. Another benefit was that she could carpool with Tomas Hartman to work. When you're single with two children you have to count pennies. Besides, a number of minor matters and police formalities could be taken care of in the car. And Emil was within walking distance of the soccer school in Klinte. All told this had outweighed the advantages of living for almost free in Eksta.

"I bought the book we were talking about yesterday, Marianne. You can read it first, and I can borrow it when you're done if it's good. I felt like I wanted a little escape from reality, so I got a mystery for myself. *The Myths of the Plagues* sounds a little too real. On the back cover there's something about the Black Death and the Spanish flu. It says that new figures show a hundred thousand people died in Sweden alone. Sounds a little heavy. We'll have to see what you think of it."

"Nice of you. Listen, I heard that Berit Hoas is in the hospital. My girlfriend told me. It's not anything serious, is it?"

Chapter 8

Petter Cederroth was lying in bed in a half-stupor, squinting toward the narrow crack of gray daylight coming in at the lower edge of the blind. Sonja had been in twice to wake him, but he asked to be left alone so he could sleep a little longer. The police were looking for him, she said, and then a nurse at the hospital had called and wanted to talk with him. It was something about Berit Hoas.

People don't get what a night shift means. If you get home at seven you fall asleep by eight o'clock at best. By twelve you've managed to sleep for four hours. Four hours! When someone calls and asks, "Are you still asleep?" you can't help but get mad. No one would call a day worker at two in the morning and say with surprise, "Are you still asleep?"

It's a lack of respect, damn it! Driving a taxi on a weekend night is not exactly a lazy man's job! Besides all the passengers arriving on the night boat with enough baggage to spend the winter on Sandön and arguing about where the taxi line is and who was first at the sign, there were talkative people going home from the bar who haggle about the fare or people going to the hospital to give birth or women who've argued with their husbands and intend to spend the night with their sister and left their money at home.

When you sleep during the day, the events of the night get mixed up. It seems like you sleep lighter and dream more.

Petter woke up because he was cold. When he went to pull up the blanket, it was on the floor and completely damp with sweat. It was cloudy outside and not particularly warm in the room. He wasn't getting sick, was he? Petter leaned on his elbow and took a gulp of water from the glass sitting on the nightstand. It was lukewarm and stale and his throat hurt when he swallowed. It was not good timing if he were to get sick now. Here he had carefully instructed Sonja in how she should take in the homing pigeons and put the rings in the pigeon clock each time after they came home from the competition. That task demanded a trained educator, but it meant he could take yet another extra shift with the taxi. Money that would go for a vacation in the fall when the flow of tourists subsided. Sonja wanted so much to travel to China.

Petter leaned his head against the pillow again and shut his eyes. The events of the night were still spinning in his head. When you've been driving a taxi a long time you recognize the people you drive often. Yet a taxi driver is sometimes a non-person, an observer. Once the passenger gets into the taxi and gives the address, the driver doesn't exist anymore. That's how it was last night when he drove one of the doctors of the new healthcare center. Private facility, of course, where the nurses look like airline stewardesses in their well-tailored uniforms and speak clearly and courteously as if they were always being monitored. According to Sonja they had to submit voice tests—whether that was true or not was hard to say. Reine Hammar was his name. Petter had seen the article about him in the newspaper. He was tall—maybe as tall as six-foot-six—perfect suit and perfect hair, but with a cold or allergy. He didn't blow his nose, it was more like sniffing and constantly clearing his throat. After ten minutes in the car with him, the sound got on Petter's nerves.

His wife had also been in the picture in the newspaper, a charming woman who looked like she knew what she wanted. She was a doctor too, but she wasn't the one with him in the taxi last night. This woman was young, with long blonde hair, a short white skirt, and high-heeled boots. Could have been his daughter, if you let your kid go out in such an outfit. The address was Jungmansgatan. Hammar lived in a little house worth over four million kronor in Norderklint, if he hadn't recently moved. That had also been in the newspaper.

At the risk of running over pedestrians and bicyclists Petter observed the couple's doings in the rearview mirror. There was no hesitation, no uncertainty as she pulled down the zipper on his pants. This was clearly not the first time. When she leaned her head down she made eye contact with Petter in the mirror and winked at him with an amused smile. This was when he missed the turnoff in the round-about, but they didn't seem to mind going around again.

When they got out of the car Hammar pressed a five-hundred kronor bill in Cederroth's hand. "You'll keep this confidential, I hope."

"Of course!" he answered and put the bill in his pants pocket with a shrug. A tip is never a bad thing.

The rest of the night had not been as entertaining. When the ferry came in at midnight he drove an elderly woman to Fårö. She was going to stay by herself in a cabin on Skär that she was renting from a distant relative. But when they got there, in the dark she was unsure which house it was. It was already almost one-thirty in the morning—not exactly a good time to knock on anyone's door—so the woman went back to town with him and checked into a hotel in Visby. The money some people had!

She thanked him for the conversation and said it was worth every penny. Petter had a vague feeling that maybe there never was any relative on Skär. That she was paying him for the conversation and a little nocturnal sightseeing tour—an adventure for the two of them. Even so Petter had hardly said a word, only listened to the amazing tall tales and thought that he actually would have driven her for free, it had been that interesting to hear about what it was like in the past. About the new minister who took a shot right through the ear when he came to Fårö and proclaimed that they ought to pay a tithe like other people in Sweden. The bullet was still in the altar painting below Judas as a warning to future ministers, the lady said.

Laughing, she also described the real eccentrics who never once in their lives left Fårö. Why would you do that when you're at the center of the world and everything else is only periphery? And about the vicar whose foot slipped off the pedal after a party and he crashed his car through the fence to Hulda's place at the bend.

"It's your pastor coming, dear Hulda. Just take it easy, it's your pastor coming." The lady was an amazing impersonator and he laughed heartily at her mimicry.

Best was the story about "Everyone's Dad," the man who claimed all paternity on the island so that no one would grow up without a father. That's why everyone on Fårö is related to everyone else.

After dropping off the woman, he drove a man with a cramp in his chest to the emergency room, where they were at full capacity. Petter really wanted to hear how things stood with Berit, but no one paid any attention to him, and afterward he was grateful that the man survived the ride, despite his severe chest pains. The guy should have taken an ambulance, of course, but did not want to be any trouble. Between three and four o'clock it was quiet and Petter nodded off for a while at the steering wheel. He admitted that straight out when the infectious disease specialist questioned him later in detail about the night's events. But that was much later and for the moment Cederroth had no idea what a commotion there would be.

"Now you've got to drag yourself out of bed, Petter. The police are here. They want to talk with you. I've put the coffee on." Sonja pulled the cover off and tugged on the shade so that the roller flew to the top and revolved an extra turn. He hated it when she did that, it always meant more work when the blind got stuck and had to be taken down and re-attached. The light cut into his eyes—his whole body ached.

"If it's about Ruben I have nothing more to say. He was dead in his bed upstairs. I don't know any more than that."

Police Inspector Jesper Ek sat down at the kitchen table and observed Sonja Cederroth as she moved between the pantry and the kitchen table with the cookie tins. He recognized the red, green, and yellow container, where the tins could be piled on top of one another, from his grandmother's house. Sonja had set out crullers and nut cookies and almond tarts and gorån and enormous saffron buns. Then there were mocha squares, chocolate Swiss roll with homemade butter cream icing, shortbread, and coconut bars.

"Please, don't go to any trouble on my account," Ek attempted, but Sonja just smiled.

"On the mainland perhaps you're content with seven sorts of cookies, but we're on Gotland now! We don't skimp on the good things in life.

"It's just too awful what happened to Ruben! You can't believe it's true. First he kills all his pigeons and then he eats poison mushrooms, and to top it off he invites Berit Hoas over. She can't have done him any harm, that nice little person. What would he do that for? What a frightful mess!" Sonja turned on the kitchen faucet by using the hand towel—if anyone had touched it with dirty hands it was best to protect yourself. She was meticulous about such things.

"Sonja, that's not correct." Petter Cederroth had put on pants and a shirt but no socks. His back and arms ached when he tried to pull them on and finally he rolled them up into a ball and threw them at Sonja when she came in and nagged at him for the fourth time. It struck her in the small of her back, but she didn't even notice.

Ek took out a pad and pen and noted the necessary formalities.

"Tell me now from the start what happened. So, you went to Ruben Nilsson's house at ten o'clock in the morning. What was your business?"

Petter told about the deployment of pigeons for the competition where Ruben did not show up, and about the horrible sight in the dovecote. That he went over to the neighbor, Berit Hoas, and that then they broke a window to see what was up with Ruben when he didn't come to the door.

"It may be as Sonja says that he took his own life, but he wasn't the one who treated the mushrooms. It was Berit. I've had creamed morels at her place before and there's never been anything wrong with them. If anyone can cook, it's Berit Hoas."

"You have?" said Sonja. "When did you eat at Berit's? You never told me that, Petter. Maybe you should eat there from now on. Move there; see if I care. That was probably what you wanted before you got me around your neck. Then she didn't want you, but maybe she's changed her mind now?"

"Perhaps we should stick to the subject," said Ek when he heard Sonja getting ready to continue. Without meaning to, Petter had hit her sore spot. If Sonja Cederroth had any pride in life it was what she put on the table, and she tolerated no comparisons. Petter seemed completely unmoved. Presumably this wasn't the first time the subject had come up. He sat down at the table and leaned his head on his hands. Ek observed him. He really did not look well.

"Did Ruben Nilsson have any enemies?" Ek continued. There was really no suspicion of a crime, no external injuries on the body. The wallet, money intact, was under the victim's pillow, but the question still had to be asked.

"No friends, and no enemies. There was a painting salesman here a few days ago, otherwise we haven't seen any strangers." Sonja remained standing with the coffeepot in her hand and thought about it.

"Ruben was an extremely solitary person. It was like he never let anyone get close to him. I thought about the pigeons being dead. I read in a magazine that there's a venereal disease called chlamydia, a kind of parrot disease. If pigeons get it they can get pneumonia and die. Darned if I know how they get it," said Sonja thoughtfully and then shuddered.

"That's not the way it is, Sonja. When Björkman got pneumonia from his pigeons it was called parrot disease and it's not a venereal disease. You're mixing the two up. You can't just go saying things about people when you don't understand what they are."

"So what are you going to do now? Who is his heir, is it the brother?" she continued in a slightly sulky tone. "Or the niece? You probably know that it's Mikaela Nilsson, the one who's in the Cabinet. Minister of Equality. Although I'm sure she has money anyway. It was never really clear which of the brothers was her father, Ruben or Erik."

"We have nothing to do with that, Sonja." Cederroth shook his disheveled head.

He was noticeably embarrassed on his wife's account, but answered her anyway. "Ruben wouldn't want Erik to be his heir, you understand that, don't you? I'm sure he has a will hidden somewhere."

When Ek refused a second refill and was getting ready to go, Petter Cederroth followed him to the door. Courtesy required it, but it was hard work getting up from the table. His head ached and every muscle in his body was stiff and tense. The last half hour all Petter wanted to do was go lie down again, but Sonja had set the table with everything the house had to offer. She wanted to show the police that she was no worse a housewife than the cook. In the doorway he called after Ek.

"What happens now? I mean with the funeral and that? Who takes care of that?"

"It will be whoever is the closest relative, if it doesn't say otherwise in the will. But he can't be buried until the investigation is done. We'll be in touch. There's nothing in the present situation that indicates a crime, but we'll wait for the autopsy."

"So he's going to have an autopsy?" Petter drew his hand over his beard stubble. "Is it necessary to waste tax money on such things? He was old. Everyone dies of something, don't they?"

Chapter 9

Dr. Jonathan Eriksson, infectious disease specialist at Visby General Hospital, put down the receiver and rested his head in his hands. He felt like he wanted to cry. If he had been alone he would not have resisted it. The fatigue and a steadily grinding anxiety were making him sick to his stomach. The recreation center assistant, the blonde girl from Burträsk with slightly protruding front teeth, just wanted to let him know that Nina had not brought Malte and that everyone was waiting to go on a field trip. Yes, they had tried calling home several times, but no one answered. Could they have overslept? It was very unfortunate if that was the case. Malte's mother had promised to drive. It wouldn't be easy to find another parent at this time of the morning. Damn it all, so little was required to set off the worry that was always there like a dull ache in his belly. The worst must not have happened. They really might just have overslept.

Jonathan logged onto the computer and picked up the digital microphone, but could not come up with the words. Several days without sleep produces a peculiar form of aphasia, you fumble for nouns and don't remember the name of your closest co-worker. If ordinary people grasped what miserable condition their doctors were in after a weekend of being on call, they would not put their well-being in their hands with any confidence. A truck driver has to take a break after four and a half hours; a doctor can work around the clock and is still expected to be empathetic. Jonathan tried to put aside his personal worries and focus on his work for the remaining few minutes before he could leave the hospital.

A woman had died in the morning and now one hour later Jonathan was sitting with the test results up on the computer screen. He backed up and read his notes in the hope that it would help him complete the patient chart note.

"Previously healthy seventy-one-year-old woman dies 6:35 a.m. of respiratory failure, heart failure, and renal failure, most likely complications of influenza type A." Pause again. The illness pattern had seemed like a serious sepsis with a very acute progression. White fluid-filled lungs on the X-ray. Peripheral swelling, the whole capillary system had run amok and opened up while her blood pressure plummeted. It had been necessary to give more fluid drip and the swelling had increased. The woman had been severely disoriented and anxious before unconsciousness set in and then death. They had not even had time to intubate her. No close relatives who had thought about coming, thankfully. A sister, but evidently she was in no shape to make it to the hospital. He was slightly ashamed of his reflections. But being forced to meet shaken, perhaps even accusatory family members and give them an involved, empathetic reception after almost twenty-four hours on duty felt almost impossible.

Berit Hoas was the name of the woman who had died. Her terrified gaze would haunt him a long time. He knew that. Perhaps he never should have become a doctor, it wasn't worth the agony he felt when treatment failed and someone died. Could you have done anything differently? Thought differently? Acted more quickly? The last seven hours he had done his best to save her life.

This influenza had an unusually violent progression. To start with it had only been determined that CRP was over 100. Low leucocytes, nothing life-threatening in that. Flu-like symptoms. Effect on breathing. Headache. Then rapidly declining saturation, no urine production. Signs of heart failure. When mushroom poisoning had been dismissed at first his thoughts turned to an infection with legionella bacteria and then to ornithosis, when the woman mentioned that she had fed homing pigeons. She had been re-cultured and put on Tetracycline without effect. There were always a lot of ifs when you weren't able to keep someone alive. If you could have made the diagnosis sooner. If she had been sent to the ICU sooner. Instead she'd died in the elevator on the way up. If . . . Jonathan moaned out loud when the pager sounded. He dialed the number to the switchboard and waited.

"Can you come up to the ER, Jonathan."

"Isn't there another doctor . . . Hasn't Morgan arrived?"

"Not yet. He called. There's something wrong with the car again. Listen . . . a man has come in with flu symptoms. He's in very bad shape. Barely conscious. His wife is on the verge of a breakdown, talks about a neighbor who just died. Can you hurry? It doesn't look good."

Jonathan swore out loud to himself. Morgan probably forgot to fill the tank, that climber. If there was anything that got Jonathan Eriksson's gall it was people who didn't show up on time and didn't keep their promises. The collaboration with his colleague Morgan Persson would have been a marvel of smoothness if it wasn't for his poor instincts about the laws that govern the reality in which other people live. Do cars need gas? Does the phone service get shut off if you don't pay the bill? Does food spoil?

Treatment room 9 was bathed in white fluorescent light from the ceiling fixtures. A burly man was lying on the examining table in the middle of the room. His wife got up immediately from the tall armchair where she had been sitting dangling her legs—the only available chair in the room, besides a stool—when Jonathan Eriksson stepped in through the door.

"He's dying! Do something!" The woman's face was tear-stained and her eyes were wild and red-rimmed. "Won't you do something, doctor. This isn't working. He's going to die on me! Take a look for yourself. Petter, do you hear me? Answer! Don't you see, doctor? He's dying!"

"ECG not remarkable. Some tachycardia, maybe. Pulse 100. Blood pressure 90 over 60. Temp 103. Saturation 97 percent," the nurse attending the patient reported. "Admission samples taken. Is there anything else you want?"

"I want to hear what happened first." Jonathan shook Sonja Cederroth's hand and sat down on the edge of the bed. The fatigue was pressing on his head. The fluorescent light cut into his eyes. If this hadn't happened he would have been on his way home now to clear up yet another situation. Where the hell was Morgan? The woman was talking nonstop and Jonathan was almost afraid for himself when he noticed that he hadn't been listening at all.

"Excuse me. Can you take that from the beginning again?"

"Is he going to get better? What should we do? Petter was hardly able to eat today. He didn't even taste my dumplings, even though I served them with melted butter and green peas."

Jonathan could feel himself getting irritated. It was impossible to think clearly with this woman buzzing about irrelevant matters the whole time.

"First I want you to tell me what happened," he said, turning toward the patient. "How long have you had a fever?"

Sonja Cederroth answered in her spouse's stead. "He didn't take his temperature even though I told him to. He never wants to. You can tell if you have a fever, he always says. I think it embarrasses him that he has to put it in his bum, you understand, doctor. He's funny that way. I heard from the nurse that Berit Hoas is dead. She called when we were on our way to the hospital, she's sickly, poor thing. The nurse called, that is. That turned out wrong, excuse me. Is that right? Is she dead? Berit is almost a neighbor to us and Ruben, Ruben Nilsson. They put him in a black bag with a zipper, Petter said. And all the pigeons, can you believe that, doctor? He had over sixty pigeons. What should we do?"

"Take it slowly so I can follow along." Jonathan placed his hand on the woman's arm to calm her if possible and get her to be a little more coherent.

"Ruben's pigeons are dead and Ruben and Berit are dead too. It's like the plague. Do you understand what I'm saying, doctor? It's like the plague! Petter is going to die. He's barely getting any air and his heart is pounding in his chest something awful."

"Have you been in contact with pigeons?" Jonathan asked in a new attempt to communicate with the patient.

Now Petter Cederroth looked up. He exerted himself to get out the words.

"I went up the stairs to the dovecote and saw that they were dead. Every single one. And then Ruben. He was lying stone dead in his bed." Petter sniffled. "Our pigeons have survived."

The thought Jonathan Eriksson had in his mind was a pure nightmare. For a period of several minutes he did not hear what the people around him were saying. The sound came and went in waves. Sonja's perplexed face. The nurse's hand on his shoulder. They didn't reach him. I'm working at a soccer camp, as the cook, Berit Hoas's voice echoed. I have to get better so I can come back after the weekend. Fifty children are counting on me. Fifty children! Jonathan backed out of the room. Excused himself. Pulled the nurse with him. Out! Away! He covered his mouth and tried to keep from breathing until they came some distance out into the corridor. There he stopped and stared at the skeleton the orthopedists use for patient instruction. Suddenly completely lacking in initiative and empty. He gasped for air.

"What is it, Jonathan? You look so strange. Tell me what it is! Are you sick? You're scaring me, tell me what it is!" said Agneta.

"I hope I'm wrong. But I don't dare trust that. Perhaps I'm going completely crazy, getting the creeps, but right now I want us to bring out whatever breathing protection is available. Preferably P3 masks, 3M with tube filter last for eight hours, otherwise duck beaks. All personnel who go into the treatment room should have protective clothing, gloves, and the best possible breathing protection. The patient and his wife likewise, until we know what it is. Find the disease control officer for me. Now!"

"What do you think it is, Jonathan?"

"It may be bird flu. I need a register of all individuals that Petter Cederroth has seen in the past five days. Good Lord! He was in the waiting room at the ER. How long was he sitting there? I saw him give a piece of candy to the little boy with the tractor."

Chapter 10

"*A* *case of suspected bird flu has been discovered on Gotland.
For this reason any tourists planning to go to the island are
asked to postpone their travel if possible. We also want to ask any
passengers who took a taxi in Visby on the evening of July 1 and
the following night to please call the Infectious Disease Clinic's
new telephone line 0498-690 001. There is no cause for alarm,
but to avoid lines we are asking individuals with flu-like symptoms not to visit a health center or hospital. Instead a doctor will
be making house calls as needed. To get in touch with a nurse
and schedule a doctor's visit, call 0498-690 002. For general
information, call 0498-690 003. The report of a case of bird
flu has not yet been confirmed, and we repeat, there is no cause
for alarm.*"

Maria Wern turned off the radio, which continued with
a broadcast from Almedalen Week and a female journalist's complaints of sexual harassment by a number of named
politicians from both sides of the aisle. Minister of Equality
Mikaela Nilsson was merciless in her judgment. It reeked
of a major scandal. Maria logged onto her computer. In the
room next door was Tomas Hartman. She could hear him
talking with his wife on the phone. Words of love.

Everyday agreements. A number of affirmations of love. I love you too. Not bad after thirty years of marriage. Happy people. Of course you think it will last the rest of your life when you promise one another eternal fidelity. But life doesn't always turn out the way you imagined. And when it doesn't turn out the way you imagined it, it's just as well to drive away your self-recriminations. Pulverize them in your clenched fist and blow the dust out the window. Because they don't lead anywhere, they only bring you grief. The most painful thing is seeing the happiness of others and thinking that you have failed. That maybe you're never going to find someone to trust and live with. She heard Hartman hang up the phone and then whistle enthusiastically. Not the melodic line itself but a harmony he was trying out second hand, with the same effect as when someone is humming to their iPod and you hear only the naked voice and not the song itself. Now he was getting up, the chair legs scraped across the floor and a mop of gray hair became visible in the doorway.

"We've got a preliminary autopsy report on the man from Värsände. He was knifed in the throat sometime in the night between June 28 and 29. On his heels he has dirt-soiled scratches as if he'd been dragged on the ground. Then he has a small, barely noticeable cut on the upper left arm and an old scar on his chest. We don't have any results on the chemical analysis yet. We don't know more than that right now. We still have no idea who he is. In age and appearance he doesn't tally with anyone who has been reported missing. The black hair may indicate that his ethnic origin isn't Swedish." Hartman glanced at the clock. "I was thinking about having my lunch on a bench by the ring wall in Östergravar, do you want to join me? It would feel good to get away from here for a while and return to the Middle Ages."

"Sure." Maria was getting up to go with him when the phone rang. She asked him to wait while she took the call, and he returned to his office, still whistling, to get his lunchbox in the meantime.

"I'm looking for Maria Wern, Emil's mom. Is this the right number?" asked a female voice.

"Yes." Maria started feeling worried. Had something happened? Did Emil hurt himself? Hit his head? Get sick and had to be picked up at the soccer camp? Or was he just homesick? Perhaps Emil was jealous that Krister had taken Linda and not him. But that's what he'd chosen. Maybe he'd changed his mind and wanted to be with his dad instead?

"My name is Agneta and I'm a nurse at the Infectious Disease Clinic. This evening we're having an informational meeting about bird flu. This concerns the children at the soccer camp at Klinte School. There is no cause for alarm, but we must take certain precautionary measures."

"What do you mean by that?" Maria felt that she had to sit down while the words worked their way in and assumed their full significance.

"We'll go into that in more detail at the meeting this evening. It will be at Warfsholm."

"No, I want to know now." Maria felt her face turning red and her neck flushing. The sense of an incomprehensible threat coupled with powerlessness made her agitated. "Do you think the children may have been infected by the bird flu? The cook, Berit Hoas, has it, doesn't she? She wasn't feeling well; I know she was taken to the hospital. Does she have bird flu? She does, doesn't she? Answer me!"

"I have no authority to answer that. If you have any urgent questions before the meeting, you may contact Dr. Jonathan Eriksson at our information line."

The nurse sounded stressed. Maria suspected that the situation was worse than she wanted to let on.

If she says there's no cause for alarm again I'm going to scream, thought Maria, feeling a rush of hatred toward the woman, even though she was only doing her job according to the directives she'd been given. She could at least talk like a real person, so you felt like it was a fellow human being talking to you and not a bureaucrat. Emil, what's going on with Emil? Maria felt worry like a clamp pressing around her neck.

"What do you intend to do? Take samples? Vaccinate them? Does the vaccine help if they've already been infected? Is there even any vaccine? Or medicine?"

"As I just said: If you have questions, you have to speak with our doctor. There is no reason to worry. The measures we have taken are simply to be on the safe side, if it should turn out that this is bird flu, that is. We still don't know that."

"But you must have a strong suspicion of that if people are being asked not to travel to Gotland. Right? That's not a small amount of money you're talking about, if the flow of tourists stops." Maria felt harsh, but she did not intend to let her off that easily.

Hartman was in the doorway again, this time with his lunch in hand. He appeared to be in a marvelous mood.

"Are you coming?" He took a step into the office. "What is it, Maria? Has something happened?"

"Listen, I can't come with you. I've got to make a call. It's about Emil. I'll explain later." But instead of leaving the office Hartman sat in the chair by Maria's desk with his lunch in his lap. She was glad he was sitting there; it felt like a guarantee that nothing too terrible could happen, a link to everyday reality where things such as children being infected by fatal diseases don't exist. Maria dialed the number she'd been given to the infectious disease doctor. There was a busy signal. Most of all she wanted to go to Klinte School and make sure that Emil was doing fine. Right now. Her thoughts were whirling. What would she do if he were sick? She had to know whether he was infected, didn't she? The line was still busy and Maria was happy that Hartman was sitting there, so there was someone to share her worry with.

"I was thinking about the neighbor to Berit Hoas, Ruben Nilsson, the one with the homing pigeons. He was found dead in his bed. This is bigger than they're saying. What aren't they telling us? They must understand that people will get upset and demand to find out what's going on. This concerns my child!"

"So how contagious is it?" asked Hartman, for lack of anything better to say. It was more like evidence that he was listening.

"I don't know, but if it spreads like the common cold I've heard that a sneeze reaches ten meters. Then I guess it depends on how much resistance you have. There is medicine that stops viral infections."

"Tamiflu. A decision was made that Sweden should buy up a million treatment rounds of ten doses a year ago, when there was an outbreak of bird flu in Southeast Asia. An emergency supply was supposed to be built up. I hope that happened."

"Yes, I remember reading about that. The doctors had prescribed medicine on fairly shaky grounds and those who needed medicine for real afflictions had to wait, because they ran out at the pharmacy. Why doesn't he answer? I think this shows a lack of respect! They have to set up more phone lines. They have some irritating music playing. Someone's pounding on a piano and then there's a catchy fiddle that stirs up the tempo even more. No doubt for a calming effect. It's not making me calm. I'm getting mad."

Tomas Hartman was about to say something when Maria was connected to the infectious disease specialist. She made a dismissive gesture with her hand and clamped the receiver under her chin while she reached for paper and pen.

"I want to know the truth," said Maria when the introductions were over and she had asked about Berit Hoas.

"I have an obligation of confidentiality and I can't say anything about a particular patient, I hope you'll respect that. The truth is that we don't know—and when we don't know for sure it's better to take precautionary measures than to stick our heads in the sand." She heard him sigh heavily. What reason did he have to sigh? He probably didn't have a child who was in danger. Conceited ass! Maria imitated him to herself . . . I hope you'll respect that. Why did he have to hide behind such pretentious words? That way of talking creates distance. What you need is understanding and a sense that someone really cares.

"Okay. And what do you intend to do with the children if they're infected? I want to know that now. Then I intend to bring Emil home from the camp. I don't want him there if there's a risk that he'll get sick."

"It's not that simple. The disease control officer has decided to have the children remain at the school in quarantine. If any of them are infected we can't risk spreading the infection further into the community. The children will be given medicine for bird flu."

"In quarantine. What do you mean? That he can't come home? What happens if he's not infected now, but gets infected by someone in there? Let's say tomorrow, because I couldn't take him home. Do you have a legal right to do this? Otherwise this is unlawful deprivation of liberty, that's a felony. I hope you understand the seriousness of this." Maria felt anger suddenly flare up. She would have preferred being face-to-face with this guy so that he couldn't escape or turn his eyes away.

"To put it in plain terms, if we don't do this and it should turn out to be bird flu in a mutated form, which we have feared for a long time, it may mean thousands infected. The disease control officer has a legal right to hold people for taking of samples. We anticipate needing to keep them for five days if none of them become ill. So that they won't infect each other, the children will each have their own room, where they should stay and breathing protection when it is necessary for them to leave the room. We will have health-care personnel on site and all the children will be followed, their temperatures taken morning, noon, and evening. The children will have cell phones so that they can maintain contact with their families. I understand that this is difficult," he added in a somewhat softer tone.

"So how long do you intend to keep my son there?" Maria sought Hartman's eyes for reinforcement.

"In the best case we can call off the entire action as soon as tomorrow. That's the earliest we can get a definitive answer as to whether or not this is bird flu."

"But you believe that it is."

"Unfortunately, yes. But I hope by all that's holy I'm wrong."

Chapter 11

Jonathan Eriksson was staring out the window from his desk at the Tallbacken assisted living facility in Follingbo. The magnificent rainbow arching across the sky and the expansive view did not lighten his mood, feeling like a prisoner in his office. Just like back in the day when the building was a sanitarium and the feared tuberculosis spread with awful speed, they did not want to let anyone who was infected into the hospital in town. So the residents at the Tallbacken assisted living facility had now been moved to Tingsbrogården or evacuated elsewhere, to make room for those who had been brought in for observation and almost certainly already contagious. An observation ward was set up on the ground floor and a ward for patients with symptoms on the second floor. So far it was the taxi driver and his wife, the two policemen and the ambulance personnel who had contact with Ruben Nilsson, five homing pigeon owners who had met with Petter Cederroth on Saturday evening to go over the results of the pigeon competition, the passengers the taxi driver had reported from the night in question as well as the patients who had been in the emergency room at the same time as him, and the librarian who helped Ruben Nilsson find homing pigeon association websites on the Internet.

Rigorous arrangements, but Dr. Åsa Gahnström, the disease control officer, did not dare take any risks in the present situation. Especially not with the healthcare personnel who had been in contact with Berit Hoas and Petter Cederroth. They had all been taken out of service and reassigned to the phone lines for information to the general public, each with a room where they had to stay night and day on the top floor in the main building of the old sanitarium. All had been given strict orders to use breathing protection if they left their rooms.

This also applied to Jonathan Eriksson. The phone call with the worried mother shook him to the core, and there were more calls coming. Maria Wern's worry was justified. If her son isn't infected now, but turns out to be later, who is responsible? Can you sacrifice one child to save thousands of lives? Jonathan had questioned the disease control officer's decision, but was obliged to maintain the same line with respect to the general public and the media. It was hardest to argue with his medical colleague Reine Hammar, who was clinical director at the recently opened Vigoris Health Center at Snäckgärdsbaden. A schism had immediately arisen when at the request of the disease control officer Jonathan had to question him about when and where his colleague had been taken in a taxi by Petter Cederroth.

"What the hell is this? Do you think you're some kind of policeman?"

Yes, that's more or less how it felt to chart in detail the taxi driver's doings during the night, as if you were the extended arm of the law. Pure investigative work to judge whether someone was guilty or not of carrying the contagion.

"Listen, I'm not interested in your personal life. I want

to know what time you took a taxi and whether you were alone, that's all."

"I'm going to file a complaint to Social Services about this. This is abusive treatment, damn it, and not even remotely medically motivated. I'm going to laugh my head off if this isn't bird flu. What a nuthouse!" Reine Hammar had thrown the protective mask on the desk, gone into his office, and slammed the door.

"Listen, if it's not bird flu I'll laugh my head off too. I'll laugh until I puke," Jonathan called after him behind the closed door, but was not certain that Reine heard him. A short time later he had Hammar's wife on the phone. She was considerably more collected and seemed to grasp the seriousness of the situation.

Jonathan was dragged out of his thoughts by the phone ringing again. He collected himself briefly and picked up the receiver. It was Åsa Gahnström, the disease control officer for the province of Gotland. He exhaled. He shouldn't have done that.

"Just a brief bit of information. We have a problem."

"A problem. Okay." He tried not to sound sarcastic, but the undertone reached all the way to Åsa.

"I would hope that you at least would realize the seriousness of this. I'm the one who's responsible and I'm the one who'll be hung out to dry. Oh well, posterity will have to judge me. The big problem right now is that we have far too little Tamiflu in the emergency supply to do any preventive treatment. Word went out to the general public that a million rounds had been procured, but not everything that was purchased is Tamiflu, far from it. Only a fraction, really. So my strategy is, treat those who have symptoms and those who are latent with the drugs we have and keep them under careful control. It's hard to believe it's true, but that's how bad it is."

"But then what's been procured?" he asked.

"The remainder are other anti-viral drugs, without real effect on the bird flu we fear. I've been in contact with the procurement managers. They haven't bought anything at all the past year. Nothing. The money is there, but they haven't pulled the trigger and purchased any medication. Sweden has simply put itself in line."

"What do you mean by that?" Jonathan noticed that his hand had left a damp mark on the desk pad. Suddenly the room felt stuffy and enclosed. The collar on his T-shirt was choking him, his pants felt tight.

"For a tidy sum, most other countries in Europe have already signed contracts for a place in line to purchase Tamiflu. We're extremely late getting started. All we can do is appeal to the outside world for help—discreetly. If this leaks out to the press we'll have a panic situation. Can you imagine what it would be like—what the terror might do to people, what a strain there would be on the healthcare system if thousands of people called at the same time or showed up at a hospital demanding treatment? Just this morning the general director of the Swedish Institute for Communicable Disease Control issued strict directives to the pharmacies that only disease control officers should be able to prescribe Tamiflu. This should have come much sooner. Unfortunately a number of doctors have been very quick with their prescription pads once the news was released. I've assigned someone to review the prescriptions and if possible effective immediately recall the filled prescriptions that are not medically motivated. The new system where the pharmacies register which medications are picked up isn't so bad after all. This is a typical example. When it really counts you look after your own first."

"When will we know with certainty that this is bird flu, when can we have an answer from Disease Control?"

"Normally it takes two or three days to type which strain of influenza we're dealing with and get a resistance determination. It has to be done at a level-four biosafety laboratory, but they think we can get a preliminary answer sooner. The national epidemiologist has ordered in extra personnel. Maybe we can get an answer as soon as this evening. It has top priority and they're doing their best. They'll call. I'll be in touch as soon as they do."

"What should I tell the parents? I have to be able to give them clear answers when they ask me whether the children at the soccer camp will receive treatment."

"Say that the children will get medicine. We'll dole out what we have for as long as it lasts. The most important thing is for them to remain calm. Otherwise we have to act as if we're dealing with bird flu until the opposite is proven. That's my policy. It's hard enough anyway to motivate the observation patients to stay inside. We have to pursue this consistently."

He heard how she swallowed and then braced herself, her voice getting tense. "For your information, Jonathan, I've also requested assistance from the police. The area around Klinte School will be cordoned off and movie showings in the school auditorium will be cancelled. I don't want to risk parents coming to pick up their children. If you have children yourself you understand what I mean. This arouses strong emotions. It's not an easy decision, but the scenario that could play out if we don't show a clear line is infinitely more frightening. Is the picture clear to you? We don't have medicine for the whole population. This may mean tens of thousands of deaths."

"And if it should turn out that it's not bird flu?" Jonathan could not keep from asking the question.

"Then I'll donate my body to research and my soul to be dissected by the media, and you'll inherit my chair. The decision has support from the National Pandemic Group. Speaking frankly, Jonathan—what else could it be? The old man with the homing pigeons died, unclear why. A preliminary autopsy report should arrive before too long. I've spoken with the pathologist about the risk of contagion. Berit Hoas died; it was a flu virus. We don't know yet what type—but flu is normally not this aggressive. She was basically healthy before she was infected. Petter Cederroth has a flu virus, again type unknown. But we don't dare wait. You can start treating him with Tamiflu if you haven't already done so. I heard he was doing poorly. His wife, if I'm correctly informed, has a slightly elevated temperature and a sore throat. We're waiting to find out if this is H5N1. You should be getting that at any time, if you've set up a computer out there in the woods."

Jonathan opened the window to let in the aromas of summer after the rain. It was oppressively hot in the office; he stood in the draft and breathed in the scent of pine forest. Sweat pearled on his forehead and his clothes stuck to his body. Did his throat feel a little rough? Did he feel a little feverish? Was there resistance when he swallowed? Hopefully imagination—a mental influenza. But still—the risk was there. With an incubation period of one to three days it could still flare up. What would happen to Malte and Nina then? It was worrisome enough as it was. Jonathan tried to dismiss the fear but it ground and ground deep in his belly as soon as he thought about them and the future and what it would be like when he could no longer conceal the shameful truth about her alcoholism, lie and set things right. If only he had been home more perhaps things wouldn't have turned out the way they did, perhaps the problem never would have developed, perhaps he could have stopped the destruction in time . . . if, if, if.

The old sanitarium environment was a reminder that wiped away the boundary of time. Jonathan Eriksson thought that he might as well have been in the 1940s as in the present. A generation or two ago people died from TB in Sweden the way those affected now were dying in other countries because they couldn't afford the medicine that could heal them. Young people. Parents with small children. Schoolchildren. Entire families wiped out. If the walls of this sanitarium could talk they would tell of hopelessness and despair, but also of courage and gallows humor and defiant hope. Life changed and new perspectives open up when you are staring death in the eye. What is important when you have a week left to live? Is there anything we've missed? Those of us who believed we would live forever now face the fact that death applies to us too, thought Jonathan. He got no further in his train of thought before the phone again demanded his attention. What would he say if it was another worried parent? Had they already cordoned off the school where the children were at soccer camp? Åsa didn't say.

Jonathan wanted to escape from it all but he grabbed the receiver and said his name as calmly and with as much control as he could. Every patient has a right to an engaged reception, regardless of how you feel yourself, an elderly colleague had imprinted in his medical students. It was still there as if he heard it yesterday.

"It's Nina." He heard immediately by her slack articulation that it was as he'd feared and his stomach muscles knotted up in defense. "Malte's not here. I don't know where he is, do you think he might have gone to a friend's?"

"I asked my mother to pick him up—thank god. He fell off the swing and his nose was bleeding. He couldn't get it to stop and he tried to wake you, but you were too far gone. Did you even notice he was gone? My mother said the door was wide open."

"Well, lucky you—your mother can show little Nina what to *do* with her own child! Accuse me of being a bad mother, go ahead! It's your fault. Your damned fault, you hypocritical jerk. I never wanted to have a kid, you were the one who wanted one and then . . . What happened then? Who the hell had to stay home and take care of everything, literally everything while you were gallivanting around?"

"I wasn't gallivanting around. I was doing my specialist training."

"So goddamned charming and important, more important than my life and my plans. Nina just wanted to go to art school and play a little, dabble a little with paint."

"Listen, we can talk about this when you're feeling better. Go lie down and call me later, when you know what you're saying."

"Take two white tablets and go lie down, is that the doctor's orders? My art teacher at high school said that I could actually be something. He saw that I had talent. He believed in me, did you know that? You fucking traitor. He said, 'Nina, you have genuine talent. You really have talent!' Do you hear that, you fucking—"

Jonathan hung up, steeled himself, and pushed away the thought of Nina. He thought about Malte. If it was bird flu Malte shouldn't be at daycare. There would be major risk of infection, he thought. It must be possible to resolve this somehow, even if the days Malte spent at daycare were the only days Jonathan felt calm and could work in peace.

Chapter 12

"*It is feared that an epidemic of bird flu has broken out on Gotland. Two deaths may be linked to the contagion, and a number of persons have been taken to the old Follingbo sanitarium for observation. We are speaking with disease control officer Åsa Gahnström. Dr. Gahnström, you say you've been expecting this epidemic to break out. Why haven't you taken any preventive measures?*"

"*First, we still don't know whether these patients are infected with bird flu, and second—*"

"*Why don't you know that?*" The radio reporter's voice penetrated like the tip of an arrow.

"*It takes time to determine what type of influenza we are talking about. The analysis must be done at a special biosafety laboratory. H5N1, commonly known as bird flu, normally affects birds but not people. Generally, when people are infected they've been in contact with animals. We have only seen a few cases where the contagion has been transferred from human to human. In the case of a twenty-one-year-old in Hong Kong who drank duck blood at a Lunar New Year ceremony, the nurse who treated him and his fourteen-year-old sister died, but no other cases have been reported. What we have feared for some time is that the virus could mutate and become like a normal virus in the way it infects humans. This could possibly happen if a single individual already has a typical influenza virus and is then infected with bird flu through contact with birds, allowing the different types of flu to exchange characteristics. There is also a risk that the process could occur in a domesticated animal, for example a hog. But in the present situation I see no cause for alarm."*

The reporter pressed on: *"According to reports, 180 cases of bird flu in humans have been discovered around the world, and eighty-seven of those infected are dead. If you have feared such a development and the mortality rate is so high, why is there so little preparedness for a crisis situation? Why hasn't the entire population been vaccinated for bird flu, like with tetanus, diphtheria, and polio?"*

"Viruses change form," answered Gahnström. *"New, more effective vaccines are developed all the time but before it is known exactly what the virus is, it's impossible to make a vaccine. Even the standard flu shot is customized for each outbreak in the Southern Hemisphere. Sometimes the virus manages to change so much that the vaccine does not provide complete protection. Then it takes at least six months to manufacture a vaccine for bird flu once it is known what the virus looks like, and we no longer have those resources in Sweden. Instead we have to buy the vaccine from abroad once it's known what needs to be manufactured."*

"And this may already have affected a third of our population? Can a comparison be made to the Spanish flu that broke out in 1918 and 1919, where twenty million people in the world lost their lives? The latest statistics show a hundred thousand deaths in Sweden alone." The reporter paused for the doctor to answer.

"That is a bit drastic perhaps. There is no cause for alarm right now."

Strange Bird

"We thank Åsa Gahnström and turn now to Almedalen, where we hope to get a commentary from the Minister of Public Health, Erik Malmgren."

Hans Moberg turned off the radio and pulled back the blue checked curtain of his camper. Yes, it was definitely starting to clear up—and about time. He stretched his legs and finished up his online flirtation with "Mature Woman '53" with a phrase in French he had picked up in a previous conversation with "Dolly P.," an unemployed mail clerk from Västerås. *Damned if I know what it means, but it looks charming.* His tongue was perched at the corner of his mouth as he pecked out the sentence letter by letter. *Women like that sort of thing; in his experience, the effect usually exceeded expectations.*

Of course, he had no intention of actually meeting "Mature Woman '53," but for the moment he needed someone who would show him some maternal solicitude. "Blonde Goddess" had, upon closer examination in a cabin on the Gotland ferry, turned out to be a disappointment. But those were blows you had to accept. Hans was used to it. *The ladies seldom correspond to the image you create for yourself when you're chatting with them on the Internet,* thought Hans Moberg with a shrug. *When it came to online dating, reality tended to be far too real—especially when meeting in broad daylight. In fact, it could be a bit of a shock—for both sides,* if he were to be completely honest with himself. In those cases, it was a matter of quickly returning to the mutual understanding that existed in their intimate conversations on the Web, or giving her a kiss right away to activate the romantic hormones before she had time to think about it.

Hans Moberg, known to his friends as "Moby," stood in front of the brown-stained mirror on the door of the broom closet and combed his long, wavy hair before stepping into his boots. He inspected his face again, yanked out a few white strands from his mustache and put on his white cowboy hat. He adjusted the brim so that it sat at a slight angle over one eye. Villains wear a black hat, heroes a white one; everyone knows that. He thought he was probably too nice, too indulgent in the interpretation of "a few pounds too many" and "some problems with finances right now." Not to mention "easily offended husband," which could be pure hell. He knew that from experience. Nevertheless this was his life. Traveling around in his camper/love nest and meeting women, wherever he wanted, whenever he wanted, and for as long as he wanted. No boss. No old lady. No schedule to stick to, other than the one he made for himself, and only if, as the hour approached, he still desired it. Otherwise he could forget about it, change his email address, create a new identity on Facebook, and move on to new adventures in a new guise.

That was actually part of the attraction: the acting, getting to play a new role every time. He'd been owner of an art gallery in Paris, construction industry project manager on the Riviera, agent in the intelligence services, leader of rescue operations for the fire department, and a big-game hunter in Gambia. Everything he'd dreamed about as a young boy, but that never happened—and didn't need to either. Now he could experience everything in his imagination without getting his shoes muddy or exposing himself to physical danger.

The important thing was how others saw him, whether they believed him. That was the kick, once he'd rehearsed his role and found a suitable counterpart on the Web: actually meeting women in real life and getting to test his act with them, picking out the best ones for the more passionate scenes.

Of course, not every woman he met got the full treatment. He had little use for those who demanded clean living and fidelity up front. That got too complicated. Even if there was the time he lived on potato decoction, sprouts, and sesame seeds for a whole week because the lady in his life was a vegan. He was not even allowed to wear his leather belt! But for that one week it didn't make any difference.

The incense had been pretty bad. A camper tolerates very little of that particular product, and it drove out the aroma of his own pipe tobacco. Smoked out of his own burrow! He felt homeless. Later, she'd expected him to eat nettles she had picked behind the men's restroom at the campground in Västervik. It was all too much; there were limits to what was acceptable. Time to pull up anchor and head for a more fashionable location, thought Moby.

Last night he had parked his love nest in an industrial area east of town. If someone wants to save on the unnecessary expense of paying for a space at an RV park, an electrical outlet at a factory building is a worthy alternative, wireless Internet, too, is easily borrowed when parked in a populated area. A penny saved is a penny earned, Moby always said. It was just a matter of looking out so the barbed wire didn't rip your pants as you climbed over the fence.

He'd marked a strip of beach on the map labeled Tofta Campground. There he could shower and freshen up before the evening's encounter with "Cuddly Skåne Girl." But before that, he had a little business to take care of—discreet deliveries. Cash in exchange for romance and renewed self-confidence. It often surprised him that more people didn't get into the same line of business. Freedom, quick money, and grateful customers. As the many cases thrown out of court had shown, there was practically no danger in buying and selling medications over the Internet or just peddling them right on the street for that matter. Hans

Moberg was careful to follow the developments in the media. The legislative authority had truly bitten itself in the tail on this one! The fourth clause in the Act on trade in pharmaceutical products (1996:1152) namely refers to the pharmaceutical decree from 1962, which was terminated in 1993. No court in Sweden can judge according to a law that no longer exists—the lowliest blueberry picker can understand that!

No, Hans Moberg was not worried about his livelihood, not now and not in the near future. By the time the monotonously slow decision-making process was over and the lawmakers finally had their butts in gear, the European Court would surely have abolished the Swedish pharmaceutical monopoly. Moby often said just this to his colleague, Manfred "Mayonnaise" Magnusson, who worried about the future of their business.

It would be fun to get together at Tofta Campground and pop open a beer or two before doling out Christmas presents to the Viagra customers. Some customers wanted their medication sent by mail, others wanted it delivered right into their hands. A few customers could be picked up on the spot when the demands for satisfactory entertainment increased during a camper vacation. It was just a matter of opening the kiosk door and inviting them in. Moby was lucky—his whole warehouse fit in his camper. And he used the thrice-yearly pickups to also refill his supply of alcohol. Really, those trips were like a vacation.

Business had really been booming when he'd joined forces with Betsy, who sold underwear and sex toys. What a businesswoman! There he'd met his match. And although it had tried his patience severely to stick to schedules and routes, it was with sorrow in his heart that he dropped her off in Tanumshede when winter came and the camper became too cramped for the two of them. Freedom has its price.

"Cuddly Skåne Girl"—his date this evening—loved country and western, honesty, and evenings at home, she wrote. On the picture she sent through cyberspace she was wearing a short, fringed leather skirt. A checked shirt unbuttoned to the limit of propriety and pointed boots in white leather. Yeehaw! Her red hair was cut in a pageboy and her mouth was red and broad. A real pretty little doll. Of course, Moby had been mistaken before.

"Cuddly Skåne Girl"—he hadn't even found out her real name. She was presumably an experienced Web charmer. Total discretion. He was usually just as careful himself. His newest moniker, "Doctor M," was coined after a couple of beers and was actually not very well considered, but it would have to do for the time being. The biggest problem for the evening would be consistently sticking to a Skåne dialect. He couldn't believe he'd been so stupid as to say he was from Skåne, too. It was a dilemma that occupied him until the morning hours, when he'd come up with the solution: he was an American living in Skåne! He rehearsed an American accent; in the best-case scenario, an American might be to the lady's taste. This was part of the game. Guessing your way to her secret wishes and then fulfilling them.

With Cuddly Skåne Girl he guessed that a "tragic fate" might open doors to the paradise of kindness and sympathy. But that had also taken considerable contemplation. The result of his mental efforts: he was an American country singer with an incurable disease. After a few hours of searching on various browsers he decided on an incurable congenital disease, somewhat diffusely spread around his body. A few months left to live. Nothing contagious. To be on the safe side he thought up a Latin name. *Strabismus.* That immediately made it sound more authentic. Strabismus. Heavy! He already felt a dull enervation in his back muscles and a diffuse ache behind his forehead. His vision was getting hazy.

Soon he would no longer exist on this beautiful Earth, but in his music he would live on. And even if he could not sing his songs for her—tragically enough the illness had settled in his vocal cords—he had sent her his poetry in an email.

Chapter 13

The beautiful turn-of-the-century wooden structure of the Warfsholm Guest House was on the far side of the pedestrian bridge over Klinte Bay. During the era of the lime magnates in Sweden, there had been an old lime oven and a boatyard on the cape.

At this moment the yellow building with its charming tower and big white porch was bathed in warm evening sun, as if no evil existed in the world. Yet this was where tonight's gathering would be held to talk about the unpleasantness that had shaken the whole community, to discuss the bird flu and the children being confined at the Klinte School by the police. They had seen the pictures, the men in uniform, the dogs, and the blue-white tape cordoning off the area. Rumors were flourishing. It was said that the cook, Berit Hoas, was dead and that she had been infected by her neighbor, Ruben, the old man with the homing pigeons. There must be something to that, because Ruben's place was cordoned off, too, and men dressed like extraterrestrials were in the process of killing the pigeons at the homes of other homing pigeon owners in Klintehamn and its environs. The rumors also said that

Bengtsson's poultry farm was in danger, as well as the turkey farm in Fröjel.

Maria Wern let her gaze drift out the frosted windowpanes toward the sea and tried to calm her agitated breathing and the rapid beating of her heart. Breathe deep. The place quickly filled with people. The carefully restored fin-de-siècle decor with its sheer lace curtains and pink geraniums was inherently festive, but this evening there was anything but a party atmosphere in the room.

The mood among the children's parents was tense as disease control officer Åsa Gahnström took the podium and explained that the evening concert with the visiting ballad singer had been cancelled in order to allow this important meeting regarding the possible bird flu.

The evening lamb grilling was not cancelled however, Maria noted. Appetizing aromas seeped in from the bar, where the door to the veranda stood open. Maria could see an old jukebox next to the bar.

Just then a flashbulb went off and then another and another, until the photographers and journalists who'd shown up despite the fact that the meeting was private were asked nicely but firmly to leave.

A woman with a mop of bushy hair stood up in the front row and shouted, "We demand to bring our children home!" A murmur of approving voices ran through the crowd. Three men in the middle row also stood up and the murmur took on a threatening tone.

The disease control officer seemed to be trying to hide behind the lectern, holding onto it the way a drowning person holds onto a plank. From her seat Maria could see that the woman's legs were shaking. She was seized with empathy. They could at least listen. Maria gathered her courage and said in a loud voice, "I think we should listen to what she has to say. We have a lot of questions. If we listen we may get answers. Then I hope we'll get the chance to discuss this afterward."

Åsa Gahnström shot her a look of gratitude and started her statement with words she had considered and weighed for the past hour.

"I want the best for your children." Someone began to protest but was hushed. "This evening I have received a preliminary response from the Institute for Communicable Disease Control in Solna, which indicates that we are dealing with the bird flu. The cook who served the children's food was infected with the bird flu, and your children are now being held for observation. They will have access to Tamiflu, a medicine that inhibits viral infections. To be on the safe side the children are being kept apart from each other in separate rooms. If anyone has to leave the room, they will wear breathing protection so as not to infect another child or become infected. Personnel specially trained in the treatment of infectious diseases will take care of them. We will check the children's body temperature four times a day, and blood tests will be taken on each child to see whether they have been infected."

"Why can't they just come home?" the woman in the first row shouted. "You have no right to keep them there!" She removed her sunglasses and turned around to get support, but was silenced.

"If we allow the children to leave the premises, we will no longer have control over who may be carrying the infection," continued the officer. "Bird flu is a dangerous disease. The children's siblings or other members of the family could be infected. It is important to limit the number of infected patients early on so that healthcare resources are sufficient—both for patients who are already in the hospitals and for those who will become ill from the flu. Your children will get the best possible care."

"So why can't the whole family get medicine? Why can't you give out medicine to the whole population of Gotland?" the woman continued, taking it upon herself to be the spokesperson for the parents.

Åsa Gahnström briefly considered telling the truth: because we do not have enough effective medicine for everyone. But she refrained, considering the risk that the statement would lead to chaos. An agitated mob can be incredibly dangerous, particularly when life-and-death commodities are being threatened.

"That might lead to more people getting infected, more than we will be able to treat. And the longer a large group takes the medicine, the more likely its efficacy will diminish. We hope that within the course of a week we will be able to declare those individuals we have under observation healthy and the danger will blow over."

She also didn't mention that Tamiflu, like most medications, has side effects. She did not intend to bring that up, especially not the alarming reports about mental symptoms and suicide.

"We won't get to see our kids for a whole week?" a familiar voice called out from the back of the hall and Maria turned around. It was Krister. They must have missed each other as they came in. "It's actually my turn to take care of my boy this week and I thought we'd go to Gotska Sandön together. This is terrible! First I have to go through a horrible divorce and only get to see my son every other weekend and a few short weeks in the summer, and now this. It's tough enough going through something like that without this adding to it."

Maria felt her face turning bright red, the redness spreading down her neck. Did he have to talk about the terms of the divorce and complain out loud in front of people who didn't have anything to do with it? They had resolved most of it in mutual understanding. Typical Krister to be so theatrical. Why couldn't he just be quiet like normal people? Had he always acted that way? So dense, and with such a distressing lack of boundaries? He must have, but then she had felt a sense of loyalty toward him. Now she wished he was on the other side of the globe.

"That's exactly what I want to discuss." Åsa Gahnström allowed herself a little smile. "I plan to make sure that all the children have a phone, a cell phone, or is it better if you can reach them by computer? It's important, both for them and for you, that you're in touch. We need to work together to motivate the children to stay in their rooms and put their breathing protection on when it's needed. It's not an easy task, but together I think we can manage it."

Maria Wern saw how the disease control officer breathed out. A carefully prepared move. Now she had solid ground under her feet and the parents could participate and make decisions in a question of secondary significance: telephone or email contact. The woman knew what she was doing. A strategist to her fingertips. Soon they could discuss the phone or computer options, but first there were other matters that were more urgent.

"What if there are infected persons we don't know about? Considering that, shouldn't everyone on the island be given Tamiflu for preventive purposes?" It was the thought that had pursued Maria into the night's uneasy slumber. What if there were cases that had not yet been discovered?

"We're in the process of reviewing that. It's not good to medicate unnecessarily, so my basic approach is that only those who have been in contact with an infected person will be given Tamiflu at the present time. If there is an uncontrolled spread of infection, that decision may be revisited. But one thing is certain: if there is infection outside the barriers, your children are protected in the best possible way."

An irritated frown appeared on the disease control officer's forehead. She did not like answering that question. Maria Wern assumed there was something she did not want to tell them, part of the story she was leaving out. But Maria knew the meeting wasn't the place for provocative questions. Perhaps she could speak with Jonathan Eriksson at the information line about that instead of risking a popular uprising at the parents meeting. Yes, it would probably be wise to go that route.

When the meeting ended two hours later, Maria was in a hurry to get home to Linda. She was already tired of her dad and the camper vacation and demanded to return earlier than they had agreed. Which meant that it was Maria, not Krister, who had had to arrange childcare for the evening meeting. While Maria was at the meeting, Linda had stayed behind with Marianne Hartman. She'd been happy enough, picking out a Pippi Longstocking movie and a big bag of mixed candy for the night, both of which were presumably finished long ago.

Maria had been overly optimistic when she estimated the time of her return home. From the beginning, it was obvious that it would drag out, and after the meeting she had exchanged a few words with Krister. Brief and polite, as if they had just met and not lived together for ten years. He thought the whole thing was overblown.

"It's like we're going back a hundred years in time when a doctor's word was law," he said. "We're living in the twenty-first century, not 1900. Patients should be informed and grant consent."

"Yes," Maria had countered, "but a virus doesn't take your consent into consideration. It has a life of its own. I think the disease control officer seems competent. We should probably trust that she's doing what's wisest, no matter how much I want to bring Emil home immediately."

Both agreed that although they were worried about him and wanted him home, it seemed like Emil was doing fine. It may have been the only thing they had really agreed on in the past few months, which had otherwise been filled with minor conflicts and border disputes about the children's upbringing and living arrangements. The extent of their conversation had devolved to: "Don't call me in the evening after ten o'clock," and "Don't let the kids drink all the soda they want when they're with you."

"Do you miss me sometimes?" he asked as they were leaving. Maria was about to turn right toward the bridge and Krister was going straight into the parking lot. She stopped in her tracks and he pressed himself against her back and took hold of her arm in a caressing gesture.

"Only when I can't get the pickle jar open," she answered with a laugh, and he said that he would be glad to come and help.

Then he lost control—as usual. Why did he have to destroy the fragile cooperation they had nevertheless managed to achieve?

"Couldn't we get together and have sex? I mean, a little no-strings sex without commitment. No promises. I know what turns you on, Maria, I can still smell your scent . . ."

"Oh, Jesus. It's over, Krister; can't you get that into your head? Leave me alone!"

As expected, the added TV news broadcast at ten thirty almost exclusively concerned the epidemic that had struck Gotland. The man found murdered in Värsände in Klintehamn was mentioned only briefly, the police were appealing to the general public for leads. Linda had heard the earlier broadcast and had a hard time settling down. She had heard Marianne and Tomas talking about something terrible that had happened and she'd surmised that her brother, Emil, was somehow involved.

"Why did the police put Emil in jail?" Linda asked when Maria went into her room to tuck her in.

"He's not in jail. They're watching to make sure everyone is safe."

"My Helmer frog is sad."

"Does he miss Emil?"

Suddenly Maria could barely hold back the tears that were forming under her eyelids. Only with Linda's questions did the situation become frighteningly concrete and unmanageable. My child! What if the disease control officer was wrong? What if the medicine didn't help and Emil was right there at the source of infection?

"You know, I miss Emil too, but I think he'll be coming home next weekend and then we'll think of something fun. We can go to the Viking village in Tofta so you can try living like a Viking for a day and grind flour and bake bread and throw an ax and spin thread. I think that would be fun."

"Only if Emil goes along. Otherwise it's boring for Helmer Bryd. You know, Mommy, Mr. Hartman bought cherries and gave them to me, but I didn't want to eat them because the birds had eaten them. I said that Helmer's allergic. It's super disgusting that the birds pecked the cherries. Who wants to eat something that someone else has licked? Maybe they have that flu and then they look for worms. Yuck! There was a worm in one cherry. It looked out and shook its head. It was saying, 'Don't eat me up, don't eat me up'"

Then she sang in a pretty little voice: "Nobody likes me,

nobody cares, just 'cause I eat worms. Bite off the head. Suck out the slime. Throw the little skin away."

And within a few more minutes she had fallen asleep among the stuffed animals on the bed.

When Maria finally sank into the living room couch, she again encountered the face of the disease control officer—this time on the TV screen. She was sitting across the table from the Minister of Public Health, a representative from Social Services, and several local politicians.

The local politicians assembled in Almedalen had held an extra meeting during the evening to discuss the ramifications of the bird flu, including which individuals in the community should have primary access to Tamiflu.

The plan that the emergency management agency and Social Services prepared was severely criticized because it was so diffuse and lacked detail.

How can you pit groups against each other because there isn't enough medicine? Why should individuals over the age of sixty-five get medicine but not schoolchildren or children in daycare? They're clearly in an environment where the infection is easily transmitted—why aren't they a priority?

"First of all those who have been infected must get help," explained Åsa Gahnström. "Second are those who have been exposed to infection and those who have reduced immune defenses, have heart and lung disease, are elderly, or are medically fragile in some way."

But each politician's list looked different. First of all cabinet members, parliament, county council and municipal officials, and civil servants needed access to medication. Then there were first responders at hospitals and ambulance personnel, followed by those who worked in public utilities: electricity, water supply, and garbage pick-up. Workers who produce and transport foodstuffs also needed access to the medication.

"During the Spanish Flu, the majority of those who died

were between the ages twenty and forty. Will bird flu affect the same demographic?" the program host asked, turning toward Gahnström.

"As it appears now, we believe we have the situation under control. If we manage to hold this line consistently, the risk is slight for further contagion in the community. There is no cause for alarm right now," assured the disease control officer.

Maria could see redness spreading over Åsa Gahnström's cheeks. She was clearly under pressure.

"How do you think teachers and childcare personnel will respond when they learn you don't consider their work to be important?" the program host asked, looking challengingly at the disease control officer and the minister of public health. "How about the janitors, and the journalists on radio, TV, and newspapers? How will people find out what is happening if no one reports on it? What about the security guards—who will prevent break-ins at health centers and grocery stores if things get really bad? Is there any group in society that shouldn't be prioritized? People in the arts? The unemployed? Homeless people? Asylum seekers? Anyone with an annual income below the poverty line? Such low-paid work can hardly be very important, can it? Who will be singled out to not receive help?"

The host paused and said sternly, "Is there even enough medicine for everyone? I, along with the Swedish people, demand an answer to this question. How prepared are we?"

The disease control officer's face reddened up to her hairline. "We are well-prepared and in the long term everyone will have access to medication, should that be necessary. In the present situation, we want to be careful about overuse of medicine, considering the risk of developing resistance. So a general prophylactic treatment is not appropriate as long as we have the situation under control."

The woman was lying. Maria sensed it in her voice and

affect. This was definitely not the whole truth. Maria Wern turned off the TV wearily as the broadcast degenerated into a buzz of angry voices. She could not bear to listen anymore. Could not bear to see those who ought to be collected and decisive arguing like children.

She walked around the living room, stood a while at Linda's bedroom door, watching her sleep, took another round through the apartment.

Finally she called Emil to check that he really had been given medicine. He could tell right away that she was worried, although she tried to joke it off.

"Are you okay, Mom?"

"I wish I could be with you, Emil. I would like to, you know that." She tried to say it without letting him hear that she was crying. She had to let her nose run without sniffing.

"Don't worry, Mom, I'll manage. I talk with a kid named Zebastian; he's cool."

After hanging up, Maria wandered out into the kitchen and made a sandwich, which she couldn't swallow. The bites seemed to expand in her mouth. She stood by the window and looked at the streetlamp shining outside the library. The street was deserted. Not a car.

She had to talk with someone. Talk about her fears. She didn't want to call Krister. He would come over in a flash and think that everything was going to be like it used to be and she couldn't risk that. The Hartmans were surely already asleep and Jesper Ek had been admitted for observation at the old sanitarium. She couldn't call there after nine o'clock. So who was there to talk with?

She wondered how late the information line was open? Was it only during office hours or was it possible to talk with someone now? Maria dialed the number and waited. Jonathan Eriksson answered immediately, as if he had been sitting by the phone waiting for it to ring.

"I don't intend to discuss this with you when you're not yourself. This is humiliating for both of us. Go to bed for Christ's sake and don't disturb me anymore."

"What?" Maria wondered if she was hearing right. If this was the support they intended to offer the parents of the children being interned at Klinte School there was even more reason to despair than she had guessed! "I didn't want anything anyway," she said, slamming down the receiver.

Chapter 14

Jonathan Eriksson realized his mistake as soon as the caller hung up. The steady tone in the receiver drilled itself into his gut. What had he said? "I don't intend to discuss this with you when you're not yourself. This is humiliating for both of us." After four increasingly abusive calls from Nina he hadn't even considered that the fifth might be from someone else. This is called "logical sequence" in intelligence tests—in reality it doesn't work that way. Reality is seldom logical and he did not have caller ID so that he could even correct his mistake. Damn it, damn it, damn it, what a stupid mistake!

Jonathan walked once around the room and slammed the walls with his fist before it occurred to him that the person in the adjoining room was likely trying to sleep.

Nina's scornful voice still echoed in his head. First she'd called enraged that his mother had taken their son to her home. The old bag had no right to go into the house without her permission and take him! After the first call there were two tearful calls apologizing and promising that everything was fine. "Please forgive me! I'm sorry! I swear, Jonathan, it will never happen again. Never again. I love you. When this is over, we'll go away. We can take that trip to Paris we dreamed about. Just you and me. Malte can stay with your mother and we can have time for each other like we had before, when we couldn't be without each other a single minute. Do you remember the sandpit on Fårö? Do you remember when we made love by the sea? Do you remember the vacation in Smögen? I want us to start over. We need a fresh start. It's been tough for a while, but I promise that everything will be better. I promise."

The final call, of course, proved the opposite.

"I can tell you've been drinking. Don't lie to me, Nina. The least you can do is admit you're drunk." And then things got really bad.

"It's none of your business, damn it! You do your fancy job and I'll do mine. If you only gave me the appreciation I deserve, if you only listened to me and cared even a tiny bit about what it's like for us at home everything would be different. Of course I have to wind down with a glass of wine to relax and go to sleep after a day like this. I have to manage everything myself while you frolic in the linen closet at the hospital. I know there's someone else, or are there several? Maybe there are several, Jonathan, that's why you're never able to when you come home. I'm so tired, you say. I've been on call the whole weekend. That's what you say when you come home and we haven't seen a trace of you for days. I'm sure it was exhausting for you. . . . How many do you manage on a weekend?"

There was no point in arguing with her when she was in that state. He'd hung up and then, when it rang again . . . Well, what should he think?

Jonathan sat down at the computer to pass the time. As agitated as he felt now it would be impossible to fall asleep. He opened the window to let in the coolness of the night. The worst thing was that Malte had to experience this. The thought that Nina's emotional outbursts and lack of super-vision might damage the boy made Jonathan furious. But there was no way out, however he looked at it he was stuck. If it hadn't been for Malte, he would have left Nina long ago. After the initial violent passion there was only a gaping vacuum. The feeling of distaste when she lay in bed drool-ing and snoring, a sour stench of sweat and stale booze in the room. No, he didn't love her anymore and he was so unspeakably tired of lying for her sake, coaxing her home from parties: "You look tired, dear, maybe we should go home now." "Tomorrow will be another day. Now I think it's time to go home." "You really look tired, Nina. Perhaps we should say goodbye and . . ." "Well, Nina is not sleeping well and is so easily affected. Wine goes to your head so easily when you haven't slept."

What she said was quite true; he really had no desire to touch her anymore. They deserved something better, but you can't cut a child in two. Shared custody would in the worst case mean that he would only see his son every other weekend. But even the thought of having full custody with her taking care of him every other weekend made his stom-ach turn. Forty-eight hours without being able to check that his son wasn't in harm's way. How could he protect him, how could he keep an eye on him if they separated?

Malte loved his mother and was loyal to a fault. He always believed her promises and was always disappointed. It was painful to stand by and see it happen again and again. But a custody dispute can be so humiliatingly ugly and dirty. Nina would not hesitate to make up preposterous lies, not if she felt pressured and offended. How could he avoid that?

And how could he arrange things so that people wouldn't know? For Malte's sake more than for anyone else's, he thought about that. If only he had someone to talk with—someone who could understand what a nightmare he was living—without judging and moralizing. Someone who could help put order into the chaos of thoughts that made him live through the days in a haze.

Absentmindedly Jonathan browsed the Internet for hits on "medicine + Internet commerce"—the Web trade in prescription drugs. It was surprisingly open. Although it's illegal to purchase medicine over the Internet if you don't have a prescription, the worst that could happen is that the medicine would be confiscated. Viagra topped the list in popularity, but there was also epilepsy medicine, drugs for depression, and antibiotics for anyone prepared to pay full price for uncertain products. The quality of the medication available through the Internet varied considerably, according to several studies he skimmed. Some medications had even been revealed as pure fraud: at best they had no effect and at worst they were downright harmful. The Internet trader that Jonathan had just brought up on the screen, Doctor M, appropriately enough sold Tamiflu. It was cheap too—795 kronor for a course of treatment at 75 mg times two for five days. The dosage seemed correct. Presumably sugar tablets. Åsa ought to have someone look more closely at this immediately.

"Jonathan, you have to come!" The door was thrown open without warning and a masked face peeked in. "Now, it's urgent."

Jonathan put on his breathing protection and followed the nurse into the corridor and down the stairs.

"It's Sonja Cederroth; she's suddenly become much worse. We've injected Furix, but she has no urine output and she's oxygenating very poorly. Saturation is at 64 percent."

"Where's Morgan? Shouldn't he be working tonight?"

"Morgan is occupied at Klinte School. Two boys and one of the coaches have symptoms. They're on their way here in an ambulance. And Reine Hammar has disappeared. Karin in reception said he went out, needed to get some air. He's a smoker. I said he couldn't smoke inside. She couldn't stop him. What do we do now?"

"Prepare a respirator. We'll start with five liters of oxygen. But before that I want to retake the arterial blood gas. It can be venous," said Jonathan glancing at the slip of paper with the test results that had been put in his hand.

"I wouldn't think so," said the nurse. "She looks deathly ill, her nail beds are completely blue and her face is pale gray. It's hard to see whether she has any lip cyanosis under the mask, but we have to assume that. Irregular pulse at about 120, blood pressure immeasurable. I don't think we can save her, Jonathan."

They put on their protective gear and went into the ward while precious minutes were lost. Petter Cederroth was sitting on the edge of his wife's bed holding her hand. A nurse in protective clothing and visor was connecting oxygen to the respirator. The pulse oximeter sounded an alarm. The numbers for pulse disappeared from the display. Saturation sank further and the numbers turned into straight lines. Jonathan felt for a pulse on her neck.

"We're losing her!" He tore off the oxygen mask and pressed the bag valve mask over Sonja's face. Rhythmically he started to pump in air with the black rubber bladder in his hand while the nurse connected the oxygen. Someone brought the cardiac massage board. The pillow was torn off the bed and the board was worked in under the woman and heart massage was begun. The silence became dense. The only sounds were brief commands and necessary information exchanged. On the face of the clock, the minutes slipped by.

"Defibrillator."

It was already in place. Jonathan held the plates over the woman's chest to give a jolt.

113

"I'm firing now."

Those who were gathered around the bed took a step back. A jolt made the woman's body bounce on the bed, then it fell back just as limp as before. The room was a chaos of apparatus and hoses. On the bed next to his wife sat Petter Cederroth, frightened and abandoned. He picked at his arm; tore himself bloody with the hope the pain would wake him from this hellish nightmare. Under normal circumstances someone—a nurse or social worker—would have pulled him from the room and cared for him while the doctors and nurses tried to save his wife's life. But no one had time for him and there were no normal procedures to rely on. With the risk of infection, the routines were considerably more elaborate and time-consuming and empathy came in second place where saving lives was concerned.

"Is she dead?" His voice was very weak and could barely be heard through the protective mask.

"Yes, I'm very sorry. We couldn't save her." Jonathan sank down next to Petter on the bed and put his arm around his shoulders. He had no words of consolation. All he could offer was his silent sympathy. It felt worse than ridiculous to talk through the breathing protection, but Jonathan resisted the impulse to tear off the mask.

"Will I be the next to go? Is it really that contagious?"

"We don't know who will be affected. I don't think there is any great danger on your part. The medicine seems to be working. You're no worse today than you were yesterday, are you?"

"My Sonja." Jonathan assumed that Petter was crying, there were no sounds but his shoulders were shaking and a clear drop fell down onto his white shirt from the edge of the mask.

"I've been thinking about something," the taxi driver said suddenly, in a completely different tone. "There's something

I didn't tell you, before when you asked me, about who rode in the taxi. I drove a girl, a nice-looking blonde, to Jungmansgatan at the same time as Reine Hammar, the doctor that is. He gave me five hundred kronor to keep quiet about it. I can pay it back. If this pestilence is that contagious, maybe you need to know about that."

Jonathan nodded.

"One more thing," said Petter, taking firm hold of Jonathan's arm. "Sonja didn't want to be cremated. Anything at all, but not that. She was scared to death of fire. Promise me that. We talked about it just this morning. You have to promise." Jonathan assured him that he would do his best to accommodate their wish. He could only guess what Åsa Gahnström would think about this promise.

"Jonathan, it's important, I have to speak with you," Nurse Agneta called from the corridor. "We've got test results!" He made a sign so that she would know he had heard.

It took a while take off the protective suit and visor. The clothes he was wearing were sour with sweat. Jonathan felt feverish and his throat felt a little sore when he swallowed. Test results. Now they had arrived. Until now he had pushed aside the thought that he himself might be infected. If he was, what would that mean? He could not bear to complete the thought. "We've got test results," she said again, meeting his eyes. During the four years they had worked together he had never seen her so jittery. He took the bundle of papers she had printed out from the computer and sat down at the desk. A policeman, Jesper Ek, tested positive. Then the older woman who took the taxi with Cederroth to Fårö, positive; the man with the heart attack, positive; the homing pigeon guys, all had positive cultures. Those who had been in the ER at the same time as Cederroth miraculously enough had avoided the infection. Reine Hammar, negative. When he picked up the next paper his eyes blurred; it was his own test results. He read through it several times to be certain that it really was negative and then he quickly scanned through the rest of the results. Four of those who had treated Berit Hoas had been infected, one of whom was Nurse Agneta. He heard her crying quietly behind him.

"What happens to me now? I'm so afraid."

Chapter 15

" *The epidemic of bird flu that has broken out on Gotland has now claimed its third fatality and another twelve persons are feared infected. Once again we appeal to the general public not to come to Visby General Hospital or the community health centers if infection is suspected. House calls by a doctor will be made instead, and appointments can be scheduled on one of the infectious disease clinic's phone lines. We are also looking for a particular person. The night of July 1 or early morning of July 2 a woman in her thirties was taken by taxi to an address on Jungmansgatan in Visby. The woman is of medium height and has long blonde hair. It is very urgent that we make contact with her or receive information about who she might be. According to disease control officer Åsa Gahnström, the epidemic is under control. She also believes that in the current situation there is no cause for alarm.*"

"Confounded lie!" Jonathan Eriksson turned off the radio and pushed away the paper plate of warmed-up beef and powdered mashed potatoes. He could not choke down even a bite. He got up and tossed the plate of cold food and the plastic utensils into a garbage bag marked with yellow tape and the words "contagion hazard". Food had no taste when

117

worry was gnawing at his stomach. It was apparent that they were faced with a very grave situation. The conversation with Reine Hammar last evening had not produced the information Jonathan was looking for. First his colleague flatly denied having been in a taxi with a blonde woman and then unwillingly admitted that it was possible when he really thought about it. After a whole evening at the bar you don't remember much. I'm only human, damn it. Reine had shared a taxi with a young woman, but he did not know her name or where she lived. They got in together at Hamnkrogen and then went their separate ways outside the Gråbo School after sharing a taxi. No, he had no idea what her name was, he already said that, he hardly noticed that she was in the same taxi. You might think that perhaps he had left a pretty generous tip. Probably mistook a five hundred for a hundred kronor note, what the hell. He hadn't intended to get out of the taxi right where they happened to be, in the Gråbo area; it was just a mistake. That sort of thing can happen, can't it?

Jonathan had no opinion about that. He was uninterested in Reine's relationship with the woman as long as they were able to test whether she was contagious. In the worst case this might mean bringing in a new batch of patients for observation and even more deaths. Jonathan leaned his head in his hands and closed his eyes. He just wanted to be away from it all and most of all from this deadly sanitarium. At the teleconference that morning the disease control officer painted a different picture of the situation than she had reported to the press. The emergency management board could not reach agreement and the division of labor was unclear. The situation was more dire than any of them could have imagined, with another twelve falling ill. How many more would be affected? There was nothing to do in the current situation other than put their cards on the table and report facts. The medicine they had was not going to be enough.

A company doctor had prescribed Tamiflu at the end of the year to all personnel in the company he worked for. Most of the employees misunderstood the instructions and took the medicine when the regular flu prevailed during the winter. It was an outright scandal given the risk of resistance development that might entail. What do you do if Tamiflu is no longer effective, if that option gets used up due to pure carelessness? The doctor was employed by a private healthcare provider and hired out to the company and told not to get on the bad side of his client but instead accommodate their expectations, despite the disease control officer's recommendations. What was left to do now was to appeal to other countries. This was a matter of saving lives. The Internet sellers of medication should undergo an immediate review, Åsa Gahnström had decided. Although the trade was not strictly illegal, in the worst-case scenario they might be forced to buy medicine from them—if any of them perchance were actually selling Tamiflu and the substance proved to be effective, that is. In that case the medicine must be tested before it was given out to patients. The question was whether it would be possible to get that process to run quickly and smoothly. It would be best, of course, if despite previous rejections they could get medicine through the usual channels. That might work out if an appeal was made in the media while at the same time the pharmaceutical companies were contacted again. At best this might produce an effect. PR and goodwill in exchange for medicine. There would be headlines, of course. People would get scared, and frightened people do risky things. But fortunately it was not Jonathan who would make that decision.

What worried Jonathan most at the moment was the

thirty-year-old coach at the soccer camp, Jenny Eklund, and the two ten-year-old boys who became ill last evening and were both taken to the old sanitarium in Follingbo with fever and flu symptoms. The woman had two small children at home age two and three and her husband Mats was in a complete state of dissolution. He had reportedly already filed a complaint with Social Services and intended to contact the TV investigative reporters if he was not given complete assurances that his wife would come home alive.

Jonathan had listened patiently and borne the brunt of the man's anger and terror, and gradually it came out that they had quarreled and Jenny had not forgiven him and he was still in shock after finding a dead man by an outhouse in Värsände—all this in an incoherent flood. Probably he was not sober. Jonathan let him talk without really having any opinions of substance. Then it simply ebbed out and something that resembled mutual understanding appeared when Mats Eklund realized that Jonathan Eriksson was an ordinary human being who was only following the directives he had been given by his superiors. It was a relief to end the conversation and return to the patients.

The boy, whose name was Emil, was so like Malte. Same coloring and body structure, and his smile was almost identical. Jonathan had seen him early in the morning. A tough little guy. Yes, there was another one too whose name was Zebastian, but there was something special about Emil. He had a liberating sense of humor and great trust. The symptoms were mild so far, fever and aching joints. The parents of the two boys had been informed and demanded to see their children immediately. Maria Wern had been informed of the reason for the transfer and was very shaken, said the nurse. It had fallen on Jonathan to take the follow-up conversation. She should be here any time now. Jonathan took a quick shower and changed his shirt. Then he had to find a time to talk with Nurse Agneta in peace and quiet. She was single with three small children; her husband had been killed in a traffic accident. Since finding out she was infected she had been in a state of shock, unable to be present in her work on the telephone information line. That was not surprising.

"How are you holding up, Agneta? I can see you're having a difficult time. Do you want to talk about it?" He didn't have much time, but he had to take a couple of minutes.

"But Jonathan, didn't you see the results from the virus lab? Check the resistance determination! Tamiflu is ineffective! Check this—resistant." Agneta's eyes were big and black and suddenly she started crying behind the mask. He placed his arm around her and pulled her into an embrace and at the same moment the phone rang. It was Disease Control Officer Åsa Gahnström.

"I presume that you just received the same information as me and keeping the lid on it is what counts, of course. If it gets out that we don't have any effective medicine to offer we will have a nightmare situation none of us can imagine."

"Don't we already have one now? Yes, I've suspected for a while that the medicine didn't help. It hasn't halted the course of any of the patients I've treated except possibly the taxi driver. Sooner or later this is going to leak out and then we will have used up our trust with the general public. I think we should tell the truth."

"My decision is that we keep quiet. If you have even an ounce of imagination perhaps you can visualize the panic such news would trigger and the consequences it would have. There is hope, however. Several pharmaceutical manufacturers are far advanced in product development where antiviral agents are concerned. We are in the process of investigating whether there are other medicines that may have effect. Until then we have to try to hold out."

Jonathan looked at Agneta, who was standing beside him and heard the whole conversation. "Can you bear to work at all?" he asked.

"There's no one else. People are afraid to come in. Moa, Per, and Karin have taken medical leave. They don't want to be infected. Mental insufficiency it said on Karin's certificate. She told her doctor she couldn't bear to see more death and illness; it was too stressful and she needed to rest. Moa doesn't even have a certificate. Her husband has forbidden her to come here. He supports her. But I don't have that option."

"What are you saying? No one's coming to relieve you?"

"No, they refuse to come in."

On the other side of the Plexiglas walls that had been hastily set up in the lobby as a corridor sat Maria Wern, Emil's mother. Jonathan vaguely recognized the voice when he heard her speaking with the nurse on the phone they used to communicate, to avoid breathing the same air.

"Is there another doctor besides Jonathan Eriksson I can speak with? I had a bad experience with him before. Can't I choose a different doctor? I don't have confidence in him anymore." He saw her pleading face on the other side of the glass. What a horribly poor basis for a difficult conversation. It struck him that she must have been the one who called when he thought it was Nina. Damn it! Why couldn't life be fair and simple, if only for a little while so you could catch your breath?

Jonathan picked up the receiver and introduced himself. "I have to apologize and I hope you can accept that. I am truly sorry that it was you I happened to snap at on the phone last night. I thought it was someone else."

"Your wife?" she asked pointedly, and he could sense the shadow of a smile. "Cozy way to say goodnight."

"Yes, my wife." There was no chance of evasive action. No time to find an acceptable white lie. "We were having a little, hmm, controversy."

"Then I'm glad I avoided getting in the line of fire when it's a big controversy. How is Emil doing now?"

"As you know, he's infected. He's carrying the virus, but he is being treated with a medicine that is effective against virus so we hope the virus will only manifest as a mild flu." While he spoke he rubbed his nose through the mask and lowered his eyes.

"Tamiflu," he added. The doctor spoke so slowly and pedagogically that her skin was crawling. She wanted to hurry him up a little; her irritation was only barely below the surface. It was not that easy to change attitude toward him, even if he had apologized.

"Yes, right now he has a slight fever and sore throat. When I saw him a while ago he was playing solitaire on the computer. What did you want to speak with me about when you called yesterday evening?" Jonathan felt himself blushing. This was still terribly awkward. He could not even remember for sure what he had said; presumably he swore at her.

"I was listening to Åsa Gahnström yesterday evening and I got a feeling that she wasn't telling the whole truth. What I wanted to ask is: Is there enough Tamiflu for everyone who gets sick? How bad is it really? How do I know that he'll get medicine and how do I know that it's doing any good? I mean, if the medicine has an effect? Why does every news report talk about how many people have died? It seems to be almost half. Answer me. What help do you have to offer my child? I have the right to know that!" She held his gaze and there was no opportunity for evasion.

"Can this stay between us?" he said, awaiting her answer before he continued. "We just received the resistance determination for Tamiflu and it doesn't work on this strain of bird flu. But there is a slight hope. There are medications under development and perhaps one of them can be released faster than they thought, and in the best case it will have an effect. We are working every minute to produce a medicine in time. Right now there is no way to prevent it other than isolation and basic hygienic procedures. That's how bad it is. But it's still better than no care at all."

Jonathan realized that he had breached the confidentiality of his discussions with the disease control officer, but this was a situation when conscience and integrity demanded plain speaking. Maria Wern said nothing for a long time and he shuddered at how she would respond. She looked at him and felt, despite her worry, a creeping sympathy. He had revealed himself and allowed her a glimpse behind the curtain.

"So how bad is Emil? I want to know the truth."

"He has extremely mild symptoms. I can't imagine anything other than that he will recover." Jonathan closed his eyes as he said this and hoped it was true. It seemed moderate at the moment, but the dreaded pneumonia or other complications could not be foreseen.

"Now I want to see Emil." Maria got up and Jonathan showed the door to the sluice she would go through.

"Put on the protective clothing according to the instructions that are on the placard on the wall, breathing protection and protective goggles. If anything is unclear you can reach Nurse Agneta by phone. When you're ready, we'll go. I know it feels a little silly to talk through the mask, but you must not under any circumstances take it off, not even when you are hugging your son. That is an absolute condition. Otherwise you'll have to stay here."

"I'd be happy to stay here if I didn't have a little girl at home too. I had hoped that Emil's dad would come here with me, but he's afraid of hospitals. Anyways, you'd only have trouble with him, so perhaps it's just as well that he only speaks with Emil on the phone."

"So he's at home with Emil's little sister?"

Maria shook her head and had to adjust the mask. "It's not that simple. We're not living together anymore. But we cooperate for the good of the children. It's not exactly uncomplicated, but if you do your part and a little more it works out."

"Sometimes I think it's stranger that people manage to stay together year in and year out than that they separate," said Jonathan. "When we're inside the next sluice you have to put on another protective coat. You're going to look like an extra-terrestrial, but the boy is starting to get used to it now."

"Are you divorced, too? Excuse me; perhaps that was an intrusive question. But the relationship between doctor and patient feels extremely unequal; it's not often it seems appropriate to ask a doctor how he's doing."

"I'm married and between you and me, it's pure hell."

"And you have no one to talk with, right?"

Jonathan tried to interpret her facial expression but it was impossible to see whether she was smiling at him under the mask.

"I guess that's the way it is. Now let's go in."

Chapter 16

Åsa Gahnström kicked her high-heeled shoes off with a snap, making them fly through the air and hit the wall. An incident at lunch had upset her badly, and since then she was having a hard time concentrating on her work.

She had been looking at the paintings in the Rainbow Café's gallery window to help her settle down after the humiliating television interview that morning. She'd lingered a little while longer to take a few deep breaths and think about something other than the approaching catastrophe, when a man came right up to her and stood so close that she could not ignore him. He looked threatening. She could not remember having met him before. He must have recognized her from the TV broadcasts the past few days.

"My wife, Jenny. You've moved her to Follingbo. What the hell are you up to? People are dying like flies. I'm going to contact Social Services. They say that high-level managers are psychopaths without normal emotions, and I believe it. How cynical can you be when it concerns saving money for the municipality? You're playing with human lives. I can pay for real medicine, damn it, as long as she survives, as long as we all survive! I've already paid for it; do you know how much tax I pay every month? Do you know that? It's us taxpayers who've hired you and you should be fired, damn it! If my wife dies"—he put his clenched fist under Åsa's chin and applied pressure—"I'll kill you."

She did not have the energy to defend herself. Choking back tears she staggered off. For her entire adult life she had balanced on high heels without difficulty, but on the cobblestone streets of Visby this proved to be hazardous. Outside the narrow little building in Hästbacken called the Flatiron, her heel got caught between two stones and she fell to her knees. It still hurt terribly and with pain the tears had come. Days of suppressed tears facing impossible demands to manage her job washed over her like a deluge, and once they started it was impossible to stop the flow. An older woman stopped and stroked her hair. "My dear girl, how did this happen?" And Åsa wept with her face pressed against a flowery skirt dress and then went with her into the Flatiron and had a cup of coffee. Once inside she felt silly and confused when she was going to tell about her sorrows and reeled off a half-truth about back problems.

"Well now, it must be something more than that?" The older woman had a serious yet friendly smile and her chicory-blue eyes looked right through the facade, saw Åsa as the little girl she was right at that moment.

"It's a bit more than that," Åsa admitted. "I'm not good enough."

Then the woman laughed, a warm and friendly laugh. "That doesn't matter, my dear, no one is. You have to try to forgive yourself for not being perfect. No one's perfect. That's the big secret. We only pretend. I decided to stop worrying about it when I turned fifty. Still working on that. When do you intend to start? If you start now perhaps you'll be free as a bird when you reach my age. Would you like a tissue?" She dug in her handbag and took out a package with a wrinkled plastic casing.

Then strangely enough, Åsa felt better, even if her problems were the same as before lunch. There was frightfully acute shortage of medicine, primarily for bird flu, but also regular antibiotics, Furix, Bricanyl, cortisone, and Theophylline. But not only that. All the passengers who had taken a taxi with Petter Cederroth on Saturday night, except her colleague Reine Hammar, were infected with bird flu—and one of them was missing. Just when you might assume that the epidemic was under control a leak had been exposed. An unknown blonde woman who shared a taxi with Reine Hammar. It had to be assumed that she too was infected until the opposite was proven. The conversation with Reine Hammar had degenerated into a real argument and it ended with Åsa threatening to contact Mrs. Hammar for more information if he didn't want to cooperate. But then his recollection got clearer and an address suddenly percolated up in his memory. With the help of the police a name and telephone number had been produced, but no Malin Berg had answered despite repeated attempts. According to her employer, the owner of a restaurant at the edge of town, Malin had called in sick on Sunday. Not unusual. It wasn't the first Monday she had not come to work. A demanding personal life, you had to assume, he said ironically.

With the approval of the prosecutor there was now a warrant to enter the apartment to see if the woman was there. But what doctor would voluntarily go in? Åsa Gahnström had expected that healthcare personnel who heard the call for reinforcements on the island would volunteer, but no one had reported, not a single one, despite repeated announcements on both radio and TV about the desperate need for assistance. One of those asked had referred to the previous SARS epidemic, where two anesthesiologists were infected from intubation of patients despite maximum protective equipment. The unions were brought in and the safety representatives, and negotiations would be initiated in the coming week. Can you force someone to risk their health, and perhaps their life? For the moment there was no one she could ask about that and the emergency group at the infectious disease clinic in Linköping had been contacted after discussions with the general director for Disease Control. They should be on site at Jungmansgatan now and a report from them could be expected at any moment. Åsa Gahnström hoped that the woman would be in shape to account for who she had seen since Saturday evening. The entire infection prevention plan hinged on that now.

Åsa thanked a thoughtful nurse for the cup of coffee she had set on the desk along with a small plate with a cheese sandwich and a few biscuits. The lovely sea view from the windows of the infectious disease department was blocked by the scaffolding climbing up the facade of the dialysis department, leaving the office in constant shadow. A narrow strip of Strandgärdet, where the Medieval Week tournament would soon be held, could be glimpsed if you stood by the window. But Åsa Gahnström did not get up; her entire focus was directed at the phone that should be ringing at any moment. A lack of sleep made her eyes sting and her whole body was on edge.

There was a vague hope. There was an antiviral medicine, Tamivir, which clearly had been pirated by a foreign company before it was ready for market. There would be an uproar if it came out that the healthcare administration was buying pirated medications, but necessity knows no law where saving lives is concerned. They were still awaiting an answer to the request to release the pirated medication for use on Gotland. For the time being, four medical secretaries were assigned to see what could be fished out of the Internet trade if there was no other option. May they never need to make use of that service.

Åsa Gahnström answered the phone at the first ring. It was Tomas Hartman from the police. None of the neighbors on Jungmansgatan had seen Malin Berg outside her door since Saturday evening. Someone had heard her showering on Sunday afternoon, but it had been silent since. Åsa thanked him and awaited further information from the emergency group. She kept thinking about Jenny Eklund—the man on Adelsgatan had screamed that she had two little boys at home. Nurse Agneta had three children who would have no parents if . . . Åsa got no further in her train of thought before the report came from Jungmansgatan.

"We've gone in. Malin Berg is dead. We're taking her body with us to Pathology. There is no sign of external violence. She had been vomiting in a bucket alongside the bed. The body is swollen." The voice on the phone was very faint and Åsa had to ask the leader of the response group to speak louder. He said that he was in an awkward spot considering the surrounding neighbors, but soon Åsa could hear the rest of the message without any problem. "The neighbors don't think she left her apartment all day Sunday. If so, that's almost too good to be true. The people who live in the adjacent apartment are worried that infection might have spread through the ventilation system and demand to have tests taken and medicine. What do we do?"

"Take samples from them and ask them to limit their association and stay indoors until we've got an answer. I'll arrange sick leave. We'll wait with medicine until we've seen whether anyone is infected."

"Is that wise? Shouldn't we be open-handed with medicine in this situation?"

"Yes, we should be, if we had that option. We don't have medicine for prophylactic purposes. If we start that in one case we'll have started the whole crazy carousel of who should be first in line. There would be no way to work in peace after that. I'll explain in more detail when you're here. Then I have a patient I want you to take to Linköping, a young woman, a soccer coach. She's in a bad way. I'm not sure we can help her here. It's hard to find more respirators and the ICU rooms at Follingbo are full."

When Åsa ended the call she felt relieved, relieved and almost euphoric that Malin Berg managed to die without seeing a single person. The thought would have been downright indecent if the circumstances were normal, she realized immediately, but in this situation it was better that one person was dead than that a hundred people had been infected.

Chapter 17

Camper denizen Hans Moberg woke up with a hang-over, a need to pee, and a strong but vague feeling of anxiety. He was thirsty, too. With his hand on the last can of beer in the fridge he glanced at the clock. It was already eleven thirty. The pounding headache almost made him lose his breath as he bent over to pick up the imported liter bottle of 50-percent vodka from the floor, in a quick inventory of what the house had to offer. He looked in the mirror and met a bloodshot pair of eyes and a disheveled flow of wavy gray hair. His tongue was like a foreign object in his mouth and he felt like he was going to retch.

"What are you doing now, Moby?" he said to himself in the mirror. Yesterday evening's encounter with Cuddly Skåne Girl had not turned out at all like he'd imagined. It seldom does, but this was one of the most awkward he'd experienced. He had truly exerted himself to make a pleasant impression. For weeks he had caressed her ear with poems, double entendres, compliments, allusions to impending love games and she had followed along every step of the way and let herself be captured. Sometimes she took the lead and he had no objection to that—variety is the spice of life. He had her photo on the table beside the bed so that she could creep down under the covers with him when he had the desire. The large breasts and rounded hips would make any fellow feel weak in the knees. The whole day before the encounter he had fantasized and planned in detail—and then she didn't show up.

Well, that was what he thought at first, before a woman who was hanging around the kiosk took hold of his arm and asked, "Are you here to meet a woman from Skåne?" He couldn't deny it.

"Here she is!" The woman gave him a radiant smile.

It must be a mistake! It just couldn't be possible. The woman who called herself Cuddly Skåne Girl was heavy-set and admittedly large-breasted with copper-red hair, but her face didn't match the photo at all. What a darned swindle.

He had decided however to make the best of the situation. His role as dying country singer was rehearsed to perfection and he could just as well act it as not.

"You said you were sick. How bad is it really?" she asked. There was something maternal and tenderhearted about her and once he had recovered from the initial disappointment a warm embrace was better than a cold camper.

"My sickness? It's incurable. The disease has spread throughout my entire body, but my music will live on."

"So what is it, do you have cancer?" she prodded. "Shouldn't you be in a hospital if it's that serious?"

The mournful expression on her face and the gentle smile were reward enough for the whole performance. It felt cozy to be the object of her concerns and worry, and to have such an obvious leading role.

"No, the doctor didn't think there was any point in being in the hospital since it couldn't be cured anyway. They released me. Take each day as it comes and thank God for the days I'm able to get out of bed. My appetite is poor. Yesterday I was so weak my legs could barely hold me. But today I feel better."

She looked at him with such tenderness in her eyes that he was sincerely moved. Right then, at that moment, he decided that she was beautiful. Yes, beautiful.

"What kind of sickness do you have? There's usually treatment for most things." Then he said it, at the same time striving for a gentle, serious expression to show that he bore his pain with equanimity: "It's nothing contagious, my dear. I have Strabismus."

The cuddly girl from Skåne put her hands to her face and took in air in sobbing breaths; her shoulders were shaking and he put his arm around her.

"Don't take it so hard; I can still enjoy life at times." At about that point he realized his fatal mistake. The cuddly one was laughing so that she could hardly breathe, she was laughing so that the couch they were sitting on rocked. Tears were running and washed away the color from her eyelashes in black streaks across her cheeks.

"So you're suffering from Strabismus, are you?" she snorted so that saliva sprayed over his face. Do you even know what that is?"

No, he had to admit that he didn't completely have a handle on it. The doctor had not really succeeded in the pedagogical task of explaining it to him.

"Strabismus means cross-eyed, sweetheart. I'm an optician. Bad."

The encounter with Cuddly Skåne Girl had been cordial but brief. There isn't a man in the world who can hold their ground against a woman who laughs out loud.

There was coffee and a roll and "let's be in touch." But he suspected that neither of them would ever entertain the thought of making contact again. Right before he was getting ready to leave he asked the question that was on the tip of his tongue the whole time.

"That wasn't you in the picture, was it?"

"No, that's my little sister. No one wants to meet me if I send a picture of myself; I'm sure you understand that. They'd rather choose an airhead in a nice wrapping. It's not fair and yet I usually win in the end. Once they're done looking at Gunilla I'm the one they want to talk to and confide in, like a mother or a dear sister. On the Internet I can pretend to be someone else for a little while and experience what it feels like to be physically attractive. You know, there are times when I hate my little sister. That, my friend, is true sibling rivalry.

"We're not going to see each other again, are we? You know, every time I do this I hope there'll be someone who might like just me, isn't that silly? So I took the chance to meet you in reality. I shouldn't have done that."

Then she started crying and the whole situation became so awkward that he couldn't get away from there fast enough.

The first thing Hans Moberg did when he got back to his camper was open a beer. He drank it in greedy gulps while he waited to get out on the Internet and flee into new lovely fantasies. When he had sorted out the junk mail selling Viagra and penis enlargement and standby vacations there was only one e-mail of interest—it was from Sandra Hägg who had contacted him on one occasion previously.

Extremely formal and actually fairly uninteresting. She did not want to send a photo, she was presumably ugly as sin. Although the really ugly ones can have unexpected talents, a devotion and gratitude you seldom encounter in those who know they have a beautiful body.

In her first email she asked questions about his company and where he got his supply of medications; now she was asking if they could meet. Could perhaps be something to try out, the evening looked pretty dreary otherwise. At the moment she had a migraine and was in bed. The key was hanging on a cord on the inside of the mail slot in the door, she wrote. The matter was urgent. Nothing she wanted to email about. It had to be discussed face to face.

This could actually be interpreted any number of ways. What was she expecting really when she wrote that she was lying in bed, waiting for him? House call by a doctor? A burglar? A secret lover in the form of a salesman? What role should he play? Perhaps it was so monotonously simple and boring as she wrote, a business contact. Or yet another circumlocution and smoke screen for what all women wanted without seeming too easy. The whole nine yards. Well, what the hell. If she was waiting for him . . .

Even though Hans Moberg had another four beers and an undetermined quantity of vodka, he disconnected his van from the camper and drove in to Signalgatan and the fashionable apartments with large glassed-in balconies facing the sea. What does it cost to live like that, he wondered. A little society bitch with a rich daddy, maybe, or did she have her own income, or even worse: a husband with income? Could get complicated. It was probably best to scope out the situation before getting too friendly.

He had to wait almost half an hour before he was able to slip through the door at the same time as a thin, elderly man in golf attire. The man gave him a suspicious look, not fearful, more like disdainful, and then confidently took the stairs in three bounds and disappeared behind his door on the second floor. Moby continued up. On her floor a curious older woman stuck her head out and watched him. The hall smelled of scouring powder and fresh-brewed coffee. He rang the bell at Sandra Hägg's, but not a sound was heard. He repeated the signal. She was probably sleeping, poor thing. It can't be easy to have migraines. When he put his hand down into the mail slot he thought that maybe this was a joke. Maybe there was a Rottweiler inside only longing for a couple of fresh, fleshy fingers to bite on. He got hold of the cord and fished up the key. First he tried to undo the double knot. Why do women always have to tie a granny knot when it's so much easier to undo a square knot. Then he gave up and put his foot against the door and pulled. There was no great resistance. He coaxed the key into the hole and turned it.

"Hello!" No answer.

"Hello!" He didn't want to frighten her. If she was in bed maybe he could crawl in and hold her awhile.

"Are you there, little darling?"

All women are whores, deep down, although they disguise themselves as angels. Treacherous, insidious schemers they are, and in their worm-eaten brains they plan how they can entrap and injure a man. What Sandra Hägg did to him that night was unforgivable and the greatest threat he had experienced to the freedom he treasured most in life. She did not do it consciously . . . and perhaps that was even worse . . . that she could never see her mistake and ask him for forgiveness.

Now as Hans Moberg was standing before the cracked mirror in his camper, the events of the night before no longer felt real. Her bloodshot eyes and the blue lips might just as well be a sequence from a film he had seen long ago, when the plot itself had faded and only the strongest visual impressions remained. And just like in any B-movie, he had wiped off his fingerprints from the doorpost and the mail slot with a piece of paper towel he had found in the kitchen.

The table was set for two with napkins, flowers, and crystal glasses, and there was a good smell from some kind of casserole. Red wine was poured in a carafe for airing. She had been expecting him. Longed for and prepared this encounter. He took the wine into the bedroom. Her short, dark hair made such a clear contrast against the white sheets. Her skin so transparent and white, the slender hands with their long red nails. The body had truly been beautiful in the thin white dress, like a bride. Still warm when he touched her breasts. At that moment her cell phone rang. At first he thought about answering but changed his mind. It was a trap, clearly. The frightening thing was that he almost fell for it. It had been that close. No one could know that he had been with her. He felt afraid and panic was approaching. His hands, which had squeezed the pillow that lay beside her on the floor had perhaps left traces. He took the pillow with him and threw it in the latrine barrel at an RV rest area. No one would think of searching there. There could be no traces.

He had a vague memory that he sat on the edge of the bed in her room and drank up the wine before the madness kicked in. Fury rushed into his veins, taking with it all reason from his brain. He smashed her TV with a chair. A vague memory from that night. There were some frightening gaps. Two children's faces had looked down at him from the stairs. Perhaps it was reality, perhaps something that was added on from TV later in the evening? Would he dare go back there to see how bad it was? In daylight and in a semi-sober condition it would be an act of insanity. Right now he just wanted to cry and preferably go off and die. No, someone might notice him if he came back. It would be enough for the hostile man in golf pants who had stared arrogantly at him or the old lady with the permanent and the peering eyes. Would they remember him and provide a facial description? Perhaps they too were part of a bad dream? When you drink too much your sleep gets disturbed and your dreams are strangely real and frightening.

He remembered he'd emptied the wine carafe himself. Her computer had been turned on. There was a bluish light from the screen. The dreams were complicated like female creatures that no sane person can understand.

But first he had to check his email. It would be a day without alcohol, a day with only light beer and cola. When he drank too much, his worlds became mixed and the evil could reach him from the other side. He shouldn't drink so much, but how else could he survive when the terror set in? There was no other relief to be had.

Chapter 18

When Maria Wern arrived at the police station on Wednesday morning, the fifth of July, she was told about the murder on Signalgatan by her colleague in reception. She hadn't had a chance to listen to the morning news.

Linda was being obstinate and didn't want to stay home with Marianne Hartman, even though they had agreed on that. In the afternoon she was to have a play date with Sofie, who lived a little farther up the street. But as Maria was about to leave, Linda hung on her mother's arm with both legs wrapped around her leg and screamed. She was a big girl now, almost eight, but what does that matter if you're little inside? Marianne tried to entice her with videos and computer games and ice cream at an increasingly frantic pace.

"You can dress up in my old clothes if you want. I have a box of old jewelry, too, don't you think that would be fun? And makeup and long gloves like ladies have on when they go to balls and a hat with flowers. That would be fun to dress up in, wouldn't it?"

"No, because I want my mommy. Don't go, Mommy. Don't gooooo . . . you can't die . . . promise me you won't die, Mommy. I want my mommy!"

In desperation, Maria called Krister on his cell phone and listened to the sprightly message that he could not take the call right now, but Someone who's waiting for something good never waits too long. It wasn't amusing even the first time, and after the fifth try it was pure mockery. It was actually his turn to take care of the kids for fourteen days and he had barely lasted twenty-four hours in adapting his bachelor existence to Linda's terms. Pick up the phone, you jerk!

"You know, Linda," Marianne's voice was calm. "We could bake sugar cookies if you want and then you and Sofie can have them this afternoon when you've dressed up like elegant ladies. That sounds fun, don't you think?"

Very unwillingly, Linda accepted the offer, waiting just a little in case more benefits might turn up. Finally she was content with the exchange: a mother for video, ice cream, dress-up clothes, and sugar cookies. Worse transactions had been made.

When Maria entered the station a good thirty minutes later than she intended, she heard about the woman who had been murdered in her apartment. Hartman was already there to talk with the policemen who had been on duty during the night and the technicians who were on the scene. It took Maria another fifteen minutes to get there. She was exchanging a few words with her colleague at the cordon, to get a sense of what had happened, when Hartman approached her. His curly hair was standing up in all directions as if he'd fallen asleep with it wet and woke up in a big hurry, which might very well be the case. His voice sounded hoarse and hesitant, as if he had still not used it except to hem and haw. He cleared his throat.

"One of the neighbors called in the alarm at midnight. There was a dreadful racket from the apartment. Practically everything in the living room and bedroom is smashed.

There's a dead woman in the bedroom. The apartment is owned by a Sandra Hägg. Previously she shared it with a Lennie Hellström. According to the neighbors she lives here alone. We'll have to assume that it's Sandra in there and . . . well, there's actually nothing to suggest otherwise."

"Can she be identified?"

"Well, it's most likely her. At first glance she appears to have been strangled, according to Mårtenson. The medical examiner is on his way."

"Do we know if she has any family? Lennie, you said, is that a boyfriend? Are there others?" Maria sat down on the driver's side in Hartman's car when he opened the door.

"We've tried to talk with the neighbors about that. Sandra Hägg seems to have a lot of visitors both during the day and evenings. No big parties, they come one by one. More women than men and always alone, says the next-door neighbor. Three years ago she and Lennie Hellström moved into this two-room apartment together, but for the last month he hasn't been seen. The neighbors assume they separated but no one has asked directly. We're trying to get in touch with him. The name is fairly uncommon. We have a couple of phone numbers for a Lennie Hellström on Rutegatan. Cell, work phone, and a number to a landline in the apartment we've located, but so far we haven't been able to reach him. It would be good if he found out what happened before the media gets hold of this."

"Do we know anything about her? How old is she?"

"According to her driver's license she would have turned thirty-three in August. I have Mårtenson's digital camera here so we can see the pictures they took from the apartment. The fewer people who tramp around in there the better." Maria took a deep breath and forced herself to look at what she couldn't avoid seeing. The woman's face was mottled blue. Her tongue was hanging swollen out of her mouth, and her bloodshot eyes were staring. The next picture showed the bruise on her neck.

"So repulsive." Maria closed her eyes and swallowed.

"Horrible. You never get used to it. If you did maybe it would be time to quit." Hartman continued the display with a series of pictures of the interior. "It looks like she did massage. There's a massage bench set up in the living room—otherwise it's furnished like any other apartment. That might explain the number of visitors."

Maria looked at the pictures with dismay. The destruction was incredible. Not one chair whole. The TV screen was smashed and the glass doors of the sideboard broken. Otherwise the living room was light and sparsely furnished. One side of the room faced out toward the large balcony with a view of the sea and the harbor area. The massage bench was set up along one wall. It had a slipcover and pillows, hot water bottles, and buckwheat pillows, and at the foot end was a large welded floor candleholder. Tea lights were set out all over the room in elegant small steel-wire candle lanterns. Two large ceramic bowls of fruit decorated the low coffee table and everywhere were expensive flowers in vases. White lilies, white roses, and other tall white flowers, the names of which Maria did not know. Strangely enough, these had been left untouched.

The opposite wall was covered with bookshelves and the books were sorted by subject and in alphabetical order. Two shelves were swept out onto the floor. Mostly fiction, but also professional medical literature and books about herbs and art, Maria noted while she tried without much success to screen off the intrusive visual image of the dead woman. The thought of the violated body, the bruises. A woman thirty-three years old, a woman younger than herself. There was a bundle of papers on the desk. Photocopied newspaper articles about EAN codes and chip marking of animals.

There were no signs of any pets in the apartment. No food bowls, leashes, or scratching posts.

"Is there a photo of her?"

"The driver's license. Do you want to see it?" Hartman pulled a plastic bag out of his briefcase with a gloved hand and showed the photograph through the plastic. "She was very nice-looking."

"Yes, very." Maria studied a friendly, open face with regular features and a nice smile. "I've seen her before. Only in passing, but I remember it quite clearly. She left her wallet in the store. I couldn't catch up with her then, but she got her wallet back anyway.

"I noticed she had a computer in the bedroom. It was even turned on."

"Yes, I hope it can give us some information. On the floor in the bedroom was a ceramic carafe. There has been wine in it, and it looks like she drank straight from it without a glass. The technicians took it with them. I don't think we have much more to do here, or what do you think? Lennie Hellström next, shall we head over to Rutegatan and question the ex-boyfriend?" Maria agreed and let her eyes pass one last time over the picture of the living room.

"I'm wondering about something. It looks like the massage bench is easy to fold up and put away. But it's set up. Could she have been expecting a client? Both men and women come here, you said. The apartment is rather small and the bench takes up space. I would have folded it up if I wasn't working." She continued thoughtfully. "I wouldn't dare be a masseuse and let strange men into my home. I mean, being home alone and letting a man strip down to his underwear and then massaging him; it seems risky. Was she forced to see clients at home for financial reasons, do you think? I'm just thinking out loud. We should probably assign someone to check up on her clients."

"If her live-in moved out, the rent for this apartment must cost a bit every month." Hartman was silent a moment, thinking about what the monthly expense for an apartment with a sea view in Visby might be. "Wonder if she's a masseuse in her spare time or is that her real occupation?"

They went into the building to return the camera. "No Solicitors" it said on a neatly handwritten piece of paper right below it. Maria could not take her eyes off the woman's sturdy permanent. Close to her scalp it was straight as an arrow and then it became a thick headband of steel wool.

"I need to talk with you, Mr. Policeman. You are a policeman, aren't you? It's hard to tell if you're not wearing a uniform."

Yes, he was.

"Is it true that she's lying dead in there, the poor girl? Imagine, I wondered what kind of terrible commotion there was when I got up to use the bathroom. It sounded like someone was smashing apart all the furniture. This is just too terrible. How did it happen? What was going on? Well, what I want to say is . . . perhaps you could come in so I can offer you a cup of coffee on a day like this . . . you might really need it. I don't have much to go with it, but there are always rolls if that would taste good. Gotland rolls."

"I don't think we have time for that right now. If there's anything you forgot to tell the policeman you spoke with here earlier this morning please say what's on your mind, but we don't have time for coffee."

"Oh no, there's always time for that. You have to give yourself time for a cup of coffee so you can keep working." Without Maria really understanding how it happened, soon they were sitting nicely next to each other like two schoolchildren on Aunt Ingrid's kitchen bench. "Well, what I wanted to tell you was that Sandra Hägg is a clean-living person and a teetotaler. I know that, because I'm involved in the Blue Ribbon Society and we've talked about these things on many occasions. I know her mother; she was also active in the temperance movement. Where is society headed when the social democrats want to lower the alcohol tax? Who's going to pay those bills? If we're going to take care of everyone with alcohol damage, municipal taxes will have to go up if folks with other complaints are going to get any care at all. The money has to be there. Sandra Hägg is a nurse and has worked with smoking cessation. A combination of massage and smoking cessation. She worked at that health center that recently opened at Snäckgärdsbaden. I can barely pronounce the name: Vigoris Health Center. It's a kind of community health center, but private. For people with money."

"Do you know where we can get hold of Lennie Hellström? If we're not misinformed he doesn't live here anymore." Maria refused a refill. Her stomach was aching. Onset of gastritis again, presumably. Linda's reaction that morning was still in her body—Promise you won't die, Mommy—and the constant thoughts of Emil. She needed to be with him.

"Lennie, that's very sad, I don't understand what made her break off the engagement. They were so in love and he's such a nice young man. So considerate and friendly. If he saw that I was carrying heavy bags from the store he helped me up the stairs with them, and if he was going into town he always offered me a ride so I wouldn't have to walk. Yes, she was nice too, she really was. I thought they were so well suited for each other and then they go and make a mess of things. I have to be truthful. When she broke up with him he was sitting there on the bench, right where you're sitting now. He was completely pale, the poor boy. He couldn't understand it. He simply could not understand what he had done wrong. Things were going so well for them, a nice apartment and both of them had jobs, a car and everything. It was as if she wasn't really herself anymore. He didn't recognize her, he said."

"In what way was she different?" Hartman swept the crumbs into his hand and put them on the plate. He was getting ready to say thank you and leave when he got an answer to his final question.

"Yes, in what way? No, he didn't say. So you haven't got hold of him yet? Well, but then he doesn't know . . . that's just terrible! He lives on Rutegatan."

"We know that, but he doesn't answer the phone."

"That's not so strange. He works nights at a security company. That was how they met and he became her personal bodyguard. They used to joke about that and now she's dead . . . it's just so horrid and he doesn't know anything yet, poor boy."

"What's the name of the security company where he works?"

"Guard something, that center and the security company are related in some way. They're owned by a foreign company, I think. It was so romantic when Sandra and Lennie met. She got locked in the laboratory. There was something wrong with her access card so she couldn't get out, and he had to come and rescue her on a ladder through a window so that she could get back to her patient who had just had an operation. She worked nights at that time and was the only nurse on the ward. She had to get out so she could do her job. Sometimes Lennie works extra as a bouncer at the bars in town. I know that. He's probably working more now that they're no longer together. He's got to do something. He can't just sit alone at home staring at the wall."

"I assume you've already been asked whether you saw anything unusual yesterday evening, saw anyone on the stairwell who doesn't live here, for example, or heard anything unusual."

"Yes, I actually did. I have such a hard time sleeping when it feels like there are ants creeping up my legs; I walk back and forth in the apartment. I'm sure I've walked several thousand miles this month alone. Of course, you have to take a look at who's on the stairs. The Perssons below aren't home. They've gone to Greece and you feel a little responsibility. There have been a number of apartment break-ins recently when people have been away . . . and then I read in the newspaper about the old man who let two strange women in who wanted to borrow a pen and paper to write a message to the neighbor upstairs. He wasn't at home and they had just stopped by. While they kept the man busy a third person sneaked in and took his wallet and other valuables. It's just shameful to do such a thing to old people. Well then, I do keep an eye on the building."

"And what did you see," said Hartman in an attempt to hasten the testimony somewhat if possible.

"First some children came who were selling peppermint sticks. A boy and a girl. The girl had long blonde hair and was a little taller than the boy. He was dark and had big brown eyes and said his name was Patrik. They were in third grade and were going to Denmark. It's awful that they have to work so hard to go on a school trip. We never went on school trips when I was a child. We just bicycled out to the beach and camped. Right after the children rang the bell a man came by in a cowboy hat and boots. I've never seen him before. He had a beard or long mustache anyway. Henriksson saw him too. He may have been forty-five or fifty, perhaps. Burly. Grayish blond long hair. He reeked of alcohol, I noticed it far off."

"You didn't see anything else?" asked Maria when Ingrid Svensson paused to refill their cups.

"Well, there was another man, I think. I heard a man's voice outside. It may have been the same person, the one with the cowboy hat—but I got a feeling somehow that it wasn't. I thought that such a big fellow can't have such a squeaky voice, you imagine that the voice and the person go together, if you understand?"

"Did you hear what he said?" asked Hartman.

"No, I didn't. It may have been the same man of course, I won't say otherwise, but the voice was extremely high-pitched."

Chapter 19

"*The bird flu on Gotland has claimed yet another victim. The thirty-year-old female coach who was infected at a soccer camp in Klintehamn died at three o'clock this morning. According to reports from a reliable source, the supply of effective medicine is no longer adequate, and today the Minister of Public Health will make an appeal to the World Health Organization for help. The situation is serious. We also have information from unconfirmed sources that eleven more of the children at the soccer camp have become ill with flu-like symptoms and will be transferred to the old Follingbo sanitarium today with the help of a response team from Linköping. We have disease control officer Åsa Gahnström with us in the studio for commentary.*"

"*The fact is that the antiviral medications we have do not work on the strain of flu virus that has struck the island. We can treat complications like pneumonia with antibiotics, but Tamiflu and the other medications that were procured for the emergency supply are ineffective.*"

Maria turned off the radio and covered her face with her hands. So now they were admitting it. Emil! It was as if only now had the shock subsided enough for her to understand what Jonathan Eriksson said to her last night. She couldn't bear to hear more. The sound came and went and a powerful attack of vertigo made her take desperate hold of the handle to the car door while she supported herself with her other hand against the instrument panel. She should be with her child and not at work! A moderate infection, Jonathan had said, but he hadn't look her in the eyes when he was saying it.

"What's going on, Maria? Are you thinking about Emil, or what? I understand if you are. You can't work under such circumstances. I can speak with Lennie Hellström myself. I'll drive you to Follingbo so you can see how the boy is doing, then you can call me when you want to return to Visby. Okay?"

"Yes, I have to be with him now. I can't think about anything else. It's like a nightmare. They said that eleven more children . . . eleven children have gotten sick and there's no medicine to give them. There aren't enough respirators on the island or personnel if they get really sick, there may even be a shortage of beds, the doctor said when I pressed him. What happens now? If Emil had remained at the soccer camp I would have picked him up after this. I would do it even if I had to force my way past my colleagues. I would have fought to get him out of there and I don't think I'm alone in feeling that way. I feel sorry for the police officers standing guard outside the school—what will they do if parents demand to pick up their children to save their lives? It's an unreasonable task. They won't be able to hold a unified front. There'll be chaos. What will happen to the parents who try to get past? Tie them up? Hit them with batons? Arrest them?"

The row of apartment buildings on Rutegatan looked orderly,

no graffiti or any visible damage. The bicycles were parked neatly in a rack, except for one rusty child's bike with training wheels that was tossed on the lawn outside. A nice area, if not as exclusive as Signalgatan. When Hartman got out of the car at the indicated address he wondered how the division of property was worked out between Sandra and Lennie. Who earns more, a nurse or a night watchman with extra income? Perhaps Ingrid Svensson's view of Sandra Hägg as a clean-living person did not exactly add up. It's not a given that you tell your neighbors everything, especially not if they're in collusion with your mother.

Hartman read the blue directory by the entry and then took the two stairs up to the floor where Lennie Hellström lived. He rang five or six times before someone opened the door. A man with a large head of coal-black hair dressed only in underwear opened and assessed the intruder with squinting, tired eyes.

"Tomas Hartman from the police, may I come in?"

"What's this about? If you're selling something I'm not interested. You woke me up actually. Is anything wrong?" said Lennie Hellström when he saw Hartman's serious expression. He combed his hair back with both hands and yawned so that the black fillings at the back of his mouth were visible. "I've only slept for . . ."—he squinted and looked at his watch—"barely three hours. Is it something important?"

"Yes. Perhaps it's best if we go in and sit down." Hartman showed his identification. Still hesitant, Lennie opened the door so that Hartman could barely squeeze in under his hairy armpit. The stench of old sweat and beer became stronger. The whole apartment had a stale odor of unwashed workout clothes, moldy garbage, and sour milk. Hartman took a step over a large exercise bag and a pile of clothes on the hall floor and followed him into the kitchen, where

Lennie immediately went up to the fridge and popped open a beer that he drank straight from the can.

"Would you like one?" he asked, reaching for another beer. When Hartman declined he continued drinking in silence and stifled a belch with puffed-out cheeks. "Okay, what do you want? Hartman, was that your name?"

"I've just come from Signalgatan."

"Good Lord, Sandra! Is she okay?"

"We've found a woman in her apartment. Dead—and yes, we believe it is Sandra Hägg." Hartman paused so that the words could sink in. "Do you know of any distinctive marks on her, a scar, birthmark or the like?"

"This isn't true! Marks? Sandra has a bar code tattooed on her butt. She did it last summer; she thought it was cool. I don't get it! What happened?"

"A neighbor of Sandra called the emergency service center last night. She was wakened by a noise and was trying to figure out where it came from. The door to Sandra's apartment was open and when she came in she saw the destruction. By then she was already dead. She was lying in her bed. Strangled."

Lennie stared straight ahead, not understanding, as if the words went right past him. He went over to the refrigerator and opened another beer and emptied it in three large gulps. Hartman waited. Lennie remained by the refrigerator door without closing it. He stood there staring at the bare wall without showing a single reaction to what had been said. Hartman remained sitting quietly and waited for the outburst that might come without forewarning.

"Dead?" Lennie whispered in a voice from far, far away. "Is Sandra dead? She can't be dead. I just talked with her. You're lying, damn it, I just talked to her." His tone was threatening now and he came quite close with his face bobbing from side to side to stand his ground and demand an opponent, someone to fight with to regain what he had lost. Tomas Hartman did not turn his eyes away.

"Yes, she's dead. What time did you speak with her? Do you remember that? What time might it have been?"

"Damn it, I wanted to go home to her. It was right after eleven last night. I'd done my rounds at Vigoris and I just wanted to see her so I called . . . Excuse me, I have to pee."

Hartman looked around the sparsely furnished kitchen. A small round wine-stained pine table with two chairs. No flowers in the window, no curtains. A pile of dirty dishes—several day's worth of plates and glasses—were heaped in the sink and on the counter. A temporary residence, not a home. Above the kitchen table was a carelessly nailed-up cork bulletin board with a light-blue wooden frame. In one corner was a reminder of a dental appointment and below that a recipe for Flying Jacob casserole fastened with May Day wreaths. There was a photo, almost completely covered by gasoline receipts. Hartman folded back the strips of paper to see better. A snapshot of a happy couple. A Lennie with somewhat lighter hair stood behind Sandra and held her, and she was looking up at him from the side and smiling. A marvelous image showing warmth and love, it couldn't be mistaken. At one time they loved each other a lot; what happened? Lennie was taking a long time in the bathroom. Conceivably he was crying and didn't want to show it. After ten long minutes he was back. His movements were slow and disjointed but now his gaze was present.

"Are you completely sure she was dead? Did you see it yourself?" A low-pitched plea. Say it isn't true.

"She was dead."

"She can't be, she has courses in how to stop smoking. She's teaching a class this evening and I planned to go. The first thing she did when we started seeing each other was to throw away my pack of cigarettes. You have to choose, she said. Nicotine or nooky. Men who smoke become impotent. Do you want me or your cigarettes? She was non-negotiable on that point. If I wanted to be with her, I had to stop smoking and drinking. But it was worth it as long as it lasted." Lennie smiled a sad smile and shook his bushy black hair. His big gray-blue eyes looked very, very sad now.

"What happened then?"

"Happened?" Lennie picked at something under his thumbnail for a while and tried to find words. He leaned his face on his hands so that only his hair was visible and sighed heavily. "What happened? I still don't understand that. We didn't argue about money, we didn't argue about sex, we didn't even argue about who should do what. But she got strange. Absent. She could sit and stare out the window for an hour at nothing. Or sit and think, and when I asked what it was she said it was nothing, although I knew there was something of course. She wouldn't let me into her thoughts anymore and of course I got worried. Started wondering whether there was someone else. She worked a lot. Extra shifts. Overtime. Had sleepovers with her girlfriends. I didn't want to control her. She said right from the start that freedom and trust were the most important things in a relationship. Her ex checked up on her and spied on her. That was why she broke up with him, she said. Her logic was a little strange on that point. She said that as long as she was left alone she took responsibility for being faithful, but if anyone dared check up on her they took over the responsibility and then her inventiveness and creativity were almost unlimited where finding opportunities was concerned. That's exactly what she said and maybe she said it as a joke. I don't really know if she meant it. Or if it was the first sign that she was starting to get tired of me."

"So what happened? Did you start checking up on her?"

"What the hell, I guess I did. I got so fucking jealous. I checked her email. It was mostly from some freelance journalist named Tobias Westberg, a fucking bore. I've read a couple of his articles. He writes about medicine, I don't get half of it. A know-it-all who likes to throw out fancy words, you know the type. Do you know what he calls himself on the Internet? Mr. Logic. So fucking ridiculous. Mr. Logic! Then I checked her calendar on the web. She had scheduled him for massage. We had a hell of a fight. There are limits and I think she respected the fact that I got angry, anyway. After that, it was calm for a while until I noticed that unexplained Ts started showing up in her calendar, the one she carried in her purse. But I didn't say anything. I didn't dare. And now she's dead. Damn it. How did it happen? Strangled, you said?"

"We don't know yet. The door was open; it wasn't broken down. We assume she must have let someone in who then strangled her."

"Was she raped?" Lennie's voice betrayed him. He looked pleadingly at Hartman, as if he was capable of controlling fate.

"It's too soon to say. It may take several days before we know. What happened after you started checking her calendar? Did she find out?"

"I started checking whether she was at work when she said she would be there. That was a few months ago. She was going to work overtime the whole weekend, she said. Between two of my inspection rounds at night I went to the ward. It seemed like she had told the truth, because her bag was in the staff room. But I was crazy with jealousy, can you understand that?"

"Yes, I think I can understand what you were thinking."

"Well, I took her cell phone out of her bag and checked who she had called and right then she came in. Do you understand? She saw what I was doing and got furious. Then she barely spoke to me for a week. Changed passwords on the computer and did not let her cell phone or calendar out of her sight. She got stranger and stranger and didn't say where she was going anymore when she went out in the evening. I didn't know what the hell I should do, so finally I threatened to move. Go ahead, she said, just as indifferent as if I'd said I wanted to change channels on the TV. Go ahead."

"And then you moved?"

"Yes, what should I have done? I could have begged and pleaded that everything would be fine, but I couldn't. Not then, and now it's too late." Lennie got up and went to the refrigerator again. Opened the door and took out the last beer. "How could it get like this? I need a whiskey instead of this pissy beer."

Hartman agreed. There are times in life when an anesthetic may be required to endure. Lennie sat down at the table again and started weeping like a child. Hartman placed his big hand on his shoulder and waited for him to finish crying. When Lennie raised his head, Hartman's arm was stiff and his fingers were numb. He tried not to show it.

"Is it even possible to understand women?" said Lennie, and Hartman noticed that his voice had become noticeably slurred and drawling.

"Understanding women is probably something a person could devote his whole life to," said Hartman.

They were silent for a time while mutual understanding settled over the sorrow.

"I'd like to talk to you about your night shift yesterday," Hartman continued. He picked up his pad and borrowed a well-chewed pencil from the windowsill.

"What? You don't think that I . . . that I killed Sandra? Is that what you think? Say it right out in that case." Lennie's voice was full of anger and the outburst Hartman had feared earlier felt imminent now.

"Do you think I would've come here alone if I thought you took her life, do you really think so, Lennie?" Hartman was a little ashamed of his white lie, but it worked. Lennie, who had gotten halfway out of his chair, sat down again and his eyes became gentler.

"I started at nine o'clock and went through the laboratory and the department where they manufacture computer electronics, don't ask me what they do, I don't understand such things. The security manager for the whole company has his office there. We call him Five-Fault Finn, because he's a nitpicker—so fucking meticulous. He looks for mistakes as if they were rewards, he micromanages. Nobody likes him. He really wanted to be a police officer but didn't get in. These are really sensitive things to talk about. He's so prestige-conscious that no one can stand him. If I'd been the one to decide we never would have bought the apartment from him. He was there to pick up his cell phone that he forgot. I teased him a little about that—he never makes mistakes, never forgets anything, you know. You can ask him yourself and he'll tell you that I was there. Then I continued to a warehouse that is also owned by the group and then to Vigoris Health Center—the whole facility. Walked down every single corridor. We have access cards so that it shows when you go in and out. Then I called Sandra, because I was anxious just to talk with her, but no one answered. So I don't work for a security company. The group has its own security guards. They want to use people they can trust and they want to approve who moves around on their premises. Actually it's strange that more big companies don't have their own security guards. Then I did the rest of my shift with a final round at the office on Brovåg and turned in my keys to the day guard. When I came home it was almost six thirty. I didn't know about Sandra. I swear it. I didn't know until you got here."

Chapter 20

Jonathan Eriksson closed the door to his office, took off the damp protective mask and sat down at the computer to do the necessary patient chart notes. His shirt was sticky with sweat and his hands were shaking as he picked up the microphone and dictated the measures he had performed the past few hours. Eleven new children, all with fever, sore throat, and aching joints, had come to the sanitarium in groups during the morning from the soccer camp in Klinte School. There were no longer separate rooms for all of them. They had to share rooms, with the risks that entailed if any of the children had flu-like symptoms for reasons other than infection with bird flu virus. The parents were upset, to put it mildly, and needed time to talk. The majority of them wanted to stay with their children but it had been necessary to make a decision that in principle this could not be allowed. There was not enough protective equipment, masks and protective clothing for everyone. The supply of adequate breathing protection was starting to run low and what masks there were had to be assigned and reused by individuals. A new shipment of breathing protection could not be expected until next week; the supplier was out. Changing to regular paper mouth protection would involve a great, unnecessary risk. Naturally the children's need to have their parents nearby had to be considered, not the other way around, and weighed against the risk of infection. That had been the decision in the personnel group.

The situation was starting to get overwhelming. Staff who were not sick were working day and night. The extra staff who should have come and relieved them yesterday had not yet arrived, as negotiations were being conducted between Social Services and the respective unions to determine whether or not it was refusal to work to turn down compulsory service when the risk of contagion was so imminent and the medical absences among the personnel continued to increase at the hospital and sanitarium. It would be preferable to have staff with experience working in an infectious disease department. Presumably they would have to abandon that ambition as soon as this evening and take the hands that were willing to help.

Jonathan could understand those who refused and wanted to negotiate; being in a contagious environment meant risking your life. There are also limits to how loyal nursing staff can be. Someone has to do it, but why me? Why just me? He had asked that question himself. Maybe it was a combination of death wish, guilt, and duty when he chose to stay in service.

The ICU at Follingbo was unable to take more patients, nor could the infectious disease department, and the pressure from the general public on the health centers threatened to cause the whole healthcare system to collapse. A man with flu symptoms and a heart attack had died that morning waiting for a doctor at his home. A woman with a burst appendix had not received care in time either and died on her way to the hospital. And in the tent that had been set up outside the hospital to check temperatures and other signs of flu, tumult had broken out when patients were refused entry to the emergency room.

The media were in search of scapegoats. Social Services would be getting heaps of reports. The doctors who were supposed to make house calls couldn't keep up, of course, and the team of doctors that was supposed to see other patients at the health centers was hard pressed even before the flu epidemic broke out. Morgan was badly needed at the sanitarium but was forced to go to Klintehamn to calm the parents of the children who remained at the soccer camp.

What worried Jonathan Eriksson the most at the moment however was that one of the two ten-year-old boys who had arrived yesterday, Zebastian Wahlgren, was doing very poorly. Emil Wern seemed to be handling the infection better. Zebastian's parents had been contacted and would be there at any moment. Jonathan shuddered at the thought of this conversation. Sorry, we don't have anything to offer besides general care and encouraging words. He may need to be on a respirator and there are no more respirators on the island. The coordination of resources from the mainland is not working. For best possible care he must be transported to Linköping. There is an available place, but they don't have any antiviral medicine to offer either.

Letting the patients leave the island was also a risk that in the present situation they were forced to take. As Åsa put it: That way we save a few more lives, but we don't hold the barriers and risk an epidemic. But when you are standing there by the bed and see a ten-year-old boy getting worse and worse and know that the chances of his survival are greater if he leaves the island, what do you do? A slight chance, but of course you take it. His coach, Jenny Eklund, had not survived despite intensive care. There were no guarantees. But if it were your child you wouldn't hesitate, even if it meant risking other people's lives.

For the eleven new arrivals there was no effective medicine to give. Jonathan had explained his work situation in sharp terms to Åsa Gahnström and she protested that the national pandemic group was doing its utmost to produce Tamivir. A medicine that had been demonstrated in tests to have effect on the bird flu that broke out in Vietnam and later in Belarus, before it died out completely and the feared pandemic did not occur. But things looked dismal. The doses that had been purchased from an Internet dealer proved to be completely worthless sugar pills with additives of cortisone and anise.

There was a knock at the door and Jonathan put his mask on again.

"Zebastian's parents are here now." By the voice he recognized Nurse Eva, otherwise they were very alike, she and Agneta, when they were wearing a mask. Jonathan felt a twinge of guilty conscience. He should ask how Agneta is doing. It was his confounded duty as a supervisor and friend. What could he say in consolation? Not much. And his fatigue was paralyzing. If he got out of this inferno alive he would hide from people and not talk to anyone for an eternity, sleep for days, quit being a doctor and do something different, and never, ever make decisions that concerned the lives and health of others.

"Help them with the protective clothing. I'll call Åsa and see whether they've gotten anywhere in the negotiations, if anything new has happened. How do they seem to be taking it?"

"Of course they're very worried. Did you tell them that he has to be moved to get access to intensive care?"

"I said that he's worse, not how bad it is. I'll inform them now. I didn't want them risking their lives in traffic to get here. It's better to do it face-to-face and take their questions calmly."

"I was just wondering, so I know what I can say when they ask me." Eva disappeared again and the air thickened. Jonathan took a deep breath and felt the pressure over his ribcage; it wasn't possible to take a deep breath. A stitch in the spleen presumably or the start of a heart attack. In the present situation it didn't matter which—death as rest and liberator from all the misery was no longer frightening. He picked up the phone to dial the direct number to disease control officer Åsa Gahnström but instead his associate Morgan Svenning was suddenly on the line.

"Everything is falling apart. I'm not able to hold the positions out here. The parents are demanding to pick up their children. The barricade is crowded with people who intend to help them free the children. They are extremely agitated, it feels like they might start throwing rocks or let the dogs loose on the police at any moment. They don't understand what they are risking if the infection gets out and there isn't any medicine. We'll have to cordon off the whole damn island with the help of the military if we're not able to keep the infection enclosed, and people are going to die like flies in their homes because there aren't any available hospital beds. Maybe it's time to announce that in the media now, maybe it's time to speak plainly. Åsa Gahnström is on her way here. The enraged crowd outside has promised through their spokesperson to wait for what she has to offer. If there isn't anything to give the children, all hell is going to break loose. What should we do? This can't be happening – it's a pure nightmare."

"I don't know what we should do, Morgan. I really don't know."

"Listen, one other thing that perhaps I shouldn't burden you with right now—but I think you ought to know anyway. My wife was out with her co-workers at a bar yesterday celebrating with a colleague who is leaving. She saw Nina. I don't know how to say this so there won't be a mistake, but Nina, your wife—"

"Yes, what about Nina?" Jonathan was cowering from the pain in his chest. It almost took his breath away, an explosive ache that radiated all the way out to his back. And now this too . . .

"Nina was drunk off her ass and was ejected because she was loud and, well, rowdy. She was arguing with other customers. I'm really sorry, Jonathan. But I thought it was only fair for you to know—"

"Thanks, Morgan. Of course you did the right thing. Nina hasn't had an easy time of it lately. Is Åsa there now? I need to talk with her."

"No, and the line is busy when you try her cell phone. What's she doing? She has to come soon; otherwise there'll be a riot. I can't take responsibility anymore. I'm trusting that you'll pass this on to Social Services. I said that I can no longer take responsibility and you heard me."

Jonathan dialed his home number. He let it ring eight times before he called his mother. She promised to find out where Malte was. His mother's voice sounded so small and anxious that it hurt him.

"It feels terrible to have to ask you for this, Mom, but I can't think of any other way. I know how Nina behaves toward you. When all this is over I'm going to do something about my life. It can't go on like this."

She reassured him by saying that she would do her best.

"I'll find Malte and bring him home with me. You take care of your work, Jonathan. I'll take care of this."

Zebastian's parents were sitting in the sluice on the other side of the glass wall dressed in protective gear. They were holding hands. Young and helpless. But they had each other, that was clear. He went over to them and explained the situation in the gentlest terms possible.

"Zebastian has to be moved to Linköping. We're able to let one of you go along."

"But he is going to get better?" The woman's voice was only a whisper from inside the mask but her eyes were all the bigger. When Jonathan did not answer right away she started to cry.

"I hope he'll get better. We're doing our very best but his kidneys are working poorly and his heart is failing. He's pretty swollen; you're going to see that. Whatever happens in there and however difficult it may feel, you must not take off the protective equipment or lower the mask."

When Jonathan had their promises they went into the room where two nurses were in the process of getting the boy ready for transport with oxygen tubes, emergency bag and bag valve mask. Zebastian looked at them. Then he shut his eyes again. He did not have the energy to talk with them. His cheeks were red with fever under the breathing mask. Carefully he was moved with the help of a draw-sheet to a wheeled gurney. His parents looked lost and seemed mostly to feel like they were in the way. Jonathan interrupted the preparations to give the father a brief moment to say goodbye. Zebastian's mother would go along to Linköping, they had decided.

"Hang in there, kid. I'll see you when you get back." Zebastian's father gave him a friendly tap on the shoulder and Zebastian looked up and nodded. Then the sporty attitude broke down and the father put his head against his son's stomach and cried. Before anyone could stop him he had removed his mask and pressed his cheek against the boy's so that Zebastian would really hear. "We love you so much."

Chapter 21

From the window Maria Wern watched the ambulance disappear between the pines, stirring up a cloud of dust on the winding road from the old Follingbo sanitarium. The heat shimmered through the trees.

"That was Zebastian," said Emil. "I didn't get to say goodbye to him. He's going to another hospital. Is he going to die now? My coach went away in an ambulance and now she's dead."

"I don't know, Emil, we don't know what will happen. We can only hope that he comes back soon, very soon, and that all of this horrid stuff will be over so you can play soccer again. We have to think it will turn out that way."

"I don't want to be here anymore, Mom. It's boring and everyone is serious and sad or sick. There's no one to be with. I want to go home! Right now I want to go home. I'm not going to stay here any longer because everyone just dies, and it's quiet and horrible and at night you hear sounds. There are sounds by the windows and in the walls. Some-one's whispering or creaking or screaming when it's windy outside, because then they have air in their voices. The ghosts. They're the ones who died here before. People have died in this room; did you know that? Zebastian said so. He knows because his aunt works at a hospital. Maybe someone had this pillow under their head and then just died and they put a new pillowcase on like nothing happened. They died from TB, back then. There's a little boy on the other side of the wall who shows up at night. He's trying to warn me and says I should escape from here. Run away from here as fast as you can! He's a little smaller than me and has a nightshirt and bare feet."

"You must have dreamt that, Emil." Maria adjusted her mask. It felt so silly to talk to each other in protective goggles and masks, especially about such serious matters as death.

"What do you mean? He's warning me in the dream. It counts as a warning. He told me that his mom and dad and all his brothers and sisters died and he was left alone with his grandmother. Just as alone as I am at night. I used to text Zebastian, but then he didn't have the energy to answer. I think he's going to die, Mom. I heard on the radio that half the people who get infected die. Zebastian said that he was really sick and swollen up like a Michelin man. Am I going to swell up too?"

"I don't think so. I think you're going to get healthy."

"But you don't know that. You can't know that. No one knows who's going to die, Dr. Jonathan says. He knows almost everything. But even he doesn't know who's going to live and who's going to die."

Maria sat down on the other side of the glass wall and picked up the phone to speak with Jonathan Eriksson. An additional safety measure, she assumed. Even if the doctor said that his tests showed he was not carrying the infection at the moment, he was living with the constant risk of being infected at work. That's why he chose to stay at the sanitarium. He looked really tired and sad, although he made brave attempts to be present. His eyelids lowered slowly while he listened to Maria's apprehensions and with a jerk he came to and pulled himself together when he was going to respond. This was surely only one of many difficult meetings today.

"I want to know the truth. How bad is it? What do you think about Emil?"

Jonathan wiped the sweat from his forehead and looked at her with a gaze so full of pain and resignation that she was startled.

"There is an approved medication, Tamivir, which may help. But we can't get hold of it within a reasonable time. Dr. Gahnström has been in contact with the manufacturer and tried to reach an agreement, but they say they sold their patent and all of their production and that there isn't any left in their warehouse. They went bankrupt when there was no outbreak and they had invested everything. Now we're trying to find out where the medication went."

"This isn't true! But Emil—"

"There is no next dose to give him. Nothing that has an effect. That's how bad it is. He's still more fortunate than most, it seems like his flu is progressing more calmly. I think Emil's chances of getting through this are good. But there are others—"

"Forgive me. I can see that you're completely overworked and I sense how hellish this is for you. Forgive me. Is there anything I can do that would make a difference? Anything at all. It looks like you're working around the clock. Can I help you with anything?"

He looked searchingly at her. Deliberated with himself.

"You're a police officer, right?"

"Yes." Maria did not understand where he was headed.

"I can't believe I'm asking you this, but I see no other way out." He hesitated another moment and then gasped audibly for air before he continued. "My wife is an alcoholic. I think this is the first time I've used that word about her, but that's the way it is." He waited for a reaction from Maria. He had just let out the deepest secret and biggest failure of his life. Why was she just sitting there looking kindly at him, when the earth ought to be shaking?

He continued. "I have a son, his name is Malte; he's seven. Right now I don't know where Malte is, because he's run away from home. My eighty-three-year-old mother is searching for him in town. Nina is probably in bed sleeping off her drunk. Is there anything you can do to find him, discreetly, without shouting it all over Gotland, and then see to it that he stays with my mother, or some other safe person until this is over? Preferably with someone else. Nina can get very nasty when he's with my mother and she's old and has a bad heart and doesn't really have the energy for this. I'm stuck here in Follingbo, as you know, and I could give the people I'm treating more undivided attention if I didn't have to think about how Malte is doing. Most of all I would like to forget about all of it and go home and take care of my family, but of course I can't. Forgive me, I'm behaving in a completely confused and unprofessional way, but your question threw me off balance. Forget what I said, it's completely absurd. I'll have to try to resolve this some other way. I have no right to burden you as the relative of one of my patients. Forgive me. I don't know what got into me."

"I'll do my best. You take care of my son and I'll take care of yours. I'll inquire with a wise friend of mine at Social Services how to resolve this in the best way. I have a girl who is almost the same age as your son. Malte can stay with me until this is worked out, if he wants to."

"I have no right to take advantage of you like that. Under

normal circumstances I would never, ever, do you understand that?"

"These are not normal circumstances. There's a curfew.
I'll be in touch as soon as I know anything about Malte. Do
you have a photo of him?"

"Yes." Jonathan took his wallet from his pocket and
showed the picture against the glass. "He's very like your
son. I would guess that Emil looked like this when he was
a little younger."

"Yes, yes, actually he did. Although he was a little rounder."
Maria felt the worry swirling in her belly, round and round
in an aching circle. With all of her inner strength she controlled her exterior, smiled and studied the picture as if it
was a day out of the past, when nothing was really serious
or dangerous yet. She would have preferred to scream and
cry and be comforted like a child, but that option was not
available.

Maria called Hartman and explained the situation when
she had come out onto the drive. The heat was almost unbearable on the dry pine-clad hill. She decided to take a taxi
into town so as not to obstruct Hartman in his work.

"Take the time you need and come back when you can."
There was a lot of warmth in his voice and Maria would
have hugged him in gratitude if he had been nearby.

A sad little boy was sitting on the wall down by St. Hans
Café with his cap on backwards, throwing rocks at the pigeons. His grandmother said he usually went down there
when he had run off and got hungry. There were always nice
people who ask a little boy if he wants a roll if he stares at
them long enough when they're having coffee. There he sat
with his legs dangling a foot or two above the grass. Maria
sat down beside him.

"My name is Maria and I'm a police officer. I just saw your dad. He misses you very much, Malte, and would like to be with you if only he could. But there are other children who are very sick that he is helping get healthy again. When this bird flu is over—"

"That's not what he's doing; it's because he doesn't care about me and Mom."

"Does your mom say that?"

"Mom doesn't say anything, she just sleeps. I tried to wake her, but I couldn't. She just sleeps and sleeps and sleeps . . . She fell asleep on the floor in the bathroom and she threw up all over herself. I stepped in it. Yuck! I wanted her to wake up. I shook her head and pinched her on the nose. But she didn't even open her eyes. Because she'll sleep and sleep and sleep for a hundred years."

"If you sit tight here I'll ask your grandmother to get out of the taxi. I brought her with me. If the two of you stay here a while and have a snack, I'll come back soon and pick you up. What's your address, do you know that?"

Maria felt a creeping sense of worry, a thought that turned into images of a dead woman on a bathroom floor. Maybe that's what happens when you've worked in this business a long time, an occupational injury.

"Of course I know. I live on Vikingagatan."

"Do you have a key?" Slowly the boy emptied his pockets of plastic toys and Playmobil figures and chewing gum and found it. Maria hurried back to the taxi. The meter was running and she was no longer sure she had enough money in her wallet to pay.

The white villa was bedded in greenery. A few children were riding their bicycles on the sidewalk. They had put stiff pieces of paper on the spokes of the wheels to make a whirring sound. The little boy who cycled past had his head turned toward the back wheel and was heading straight for Maria, who took a step to one side at the last moment. A peaceful idyll. Maria paid the taxi and continued into the yard, where the lawn had not been cut for a long time. On the blue-painted garden table were an empty wine bottle and some plastic toy cars. A forgotten child's jacket was tossed over the wooden bench. The front door was locked. Maria rang the bell, wondering what she would say to Malte's mother if she answered. She rang again, a little longer this time. No signs of life from inside. Using Malte's key she went in. A sharp, slightly stuffy odor met her in the large, light hall. She called to Nina. It was completely silent, except for the stubborn buzzing of a fly in the window. Fresh flowers in a vase on the bureau by the mirror. Expensive furniture and irreproachably clean floors. It did not look like they were living in misery. What Malte said of course could be fantasies or something he had seen on TV or dreamt. She hurried on to search for the bathroom. Passed a living room that was covered with bookshelves from floor to ceiling and with a gigantic leather sofa in the middle of the floor, large green plants, and exclusive floor vases. The door to the bathroom was open and there on the dark-blue tile floor was a blonde woman on her back with her legs placed at an unsightly wide angle. Her mouth was wide open. Maria knelt down beside her. Felt a weak pulse. Barely noticeable breathing. The woman was short and slender and she had no difficulty putting her in a three-quarters prone position. As best she could she tried to pick out old food remnants from the woman's mouth. The T-shirt, which was the only clothing she had on, was brown with vomit. The stench almost made Maria throw up herself. She retched and turned away to take the next breath. Happened to put her hand in something sticky and got up to rinse her fingers. The woman was alive anyway. The thought of what she would have done if there were no respiration or pulse made her retch again. The very thought of making resuscitation attempts, mouth-to-mouth, on someone who had just vomited was nauseating. Maria took out her cell phone and called the emergency number. Busy. Even though she tried again and again.

Could she have dialed the wrong number or were there just that many calls? Maria crouched down again and felt the woman's pulse. A thin, irregular flutter under the skin. Answer already! Emergency center. She got through and stated her errand. They promised to send an ambulance. But it might be awhile, if the condition was not immediately life-threatening. All ambulances were out at the present time.

"I can't determine if it's life-threatening. She's not breathing very often—" The call was broken off before Maria finished the last sentence. She wet a towel in cold water and bathed Nina's face to get her to revive. The woman's skin felt so warm and sweaty. A thought began to take shape. What if this wasn't intoxication. Perhaps she had a fever and was really sick. Contagious? How could you know whether or not she had the flu?

Chapter 22

T he first thing Maria did when she got to the police station, after Nina Eriksson had been taken away in an ambulance, was to take a hot shower and scrub herself red under the stream of water. She gradually raised the water temperature to the limit of being bearable, as if the contagion had settled on her skin and could be washed off. On a rational level she realized that wasn't the case. But a purification ritual was necessary anyway. There was no evidence that Nina might have been sick with bird flu. That was just an idea, or even more a sense of illness and death and decomposition, that flowed together with the morning's horrible experience of the woman strangled in her apartment, Sandra Hägg. The pale yellow face of death. The photographs on the bulletin board of the dead man found in Värsände made her flesh crawl. His curly black hair, the scar on his chest and the broad slit on his throat, the open eyes that looked right at her. There was too much sickness and death. A terror that could no longer be controlled with reason. How do you protect yourself? How magical can you be in your strategies for avoiding death and accidents? Maria resisted an impulse to put herself under the purifying water again, pulled her wet hair into a ponytail, and went to her office.

The reception desk reported that Sandra Hägg's sister was in the lobby. The patrol officers had informed her of the death earlier that day. Maria met Clary Hägg in the corridor. A slender woman with dark wavy hair in a style that was modern in the eighties. Poodle cut. She appeared to be in her mid-thirties, wore no makeup and was not particular about her choice of clothes. Her T-shirt had ketchup stains and the baggy pants were wrinkled at the knees. She looked at Maria with brown eyes, large and shiny, as if she was about to start crying at any moment. She did not blink, simply looked at Maria's face and waited to be addressed. Maria turned on the tape recorder and asked the standard questions after having said a few introductory words of consolation. It felt shabby and flat. A cup of coffee or an arm around the shoulders usually did more good. But Clary had refused both and sat, reserved and hunched up, in the visitor's chair. Not everyone appreciates physical contact; for some it is only troublesome and embarrassing if a stranger touches them.

"I haven't seen Sandra in over six months. Not since Mom's birthday. We haven't even talked on the phone since then. We had a falling out; it feels so awful now—with what happened. Well, I've tried to maintain contact, but Sandra didn't want to. Not since I told her she should leave Lennie. That was before Christmas."

"Was there anything in particular that happened then?"

"No one in our family liked Lennie very much." Clary was about to say more but hesitated. Maria waited for a continuation but was forced at last to ask the question again. Clary sighed heavily and lowered her eyes toward her hands resting in her lap while she thought about how to put it. "He was so cocky and unpredictable and temperamental.

One minute he was charming and the next a real jerk, if you ask me. He would suddenly flare up over nothing. I don't know how it came up but—well, I think it was Mom who started talking about Sandra's old boyfriend and how silly it was when they were going to camp on Fårö and forgot the tent pegs at home. They only had the tent with them and it started to rain. So they rolled themselves up in the tent and slept under a spruce. We joked about that and about other things. Lennie got really mad and twisted Sandra's arm so that it cracked when she followed him out onto the balcony. I came out right after that so I saw it and told him to knock it off, and then he pushed me backward. I fell down and sprained two fingers on my left hand trying to stop the fall." Clary showed her hand, although there was no longer any bruise or swelling to see.

"Did anything similar happen at other times? Do you think Lennie hit Sandra?"

"I don't know." Clary rubbed her eyes when she could no longer hold back the tears. "I loved my little sister and I only wished her well. But after that I got a feeling that Lennie gave her an ultimatum: him or the family."

"And she chose Lennie?"

"Yes. Then he didn't tell the truth. Lied about little things that were pretty easy to check. He'd been there when there was a traffic accident and saved people before the ambulance arrived, although he wasn't even in the area. He bragged that he had met celebrities who were touring outside the country at the time. If you told something interesting that happened to you, he'd always been involved in something even bigger or worse, and if you asked follow-up questions he got sore. I wanted something better for Sandra. Truly. I was happy when I heard he moved out and I thought that we could be sisters again, like before. And now she's dead. It's so unbeliev-able. She can't be dead. She had such a zest for life, so full of life and energy. Do you know how it happened—what happened?" Clary's body was shaking and she curled up in her chair. Maria felt a sudden tenderness for her.

"Everything indicates that she was strangled."

"Strangled? Why? Had someone . . . touched her? I mean, raped her?" Clary had a hard time getting out the words.

"It's too soon to say. I'm sorry. Do you know whether Sandra knew anyone by the name of Tobias Westberg, a journalist?"

"No." Clary shook her curly head. "I've never heard of him. If Lennie said that you should take it with a grain of salt. He wanted to believe that Sandy was seeing others to have an excuse to fuck around himself. If you'll pardon the expression. He was like that as soon as he'd had a little to drink. Sandra stopped going out with him. She would rather stay at home than risk watching him make a fool of himself. I was so happy when I heard she'd had enough, that she had dumped him. Finally, and now . . . I'm so sorry, so sorry." Then came the tears. It felt liberating in a way. The shaking in her body ebbed out and when she got up to leave after Maria had asked a few more questions she seemed collected anyway.

When Clary Hägg left the room Maria remained sitting at the computer, feeling unable to move. It was as if the grief refused to leave the office, like a paralyzing draft in the air. Thoughts of Emil were there as soon as she did not have to think about other things. With an exertion of will Maria let the phone be; Jonathan was fully occupied as it was and they had promised to phone if Emil got any worse. Maria logged onto the computer. Stared at the screen without seeing while she thought about the information about Lennie, what the neighbor had offered and what the sister had just said. Which was true? Two different pictures. Incompatible. Or is that how complicated we all are, paradoxes, depending on who we're interacting with? Maria continued typing and searched in the registry of individuals for Tobias Westberg and brought up two candidates of suitable age. One was a journalist. No previous convictions. Perhaps there was some truth in what Lennie had said anyway. Just then Hartman came in and sat down on the chair in front of her with a half-eaten baguette in his hand and cucumber mayonnaise around his mouth. Maria remembered that she hadn't eaten anything all day. She had just not been hungry.

"I've spoken with Håkansson. He's done an initial review of Sandra Hägg's computer, which was on. She was logged into Outlook. There are a few things worth studying more closely. Yesterday evening she exchanged email with a Hans Moberg, who sells medications over the Internet. They arranged a meeting for that evening. She evidently had migraines and hung the key on a cord that he could reach through the mail slot. It sounded like she was extremely anxious to meet him, even though she was confined to bed with a severe headache. My wife has migraines sometimes and then you can barely have the TV on. No sounds, no light. She would never invite anyone in when she has a headache. You might wonder what was so important. The tone was formal, so it wasn't a romantic encounter, although there's no way to know that for sure. It's clearly urgent to get hold of him as soon as possible. Hans Moberg has a website where he promises his customers endless potency, eternal youth, and remedies for all the ailments in the world. He calls himself Doctor M. Lots of pictures of beautiful young people. Apparently he travels around in a camper selling his wares. It doesn't sound legal exactly, but we'll have to check with the prosecutor. Sandra had no alcohol in her system. We have secured fingerprints on the carafe and all I can say is that they aren't hers."

"Sandra worked at the health center at Snäckgärdsbaden. It's a private health center and luxury clinic. They offer rejuvenation surgery and beauty treatments, and they also have a vaccination clinic. I saw the advertisement in the newspaper today. Only the name is flashy. They also do operations for hip joints and cataracts. I thought we could take a look around over there and talk with Sandra's co-workers."

"As far as I can see on the list of Internet contacts, Sandra has had fairly regular email contact with someone with the email address "jessika.wide@vigoris.se," probably a co-worker. Sandra uses the same domain name when they email each other. It feels a little embarrassing to peek into people's personal lives like this. The two ladies gossip a bit about men they've encountered out in the bars. I didn't think women . . . well, used such language."

"Such language?" Maria could not keep from smiling at Hartman's bewildered facial expression. "Should there be any difference in men's and women's ways of expressing good luck in the hunt, you mean?"

"Yes, but you wouldn't . . . write . . . well, forget about that. Then we've got a little more to go on as far as the Värsände man is concerned. In the door-to-door in Klinte-hamn several people have stated that they had a visit from a painting salesman. A short dark man. In Berit Hoas's house there was a picture that she reportedly bought from him. There are fingerprints on it, in the paint itself. Our technicians have made a preliminary investigation of the prints. It's not that easy but Mårtenson has a particular interest in such things and sees agreement in the prints on several points. Although the final answer may take a week or two. We have a hypothesis to work on in any event. Then we have a witness account from a neighbor in Värsände. He thought he saw someone in the little farm by the historical society building and shouted. A male figure ran toward the smithy and then was gone. When we investigated the area we found that very likely someone had been hiding inside the smithy.

Chapter 23

Maria thought about Emil and could no longer restrain herself. She did not know how many times her cell phone had traveled in and out of her pocket in the past hour. She shouldn't disturb them, but she would have no peace until she found out how he was doing. She entered the number and got to speak with Nurse Agneta. Emil was sleeping. The fever was the same as before, with a temperature just over 100.

Maria thought the newly built facility by the sea shone like an enormous white piece of seagull shit in the afternoon sun. She looked with disfavor at the pompous entryway and tried to explain to herself what it was that aroused such feelings of antipathy. The injustice in that someone can buy themselves a place before others in the line for healthcare, faster diagnosis, faster treatment. And yet. If you were in that position yourself and had the chance to pay to be rid of pain in your hip and return to work, wouldn't you do it? Presumably, if you had the money. Who would lose in that? Someone else would get your place in line and you could start paying taxes again. And yet you would hope that the public healthcare system could offer the optimal treatment, that solidarity would somehow find a way.

A showy neon sign on the white-plastered wall above the entry said Vigoris Health Center. To the left, behind the low, newly planted hedge, a swimming pool area could be seen, a Mediterranean-class bathing landscape with a juice bar and lounge chairs and offerings of spa treatment, massage, chi gong, and yoga. To the right a restaurant with Japanese decor and a flower shop with artful and certainly very expensive flower arrangements. Maria Wern could not help being impressed by the reception area's exclusive furnishings in pink marble and mahogany. The nurse behind the counter wore a light-green suit, white blouse, and scarf, like a flight attendant. Her hair was upswept in a fashionable hairstyle and she wore high-heeled shoes. It was the same with the other nurses. Well-dressed. Soft voices. Gentle, graceful movements. No hurrying. High heels that tripped against the floor. You almost expected the airline pilot to appear in full uniform with wings of gold on his jacket lapel. But he never showed up and the doctors passing by seemed to have completely missed the dress code as they shuffled along in clogs and wrinkled white coats.

Maria asked for Jessika Wide and the receptionist asked them to sit down and wait a moment. After ten long minutes they were guided through the facility to the vaccination department and into a large, light conference room with dark-blue leather armchairs arranged around a table with a smoke-colored glass surface. The first thing Maria was struck by was the strange but undoubtedly expensive art on the walls. Barbed wire and fringed strips of fabric in symbiosis with thick layers of paint applied with a rough brush. It could have been horribly ugly, but somehow it wasn't. There was something thought out and attractive in the madness. At the desk sat a woman in her mid-fifties. She got up and came toward them. Her entire posture radiated charm and confidence. The ash-blonde hair was cut in a daring style lopsided to the right. The reading glasses were hanging on a chain around her neck and she was dressed in a chalk-stripe black dress with a white scarf around her neck. The thought that this was Jessika Wide who had written the day-after-the-bar email caused Maria to purse her lips to keep from smiling. People are not always the way you think they are at first glance. That the woman standing before them right now would describe men's rear ends and other merits in the terms they had just seen on the computer was almost absurd.

"Viktoria Hammar, managing director here at Vigoris Health Center." The boss that is, Maria translated to herself. Why couldn't she just say that? I'm the boss here at the clinic.

"You're looking for Jessika Wide. Perhaps I can help out by answering your questions in the meantime. Jessika will soon be done with her shift and then she's coming here. You're from the police if I've been correctly informed. What's this about?" Viktoria indicated with a gesture that they were welcome to sit down at the table.

"We have the sad task of reporting that one of your employees, Sandra Hägg, was found dead in her apartment this morning."

"I heard about it this morning from her sister Clary. It was brave of her sister to do that and considerate of her to think that we would wonder where Sandra had gone. This is simply awful."

"We would like to ask a few questions."

"What do you mean? Do you think she was murdered? That someone would have . . . Why? She didn't associate in such circles. I mean, when you read about women who are murdered in their apartments there is often drug abuse involved, social misery, and well . . . You know what I mean," Viktoria continued unperturbed when she saw Maria's expression.

"Sandra was a very competent nurse. We are extremely careful when we hire our employees. You have to be, especially when you are doing business in a country like Sweden, with such an inhospitable business climate, where you don't have the same leeway to replace personnel who prove to be directly unsuitable for work in healthcare." Viktoria Hammar made a gesture in the air and a discreet figure placed a plate of fruit and several bottles of mineral water in front of them and disappeared. "Sandra has worked with us from the beginning. Before that she was at the hospital for several years, at the infectious disease clinic. We actually wanted someone with broader experience, but Sandra had a very winning way and learned quickly."

"What kind of work did she do here at the center?" Maria asked.

"We have a policy that everyone should be interchangeable in their functions. That makes the system less vulnerable. All nurses should be able to assist with operations and take care of patients in medical consultation and work with diet and health advising. We see overweight patients for care and treatment and have extremely good results. In the most recent issue of Medical Journal our clinic is mentioned as an example of—"

"What work responsibilities did Sandra have most recently?"

"I can't tell you that right off, but I can find out during the day. There's been a lot to do here since my husband, Reine, ended up at Follingbo sanitarium for observation. With the number of doctors we have employed here it's noticeable when someone is gone. Very noticeable. That's how it is when you're a for-profit company that has to deal with competition, while the tax and fee system does everything to suppress the expansion of the operation. You have to work with small margins to remain profitable."

Hartman made an attempt to interrupt the monologue, but failed. Viktoria raised her voice and talked without pausing. She was used to finishing what she had to say. "I hope that he can return soon. We don't have the means to pay for his absence and hire someone else in his place. I'll tell you that socialism is nothing but pure envy. Why should you share with those who don't do any work? And this fear of bird flu is taking completely unreasonable proportions, which may have repercussions for the business community."

Maria could no longer keep her comments to herself. Worry for Emil meant that she could not control herself as usual. "Strange that you should say that. I thought that a doctor first and foremost thought about her patients."

"But exactly." Viktoria did not seem to understand the difference or hear the criticism at all. "If it had been seen to in good time that there was medication for preventive treatment this never would have needed to happen. That's the kind of incompetent authorities we pay with our tax money. But here's Jessika. Come in now and don't just stand there in the doorway. Come and sit down."

A red-haired woman around thirty stepped into the room. Her hair was long and pulled together in a loose ponytail. The hairstyle emphasized her heart-shaped face. Her face was made for advertising: it was beautiful and made you think of fitness and red apples.

"We would like to speak with Jessica privately." Maria saw the dissatisfaction on Viktoria Hammar's face. Just a slight shift. "In this clinic we have no secrets from each other." Before the authoritative look Jessika shrank, becoming an obedient schoolgirl who had to apologize to the teacher in order to leave the room.

"That's how we work," said Hartman. He didn't seem to feel any need to explain himself. He expected respect.

They found a bench to sit on behind the restaurant, out of earshot of the serving personnel. That was a request from Viktoria Hammar, who did not want the police to be seen at her facility and make people wonder. Even if they were in plain clothes someone might recognize them and wonder what the police were doing at Vigoris Health Center. Naturally she did not put it that way, but that was the gist of it.

"The decor is truly lovely. It must be enjoyable to work in such new facilities."

"Yes, and even so they've replaced every single doorframe. It was oak before and then Viktoria got the idea that cherry wood was prettier. From one day to the next, just a whim. It was really tough; the workers were all over the place. Thank God it's finished."

After a few more genial exchanges, Hartman informed her of Sandra's death. Jessika cried without covering her face. The big gray eyes filled with tears and swam over. Maria handed her a tissue, but she didn't dry her face with it. Instead she squeezed the tissue in her hand into a ball.

"Sandra was my best friend here at the clinic. I can't understand it . . . I can't fathom . . ."

"You socialized a bit in your spare time, if I've understood right." Maria could not keep from looking at Hartman when he asked the question. His face did not reveal anything about the email he'd read. "Do you know whether there was any man in her life? A friend, or someone closer than that?"

"I don't know, but I think so. I think her relationship with Lennie ended because she fell in love with someone else. It was so obvious. She hardly answered when you talked to her and she slipped away to talk on her cell phone, and when you came anywhere near she ended the call abruptly. It was the same when she was sitting at the computer.

When you came in she changed programs. You can't help but notice things like that. I thought it was good for her. Lennie wasn't right for a girl like Sandra. They were such a poor match. She was intelligent and well-educated. I think she was embarrassed of him sometimes—he can be pretty dense. He probably felt that. You have to be proud of the person you're with for it to last in the long run."

"Do you know who she was in love with?"

"Well." Jessika inhaled and looked anxious. "I know someone who liked Sandra. But I'm not sure. Maybe I'm wrong; I'm just guessing."

"It may be of value anyway. Who do you think it was?"

"Reine Hammar was a little weak for her. She got looks from him sometimes that . . . well, you know what I mean. And he could think of thousands of reasons why he needed to go into her office. Then he dyed his hair black because she said she liked dark men." Jessika laughed, and the laughter changed into a new crying attack. "He's the clinical director here and he's married to the big boss. Good Lord, it won't come out that I said that, will it? He was at home with Sandra once when I called her. I heard his voice and recognized it. But I don't think she was particularly interested in him, it was someone else. She didn't want me to know who. And Reine is who he is . . . he had an affair with a girl who used to clean here and then there was one of the girls in the restaurant . . . and then Mimmi in the kitchen said that she saw him out at the bar with a blonde woman. They took a taxi together, presumably to her place. But I don't know whether that's true, that's just what Mimmi said." Jessica sniffed, dried her eyes and around her nose and sat up straighter.

"I actually asked Sandra whether there was anything between her and Reine, but she flatly denied it. 'Confess, you coward,' I said but she just laughed." Suddenly Jessika opened her eyes wide and stared right through Maria as if she had seen a ghost. "So Reine doesn't know about it. He's at the sanitarium and doesn't know that Sandra is dead. So terrible. Who's going to tell him? Me? I couldn't. I don't think I'd get a word out. Poor Reine." She looked thoughtful. "But no, there was someone else. A journalist. She talked one time about a journalist she met at a party and I had the impression it was something serious."

"Do you know what kind of a party it was?"

"A birthday party for someone turning forty. His sister, she worked at the infectious disease clinic. His name is Torbjörn, I think."

"Are you sure of that? That his name is Torbjörn?" asked Hartman.

"Well, maybe it was Tobias. Although it was a while ago, I don't think anything came of it. Then she Internet dated—she may have met someone that way."

"Do you know if she knew anyone named Hans Moberg, 'Moby'?"

"Don't know. But I got a feeling someone was coming to see her, last night. I asked if she wanted me to be there. You know, the first date you should be careful and not meet alone and that. But she said that I absolutely couldn't. She was really strange, angry really, even though I hadn't done anything. She almost screamed at me, 'I want to be alone.' I got a little worried and actually thought about showing up anyway, but then after my day shift I was called in to work the evening shift in the surgery department. After that I just didn't have the energy. I called several times, but she didn't answer. God, I hadn't thought about that . . . if I'd been there maybe she would be alive now!"

"I was thinking about Sandra's apartment, it must have been expensive for her." Hartman followed two young nurses with his eyes and cleared his throat when he felt Maria's eyes on him. "I mean, I'm guessing your salary is no higher than the nurses who are employed by the county council?"

"No, we have roughly the same salary. I actually asked Sandra how she could afford it and then she smiled in a sly way and said that she had an ace up her sleeve and that in time she might even get a three-room apartment or her own house."

"So she was counting on coming into a lot of money soon. Did she say how that would happen?"

"No," Jessika shook her head and bit her lower lip as she thought. "No, she didn't say."

"How often did Sandra have migraines?" Maria asked.

"What do you mean, migraines? Sandra never had headaches. She was in good shape and never sick, and actually Viktoria's favorite in that respect. Viktoria would point her out as an example of how you should take care of yourself to keep up with a demanding job." The last part Jessika said with a grimace.

"One last question: What kind of work was Sandra doing most recently?"

"She was in the surgery department, too, but she wanted to move to the vaccination clinic. She asked Viktoria about that several times."

Chapter 24

Hans Moberg was just passing Tingstäde on Highway 148 when he heard the wanted-person bulletin on the radio. Name, car registration number, and a fairly unflattering description of his appearance and high-pitched voice followed by a sea report.

He realized his hands were shaking on the steering wheel before he really understood what he had just heard. How could they know who he was? And that he'd been there, with Sandra Hägg? Had someone seen him and recognized him? Not likely in the disguise he was wearing. Damn it all, they must have gone into the computer and then contacted Telia. Hell and damnation! The computer had been on in Sandra's apartment and he had played with the keyboard.

It was impossible to breathe in the car, the air was stagnant, and his ears were buzzing, roaring like a waterfall

The road was dancing before his eyes—he couldn't tell which side of the road he was on. A blurry green embankment and gray fields were twirling in his field of vision. He had to collect himself. Settle his wild heart. Slow down, assess the situation, and make reasonable decisions. The fuel gauge was approaching empty. He had to fill up in Lärbro, try to hide the camper in a safe place and then change cars. No, he couldn't rent a car; he'd have to show identification. He'd swipe a car from someone away on vacation. In town there were cars on virtually every driveway during the day. But where could he stow the camper? The landscape was so flat. Wasn't there a little forest road where no one ever went? No, then it wouldn't be a road anymore but overgrown forest. His stomach cramped. The nausea came without warning and Hans Moberg had to stop the car and throw up by the side of the road.

His whole body was shaking now and the images of the dead woman could no longer be kept out. The dark hair against the white sheet and the mouth he had wanted to kiss, even though all life had escaped and been replaced by a damp chill. Life had never granted him such a beautiful woman, but in death he could possess her a little while. The slender shoulders. The curve right at the collarbone that he simply had to caress. The touchingly small breasts he had been able to cup with one hand. He lay down beside her and imagined that they were together and had just gone to bed, just like they always did after turning off the TV. If he had only been sober the worlds would not have mixed together. Then he could have stopped in time. She went to bed first and was waiting for him. Set a table for two.

The ideal woman, the dream woman he had been seeking in all these women. Just like she had always been waiting for him. Always would wait for him. Everything else was a game. With new disguises and new meeting places, but she was the one who was waiting. Always her. If he had only refrained from drinking the wine with Sandra Hägg, he would have discovered the danger in time. Then the worlds would not have mixed in layers on each other, becoming an unbearable reality that was then devoured in the black emptiness from which he could not remember a thing. Not remembering what happened was the hardest of all. It produced an intolerable anxiety that could only be deadened by getting drunk again.

It was then, his fist full of the grass he was using to rub his worn athletic shoes clean from vomit, that he happened to think about Cecilia with the horse face. They had met at Gutekällaren earlier that summer. Emailed awhile before they met, and the encounter had been enjoyable for both of them. They talked about meeting again, but the second time is seldom as good as the first time. There's something second-hand about it. Once the conquest is complete, the curiosity fades. Cecilia was just like other women, a disappointment in a number of ways. Thin, she had written. Thin was a gross understatement. He could have cut himself on her pelvis and her cheekbones stuck out like sturdy bits on either side.

But the fact that she lived in the vicinity—now when he needed her—was an extenuating circumstance. A reunion was not a bad idea. Besides, she had a big barn and a double garage on the lot. That was extremely convenient.

Hans Moberg paid cash for the gas. Sure, the car's license plate number was noted until the gas was paid for, but then the slip of paper was thrown away. The woman at the register at the Lärbro gas station did not appear to have heard the wanted-person bulletin on the radio. She hardly looked at him, but kept a watchful eye on two urchins who were sneaking around between cars waving water pistols. She was probably afraid that someone would back over them while they were hiding from each other.

The woman at the register was not bad looking at all. Another time, maybe. After buying beer, cigarettes, and a bouquet of flowers at a convenience store, Hans Moberg continued on 149 toward Kappelshamn. As he approached Cecilia's place he stopped at the side of the road a little while. Perhaps it was best to call Horseface first and check that she did not have any visitors. No one answered and it suddenly occurred to him that perhaps she had gone on vacation. She had probably talked about doing that. He would have to read her latest email a little more carefully. Hans Moberg backed the camper into some bushes by an old outdoor dance pavilion, waiting for darkness.

He heated a can of pea soup on the stove and ate it right from the can, then took a dip in the cold, shallow water on the other side of the road before he put the coffee kettle on and checked the email inbox. He had deliberately saved his messages from Cuddly Skåne Girl. There was a warmth in her writing that he wanted to experience again. And there it was . . . the email that Sandra Hägg had sent. He could have sworn he'd deleted it. Why the hell had he gone there when he was drunk? So stupid and now the police were after him. If he had only been in his right mind he wouldn't have smashed up her furniture. How could his brain come up with such a sick idea? Panic, of course. He should have just left. He should have . . . Why, why, why didn't he just go home and go to bed after the failed date with the woman from Skåne? It was all so damn unpleasant.

Under cover of darkness Hans Moberg drove the car and camper into Cecilia Granberg's barn. He felt more collected now. Perhaps he would be able to manage if he lay low awhile. With this bird flu the police would have no time to look for him. If it got really serious, they would be fully occupied with protecting food shipments, stores, and pharmacies from break-ins, and a criminal or two would probably die too. Then he could make his way to the mainland and later . . . well, who knows if the world would even be here tomorrow. Sufficient unto the day is the evil thereof, as his mother always said.

It was obvious a single woman with no interest in cars

owned the property. The barn was empty except for a loom, a stone mangle, and a heap of birch wood. It was better than he had dared hope for. He was in one hell of a pinch. But it wasn't the end of the world. According to the emails he'd saved, Cecilia had gone to Greece on vacation for two weeks.

Moby carefully loosened the putty on a window on the south side of the house, pulled out the glass, and climbed in. She could not have been more welcoming if she were home. The pantry was full of canned goods. In the cellar there were fifty bottles of Gotland ale and in the freezer a splendid supply of homemade dishes in single-portion packages: mutton with dill sauce, beef stew, stuffed cabbage rolls, lamb cutlets, dumplings, and ground lamb. Life was not always terrible; sometimes things did work out.

The only thing he could not find were the keys to Cecilia's car. The thought that she had taken them with her was a little worrisome. He mumbled a quiet incantation to himself while he dug around in her handbags that were hanging in the bedroom. Shoes and purses should match, he had read in a ladies magazine on the Internet, but there was a plague of shoes and bags in this house. How could she find two matching shoes in this pile? It would be like looking for a needle in a haystack.

Where could she have put the keys? He did not dare turn on the light in case some neighbor knew that she was away and came over to see what was going on. Outdoor clothes were hanging in the hall below the stairs. He groped through the pockets and suddenly something rattled. He felt along the row of buttons. In the pocket of a long light coat was the bunch of keys he had been hoping for. Car key, house key, and two or three other keys, who knows what they were for. It was almost midnight when Hans Moberg sat down to read the latest news on the Internet.

The Prime Minister's appeal to the World Health Organization for assistance and help with medications was the evening's big headline. Another two people had died from bird flu, one of them a little boy. Zebastian was his name. The parents were pictured. Outside the school in Klinte a scuffle had arisen between police and parents who wanted to take their children home. There was a picture of the disease control officer standing erect and full of authority on the steps above the agitated mob. In the foreground a man with rocks in both hands. The police were a black mass in the background and looked like the real prisoners behind the barricade tape.

There was also a brief report in the online edition about a thirty-three-year-old woman who was found dead in her apartment in Visby. No nationwide alert for an overweight, thin-haired man in his mid-forties. He checked the local news to be on the safe side and the wanted-person bulletin was included there. A shudder of discomfort passed through his body. The headline was large and seemed to creep inside him and nail his eyes to the screen, accusing him of the murder of Sandra Hägg. Now they were on his trail. He had been granted a brief respite. If he could just get a good night's sleep and then think without being disturbed, he would find a solution.

Hans Moberg took a gulp of the Gotland ale and grimaced. Cecilia had bragged that she came in third in a competition for her Gotland ale. Jeez Louise. What the ales that didn't win a prize tasted like, he didn't even want to think about.

Life was hell. It all felt so unspeakably lonely and sad. He really needed someone to talk with. Cuddly Girl from Skåne was online. She had changed her email address, he noticed. She was a professional Net charmer, just as he'd thought from the very start. A friendly embrace was what he needed. It didn't matter that she had laughed at him.

There was a tenderness he liked a lot. Her way of writing: My dear and sweetest friend. He threw out a hook and she bit immediately.

"Just wanted to talk a little, it feels so lonely without you."

"You say that to all the ladies."

"Not at all. There are many women I still haven't had time to say that to. I miss you in particular. I think about you all the time. This morning I put the dirty laundry in the refrigerator and poured the dishwasher detergent in the coffee filter and just sat and dreamed away the whole morning and fantasized about what I would do with you if you were here. I think I'm falling head over heels in love. Say something nice to me; I need it. I miss you. Answer, otherwise I'll die!"

"It can't be that bad. Where are you?"

"Staying with a friend, he's asleep right now, so I'm trying to be quiet."

"With a friend. Where? Are you still on Gotland?"

"Yes, damn it. I'm in Kappelshamn. Can't you come here, it's lonely and boring."

"So you haven't heard the latest news? I have the TV on now. I can't believe it."

"No, what about it?" He felt the rushing in his ears and his face turning bright red. Answer then; just say it. You know they're after me, don't you?

"All hell has broken loose. Traffic to and from Gotland is closed. The epidemic is no longer under control. Twenty-four new cases, apparently they were infected by a woman on Jungmansgatan in Visby. And these people were around any number of other people the past few days—and those people were with other people! The parents have broken into the camp in Klintehamn and picked up their children. Everything is chaos. Almedalen Week is going to be cancelled and the politicians are flying back to the mainland early tomorrow. When the rats leave the ship, you know."

"Can we meet?" It was a long shot. He did not have any great hope of it coming true, but sometimes luck surprises you.

"At midnight in the industrial harbor in Kappelshamn."

"At midnight."

Afterward he felt almost happy, and a bit less downhearted despite everything. Cuddly Skåne Girl understood discretion. It could be a pleasant break in the solitude—that was starting to get on his nerves.

Chapter 25

Jonathan Eriksson removed his mask and collapsed onto the desk. He was finally alone and could let out his suppressed emotions. He cried like he hadn't done since he was a child and had been bullied into pulling his pants down in front of the big boys at school. The feeling of impotence was just as strong now as then and he wished himself far away from his body and the torment of life. The thought of escaping from everything, simply disappearing into nothingness, no longer felt frightening, but more like a preferable option. A death wish. It surprised him that the thought felt so appealing. He simply let it come without evaluating it. What was there to live for? Malte, of course. But otherwise . . . nothing at all.

Meeting Zebastian's father to tell him that the boy was dead and seeing the reflection in his eyes—the mistrust, the anger, and the anguished sorrow—made his own grief break loose with full force. But at that moment it was not about himself but Zebastian's relatives. And this was only the beginning. Just an hour ago he had been in a meeting with the other doctors and the members of the emergency management board who were not on vacation. The chairman of Social Services took part by phone and together they had made the unprecedented decision to close the borders of Gotland with the help of the police and military. The Coast Guard would be given added resources. The ports in Visby, Slite, Kappelshamn, Klintehamn, and Ronehamn were already under surveillance and Visby Airport was closed. That decision had been made in the national pandemic group. The government was informed.

"And what powers do the police and military have to prevent people from defying the prohibition?" Jonathan had asked Åsa.

"All powers," she replied and her voice became extremely thin and faded away before she collected herself to continue. "We've failed. In hindsight, we should have done better at tracing Malin Berg's contacts. What can be said in our defense is that we weren't given the resources we needed. We haven't had support personnel from any other county council. Not a single doctor, nurse, or nursing assistant. No anti-viral medicine with effect on this type of bird flu, a few respirators, insufficient breathing protection, insufficient medical alcohol, the supply of antibiotics is seriously delayed and we don't have enough clean linen and other supplies, even if they are on their way. We need major resources immediately—not in a week or fourteen days. Now! And the cleaning staff refuses to come in. They don't want to handle hazardous waste or clean the patients' rooms because they don't think they've been given sufficient directives and guarantees that they won't get infected. We're going to be drowning in trash and dirt and someone has to take action immediately."

"Yes, it's really bad. I've seen the garbage. It's frightening," said Morgan, rubbing his swollen cheek where a stone had struck him at the disturbance at Klinte School.

Åsa leaned back in the chair with a heavy sigh. "When

Malin Berg's neighbors said they were sure she hadn't left her apartment all day Sunday, I really wanted to believe that. It was a relief to be able to let go and focus on something else at least as important, producing medication, nothing less. In the present situation we would need to give medicine for prophylactic purposes to the whole population, and preferably start mass vaccinations all over the country if we're going to have a chance."

"The Minister of Public Health actually promised a vaccine for everyone back in February, when the emergency preparedness plan was presented," Morgan added.

"Laughable, if it wasn't so serious. In the current situation we would need to vaccinate the entire population twice, that means eighteen million doses. Of course he didn't say anything about where that vaccine would come from." Åsa sighed again and rubbed her throbbing temples.

"No, it was pure bullshit to keep people calm. Calm! If there's anything that creates confusion it's mixed messages. The newspapers reported at the same time that it takes from six months to a year to produce a safe vaccine, and once it's available that doesn't mean we can buy it. The producing countries will most likely vaccinate their own populations first. I'm sure that's why we're not getting clear answers from them. What do we do now? What's the best possible way to meet the new situation with the disastrously meager resources we have?" Jonathan heard his voice rising to a shout. His anger at the overwhelming situation was causing him to come close to losing control.

"This is still about trying to avoid panic," said Åsa. "First and foremost we have to keep people calm and help them follow the directives we provide. I have nightmares about this, believe me."

"There must be a way to get more administrative personnel to help acquiring and coordinating resources. Retired medical secretaries, nurses, unemployed nursing assistants. In a situation like this it must be possible to order them in, not just in the event of war or force majeure." Morgan, who usually seemed to be daydreaming or half asleep, had in recent days shown a new sharpness and intensity. As if he had been on the back burner for years waiting for a moment when he'd be needed in full capacity, Jonathan thought.

The most burning issue other than procuring medication and personnel concerned hospital beds.

"The sanitarium is not big enough if there's a mass epidemic. We need functional premises, oxygen, beds. I don't know how we'll reach the staff on sick leave. People are afraid of infection and are staying home. There will be total collapse if we don't manage to do something about the work ethic. Those who are working now can't keep going indefinitely." Jonathan visualized Agneta's tired face and felt a lump in his throat. He had to find time to talk with her. Once this meeting was over nothing would intervene.

"Years ago, when tuberculosis was raging, people still went to work," said Morgan. "But those were different times, there was a different respect for authority and it was considered honorable to think of others and forget yourself."

"You didn't get paid and you didn't have a livelihood if you didn't work. Although it doesn't seem politically correct to say that." Åsa let out a short laugh, which was more like a coughing fit. "You either starved or died from TB."

"If there is an opportunity for relatives to take home their elderly, we can make use of those facilities. I was thinking about St. Göransgården, Mariahemmet to start with," said Jonathan. "But they're in developed areas and that involves a risk. The best is if we can use facilities in the country."

"I've been in contact with a representative for the county funeral directors just this morning," said Åsa. "They fear that there will be problems taking care of all the dead. There isn't enough refrigerated space and their employees don't know how to protect themselves against infection. We have to consider that aspect too, ASAP. The relatives don't know whether they can have a funeral or whether the deceased can still infect them, and so on. Information is needed. Do you think you can take care of that, Morgan?"

"May I interrupt you a moment?" A nurse was standing in the doorway. "The county governor is on the phone, Åsa. Can you take the call?"

"We'll need to have another meeting with the crisis management board tomorrow morning. Nine o'clock in my office," she said, turning toward her colleagues.

Jonathan heard the knock on the door, but did not respond. There was another knock and he murmured to wait while he put on his mask.

"There's a woman looking for you. Her name is Maria Wern. Can you speak with her?" It was Lena's voice inside the protective get-up this time.

"Yes, I'm coming in a moment." Jonathan went up to the sink and rinsed his face in cold water, looked at himself in the mirror and moaned audibly. His face was blotchy and his eyes were swollen. For once it felt good to put on the mask. In the conversation with Agneta he had not been the strong one. He tried to say something, but his voice disappeared in tears and she said the words he needed to hear most of all, that it was not his fault, that he had truly done his best. Afterward he was ashamed.

When Jonathan appeared on the other side of the glass wall, Maria stood up and came to meet him in the room set up for conversation. A room with an open fireplace, a simple lounge suite with large windows that looked over the level area below the sanitarium.

"I heard about Zebastian." She said no more before she suddenly fell into his arms and he had to mobilize all his strength not to take the consolation he himself needed so much, cross the boundary of what was appropriate and let his body live its own life. He took hold of her shoulders and pushed her gently away to be able to see her eyes above the mask.

"How is Emil taking it?" he asked.

"He's sad, but he can talk about it. I came to tell you that Malte and your mother are at my house right now. She is spending the night and taking care of both kids. Nina is somewhere in the hospital. I don't know how she's doing. I mean, I can't tell whether she's sick or whether she drank too much, or how serious it is."

"Thanks, I don't know how I can—"

"I would like to stay with Emil tonight. I know that your policy is that parents can't stay, but he needs me now. I have to be with him, please don't deny me that." Maria's eyes got large and round and flooded over. "I have to be with him. His fever has gone up and . . . there's still no medicine to give him, is there? What's going to happen, Jonathan? I'm scared and I see that you're scared, too. That frightens me even more."

"Is it that obvious?"

"Yes. Why isn't any help coming from outside? Other countries must have emergency supplies to help us. From pure instinct for self-preservation, if nothing else. Why isn't anything happening?" Maria could hear that her voice had become accusatory and hard. She noticed that he pulled back, crossed his arms over his chest, and avoided her eyes.

"Administrative mills grind slowly. We have a semi-promise to get a small quantity of medication when they start up production again. But it's not going to be enough for every-one. Not by a long shot. We would need medication for the entire population of Gotland as long as the bird flu persists."

"By the time it has been produced and we finally get it here, how many will have become sick? How many are going to die, is there any prognosis for that? I'm sorry, Jonathan, I see that you're tired. It's not my intention to . . . but I'm so worried that I don't really know what I'm saying. Forgive me."

"Stay with Emil tonight, but don't tell anyone. We don't have room for the parents that want to sleep over with their children, no protective equipment or bedding, and the risk of infection is imminent for you too, you realize that?"

"I realize that, but I need to do this." She opened her arms again to give him a hug and this time he let himself be embraced. There was consolation in her gentleness, in the warmth and also in the tears.

"I read a book about the plague last summer," she said when she had calmed down and was seated on the couch. "It sounded mostly like an exciting fairy tale. I never thought about it as the reality of living people. Maybe you can't un-derstand history without experiencing it. That's why mis-takes are repeated over and over. It's not just about reason. The author had a theory that the plague spread so quickly because people fled from death. They didn't know that they were infected themselves and so it spread like wildfire. That is exactly the mistake you're trying to prevent by closing the island's borders. Is there going to be a VIP line out of here for those who can pay for it? I heard that the Cabinet is going to be evacuated early tomorrow morning, it was announced on the news. Who else?"

"I don't know, Maria, I'm just an ordinary doctor. Those kinds of decisions are far above my head." He could not keep from touching a strand of her hair that had fallen down on her face, he caressed it and let it glide between his thumb and index finger. "Go now. I think you'll find a mattress in the closet in the room, but unfortunately we're out of blankets."

Maria got up and went toward the door, where she remained standing a moment without really being able to get out what she wanted to say. He looked at her searchingly. Wondered if she was smiling behind her mask or if she was going to start crying again.

"I like you, Jonathan Eriksson, I just wanted to say that, that is . . . hmm, that sounded really stupid."

"I like you too, Maria."

The room was in darkness. Only a small nightlight was shining over Emil's bedside table. He had kicked off the blanket. His forehead was shiny and his bangs swept back and sweaty, yet his skin was covered in goose bumps. Maria held back an impulse to hug him. He might wake up and he needed to sleep. He must have sensed her presence anyway and opened his eyes.

"It's just me, Emil. I'm sleeping here with you tonight."

"Am I going to die now, Mom?"

"No, don't talk like that."

"Parents can only be here if you're going to die."

"I got special permission from Jonathan to be here, even though you're not that sick, but it's a secret. We can't tell anyone."

"I saw Zebastian. He came and sat down right there on the chair where you're sitting now. He didn't say a thing, he just sat there."

"Did you dream that? Did you think it was creepy?"

"I didn't dream it. I saw him, although he was little—no bigger than a first-grader. I asked how he got here. If he flew.

206

And then he laughed. Not so you could hear it, but I saw that he was laughing. I didn't get scared, I was happy about that. He didn't look sick. He looked like he always does. I wonder what it's like when you're dead. If you're a kind of vapor, if you can decide for yourself if you want to be fog or a person or like a cloud that can be whatever—an old man's face with a big nose or a witch or a cream cake or a skinny beam that can go through a keyhole. I wonder if you decide for yourself where you'll be when you're dead. Then I want to be away from here. What do you think, Mom?"

"I hope that we are, that we exist I mean, because I hope that people can meet again when they've died. I would like to see my grandmother Vendela again. I loved her so much. At the end she was very forgetful and confused, but still kind. I would like to see her the way she was when I was little and I would crawl up in her lap and nothing felt scary."

"Do you think it's scary now, Mom?"

"Well, Emil, this isn't at all how I wanted this summer to turn out."

"If you're afraid, Mom, you can sleep next to me. I'm a little cold. Will that make it better?" She heard him laughing behind the mask.

"Yes, that will make it better."

When Emil fell asleep Maria curled up on the lumpy mattress on the floor. It was cold even though she had her jacket on and the window frames in the old building creaked eerily when the wind blew. Here Emil had been lying alone listening to the sounds.

Now when Maria no longer felt his warm body against hers worry came over her without mercy. His fever was higher now. He was like a stove, yet he was cold. Maria asked to speak with Jonathan again, but the nurse said that he was sleeping. He had to sleep the few hours in order to cope the next day. And of course Maria understood that, although the worry made her twist and turn on the mattress and listen to every breath from the boy. He was breathing much too fast. He tossed and turned and whimpered in his sleep, raving about Zebastian. Maria got up and felt his forehead. He was sweating profusely, but did not feel cooler. She tried to calm herself but could not stay still. She walked back and forth in the room and finally stood by the window. She looked out over the garden, lit up by moonlight. A white coat fluttered between the trees. Jonathan. On his way to one of the barracks. How long had he been able to rest before he was wakened, two hours, maybe three? I like you a lot, Jonathan Eriksson, can you feel it? Can you feel my hand on your back and my arm around your shoulders when you need strength?

Maria had tried to call Krister earlier in the evening to vent her worries, but he had not been receptive. Just drunk and stupid and cowardly as usual.

"Do you understand that this is serious, that your son is sick?" she'd asked him. Then he had reversed himself and became tearful and childish and ridiculous and needed a thousand assurances that everything would be fine again. He would never be bigger than that. Now when she really needed him he was not even in any shape to look after Linda.

Maria saw the headlights from a car on its way to the sanitarium. As it drove past the parking lot and up toward the barracks where Jonathan had gone at a jog, Maria saw in the glow from the streetlight that it was an ambulance without flashing lights and sirens. Two persons in what looked like spacesuits went into the building and came back after a little while with someone lying on a stretcher. Jonathan followed with an IV bottle in his hand. She saw him walk slowly across the courtyard as the car left the area at high speed. He looked lonely. His head was hanging. She wished he would look up toward the window, that he would see her and know that she was thinking about him. If he even cared about that.

Slowly the hours crept toward dawn. By two o'clock there was already a lighter tone in the sky. Maria could not sleep when worry was rushing in her blood making her fingers tingle. Convulsively she opened and clenched her ice-cold hands. The tension headache made her feel nauseated. Good Lord, let Emil get better. Nothing else is important. Emil and Linda, if we only get out of this torment alive I'm going to be a much better mother. I'll spend more time with my children and never quarrel with them about trifles and I will never . . .

What would happen if a bird flu epidemic advanced across the island with full force? How many would get sick then? How many would survive? Would you dare go places where people gathered? You would have to go to work, of course, and to the store. There would be long lines for everything if almost all the workers in the grocery stores were bedridden. If healthcare personnel could no longer come to work or were caring for their own sick relatives what would be done with all the sick and dead? All the old people who needed care? How would anyone dare leave their children at daycare and then at school? Who would dare ride a bus where everyone was breathing the same air and sitting close together, or go to concerts, or to an athletic event? And if the contagion spread further over the rest of Sweden and Europe—what would happen to food supplies when we've made ourselves so dependent and no longer produce our own food? There was something to what Arvidsson always said, that he intended to invest in pension insurance in the form of chickens and potatoes and his own woodstove and his own water. Well, maybe not chickens—but there was something to it. Maria sat carefully on the edge of Emil's bed and leaned her head against his back. If only you get better, my love, nothing else in the world really matters.

Chapter 26

When morning came, Emil's fever was almost gone and Maria could no longer stay with him. A mouth protector is effective for eight hours and the supply was limited. Although she pleaded and cried and begged to stay, now it was someone else's turn to sit with their child. Nurse Agneta promised to call if there was any change.

So Maria was at work when she heard the news. The TV was on in the staff room and everyone had gathered to hear the newest update. Maria remained standing with her coffee cup in hand and screamed out loud when she heard: access to medicine was secured. Viktoria Hammar was shown in a close-up. She smiled into the camera and her smile was like the sun as she relayed that a large shipment of an effective medication, Tamivir, had been received that very morning, which would be distributed through Vigoris Health Center in consultation with the county disease control officer. Approved and ready. Vigoris Health Center could also supply an effective vaccine.

"I can't believe it! Shouldn't it take at least six months to produce a vaccine?" The reporter's eager face was glimpsed from the side.

"We did not dare release the news before we were completely sure that the vaccine would work on the epidemic that has just broken out on Gotland. Fortunately this is the same virus that caused problems in Vietnam and then in Belarus a year ago. The company that manufactured Tamivir went bankrupt and our corporate group then bought up the patent and the medicine in the warehouse because the epidemic died out on its own. We had vaccine production of our own previously, but there was no mass vaccination either and there was a considerable quantity of vaccine remaining."

"Do you mean that all the general public needs to do is make an appointment for vaccination and possible prescription? This is amazing." The reporter's voice was shrill and excited.

"To start with we want to discuss the matter with Social Services and the responsible disease control officer, and give the health and nursing administration on Gotland an offer. A package solution. And in parallel we are going to operate our vaccination clinic here at Vigoris Health Center as usual."

"What do you mean? Could you please clarify that a little?"

"It will be possible to buy vaccine and medication at market price without waiting for a decision from Social Services to get a prescription from your county physician. Production of these products is not free of course. Naturally the company has expenses for product development, administration, tests. Costs we must recover, to put it simply. But we will surely find a solution together with the affected authorities."

"So it will be possible to pay for medicine and vaccination and get it without having one of the county physicians prescribe it? Is that what you mean?"

"That's how it has always worked with us. This will not

happen uncontrolled, obviously. We have our own private physicians who in each individual case will recommend what vaccinations the patient should receive."

"So how much will a vaccination cost?"

"We were thinking twenty-five thousand kronor per injection. The protection is calculated to be eighty-five percent and full effect can be counted on after two to three weeks."

"That's a large amount. I wonder if regular people can afford that much. Doesn't it seem extremely unfair if those who can pay move to the front of the line?"

"We anticipate that the government will step in and subsidize this. For an individual that can be a lot of money. But if someone wants to pay for themselves and not burden the tax system I see no injustice in that, on the contrary. Then there will be more money left over for the healthcare administration to buy medicine with. We expect the same thing with the antiviral medicine. A course of Tamivir 75 milligrams morning and evening for five days will cost ten thousand kronor. Then we will see how much may be needed, that depends on how long the epidemic continues."

"Ten thousand? If I remember correctly, the price of a course of Tamiflu was less than a thousand before. Why is Tamivir so much more expensive?"

"As stated we have our development and production costs and this is the current price on the market. I'm pleased that we can offer this. Things were truly looking grim. If Vigoris Health Center can save people's lives and health through its efforts and prevent the community from being isolated from the outside world, with major financial and purely private losses as a result, we're pleased to offer our help."

In her joy Maria tried to immediately contact Jonathan Eriksson. The line was busy of course. What had she expected? That she would be the first to talk with him about the news? Clearly he had been given first-hand information. Actually it was just as well that he didn't answer, it would only be awkward. She was simply so relieved and grateful that the dark hell she had pictured to herself as she was lying on the floor next to Emil's bed seemed to have ended. She wanted to share her joy with Jonathan. Very silly and like a teenager, if you thought about it. He obviously had other things to do. Instead she got to speak with Nurse Lena, who confirmed that a first shipment of Tamivir had arrived at the sanitarium and that Emil had received his dose.

"Maria, phone for you." Hartman's gray-haired head appeared in the doorway and Maria followed him out to the corridor. "Yrsa Westberg, do you know who that is?"

"Isn't that Tobias Westberg's wife?" For a moment she had hoped it was Jonathan. Why was she thinking so much about him? Emil's health and future was in his hands, maybe that sort of dependent position produces an attachment that borders on love. This was as far as Maria could take that thought before she picked up the phone.

"Yes, this is Detective Inspector Maria Wern."

"My name is Yrsa Westberg. I've been gone for a week and just returned. I'm concerned because I was expecting my husband, Tobias Westberg, to be here when I got back, and no one seems to know where he is."

"Yes, we've actually been trying to get hold of him."

"He's not at home. I came home yesterday evening and he wasn't here. He didn't leave a note and hasn't called and I don't know where he is. It doesn't look like he slept here last night . . . he's not the type who would . . . sleep somewhere else."

"What do you think?" said Hartman later when they were in the car headed to Yrsa Westberg's home. "Straying married men usually turn up at dawn when they've woken

214

up in the wrong bed, but perhaps this is something different."

"Do you think he had a relationship with Sandra Hägg? I mean, is there any evidence of that?" Maria took out the directions to the house in Kappelshamn, although she doubted they would need it. Hartman knew the area well, having grown up nearby.

"We have nothing that indicates they knew each other, actually. No more than the suspicions Lennie and Jessika expressed. And Jessika was not even sure of the name. At regular intervals there's a 'T' in Sandra's calendar and a time. 'T' might just as well stand for therapist or trainer, but how likely is that? 'T' may be Tobias or someone else. And if it is the case that she's been seeing him, they had a meeting just over a week ago and one on July 4. We don't know if he has anything to do with her being murdered. We don't even know if he was there."

"Was she raped?" Maria wondered how much important information she missed when she was with Emil. "I think you should take this from the start," she said.

"The medical examiner's preliminary report says that Sandra Hägg was strangled. There are no traces of sexual violence, no semen. On her left upper arm she had a small scratch. So we can assume that the perpetrator was also carrying a knife. Just like Lennie said, she had a bar code on one buttock. No skin scrapings under the nails. It doesn't seem like she put up much resistance if there was a struggle. But as you saw, the furniture was smashed. We don't know how long the murderer chased her around the apartment. My first thought was that she was struck in the head with a blunt object and then strangled. The medical examiner confirms that theory. She was struck on the back of the head. There is a contusion."

"But no one heard her scream for help. If she was chased

in her apartment she would have tried to attract attention, don't you think? What about Hans Moberg? The guy who sells medicine on the Internet? Where is he?"

"It's like he's been swallowed up by the earth. We have the registration number for both the camper and the car and we have surveillance down in the harbor now, but he may have taken off before everything was closed, of course. In the past you always had to provide a registration number when you reserved a car place on the ferry over to the mainland, so we could've looked at the reservations, but it's not that way anymore. He could have made his way to Nynäshamn or Oskarshamn under a false name or else he's still on the island hiding out somewhere, and if that's the case we'll probably find him soon."

Yrsa Westberg lived in a small white-plastered house in the town of Kappelshamn, twenty or thirty scenic kilometers north of Visby, past the Lummelund nature reserve, Lickershamn's limestone pillar area, and Ireviken Bay with its greenish blue water. From a distance they could see her running with three border collies on an obstacle course in the shady yard. Morning light filtered through the trees and played in her blonde hair. An energetic woman of about forty with her hair in a ponytail, dressed in jeans and a big hand-knit wool sweater. The dogs obeyed her slightest hint and stood motionless as Hartman and Maria got out of the car and walked up toward them. Not until Yrsa asked whether they liked dogs and wanted to greet them did she give the dogs the sign to move and carefully nose them.

They were shown into a comfortable kitchen filled with the aroma of fresh-baked bread. The morning's loaves were on checked hand towels to cool. While Yrsa set out coffee and home-baked sourdough bread, she told them in a calm, controlled way why she had contacted them.

"Tobias is a freelance journalist. Sometimes he goes away to work on a story, but this week he was going to be home. I'm a graphic artist and had an exhibition in Skagen this week. We've been texting every evening to say goodnight. He's been at home or in town or at least sent texts from his cell phone. I came home yesterday evening and I expected him at any time, so I made osso buco and opened a bottle of wine. But he didn't come and I couldn't reach him by phone either. The strange thing is that he had left the dogs with his sister the whole time I was on the mainland. She called yesterday evening and that was how I learned that she had the dogs. She hasn't seen Tobias all week—not since the day I left. He must have gone there right away and dropped them off. Without saying anything to me."

"Did he usually drop off the dogs when he had a lot of work?"

"Only if he was going away, never if he was at home. He would never bother his sister with that unnecessarily. Besides, Tobias thought he needed the exercise he got from walking them in the morning and evening. I'm so worried that something has happened to him. People drive like lunatics and I suspect there are a lot more drunk drivers now that it's summer. You imagine all sorts of things. That someone mowed him down in a ditch and ran away or he had a heart attack . . . I'm terribly worried."

"Do you know what he was working on right now?"

"We seldom talk about work. He's not particularly interested in my art and to be honest I must say that I'm not terribly interested in his medical articles either. Yes, one thing is strange. The computer is gone. The desk is empty. The keyboard and monitor are still there." Yrsa got up from the table and led them into the study. "I thought about that right after I phoned you, then I went out with the dogs and then it disappeared. I thought, how strange that he took the computer when he has a laptop. But maybe he took it in for repair somewhere. It's a few years old. Although Tobias hasn't mentioned that there was anything wrong with it. I think he would have said something."

Maria looked around the room. There was a balcony door on one side. A peculiar drapery of bottle caps and corks was hanging in front of it. Maria could not decide if it was bold or just terribly ugly.

"You haven't had a break-in, as far as you've noticed?" She inspected the doorframe and gave the door a slight push with her shoulder. It opened. On the balcony floor outside a pile of shavings could be seen and there were obvious cut marks on the wooden frame.

"No." Yrsa looked alarmed. "We live out in the country. I don't even lock the bicycle. Nothing ever happens here."

"Is anything missing besides the computer?" Hartman inspected the damage to the door. "Looks like they used a knife and a crowbar."

"I don't understand what they would do with the computer; it's over ten years old, now that I think about it. You can probably get one like it for free. No, nothing seems to be touched," she said when she had checked whether the bankbooks were still in the top desk drawer. "We don't have anything valuable in that way. I've never been much for jewelry. Tobias's only major interest is music. He has several shelves of CDs, but it doesn't seem like any of those are gone either. Maybe they just didn't find anything else to take."

"You have no idea what he was working on right now, not for which magazine or what subject it concerned?" Maria asked.

"Not a clue, but you can get the telephone numbers for the publications he usually writes for." Yrsa was about to sit down at the computer when she recalled that it was no longer there. "He must have taken the regular address book with him, it's not here either."

"Does he have a calendar we can look at?" Hartman caught sight of the little blue book just as Yrsa put it in her hand. She browsed absentmindedly in it until she found the day's date.

"No, there's nothing marked down—nothing he wrote down that he was going to do this week. Why are you looking for him? Do you know something I don't know?" Yrsa's face underwent a transformation. "If something has happened to him you have to tell me, anything else is cruel and inconsiderate."

"We don't know where he is," Maria hurried to say. "But we would like to get hold of him to find out if he knew a woman whose name was Sandra Hägg."

"Name was? What do you mean?" Yrsa stared at them, first one and then the other. She looked like a child who had fallen down and had the breath knocked out of her, the moment before the wailing starts.

"Sandra Hägg is dead. We're trying to figure out how it happened. Did your husband know Sandra?"

Yrsa sank down on the chair by the desk. She suddenly turned very pale. "I know that they met. They had some kind of relationship. He was not himself. Not at all. He was up pacing around in the living room at night and sometimes he slept on the couch. Of course I got worried. I asked him if there was anything between them, but he denied it firmly. Good Lord, she's dead! And Tobias is gone . . ."

"There doesn't have to be a connection." Maria carefully placed her hand on Yrsa's shoulder. "Could he have gone somewhere and forgot to mention where he was going?"

Yrsa shook her head so that the ponytail bobbed, incapable of getting out a word.

"Do you know where he usually keeps his passport?" Yrsa

nodded and got up without a sound. After a while she came back from the bedroom. She had a determined look on her face; she blinked often to keep the tears back.

"His passport is gone. He didn't say that he was going anywhere. If he were traveling abroad he would have told me." Yrsa burst into tears. "Here you've lived with someone your whole adult life and think that you know him as well as you know yourself. And then it's not that way at all."

"Is there anyone you can ask to come here, someone who can be with you? I understand that this is hard."

"Tobias's sister. Good Lord, what could have happened? You don't think he could have . . . no. No, there's no way. Tobias would never hurt anyone physically. He's not that strong and he has always avoided contact sports and physical exercise, he's not that type at all. He always jokes that when you sweat your muscles are crying."

"What do you think?" said Hartman when they were back in the car on their way into town.

"I just compared Tobias's calendar with the times in Sandra's. Tobias has written X and the dates agree with Sandra's calendar in every case. A love affair, or could it be something else? Appointments for massage perhaps? There is a time the evening she was murdered. It says T on the edge for 12:00 a.m. A little odd for a massage appointment." Maria opened the side window and let the air stream in. What a summer!

Chapter 27

Yrsa Westberg watched the police head toward the main road. She caught a last glimpse as the white Ford passed the neighbor's maple trees and the tall privet hedge. Then they were no longer there.

The dogs came close to her, put their noses on her lap, and looked up at her with gentle eyes. Instinctively they sensed her worry and tried to console her. She burrowed her head in Rex's black-and-white fur and let the tears flow. Felt the warmth and devotion, his silently present consolation, which people are so poor at giving. Words create distance and close others out, limit and steal attention from emotions. Only without words and in the warmth from another body is there relief. Dogs never question, never assess, they simply are.

Even when she left for Skagen she'd had vague misgivings. There was something about the way Tobias quickly kissed her goodbye. He was constantly glancing at his watch. He helped her pack the paintings into the van and there were a few minutes to spare before it was time to leave. She was always punctual. He often teased her about that.

Perhaps it was just that last half hour that made her

wonder later and once again question her marriage. As soon as Tobias did what was expected of him—carried out the paintings, kissed her quickly—he sat down at the computer. Logged in and sat with his hands in a ready position waiting for . . . for her to leave. It was so obvious that he wanted her out of the house. She stood by the window and watched him, the man she had chosen to live with. For his sake she had moved from the village in Kalix, where her whole family lived, where her best friends were, where she was Yrsa without having to prove anything.

"We'll keep in touch," they promised each other. "See you!" But it was not the same to visit once a year as to share everyday things. She had been so madly in love and young and full of expectations. She had never met a man like Tobias—never loved so much and been so validated and felt so whole. Right then the choice had been easy. Afterward came the hard part. Tobias did not want to have children. He could not imagine it, and his conviction was unshakable.

Yrsa met her face in the hall mirror and smoothed her flat stomach. Soon it would be too late. This year she turned forty. It was the biggest compromise of her life and in the beginning she hoped he would change. Thought that it was a question of maturity, that the desire would come when people around them had children.

"Why don't you want to have children with me?" she pleaded. "How can you deny me this, when I want it so much? Don't you understand how important this is to me? Answer me! I have to know why."

He tried to explain that he was unwilling and he didn't want the responsibility, but for her that wasn't enough. It was not the whole truth. Bit had been joined to bit. A sudden silence when she asked about his mother. The family photographs he should have had. What does the past have to do with the present, your parents' lives with our lives?

He could not put it into words until she finally confronted him with it. Tobias's mother died during his birth. Tobias's father never got over it. It remained as a silence, a yawning abyss, over his entire childhood.

"You should get help. It wasn't your fault. You can't do this to me just because you're afraid. Tobias, listen to me!"

It was the moment when anything could have happened; she thought they had arrived at a breakthrough. His pale face in striped shadow from the blind. His mouth opening. The answer that never came. Instead he left her alone. She heard the outside door shut and then . . . she waited, first angry, then anxious and desperately sad for hours before he came home again. She did not dare bring it up. Not then, and not later.

She remembered what he said almost word for word: "If this is so important to you, you'll have to find another father for your child. You're free to go—go if it's so important to you. I don't want to stand in your way if it would make you happy. Stop your crazy psychologizing and digging into my childhood. It doesn't concern you and you're wrong."

He didn't touch her. When she tried to get comfort in his arms he pushed her away from him so that she would understand that he was serious. And the seriousness was still there as a guardedness in his eyes when he saw how she longingly watched children at play by the water or turned away with misty eyes when she saw a pregnant belly.

"Go then if it's so important to you, Yrsa, but don't blame me." And now, where was he now? Aunt Edla in the house next door wondered when she brought in the newspaper because the mailbox was overflowing. "I didn't want anyone to see that no one was home, considering burglars and such," she said in passing.

No, she hadn't caught a glimpse of him all week. Not the car either.

Yrsa went up to the pantry under the stairs and opened it to see if his suitcase was gone. No, the chipped old bag he inherited from his sister when she bought a new one was still there, but Yrsa's own little black weekend bag was gone. She continued into his closet, trying to determine what was missing. The black suit was hanging there and the blazer with leather patches on the sleeves. He must have been wearing jeans and a leather jacket. A couple of black T-shirts were also missing, and his gym shoes.

The police had asked her to think about how he might be dressed when they asked for a photo. What was this about? Where could he be, and why had he taken his passport? His aroma lingered in the clothing. Yrsa pressed his sweater against her face and closed her eyes. Let herself be embraced by his scent. There was an ounce of security in that. A feeling that at any moment she might hear the sound of car tires on the gravel road and that moments later he would be holding her in his arms and have an explanation.

A sudden impulse made her dig through the pockets of his pants and jackets to find a slip of paper with an address or telephone number or a receipt from some strange place. She did not really know what she was looking for. Nothing. She had called around to everyone she could think of before she contacted the police. Without any results. No one knew a thing.

The police said they were searching for him because Sandra Hägg was dead. Only now was she able to take in that thought. Sandra Cassandra with the black pixie haircut and the smile that made everyone melt. Yrsa had been completely enchanted herself and could not take her eyes off her. It was not just the smile, it was her entire way of moving. She radiated self-confidence, sensuality, and joie de vivre.

Tobias had not been unaffected. It just happened. Right in front of her eyes it happened, and she did not have the power to do anything about it.

Yrsa poured another mug of coffee. It had been standing on the hot plate and tasted harsh. She sat down at the kitchen table but quickly got up again. It was not possible to relax. She took the mug with her and went into the living room. Searched through the drawer of photographs and found a portrait taken of Tobias a year or two before. He smiled at the camera and revealed his gold tooth. She always thought it looked mischievous, a little insolent. As she looked at the picture worry struck her again like a fist in the stomach. Tobias, where are you? She tossed the photograph away from her, could not bear to look at it.

The monitor and keyboard were still there. That was why she hadn't noticed that the computer was gone at first. Right at that moment a memory came back to her. The week before Tobias had been sitting at the computer and when she came into the room, just as she was doing now, he changed programs. She tried going out of the room and then quickly came back in again. The same thing happened. He changed programs. She'd asked who he was writing to and he evasively mumbled something about work and confidential information.

Sandra Hägg. The first time they met was at Tobias's sister's house. Ebba worked at the hospital and had invited her co-workers to celebrate her fortieth birthday. Yrsa helped her with the buffet. Ebba was not particularly domestic and planned to hire a caterer to take care of the food, but Yrsa insisted. A caterer was unnecessarily expensive. It was no problem: just a couple of quiches, some cold cuts, and a big salad. Of course there was a lot of healthcare talk, bodily fluids and excretions and other intimacies that people not involved in healthcare usually avoid talking about at the dinner table. The guests seemed to lack such barriers completely.

Sandra vividly described a man who peed in the sterile storeroom and then continued around the office marking his territory. She laughed out loud and everyone laughed along. Tobias asserted that it was a completely rational action and that the piss-marker would be an excellent model for the Swedish pharmaceutical industry. For the sake of its own survival it ought to have made its mark by peeing instead of selling off its know-how.

The discussion quickly escalated past the puerile to intellectual heights that only Sandra and Tobias seemed to understand. The others listened politely as they discussed vaccine production, randomization, ratification, and global patents. Yrsa quickly got tired of it and disappeared into the kitchen to join Ebba.

"Who is she, the dark woman Tobias is talking with?"

Ebba, who in nervousness before the party had consumed a little too much of the boxed wine, spoke deep from her belly like an oracle in a pretend ghost voice. "That's Cassandra: the god Apollo gave her the gift to look into the future if she would be his woman. She took the gift of prophecy but did not want him as a bedmate, and so he punished her with a horrible curse."

Ebba nodded and pinched her lips together to appear even more mystical.

"What curse?" Yrsa had asked. At that point Ebba started slicing more bread. It was still a little frozen and her words came in spurts, slice by slice.

"The curse is that no one believes her predictions. So says the myth about Cassandra. No one believes her, except possibly Tobias, whom she has completely in her power—that

226

witch. No, my dear, it's fine. He loves you, I know he does, and he wouldn't exchange you even for a night with Cindy Crawford. You should probably take Cassandra with a grain of salt. She's a real Debbie Downer who sees dangers and evil omens everywhere. At the turn of the millennium she got the whole department to stockpile iodine tablets, in case there was an accidental nuclear explosion. Then she scared us with Ebola virus and mutant-resistant TB and now it's the bird flu. Bird flu, my foot! What will she come up with next? Grasshoppers and ladybugs and Ragnarök?"

When they had served coffee and Yrsa was announcing that they could get cake in the kitchen, she discovered that the guests had opened the balcony door and spread out into the garden. She called to them that coffee was ready and soon everyone was sitting at the table with cake. Sandra and Tobias were missing. It was not just awkward; it was a betrayal. They were gone and no one knew where they were. The comments were not long in coming. Small, mean taunts. "You have to keep an eye on your husband." "Sandra eats men. Bites their heads off. Have you heard about the Black Widow?" "Did they both get a headache and go home at the same time? Didn't even say thanks and goodbye to Ebba?"

By this point in the night Ebba was in no shape to answer that question or any other questions either for that matter. She was sitting on a stool in the kitchen, laughing at everything as if someone was tickling her. She choked with laughter when the dishrag fell on the floor and then she tried to use it as a hand puppet and turned it into a bleating lamb.

When the guests were ready to depart Tobias and Sandra came walking with their arms around each other, eagerly engaged in a discussion. Yrsa pressed her face against the glass although she really didn't want to see.

"Where have you been?" She didn't even have to ask—another guest beat her to it.

"Been?" repeated Tobias. "Do I have to account for every strategic maneuver to the group chief? We were just at my house for a while. I wanted to show Sandra a research report."

There was crude joking about that too. Research? Wonder what you've been investigating? Anatomical differences?

Ebba laughed so hard she peed her pants and had to change—a grown person. Tobias's face turned bright red and he took the papers out of Sandra's bag, as evidence. But all he produced was a newspaper article about chip marking of household pets, which proved nothing at all. Simply a poor excuse.

That was two years ago, but as Yrsa stood by the damaged balcony door in their living room it was as if it had happened yesterday. It still hurt. It was never explained. Tobias had said that he had not seen Sandra again and she'd believed him.

Chapter 28

"Things are moving quickly here. We're going to get vaccinated. There's a nurse in the staff room. All you need to do is go in there and have it done. Pettersson almost fainted. Those are some big-ass syringes. Yes, you know you did." Haraldson tousled his colleague's hair and nodded to Maria. "Ladies first?"

"What's this, what do you mean?"

"All police officers will be vaccinated against the flu virus. The police and the prime minister and his buddies, you're in good company. Of course. All you have to do is keep going right into the staff room, where the nurse is ready for action. We're getting this for free. Do you get that, what an investment in the police department. They think we're worth twenty-five thousand kronor each plus the tablets, let's see . . . that's thirty-five thousand. I felt a little better-looking when I saw myself in the mirror in the locker room, a little more intelligent, and definitely more appreciated as a person. You're worth investing in, imagine that. We're going to get Tamivir as long as the bird flu is going on. They're estimating another six weeks. This is real money. Although I'd happily take it as a lump sum and go to a resort by the Mediterranean instead."

Maria continued down the corridor and it was just as he'd said. A nurse dressed in the light-green uniform Maria had come to associate with Vigoris Health Center had spread out syringes on a small stainless steel cart.

"Please come on in. You know what this is about, right?"

"Vaccination." Maria felt a slight feeling of discomfort, like with the school nurse. The odor of disinfectant that you never really get used to. A little prick, then it's over. Before it reeked of ether, which reinforced the fear, and then there were all the rumors about sharp needles that came out on the other side of your arm and stinging, corrosive fluids that produced bumps the size of golf balls and fever.

"You're not allergic to eggs?"

"What?"

"Chicken eggs are used in the production of the vaccine and if you're allergic to the protein in eggs you may get a reaction, that's why we ask." The nurse gave a sweet little smile.

"No, I'm not allergic."

"Right or left-handed?"

"Right." Maria rolled up her sleeve on the left side and fixed her gaze on the bulletin board on the opposite wall. She felt the cold from the alcohol swab that cleaned the upper arm and then the stab, and the stinging sensation as the fluid was pressed in under the skin. The body remembers—this was how it felt. Maria turned her head to see when the syringe was pulled out. Didn't it seem unusually large?

"In a day or two you may feel a local reaction, a slight swelling, and you may have a slight increase in temperature. You may feel a little out of sorts with some soreness in your muscles, but it's nothing to worry about." That sweet little smile again. "Do you have any questions?"

Maria, who at first was surprised that they would get access to vaccine so quickly, had collected herself somewhat.

"It said in the newspaper today that there are concerns that Tamivir is going to be ineffective too and that it is being prescribed too liberally. Is that so?"

"The virus that a person is carrying may become resistant if the medicine is used for a longer time and when it isn't needed, unnecessarily that is. But a person doesn't become resistant. Sometimes the newspaper reporters are in such a hurry they don't really listen to what's being said before they start writing."

"Do you think it will be that way—that the medicine will become ineffective?" Maria saw that the question bothered the nurse. The sweet little smile faded a little and she suddenly looked at the clock. Probably ordered to finish X number of vaccinations before lunch. She glanced toward the door, where Hartman stood ready with his shirtsleeve rolled up.

"I think you'll have to bring that up with Jonathan Eriksson. You can reach him by phone."

"I know." Maria felt like a nuisance who took up the nurse's time unnecessarily and prevented her colleagues from coming in.

"Thanks. I guess it's your turn now, Hartman."

"They had a break-in at Vigoris Health Center late on the evening of July 4 but didn't report it," said Hartman when he came out of the staff room and they were walking down the corridor together to the technical department. "Apparently nothing was stolen. They didn't want any attention drawn to it. I just found out when I asked Lennie Hellström a few follow-up questions. He was on guard duty that night and got an alarm from the clinic. When he did his rounds he discovered that a window was broken and then he called Viktoria Hammar instead of the security manager, as had been agreed. Evidently they don't get along too well."

"A number of health centers had break-ins before we brought in police surveillance. People are desperate."

That's not strange, thought Maria. The newspapers are talking about the threat of fatalities and before the news came about medication for the whole population of the island there was no help to be had, other than what you could get for yourself via contacts. Strange that it doesn't happen more often. That more doctors aren't threatened with their lives to prescribe medicine, or because it's believed that they've stockpiled medicine at home. Earlier in the week Maria received a report from a district physician who was assaulted in his home by a desperate neighbor. His wife had a fever and no doctor had come to see her as promised. The telephone line was blocked. The doctor said that he was not on duty and he needed to sleep, but the neighbor tried to force him to come over.

"When will people be able to travel freely again?" Maria asked.

"In the last news report they were talking about five days but you must have a certificate that shows you've taken medicine. Presumably there will be a mass exodus from the island once the travel ban is lifted."

"I think so too." Maria thought about Krister, who was supposed to start work again in a couple of days. His situation was hardly unique. Most people were actually here on vacation. "But the Cabinet members got to leave."

"I heard the discussion on *News Morning*. Every Cabinet member's contacts have been reviewed in detail and they haven't been able to trace them to any source of infection. But that can't be done with us ordinary mortals, it requires too many resources."

They sat down in the technicians' office for a quick

run-through. Mårtenson yawned and stretched to his full height. His joints cracked after sitting for hours hunched up, inspecting small fragments of textiles and skin from Sandra Hägg's apartment.

"We've found something interesting in the trash in Sandra Hägg's kitchen: a SIM card for a cell phone. I checked the most recent calls with the service provider. Telia. All outgoing calls in the past week went to Yrsa Westberg and the majority of incoming calls are from her, as well."

Hartman was rocking on the chair as he listened, as if he couldn't find out quickly enough what he needed and that the movement could hasten the technician's account.

Mårtenson continued. "You get a feeling that it may have been in Tobias Westberg's cell. One call was from a former employer at a provincial newspaper, one from a medical magazine, and one from a seller of telecom services who wanted to speak with the company's procurement manager— that must be Tobias himself, since he didn't have any employees."

"Yrsa?" Maria felt her thoughts racing. "The card was found in Sandra's apartment, but not the cell phone. Either Tobias has been there the whole time and texted his wife as if he were at home. According to the provider, the calls were sent from that area. Or else he hasn't been there at all, but instead he had Sandra send text messages to Yrsa. But where is Tobias? His passport is gone and both his desktop and laptop computers."

"I just spoke with Yrsa on the phone," said Hartman. "She told me what she thought her husband was wearing when he disappeared. She's guessing he had on jeans, black T-shirt, brown leather jacket, and gym shoes. I think we have time to get that mentioned in the next news broadcast. She also continued to search through the house to see whether anything else might have been stolen in the break-in and found that camera equipment was missing. Tobias usually takes the pictures for his stories himself. Either he has the equipment with him or else you have to assume it's been stolen. Yrsa is a nervous wreck. She feels unsafe staying alone in a house where there's been a break-in. She's going to stay with Tobias's sister, Ebba. I've written down the address, if we need to get in touch with her. A break-in like that shatters the illusion that you're safe in your own home."

"Have you seen the autopsy report on Sandra Hägg? I got a copy this morning." Mårtenson reached for the papers in the pile in front of him.

Hartman shook his head. "I haven't been in my office. Did it just arrive?" He took the report and skimmed through it before handing it to Maria. "This confirms what we assumed preliminarily. She was strangled, and before that struck with a blunt object on the back of the head. No, there's nothing new. I see no motive. Not robbery, not rape. What was her boss's name, the male one?"

Hartman searched in his memory but could not think of it. That's how it always was when he slept badly. Names and places simply disappeared. Last night he woke up at two o'clock worrying about Maria's Emil and the other children at the sanitarium. He tossed back and forth in bed and wasn't able to close his eyes after that.

"Reine Hammar. Jessika Wide said he'd shown a particular interest in Sandra and that he was at her place once when she called. What about him?"

"We ought to question him as soon as he's released from the sanitarium."

"I was thinking about the painting salesman," said Mårtenson. "Have we been able to identify him?"

"We've sent the question to Europol and we're waiting for a response, but it may take a while before we get word. Of course, it would be easier if we had a name. The marks we've found are a rather ugly scar under the right ribcage—it's not a surgical scar, more like the consequences of an assault. Fingerprints. His face is swollen and badly battered, it's not easy to recognize anyone from such a photo."

Chapter 29

When Hans Moberg woke up, he didn't know where he was at first. The unfamiliar, feminine odor slipped into his dreams and colored them. In his dream he had been at a party in a big white villa by the sea. The wine was flowing and everyone was drunk, and somehow he ended up in the hostess's waterbed with three beautiful women dressed only in colorful wigs made of long metal strips. But the waterbed leaked and became a sea and suddenly Sandra Hägg was there and all desire and playfulness vanished. He tried to flee from his guilt. Turned in a different direction and tried to find his way back to the party. But the music had stopped and all around him the darkness grew denser and forced him out on the pier again. The cold penetrated his bare body and the sky arched over him, powerful and accusing. The ice-cold star-eyes were staring at him and in the moonlight her skin was blindingly white. He wanted to touch her and kiss her lovely neck. Sandra Hägg. That's what it said on the door.

He was driven to touch her. But she became afraid, took a step backward. He followed her. He reached for her and she took another step backward and fell down into the black water as though it were an open grave. The salt water splashed over his face and the cracking sound when her skull was split against the stone still echoed in the daylight. Perhaps the sound was dampened by the waves, perhaps it never reached the air, but in his ear the sound of the crushed skull was like a remnant from the dreams. The treacherous dreams that enticed him and then revealed the loathsome truth when he was defenseless and fragile. Or drunk, when he was no longer able to protect his border and was possessed by rage and smashed everything to pieces so that he would not be blown apart. Minute by minute of silence when her body was resting on the bottom. When he realized that she was dead, that time had taken her by force, he ran away. Ran in the mud without getting anywhere. Crawled until he came out of reach of her slender white arms. A secret shared by two where one was dead is a well-kept secret, he had believed. But what really happened he could not remember. He tried to breathe calmly and deeply, regain control of his runaway breathing and the hard beating of his heart.

Now he was lying down, staring at the fluffy curtains and wondering where he had ended up. In the embroidered hell of cotton curtains in the home of Horseface Cecilia Granberg—that was it. He must get something to drink, and soon. The yeasty taste of Gotland ale returned in sour regurgitations and he wondered to himself if he truly had been so desperate that he drank a whole bottle.

Hans Moberg staggered out to the kitchen to put on coffee. A new sunny day cut into his eyes making the tears run. He looked out over the neat yard with its well-tended flowerbeds and a garden where heads of lettuce and dill and carrot tops stood in straight rows. What time could it be? Only four o'clock. He had slept for three hours. It was seldom better than that and he moaned audibly with disappointment. Yesterday's encounter with Cuddly Skåne

Girl had not been what he had hoped for at all. There must have been a misunderstanding. He took Cecilia's car and parked by the lime works and waited. When the woman didn't arrive he got out and took a walk down toward the harbor. The moon was reflected in the water. Maybe that was why he had such peculiar dreams later. It was as if Sandra's pale face was there in the river of moonlight, right below the surface, to appear at any moment and accuse him with her dark eyes. As he stood on the edge of the pier he heard a car door shut. He hurried back to see whether the woman from Skåne had arrived. But he saw no sign of another car, and when he noticed the drowsy policemen watching the harbor so that no one could escape from the island he quickly left the area. It was only when he was about to go to bed that he noticed his wallet was gone. He searched in the house, but remembered that he had put it in the car. It was thick and lumpy to sit on and he took it out of his pocket and set it beside him. But when he went out to the garage and searched the car the wallet was not there. The thought struck him that he might have had it with him when he got out of the car, or else someone had stolen it. The car was unlocked. So he returned to the industrial harbor and fine-combed the area, but did not find a wallet. This was too annoying.

Hans Moberg laid back down on Cecilia's bed and turned on the radio. A heated debate was going on about the prohibition on meeting in large groups to avoid infection. Athletic events and concerts were being cancelled all over the island and restaurants could only take in a limited number of customers. Bus traffic was shut down and all schools and childcare centers were closed. The disease control officer tried to justify her decision—but people were upset. Old hags! He could not bear to listen to them but instead switched to P1. The program unfortunately was about the bird flu, too, but the conversational tone was gentler and more factual.

"A Swedish-born 73-year-old physician, Johan Hultin, made an expedition to Alaska eight years ago where he investigated a mass grave from 1918. Those buried were all victims of the Spanish flu. The purpose was to bring back tissue samples from the lungs of the deceased so that the virus that caused the disease could be isolated and studied. Johan Hultin succeeded where others have failed, and the virus strain that could be produced by means of the frozen material is now being stored at the Centers for Disease Control in the U.S. . . ."

At some point Hans Moberg must have fallen asleep and when he woke up a woman was standing in the doorway with a watering can in her hand, looking at him. She must have screamed. Her mouth was still open and the spout of the watering can was drooping toward the floor. A small rivulet of water painted her brown skirt a darker shade right in the middle.

"Who are you?" she asked in a hoarse voice after she had audibly inhaled. Her eyes were round and very blue behind the strong convex glasses, and they seemed to get even bigger as he slowly raised himself into a sitting position. Careful now, he couldn't frighten her into flight.

"I guess I could ask the same thing," he said, sounding a trifle grim. "Cecilia promised me that I would be able to work undisturbed here."

"Excuse me, I . . ." The water continued to run down in a little pool on the floor.

"Klas Strindberg," Hans introduced himself, extending his hand. He had previously adopted the role of literary author on one of his computer dates, so it was only a matter of putting on this custom-made suit. Making his vowels a bit more nasal, a slight roll to his r's and his chin arrogantly lowered on his chest produced the right image. He had practiced in front of the mirror and knew what impression it made. His hair should have been combed in a side part with a little of the long unkempt hair tossed over his forehead in shaped wisps, but that would have to wait for next time.

She took his hand in a cold, damp grip and smiled cautiously. Her teeth were uneven and overlapped slightly. It had its charm, he thought.

"I'm just a neighbor. I was going to water. Cecilia didn't tell me that—"

"Of course she didn't. If everyone knew I was here I would never get any work done. The newspapers calling. TV and radio wanting interviews. My readers don't miss a chance to get their books signed and my publisher is hovering like a vulture over my head, waiting for results." The woman followed his gesture in the air.

Simple person, he thought. She didn't look like much either. Far too reserved for it to be worth the effort to . . . but of course one might be mistaken. Simply because she looked like she came from the insurance company forms archive didn't mean she was completely unappealing.

"What should we do about the flowers?" she asked.

"The flowers?" At first he didn't understand what she was talking about. Birds and bees passed through his head. Perhaps she was retarded even though she looked normal on the outside. Then he caught sight of the watering can and understood. "You can take them home with you. I need peace and quiet, you understand. When I create I have to savor the words, let them roll on my tongue so I feel what kind of aftertaste they have. Have you ever thought that a word has an aftertaste? Tens of thousands of people read my poetry collections and I can't disappoint them. The expectations only get higher and higher."

"Amazing! Do your poems sell in large editions? Klas Strindberg, was that your name? I've never actually heard of you. I'm sorry." She got a greedy, curious look in her eyes and unexpectedly sat down on the edge of the bed. "Do you write under a pseudonym?"

"It's many years now since I published anything. Ordinary people don't understand what agony it entails to fuse your innermost dynamic impressions into static words—it's like serving your own decapitated head on a silver platter, if you understand what I mean." One of his mother's favorite expressions, she was so damn literary.

"So who is your publisher?"

"Why such a superficial question? That can't possibly interest you, could it? You're a woman with quite different depths and qualities, I see that sort of thing."

"I see, so what do you see?" She leaned forward. Her upper lip was trembling a little, not much, but he thought she looked like a rabbit and could not keep from smiling.

"What's so funny?" she asked without taking her eyes off him. A little sulky now, he truly had to be careful. "What qualities do you think I have?"

"You are reliable and you can keep a secret. Hm, I have to look at your beautiful hands. They have no calluses. They're soft. It is said that the eyes are the mirror of the soul, but that's so trite. I would say that the hands are the mirror of the soul. No rings—a woman with many possibilities." He stroked his warm hand across the back of hers and turned up her palm. "The lifeline is strong. But the line for love and desire is broken in several places." He followed it with his index finger and sensed a shiver that was transmitted through her body. Don't move ahead too fast. This should be just right. She must have time to digest the touch and long for more.

"Have you been translated?" she asked, drawing her hand back after a slightly embarrassed silence.

"But of course, what a question!"

"And you write under your real name?" she continued. Did he sense a smile? Here he had to be careful.

"Under pseudo . . . well, you know. One must have a private life."

"What do you call yourself?"

"I would prefer to keep that to myself. When I rented an apartment on Strandvägen in Stockholm last spring I happened to mention my name in passing, and then it was over. The rumor spread and I couldn't stay there. Lost three months of peace of mind in which to write and let's not talk about the rent. No—I actually came here to be incognito. That's in my agreement with Cecilia Granberg and she won't come away from this contract empty-handed. By the way, you wouldn't happen to be going past the state liquor store, would you? I was just wondering—could imagine sending along a little order . . . just in case." She shook her head.

"I think you can order through the Pressbyrån news-stand in some places, but I don't know. I've never bought on someone else's behalf."

When the neighbor disappeared with the last geranium, Hans Moberg felt relieved at first, then uneasiness came creeping in. Did she suspect something? No, she wouldn't have sat down on the edge of the bed. But what if she talked with other neighbors and they had heard the wanted-person bulletin and she started to put two and two together? Where would he go? Here there was food and electricity and a decent bathroom anyway. He must think of something. Perhaps it was best to take Cecilia's humble Saab and leave as soon as possible. But where? There was a risk that he would be infected with that bird flu misery if he encountered people. If he just wandered into a health center and asked to get medicine they would ask for identification, which was the same as a one-way ticket to prison. And no medicine, no certificate. He couldn't leave the island. Things were really a mess. It was all Sandra Hägg's fault. If she had only left him alone, if she hadn't asked him to come over this never would have happened.

She'd wanted to talk with him about vaccine against the bird flu. Perhaps he had exaggerated a little and offered information that could not be supported. But he figured if things developed favorably, in the not-so-distant future the information would not be wrong at all. At least that's how he had reasoned.

She sounded as if she were desperate to know where he got the syringes. Why was that so important? In reality, there were no syringes, but if he worked his contacts few things were impossible. Really it was almost risk-free to peddle a vaccine that had no effect for three weeks. If the goods were of inferior quality, he would be long gone. It was much worse with Viagra—his customers expected immediate satisfaction.

Hans Moberg slipped out of the house and followed the hedge to the outbuilding where he had parked his love nest. He must have a six-pack of beer somewhere—otherwise life was not worth living. A couple of beers and a little rest and then he would figure out his situation.

Chapter 30

M aria ordered a bouquet of flowers to be delivered to her colleague Ek at the Follingbo sanitarium, checked the clock, and logged off the computer. She had just come from a meeting regarding the curfew. Everyone on the force was informed that all vacation had been recalled and everyone could count on working overtime for a while. The airport and ports would be monitored, as well as the pharmacies, hospitals, and health centers. Cooperation between the auxiliary police and security guards had been established. Although as a detective the directives would not change much of anything for Maria, the situation was frightening and the division of labor unclear. The two major issues that had not yet been resolved were who would pay and who had responsibility.

As Maria reached for her jacket on the hanger by the door, she heard Hartman speaking English with someone on the phone. He was no great linguistic talent. When you're speaking in another language about serious matters with the wrong intonation and strong Gotland diphthongs, it sounds a bit strange. Hartman had grown up in Martebo and his dialect persisted, despite all his years on the mainland. Maria tried to keep from laughing—what they were talking about was truly nothing to laugh about. And in fact, she admired him a great deal. He always did his best and assumed that others did too. He was generous in his thinking to the point of being naive, but perhaps it was that very quality that allowed him to succeed where others failed. His genuine goodwill shone through and people dared to confide in him.

Sergei Bykov, Hartman spelled out with great effort. The next moment he was visible in the doorway, his forehead sweaty and with large damp stains under his arms from the exertion of speaking English, but happy and full of enthusiasm.

"The painting salesman now has a name. The scar was the tip-off. He got it in a robbery. His name is Sergei Bykov and he comes from Belarus. According to his wife he was on a short visit to Sweden to sell paintings and she expected him back on Sunday, the second of July. Her story is so pitiful that you get a lump in your throat. Sergei's son has serious kidney disease and he was going to get a kidney from his father, but the operation costs money and they were a few thousand short. Sergei tried to come up with the money at the last minute by selling his paintings. The surgery was scheduled for last Monday, but Sergei never came back."

"Do we know anything else about him? Where he lived? What he did for a living?" Maria hung her jacket back on the hook. This was a breakthrough and without a doubt required an immediate response and overtime. She would have to call home to Marianne Hartman to ask whether she could take care of Linda and Malte a while longer.

"Sergei came from Biaroza. It's in Belarus, southwest of Minsk. He raises laboratory mice and guinea pigs and other research animals for the pharmaceutical laboratories there. The corporation is called the Demeter Group and pharmaceuticals are one part of it. They are also involved in development of labeling systems for grocery and product transport, and an institute for rejuvenative surgery. From what I understand they also run clinics for overweight Western Europeans and Americans, who stay at their spa facilities. Their head office is in Montreal but they are active all over the Western world. Check the stock price in the next news broadcast and you'll see, it's a successful corporation."

"And what happens with Sergei's son now?" Maria could not keep from asking the question, although she was already sure what the answer would be.

"He's very ill. I don't know what general healthcare is like in Belarus. They had saved money to have the operation done at the private clinic that belongs to the company where Sergei worked. You can only hope they'll help the boy and that they can find another donor."

"Maybe they'll have to use the money that would have gone to the operation to buy food if Sergei can't support them any longer." Maria closed her eyes for a moment and recalled that in the break room she had just been complaining to Mårtenson that she couldn't afford to buy a house.

Maria called home and Linda answered.

"You can't come now because we're going to camp outside! We're going to sleep in a tent in the garden; we got permission from Marianne. It's really cozy and Marianne is going to sleep in a tent too and guard so no ghosts come."

"May I speak with her?" Maria waited and heard Linda run downstairs to the other apartment.

"Yes, I thought perhaps you would like an evening out. Tomas will be home soon and the children really want to camp out. I hope it's okay with you—just don't forget to leave the ball by midnight," she laughed.

"I must say I'm a little surprised. What does Malte's

dad say about this? I should probably call Jonathan and ask him first."

"He stopped by here today, and yes, actually it was his idea."

Two hours later Jonathan and Maria were at the Bister Hare in the cellar under the Freemasons Lodge at the St. Nikolai cloister ruins. The restaurant had a medieval theme, with a menu of grilled lamb, root vegetables, baked potatoes, strawberry salsa, and a chickpea stew that was very good.

"So they let you leave the hospital," said Maria.

"The tests showed that I wasn't carrying the infection. You can't hold personnel hostage. And if we couldn't rely on the protective equipment, no one would dare to work."

At first they thought about sitting in the lovely garden, where a gigantic walnut tree shaded the tables, but it was a bit chilly so they chose to be seated in the cellar, where at one time the monks who worked on the construction of the cloister lived. Still lived there, according to the waitress. One monk remained.

"He walks around down here and sees that everything is in order. If a door is suddenly open, if the light goes out or is turned on you only need to say, 'Hi, I know you're there.'"

They sat down at the long table and each ordered a beer, which was served in ceramic tankards. The many candles in the holders on the walls and the oil lamps on the tables spread a warm glow under the white arches and were reflected like little white torches in Jonathan's glasses. They made small talk about the children for a while before Maria dared to ask how Nina was doing.

"You know, it feels very strange not to lie about her alcohol dependency when you've been telling lies and making excuses for so many years. Nina is still in the hospital. She has pneumonia. Vomited and got it down in her lungs when she was lying on her back. She might have died."

"That's terrible." Maria saw the pain reflected in his face. He said nothing for a while, just looked at her with an unfathomable expression. Maria got a feeling that she was being judged. Should she have said something else? Asked more questions, or stayed quiet? She wished he would dare confide in her.

"It's worse for Malte. It makes me feel so bad and I get so angry. He thinks that's what mothers are like. He has nothing to compare her with. It's the norm to have a mother who stays in bed half the day and then suddenly rises from the dead and promises water parks and slides and computer games and new toys, and then nothing comes of what she promises. Then it changes again in a few hours. She's hungover and irritated and snaps at him and everything he does is wrong. If she had a job to go to maybe it would have been different, but that's not how it is." Jonathan inhaled in a long, trembling breath and clenched his teeth. Maria placed her hand on his. She said nothing now either. There were no suitable words.

A couple sat down at the other end of the long table. They kissed and their hands sought each other under the table. Their cheeks were glowing and eyes shining and they only saw each other. Jonathan could not keep from smiling at them.

"It's been so long since Nina and I sat like that." He placed his hand over Maria's and she did not pull away. He looked her in the eyes very seriously. "It would have been a relief for me if Nina had died. I know you think I shouldn't say that. That I shouldn't feel that. But I do. She makes my life hell and I would not stay a minute longer if it wasn't because I'm afraid of not getting sole custody of Malte."

"She should get help."

"She doesn't want help. She doesn't think she has a problem. It's like it's my problem. I'm the one who betrayed her and for that reason she has to drink herself into a stupor. There's no treatment center on Gotland either. The closest one is on the mainland. I've tried to talk with her, but she refuses to listen. If she's committed involuntarily that's a label that would give me an advantage in a custody dispute. She would not understand that I want to help her and she doesn't want to give me a trump card. We've ended up in trench warfare where every action is strategic. We hurt each other consciously even though neither of us wants to. I know it sounds sick, but that's the way it is."

"How does she think you've betrayed her?"

Jonathan heaved a deep sigh, released Maria's hand and leaned back, as if he needed distance and space to be able to think clearly.

"I was unfaithful. A couple of years ago I was at a course on the mainland with the infectious disease clinic. It happened one time. Nina and I hadn't had sex in over two years. I can't help it, but it disgusts me that she has to get drunk to feel desire. I don't want to touch her then and so there's nothing. She found out that I'd been unfaithful from a girlfriend, who heard it from another girlfriend. I was a coward and said it wasn't true. That we just sat in the hotel room and talked. But it was more than that—it wasn't the idea that it would happen, nothing planned. Both of us were starving. We could feel it already when we were dancing. We couldn't get enough of each other and the others started looking and commenting, so we decided to have a drink in my room and then . . . To be honest I would have done it again without hesitating. It was worth it."

"Do you still see each other?" Maria could not keep from asking, even though it really wasn't her business. Not at all. She wanted to know anyway. It was in the air somehow, an

249

incipient feeling that something might happen. The start of something that could be? Maria dismissed the thought. He was married, after all! And she should know better than to mindlessly lose her self-control and let herself be fooled by a man who just admitted that he had been unfaithful because his wife didn't understand him. Classic and rotten! Intelligent women don't fall for such simple tricks. Yet Maria had asked to know more, appealed to his guilty conscience and longing for absolution. Please, dear, tell me that all other women are unappreciative and ugly and untalented and that I am the only one who understands you.

"Do you still see that woman?"

"Why are you smiling so strangely? Did I say something funny? No, we don't have any contact at all. She didn't want to. There was nothing between us before; we were just co-workers . . . and nothing after. It was just right then, that moment, and I'm glad it happened. Do you think I'm awful?"

"No." What else could she say when he made himself so vulnerable? Life doesn't always turn out the way you want it to. There are seldom any simple answers to complicated questions. Who has the right to judge someone who longs for love and takes what's offered?

"How about you, though? Is there a man in your life?" He looked at her with interest when he noticed that the question embarrassed her a little.

Maria took a sip of beer and thought. It would be so simple to say: Yes, his name is Emil and he's ten years old. "There was someone, but nothing came of it. He couldn't wait and then . . . something happened. He asked me to give him confidential information about an investigation I was working on but I refused, and we haven't seen each other since. His name is Per."

"But you think about him? He still means something to

you?" Jonathan smiled and screwed up one eye and looked sly. "Am I wrong?"

"Yes, I've decided to forget him. There's no point. He's not coming back." Maria got up to go to the restroom. She warmed her hands a moment by the fire and when she came back the intimate mood was broken. Another group had sat down at the other end of the long table and the sound level was pretty high.

"Do you know what I was just thinking about?" he said once she sat down again. "That homing pigeon that came to Ruben Nilsson's pigeon loft was carrying bird flu in a mutant form and it was from Belarus. Previously gallinaceous birds spread bird flu, not pigeons. What I think is that someone may have prepared it, infected it intentionally. Do you understand where I'm going with this? Right before I met you at Österport I heard the news that the murdered man found by that restroom in Klintehamn was from Belarus. Isn't that a little strange?"

"I didn't know that Ruben Nilsson was infected by a pigeon. I thought wild geese had infected his birds. How do you know it was a pigeon from Belarus?" Maria leaned forward to hear better and Jonathan grazed her cheek with his fingers when he answered.

"He took the pigeon's ring to the library and asked a librarian for help finding out where it came from through the homing pigeon association website. It was from Biaroza in Belarus. What you ought to check on is whether Sergei, or whatever his name was, was infected with bird flu. Do you know if anyone asked the medical examiner that question?"

"My God, I don't believe it. I mean, no one was thinking about bird flu then! The newspapers were full of scary stories about multi-resistant TB and infected daycare children. This is how you protect yourself and your family—the whole list! The warning about bird flu came later. I don't think that's been checked."

"When you know I'd be very eager to hear the answer. Maybe we're working on the same puzzle, and then it will be beneficial to see each other's pieces. Are you in charge of the investigation of the murder of Sandra Hägg?"

"Yes, do you know anything about her?" Maria saw the change in his facial expression when she asked the question. This was important to him.

"She worked for a while with us at the infectious disease clinic."

An idea occurred to Maria. She felt that Jonathan was observing her while she tried to put it into words.

"What is it?" he asked.

"That time when you were on a course, for your job. The woman you spent the night with. Was it Sandra Hägg?"

"No, but I liked her a lot."

"Do you know a medical journalist named Tobias Westberg?"

"Yes, why do you ask? Does he have anything to do with the investigation of Sandra's murder? You look strange, you don't think that Tobias . . . I can't imagine that he would have killed her. Not a chance. He's not aggressive at all. We did our military service together. He had a hard time following orders, he always wanted to discuss and analyze and argue about things. He drove the officers crazy, but he was just very gentle and friendly. He went by the nickname Hamster."

"Why that name? I've seen a photo of him; he's fairly thin. Did he collect things?"

"No, he got the mumps. It wasn't really that funny. He had a bad case of meningitis. That cut short his military service. But I wouldn't have wanted to trade places with him. Once I brought him flowers and his girlfriend was there. Yrsa, her name was. She was a kind of dream girl with long blonde hair and innocent blue eyes that everyone just sighed after. Naturally pretty—a bit like you." He smiled when he saw Maria grimace. She was not very good at accepting compliments.

They got up and went out into the garden to look at the fire-eaters and listen to the jesters' music. The gate to the St. Nikolai cloister ruin was slightly ajar. They were drawn in by the magnificent sunset that was framed by the tall window arches. Solemnly they walked along the path and felt how powerfully history spoke to them from the time before the plague and plundering expeditions, when the cloister was living and magnificent.

"During the time of the plague it was believed that the infection was due to bad air. The doctors had a protective outfit with a mask that looked like a long bird beak and in the beak aromatic substances were stored that were thought to purify the air. When you see pictures of that old get-up it's like seeing the bird flu personified."

Maria said that she could picture it and Jonathan was about to continue when they heard the sound of the gate closing behind them. A key was turned in the lock. They tried to call and pound on the wooden gate, but the sound was drowned out by the music outside.

"I can wrap my coat around you, and we can stay here tonight," Jonathan quickly suggested, putting his arm around her. Maria shook her head. The idea was enticing, but not uncomplicated.

"There must be a way to get out," she said. "It's lower on the east side, if you just get under the barbed wire." She started walking down the path. He did not let go of her shoulders and when she turned toward him she was in his arms. He placed his cheek against hers, sought her mouth, and gave her a kiss. She did not respond to it, but instead stared at him with eyes wide open and lips drawn in. He started to laugh. She looked pretty funny.

"If we move a bench here and help each other we can get up to the window. If the barbed wire could be clipped off it should be possible to get between and jump down on the street, it's not very high." She was talking quickly and forcefully. This couldn't happen. She felt the longing in her body, making her an easy prey to touch. How long had it been since someone touched her like that? He's married! And this is going to do me harm, she thought over and over again like a mantra. I don't want a complicated life, I don't want to be betrayed, I don't have the energy for another guy, not now. Think about Nina, she needs him more than ever. We have to get out of here, now!

"If you really think it's necessary. I have a Swiss army knife. Although I think it's a shame. I like being locked in with you. I can't really think of anyone I'd rather be locked in with. Don't you think it's a little cozy? We're both victims of chance; no one is guilty. It's a golden opportunity, isn't it?"

"If we move one of the benches here it will be easier to climb out."

Once outside the walls Maria was about to call for a taxi when Jonathan took her in his arms in farewell and thanked her for a nice evening. She noticed that he sniffed her hair and that his hands were gliding slowly down her back. She stood completely still, unable to resist the caress. It felt marvelous.

"You smell right," he said.

"What do you mean, right?" she laughed and let go.

"It has something to do with pheromones. Do you want to come home with me . . . I mean . . . I would really like it."

"I don't think that's a good idea. I like you, Jonathan, and I'd like to see you again. But you're married and you have a wife who needs you and a Malte who loves both his mom and his dad."

"Oh, I wasn't thinking that—I thought we might play Scrabble or have a cup of coffee or something. You didn't think otherwise, I hope." He laughed teasingly and helped her into the taxi. "If you change your mind right now it will be cheaper than going to Klinte and changing your mind halfway there."

"Maybe another time, Jonathan." She felt strong and full of self-discipline as she said that, but even before the taxi pulled away in her fantasies she was in his arms, locked in the ruins where no eyes or ears could reach them. His caress along her back lingered like a longing in her skin and gave her no peace.

That night she lay for a long time in bed, listening to the rain. It was like weeping, uncontrolled and inconsolable, and toward morning it was like quiet sobbing in the drops from the trees. I am not single. A single person has chosen to take care of herself and live in freedom. I'm really just alone, she thought.

Chapter 31

The windshield wipers swept aside the rain in big, drowsy waves. Over the rooftops was a heavy blanket of clouds. Hartman was worried. Marianne had tried to reach her doctor the entire day before without success.

"She has a lung transplant and she's on medication that suppresses her immune defenses. She ought to be in a category that gets vaccine and antiviral medicine first," he said indignantly to Maria as they carpooled to the police station in Visby. "It seems like those with the greatest need for care are taking a back seat to what the politicians call social benefit. The question is whether there will be any medication left when everyone in important positions and those who can buy it have theirs. We've talked about taking out a loan. It won't be easy, because we already have a mortgage on the house. But I don't think we can wait. I would never forgive myself if Marianne got sick and we could have avoided it. Whatever the cost."

"That business of social benefit is debatable. If Marianne wasn't taking care of my Linda, I wouldn't be able to work. Everything is connected. Who's important and who's less important? You should know how grateful I am to you and

Marianne. I don't know what I would have done with Linda otherwise, when she doesn't want to be with her dad."

"The feeling is mutual. Marianne hasn't been so happy for years." He gave her a warm smile and suddenly became serious again. "I think it may be dangerous to get people's hopes up about how quickly it will be possible to get help. In the TV interview it sounded like all you had to do was go and pick up the medicine. People will go crazy when that's not the case. You know, personally I feel that I'm prepared to fight to get medicine for her. Physically fight so that the vaccine won't run out and there won't be any left when it's her turn. I feel that the barrier that keeps you from running amok is so fragile, only a little superficial veneer actually. If it really came down to that, I think I'd kill so that she could live. We're so frighteningly primitive when it comes to basics."

"I suppose. I actually think it's strange that people stay as calm as they do. It's as if the seriousness of it all doesn't really sink in. It still feels like this is something happening far away when you see it on TV and listen to the radio reports every hour. As if this concerned other people, just another report from a crisis area somewhere in the world. Maybe we've become desensitized from constantly bringing all the misery of the world right into our living rooms."

"Or else it's bubbling below the surface. Fear and the sense of injustice are going to find an expression, I think." Only now did Hartman hear the sound from the radio that had been grinding on without either of them listening. An exchange was going on between the Minister of Public Health and a spokesman for the opposition, about how to tackle the enormous costs associated with the purchase of medication and vaccine. The opposition advocated a school fee of a thousand kronor per child each semester, increased co-pays in the magnitude of five hundred kronor per doctor's visit and a thousand kronor for a visit to the emergency room or a specialist. The medication subsidies would also need to be reviewed and the rate for elderly housing adapted to the cost situation. No sacred cows. The minister spoke instead in terms of a more general tax increase and tougher, more progressive taxation so that low-income workers would not be affected too severely.

"Tamiflu and Tamivir and take that, damn it." Hartman's calm voice had acquired a sharp tone. Maria had never heard him so angry. "Why weren't we better prepared for this? How could this just happen? The bird flu didn't come like a lightning bolt from a clear sky. We've been forewarned for several years. When we hire people with our tax money to make decisions on such important questions and at such high salaries, you expect competence and responsibility. Clear directives for who should get medicine and in what order. It's a matter of saving lives."

"I read an article in a medical journal last night when I couldn't sleep. It was by Tobias Westberg. The past few years he's been promoting the idea that Sweden should start its own manufacture of vaccines along with the other Nordic countries. In the article he is admittedly pessimistic as far as profitability goes, but money isn't everything. It's about what kind of preparedness a society should have. If you're going to have resources to produce vaccine for the whole population in the event of a pandemic, this means a major over-capacity compared to what normally needs to be produced in flu season. If the project was started now it would take four or five years before a vaccine could be produced. Perhaps even longer than that."

"I read something about that. There were problems with cultivating a vaccine against bird flu."

"He wrote about that in the article. The virus is cultivated from fertilized chicken eggs. But the bird flu virus destroys the eggs so the vaccine virus can't grow there. Other methods are required and that's been an obstacle, besides the fact that the virus changes form constantly so that it can't be manufactured until it appears again. Just like ordinary flu virus changes character and the vaccine has to be customized every year. Tobias Westberg has visited production facilities all over the world. In Europe they're in Great Britain, France, Germany, Italy, Switzerland, and the Netherlands, and then there's a recently opened facility in Belarus. Listen, Tomas, last night I discussed how the bird flu broke out with Jonathan Eriksson. He said that a pigeon that came to Ruben Nilsson's pigeon loft was from Belarus and our man the painting salesman is from there too. Sergei Bykov worked with research animals. We have to find out whether he was infected with bird flu. Maybe he brought the infected bird with him. I know it's a crazy idea, but what if the company paid him to deliberately plant the pigeon here? They were sitting on an enormous warehouse of medicine and it doesn't keep indefinitely. A pandemic was required to make back the money."

"Damn it! I hope the medical examiners used protective gear when they were doing the autopsy. I'll check as soon as we get in. We probably never asked that question. What you're saying sounds a little crazy, of course. Even a little paranoid. It's hard to imagine that illness is being spread intentionally to make money."

"Are you so sure?" Maria asked in a slightly sulky tone. But Hartman had already dropped the subject.

"Tobias Westberg has still not been in touch with his wife, as far as I know. It would be very interesting to find out why he's hiding."

"People murder for money," said Maria, who felt a little offended that he so quickly rejected her line of thought. What if it really was the case that the pigeon was released so that a pandemic would break out and make a profit for a pharmaceutical company?

Maria Wern was about to go down to reception and meet Reine Hammar for questioning when she got a call.

"I think it's urgent," said Patricia in reception. "It's about the break-in at Vigoris Health Center that was never reported. We have a person who wants to remain anonymous. Can you take the call?"

"I'll take it now." Maria waited while the call was transferred. A faint voice with a Gotland accent presented her business.

"I want to be anonymous. Otherwise I can't tell you anything."

"It's okay, I'm listening."

"I clean at Vigoris Health Center and I start my work at ten o'clock so I won't be in the way when they're busy during the day. I clean all night. I can do what I want, as long as I do my assigned work. Tuesday evening I noticed that a window in the clinic was open. It was forced open. Then I heard a sound from one of the treatment rooms where patients are usually seen for vaccination. I didn't dare go in so instead I hid in the closet with the door cracked open a little. I heard a refrigerator door being opened inside the treatment room—it has a kind of smacking sound. Then I saw Sandra Hägg. Just for a moment. She had something in a white plastic bag in her hand and she ran toward the open window and crawled out, even though she has an access card. I didn't call the guard because it was Sandra, I thought she'd forgotten her code or something like that."

"Was she alone or did you see whether anyone was with her?"

"I didn't see anyone. But Lennie, her ex, came by right

after that on his first round. We usually have coffee together. I told him about it. It wasn't the first time she'd locked herself out. It was so romantic when Lennie and Sandra got together because she had locked herself in the laboratory."

"How did Lennie react to this?"

"He was already tired and irritated when he arrived. Mad at Finn Olsson, the security manager, they had met right before. He probably complained about something, said that Lennie wasn't doing his job or something. Once Finn left a window open on purpose in the laboratory to check whether Lennie really was paying attention, and Lennie missed it and Finn told Viktoria. Can you imagine what a scolding he got? He almost lost his job, and Finn was there standing behind the boss sneering when he got chewed out. That sort of thing sticks. They can't even be at the gym at the same time, because they compete so they can hardly stand up the next day. Once they even fought so hard that Reine had to intervene. It was supposed to be sparring, but then it got serious."

"What did Lennie say about you having seen Sandra?" asked Maria.

"He got mad and said I was lying, so I showed him the window. See for yourself then! I said to him and he shut up. But then he took hold of my coat and pushed me up against the wall. 'You won't say a word about this to anyone, do you understand? I'll bring it up with the boss myself. Not a word to Finn,' he said."

"Do you know whether he told Viktoria Hammar that Sandra had broken in? Perhaps it wasn't all that easy for him to accuse her, even if it was over between them?"

"I didn't hear any more about it. He must have said something about it; the window was damaged. A glazier came the next day. It couldn't be hidden. But now when she's dead . . . I've been thinking about this a lot. I don't know if I'm doing the right thing now, but I can remain anonymous, can't I?"

"You did the right thing," said Maria without making any promises, thinking at the same time that there can't be too many cleaning ladies at Vigoris who were working on the night in question. "If you think of anything else please contact me again. It was a good thing you told us about this."

Reine Hammar sat down self-consciously in the visitor's chair in front of Maria. There was antipathy in every movement.

"I really hope this conversation is necessary. I've been away from the clinic and locked up in that nuthouse in Follingbo. I'm sure you can imagine that I have a few things to do now that I'm back. It's not even really clear to me what this concerns. Am I suspected of something or what the hell is this about?"

"One of your employees, Sandra Hägg, was murdered. My job is to find out who did it, and why."

"This is truly frightful. Does that damn tape recorder have to be on?" he asked, with an arrogant expression that Maria found rather irritating.

"Preferably. Otherwise we'll have to rely on my faulty memory."

He gave her a guarded look and a shadow of a smile passed over his face. "Of two evils, always choose the lesser. Go ahead."

"What can you tell me about Sandra, what was she like as a nurse?"

"Dear Sandra," he said thoughtfully. "The perfect nurse. Always so friendly and always a step ahead. When you were about to ask her to do something, she'd usually already thought of it. The tray was set. The test samples produced.

The appointment scheduled. The referrals stamped and ready. It's going to be hard to replace her. It's always tough to teach someone new, then you have to do some thinking yourself."

"Personally . . . what did you know about what things were like at home?" Maria thought he appeared to lower his guard somewhat now, but she still waited with the most burning question until he had relaxed even more.

"Sandra was single. No children." He made a sound somewhere between a cough and a sob, and Maria had to ask him to repeat himself so that he would be heard on tape. "She had just ended a relationship with one of our other employees. Where relationships at work are concerned we have recently received guidelines from the corporate office. We prefer that employees not be personally involved in that way. In the future we're going to call the parties in for a talk if a romance arises at work and the persons in question will have to bear the consequences of their involvement."

"What do you mean by that?" Maria had a hard time concealing her surprise—and her indignation.

"There will have to be an agreement on who is most useful to the company and the other will have to resign. The work here is so important that we require complete loyalty. If you have a bond with a colleague there are dual loyalties."

"But you and Viktoria are married," Maria blurted out before she could stop herself. This was not a crucial point and the risk of ending up in a stalemate was imminent if she offered her own opinions.

"Which is just what Sandra pointed out when we called her and Lennie in for a discussion. Viktoria offered Sandra an exciting job in Montreal, but she refused and said that it wasn't necessary. They had already decided to separate. As far as Viktoria and I are concerned, this is more of a partnership than a marriage. Three minutes at the courthouse to avoid a lot of paperwork is time well spent. No, I'm joking. The company employs us both and they don't see our relationship as a risk, we've been married too long for it to be detrimental to production. Viktoria loves her work." He laughed crudely and tossed back his hair. "I'm sure you've heard of a social security marriage? No? It doesn't matter. Forget about that. Was there anything else, otherwise duty calls." He smiled at her and got halfway up.

"You've had a break-in at the clinic. But we haven't received a report about it. Would you like to explain why?"

"Where did you get that information?" He was suddenly more guarded. He sat back down. His eyes became narrow slits and his face came uncomfortably close. Maria stretched and tried not to shrink back.

"Sandra broke in," she said, and her voice was steady. "I assume you know that. What was she looking for, and why didn't you report it?" He rocked in his chair for a long time before answering. It was extremely irritating.

"The truth, you mean. Was what I said about Sandra's merits too beautiful? Why couldn't it be? You shouldn't speak badly of the dead. It's true that she was an excellent nurse, but the truth was that she was also a drug addict. We intended to send her to the company detox clinic in Montreal. Our twelve-step program has proven to be one of the most effective instruments available. It started with a colleague reporting that morphine ampoules were missing and that the withdrawal of morphine from the storeroom did not tally with what was prescribed for newly operated patients. We kept our eyes on her for a while and then held her accountable. She went along with detox, but the desire must have been stronger than reason and she broke in."

"Did she get anything?"

"We counted everything. She got some syringes and needles but no morphine."

"Does morphine for injection have to be refrigerated?"

"No, why do you ask? Who contacted the police and told about the break-in? I have the right to know, damn it! Lennie, is it him? I'm going to get to the bottom of this." The throat-clearing that followed almost made Maria hit the ceiling with suppressed annoyance. The way he sounded was completely unbelievable. Did he have a cold or was this some kind of tic triggered by nervousness?

"It's not Lennie and I'm not saying anything else. You can go now and if you think of anything else that may help us to understand what happened to Sandra then please call. Otherwise you should be prepared for some follow-up questions."

"You do realize that it was one of her doper friends who did it? Do we live in the same reality? Who do you think commits crimes? You ought to know that. She probably promised one of her buddies a little party and then there was nothing. Someone got upset and out of control, and well—what usually happens then? Why do you want to root in this dung? Can't we just remember Sandra as the capable nurse she was before she lost her grip?"

After Maria had followed Reine Hammar to the exit she picked up the phone and called Jonathan Eriksson. He sounded happy to hear her voice.

"I've been meaning to call you all morning. I've picked up the phone and hung it up again at least ten times. Cowardly. I'm not very good at this sort of thing. Wanted to say thanks. Maybe we can do it again sometime. Go out and eat, I mean. Soon. It's been ages since I had such a nice time."

"The same for me. How's Emil doing?"

"Much better. But he's starting to get a little restless. He doesn't have a fever anymore."

"Such a relief; I'm sorry for nagging. Listen, Jonathan, I have to ask you about something else. Is morphine for injection stored in a refrigerator?"

"No, it doesn't have to be refrigerated. Why do you ask?"

"I can't say. Is a vaccine the sort of thing that has to be stored cold?"

The cleaning lady had talked about the sound of a refrigerator door in the room where they usually saw patients for vaccination. Then she had seen Sandra come out with a white plastic bag in her hand.

"Yes, flu vaccine has to be refrigerated. When will you have time to see me again? The correct answer is NOW, at once. I've been thinking about something, but I want to bring it up face-to-face."

"That sounds rather intimate." Maria noticed that she got giggly and tried to pull herself together.

"Don't get your hopes up, this is about work," he said, but there was laughter right below the seriousness. "I was thinking about picking up Malte this evening about five. But Marianne has let them built a fort in a closet and the kids want to sleep there. Well, if that's okay with you, that is. And because both of us would be child-free I thought it might be nice to go out and have a nice dinner. This evening, if you don't think that's too soon?" He was talking very fast at the end and Maria could not help smiling at his obvious nervousness.

"I think that sounds perfect."

Maria returned to the pile of mail she had been sorting when she got the call from the cleaning lady. The response from the National Board of Forensic Medicine to the question of whether there were drugs in Sandra Hägg's blood ought to be there. Maria browsed further and found the envelope.

She opened it and read. It was as she suspected. Sandra was clean—no traces of alcohol or narcotics.

Chapter 32

When Maria agreed to meet Jonathan Eriksson after work, she had not yet received the call from Nordkalk, the limestone plant in Kappelshamn, a call that would change all her plans for the day and etch itself firmly in her memory for the rest of her life. A body had been found in the limestone quarry in the crater where quicklime was dumped.

Barely forty minutes later she was outside the office of Nordkalk along with Tomas Hartman. The sound from the crusher and the wind coming in from the sea almost drowned out their voices. Down in the harbor, a vessel was being loaded. A fine layer of lime dust lay over the whole area like powdery snow. Despite the rain, the roses in the flowerbeds were unnaturally pale in color. The gray trunks of the trees appeared to be cast in cement. Conveyor belts wound high above the ground between the big silo buildings. Maria followed their path with her eyes over toward the gigantic piles of limestone. She estimated them to be almost twenty meters high. The site engineer, Karl Nilsson, with whom Maria had spoken on the phone, drove her in his Jeep. Hartman followed up into the quarry on roads that passed between cliff edges and shimmering green lakes, edged by pine seedlings in a strange, barren but beautiful lunar landscape, up a steep hill where the white turbines of the wind farm creaked in the breeze. He pointed out the production ponds for steelhead and sea trout and the breeding ground for several species of wild birds. The sun was wrapped in fog and the light reflected in the white stone was magnificent, almost supernatural, like the transfigured light on an altar painting. Maria asked a few general questions about the lime quarry and was told that limestone is used in steelworks and sugar refineries, and that exports were currently three million tons per year. They talked about the risk of silicosis and Karl said that recent studies showed that the risk was nonexistent where lime dust in particular was concerned. It felt safer to stick to more-or-less neutral subjects before they reached the place where the body parts had been found.

The technicians were already there and a barricade had been set up. They stood at the edge of the dump talking to Sven-Åke Svensson, the employee who had made the macabre find. He showed them the pieces of bone, the cranium and the jaw with teeth, of which one front tooth was gold. There was a buckle that had presumably been on a belt and a zipper.

"How long could the body have been here?" Maria's guess was five to ten years. The cranium lacked hair, and the clothing was gone.

"Twenty-four hours maybe. It rained last night. The process goes faster in damp weather. Textiles can almost self-ignite. A human body contains a lot of water. When you add water to quicklime a chemical process occurs with high heat production. A full day, maybe two—max. This lime powder is like quicksand, it consumes everything, except noble metals and diamonds. Do you see how clean it is in those light bands of half-slaked lime? Compare that with the gray bands where the lime is slaked. No chemical process is going on. People dump their garbage illegally and it stays there."

Maria went closer to the edge of the crater and saw the congealed lime porridge at the bottom that turned into a whiter streak, like an inviting sandpit on the beach at Tofta. Deceptive and dangerous, a short distance from the emerald-green water. When Maria asked about the color, Karl Nilsson explained it got its special hue from the layers of limestone.

"I came here just over an hour ago to dump quicklime from the furnace, we do that once a week." Sven-Åke took off his helmet and dried the sweat from his forehead. Maria saw how he swallowed a few times before his voice steadied and he could continue. "I saw something sparkle and got out of the dumper to see what it was." He paused again to be able to continue his story without his voice giving way. "It was a jaw with a gold tooth. I called the production manager at once and got a protective suit here so that I could go out and bring in what I saw. At first you don't believe it's true. I feel better now that you two have seen the same thing. It's so unreal."

"And yet it was lucky that you discovered it," said the site engineer. "That was observant of you—in a couple of days we wouldn't have seen anything at all. If the body had ended up in the sedimentation plant for wash-water that gets emptied every three years that would have been it. Or if it had been dropped in the crusher. It's not certain it would have been discovered in loading and the parts might have been shipped to Poland and Germany and Lithuania." He grimaced when he realized what he'd just said.

"Whoever dumped the body must have had a car, but

the area is cordoned off with gates at night, right?" Hartman noticed that the road out was cordoned off when they passed the big piles of stone. "And if a strange car passed in the daytime, you would have seen that, I assume?"

"Absolutely. We don't allow anyone up here without an escort from our cars with blinking warning lights. But it's possible to approach from the other direction." The site engineer pointed toward the forest ahead of them. "We don't have permission to close off Takstensvägen to traffic. The people who live there have to get out, but that also entails a risk. This isn't exactly a playground."

"How many people work here at night?" Maria asked. The wind was cold and she felt her fingers starting to get numb, even though she tried to pull them into the sleeves of her sweater. Her hair was billowing and she pushed it away from her face.

"The mine and the dumps are closed at ten o'clock. The lime furnace is manned night and day, and we usually have two men loading out to the vessels. It was the same last night. This morning a ship departed for Poland."

"Did anyone notice anything unusual during the shift last night or the night before? A strange car?"

"Sune Pettersson, who was loading down in the harbor, found a wallet when he got off work. He was going to turn it in to the police when he got up today, he said. It was right inside the gate. He saw it as he was driving out of the parking lot. A brown wallet. There was a driver's license in it so it shouldn't be hard to find the owner. He also says that there was a light-colored car in the parking lot right after midnight and they saw a man walking down to the wharf. Then he and the car just disappeared when they went to check on what business he had."

Hartman got into his Ford and made a few notes before he called the patrol that was en route from Visby, the same patrol that had served the past two nights in the harbor. With any luck they had noticed something they hadn't reported. What was most pressing right now was to go door-to-door along Takstensvägen to ask about cars that might have been observed during the night and possibly the night before.

"It must be Tobias Westberg who was found, don't you think? On the photo we got from his wife he has a gold tooth." Maria sat down next to Hartman, rubbing her ice-cold fingers. "What do you think? A crime of passion?"

"I have no great experience in that area. I can only recall one case and it happened without premeditation. During my thirty-five years in service I've never heard of a crime of passion that was planned. But that doesn't mean it can be ruled out. Usually the victim and murderer know each other. If we assume that the same person killed both Sandra and Tobias, where does that lead us?"

"Sandra's former live-in, Lennie, or Yrsa. Hans Moberg— although we don't know if he knew Tobias."

"Yrsa has to be informed. This will be tough. And the worst of all is that we don't know whether he was dead when he ended up in the lime quarry or whether he was alive when he was thrown in. We'll probably never know whether he was tied up. A plastic or hemp rope is probably destroyed in no time in such a process. I hope she doesn't think about that." Hartman started the car and turned on the heat when he saw Maria shivering.

"The painting salesman?" Maria nodded to the site engineer that they were ready to leave and he drove ahead of them down the hill. "We still have no motive whatsoever there." The thought of the painting salesman and the pigeon would not leave her alone.

"Evidently he was not infected with the bird flu, but he had antibodies in his blood. So he has had the disease, we have to assume. There is nothing that indicates he knew either Tobias or Sandra. But we'll have to ask his wife that. By the way, did you see the painting of his that Berit Hoas bought? He was a very skilled artist. It feels like the waves of the sea are rolling toward you and you can really feel the heat in the sand. Think if he'd had the opportunity to work on his art full time."

"You have a visitor, Maria." It was Veronika's voice from the reception desk on the intercom.

"Who is it?" Maria had just decided with Hartman that they would make an unscheduled visit to Lennie Hellström to ask where he was last night. A patrol car had just been to see Yrsa Westberg; it was a relief not to have had that conversation. Maria sent her colleagues a thought of gratitude.

"He says his name is Jonathan Eriksson, should I send him up?"

"I'll come down." Maria looked at the clock. Already six thirty. They had decided to meet at the parking lot at five. Was it possible he'd been waiting that long?

"I'm sorry, Jonathan. I couldn't get away. Can we meet in a few hours?"

"Sure, call me when you're done." She searched for irritation and disappointment in his face but he concealed it well. He was wearing a blue sweater and white shirt. It suited him. Maria drew her hand through her straggly hair, ravaged by the wind in Kappelshamn, and realized that she was hardly looking her best. As if that mattered.

He's married, he's married, he's married, and you have to stop acting like a teenager, she said to herself, biting her lower lip. But when she felt his eyes on her back she could not keep from turning around and giving him a quick hug before he left.

On the way out to the car Hartman said, "Wasn't that Malte's dad, the doctor? Are you one of his patients now?"

"Oh, it was nothing, I just wanted to ask him about Emil."

"I see," he said, sounding a little disappointed. "By the way, do you know who the wallet found at the limestone quarry belongs to?"

"Anyone we know?" Maria was torn away from her self-accusations, her curiosity aroused. "Who?"

"Does the name Hans Moberg ring a bell?" Hartman was smiling like a fox. "We'll be bringing him in soon now."

Chapter 33

Ever since being surprised by Cecilia's neighbor, Hans Moberg no longer felt relaxed in the house. When he checked his email account linked to his sales activity on the Internet and saw that the police were trying to contact him, he felt even more harried. The police requested he immediately make contact with Detective Inspector Maria Wern. The matter was extremely urgent.

The message was written in a cordial tone. Not as stern as you might expect from the authorities. Even so, the request made his stomach turn. If only he had someone to consult, someone he could trust. It was not likely the police knew where he was, unless they'd gotten a tip from the Skåne woman, of course. She was the only one he had emailed from the dial-up connection where he was now. If they were using her as a tool, they would soon be here. No, they would have already come during the night. But if they were working office hours and didn't have time for criminals except between eight and five they might be here at any moment.

The more Moby thought about it, the likelier it seemed. He had to leave. Now. To anywhere. The tension was making him shake. Thoughts were whirling, but he was unable to collect them into a decision on where to go. His heart was squeezed in his chest and his mouth was completely dry. He opened a can of beer. That was just what he needed to be human again. Now his brain was starting to function. There was something in alcohol that makes the blood flow more easily, he had read, and it must be true. Oxygen flow improved and thoughts were released from their cramped prison of conventions and acquired a lower density.

Of course they had the camper's registration number on the windshield of every police car, so Moby moved the most important things over to Cecilia's rusty Saab and kissed the instrument panel when he saw that the gas tank was full. In the cellar pantry he found a couple of cans of Bullen's beer sausage, pickles, and applesauce. That would do.

He gathered up the underwear he had meant to wash and hung them over the edge of the tub in Cecilia's bathroom. While waiting for inspiration, he looked at himself in the mirror, and made a hasty decision. In a container on the sink he found an electric razor, which Cecilia presumably used for her legs—he hoped she only used it for her legs. With it he shaved off the last of his long hair and his beard. It fell down into the sink. He looked at himself. The change was not to his advantage. A big, ugly scar on the top of his head came to light and he seemed to shrivel up even more and became insignificant and gray and almost a little stoop-shouldered when his hair no longer reached his shoulders. His hair had actually been his pride. But for the moment it was an advantage to be insignificant. He put on his hat again and felt a bit more like himself, swept the hair and beard into a plastic bag and buried it in the garden. The neighbor lady waved from her window, but he pretended not to see her. Confounded curious person, that one, he thought, getting into the Saab.

By Lärbo he had already finished his last beer and then

searched frantically for the wallet to buy more. Hell and damnation, it was gone. The thought of how he would manage without money chafed at his brain and finally he could not keep from sampling some of the Absolut vodka he had meant to save until he found a new place to camp. Life is hell, you know, but it still must go on, he said to himself in the rearview mirror, turning onto Highway 148 toward Visby.

An idea began to take shape. Presumably his buddy Mayonnaise was still in Tofta. There was food, beer, and the possibility to surf the Internet, and with any luck there was a tent flysheet to curl up in in Cecilia's car after the onset of darkness. He didn't dare phone Mayonnaise, the best thing was to simply show up. The thought of company made him exhilarated after the days of solitude. Actually it was a stroke of genius to return to Tofta in a new guise, contrary to logic. There he would be safe for a while.

In pure joy at having thought of a solution, Moby took a swig of vodka and turned on the radio to listen to a little music. It was a Stone Age model with cassette player, but it worked reasonably well, even though it crackled a bit.

" . . . We haven't been given any directives on where we should dispose of the hen cadavers. Normally when infection is feared, they go to a destruction facility on the mainland, but in the present situation no one wants to take on the transport and the mountain of animal bodies is growing. Since an employee became infected, no one is willing to deal with it.

"If you've just joined us we want to say that we have county veterinarian Håkan Broberg with us in Studio X. After the decision that all poultry on the island should be destroyed, we now face the problem of where to dispose of the cadavers. Wouldn't it have been better to wait to kill the birds until there was a solution to that problem? Wouldn't it be better to have an incineration facility on site than to transport the cadavers, with the risks that transport involves? As I've understood it, the veterinarians in the county are very worried because there are no clear directives."

Hans Moberg moaned out loud. If everything had been as usual and the police weren't after him, he could have done amazing business this week. The demand for medication was enormous. Calling the pills Tamivir instead of Tamiflu didn't really matter, it was all the same. Faith works wonders. In a way he could actually see his work as a mission. A charitable deed with a good profit margin.

The placebo effect cannot be denied or disdained. If people truly believe in the medicine you give them, the body's own healing powers are mobilized. Stress is reduced. Immune defenses improve. Healing sleep comes as a result of reduced stress. During sleep the body repairs its damaged cells, seeks out and destroys cancer cells, and lets the hormones flow and produce well-being when soul and body work together. He had read somewhere that the placebo effect could be almost twenty-five percent effective. The opposite, the so-called nocebo effect, appeared if the patient did not believe in the doctor and did not feel treated with respect and courtesy. It should be punishable to treat people without showing goodwill. If a sugar pill with the help of the placebo effect is twenty-five percent effective, it must be seen as potent anyway. People need hope in times of terror and fright.

Moby leaned his head against the neck support and tried to relax. He was not an evil person; his intentions were good, considered, and scientifically validated.

The radio discussion on poultry disturbed his thoughts and he changed stations.

". . . a body has been found at the limestone quarry in Kappelshamn. The police have not released many details about the discovery. This morning an employee at the quarry found parts of a body in quicklime. The remains are of human origin. The police are very anxious to get information about a man who was very likely at the scene the night of July 5 or 6. The man is about 170 centimeters tall, burly, and when last seen had long, light hair and long sideburns or beard. His voice is described as soft. He travels in a white Chevrolet van with a Polar brand camper."

Hans Moberg felt his hands starting to shake on the steering wheel. The road ahead of him suddenly seemed unreal, like in a video game with cheap graphics. Oncoming cars came too close, the edge of the road swept in under the car and despite the straight stretch he thought the car was pulling seriously to the right. He slowed down and stopped. The bottle of vodka was beside him on the seat and he took a generous swig to clear his brain. He opened the car door to cool down. The heat in the car was on and there did not seem to be any way to turn it off. The windshield wipers were moving out of control like frightened birds across the front window. Were the cops on his trail now? The decision to leave Kappelshamn still seemed sensible and the idea of continuing to the Tofta campground was reasonable too, so he really could not say what made him so paralyzed right now. A vague nausea, a peculiar shakiness in his body. He took another swig of vodka and continued his drive into Visby.

In the rearview mirror he could see a dark car approach at high speed and then stay right behind him. It was not a marked police car but there was something strange about it. Plainclothes cops? Pass already, damn it! He braked but the car stayed behind him and increased the distance between them somewhat. It was irritating. When they reached Visby the car was still there and followed him through Öster Centrum, where he almost ran over an elderly woman with a walker. What an old hag, people like her ought to be locked up, damn it. In the rearview mirror he saw her fall and then be helped up by other pedestrians. The progress of the black car was blocked and it remained stopped at the crosswalk. Hans Moberg fumbled for the plastic bottle of vodka and found it. He brought it to his lips and discovered that it was empty. Hadn't he put the screw-top on properly? The road ahead of him was an obstacle course and soon the black car would catch up. A roundabout came toward him without warning and he was forced to drive right through it and out between the cars in the line from the ferry. If he wasn't such a skillful driver they would have rammed him, fucking nitwits. The road narrowed and the crowns of the trees dragged over the hood of the car. A car was coming right at him on the wrong side and he swerved and managed to get past it on the left side by driving down onto the grass and up again. Fucking idiots! On the road through Vibble and past Tofta Church the traffic was lighter. You really ought to lie in ambush and shoot the heads off those bastards. Several times he had to remind himself where he was going. The approach to the campground should be here somewhere. There were some campers set up in a field and there was the grocery store. Why wasn't there a clear marker of where you should drive in? If he got hold of the idiot who was responsible for the signage they could fetch his ugly head in the trunk later.

All too suddenly, at far too high a speed, Hans Moberg realized he was about to miss the approach and turned the steering wheel sharply. A red car was coming toward him. He saw it during the fraction of a second before the crash smashed the world into smithereens. I'm dying, was Hans Moberg's last conscious thought.

When he woke up he saw a steel-gray sky between all the faces leaning over him. The sound of sirens came and went in waves. Someone was touching his shoulder, asking how he felt, but he was unable to answer. Sirens; were the police on their way? How the hell would he get himself out of this? They would ask him who he was and then he was screwed. Really, totally screwed. Unless he did what that pianist who lost his memory did. How long did he get by?—six months or several months anyway before the truth came out.

"Does it hurt?" asked a woman in a white coat. He stared at her and made an indefinable gesture with his head. Neither yes nor no—best not to even understand body language. "Can you move your arms and legs? Can you try to raise your left leg now?" He stared into her beautiful blue eyes. The mouth was so soft and inviting in shape. It was almost superhuman not to kiss her when she was so close, so accessible, and her voice so friendly. He raised his head a little. Oh, dagnabbit, how his back hurt. He fell back and closed his eyes. "What's your name?" she asked.

Hans Moberg mumbled a string of consonants and looked perplexed. He didn't really know if you had a language when you lost your memory or if that went away too.

"Is there anyone here who knows who he is?" a male voice asked. Moby turned his head a little and saw that it was a uniformed policeman. Now it was crucial to play his cards right.

"That's my buddy. I said it was Moby, although he's cut off his hair. How ya doin', Moby?" Mayonnaise's face came very close as he crouched down.

"What's his name, did you say?" The policeman was there again, leaning over to hear better.

"Hans Moberg," Mayonnaise said helpfully. "Listen, that's not a good-looking haircut. What's the name of your stylist? I'd stay away from him in the future, if I were you."

Chapter 34

Maria was back from questioning Lennie Hellström and was on her way out again when her colleagues informed her that Hans Moberg had been arrested at the Tofta campground. Unfortunately he was in no shape for interrogation. He was probably just blind drunk, but to be on the safe side he would be seen by a doctor to rule out a concussion or injury to any vital organs. Maria breathed a sigh of relief and told reception that she was gone for the day. The questioning of Lennie Hellström had tried her patience. He was touchy and arrogant, and Maria was grateful that she did not have to meet with him privately. He had been at work the past two nights and could show a personalized time schedule. There was no way he could have managed the forty kilometers to Kappelshamn and back between any of his guard rounds, as long as he had followed the schedule. Finn, the security manager at Vigoris Health Center, had been asked to come in with a list of the times when Lennie used his access card.

"He's going to mess with me if he gets a chance, just to get me locked up," Lennie shouted after them in the stairwell. For the time being Hartman assigned a trainee to follow up on the matter.

Jonathan was holding an umbrella, waiting for her at the entrance to the police headquarters. She struggled to keep up with his long strides, but she didn't dare hold onto his arm. It would seem too intimate, and perhaps embarrass him if they were to see anyone. They spent some time discussing where to eat and decided to walk down to Strandgatan. Jonathan argued that the restaurant Lindgården had the best food, but Maria did not want to go there with him. Lindgården had too many memories—it was there she'd spent one magical evening with Per Arvidsson, and where he asked her what her dreams were for her life. The underlying question had been: Do you want to share them with me? But Maria started digging in her handbag to avoid answering his question, and then laughed it off. What did it help to regret it later? What was done was done and that moment never came back, but the memories were there, out in the enchanted garden under the lanterns. It felt wrong somehow to go there with someone else.

"Then there's Burmeister, Dubbe, or that medieval bar, Clematis. I hope we'll get in. They have a rule about two meters between tables and one group per table, so it fills up pretty fast."

They passed the outdoor torches at Clematis and saw the nose of a stuffed wild boar. On the walls, torches were glowing and a big fire was lit in the cellar room. Jonathan told her that the restaurant was located in an old storehouse from the thirteenth century.

"There was a ghost here named Hertvig. He was slain by his own brother when he was twenty-one years old. His wife's name was Maria, like you; she died in childbirth in 1383. I sat here one evening by the fire and heard his story. His message to the people of today was: don't get accustomed to evil, act while there's still time. And he was very worried that even in our time there are rich and poor."

"Why did he have to stay on earth as a ghost?" Maria asked when they were shown to the table closest to the hearth. A fire felt nice. The evening was raw and cold.

"Who knows—maybe to learn to forgive. It can't be easy to reconcile with a brother who has literally stabbed you in the back. It may take seven hundred years or so."

They ordered a jug of wine and a medieval plate consisting of bread, apples, nuts, candied rose petals, smoked leg of mutton, sausage, cheese, browned cabbage, lamb cutlets, spareribs, and pear toffee. They were just about to dig in with their fingers when a jester opened the door wide and declared in a loud voice:

"A shadow settled over the people when the trombone sounded over the city in the year of the plague 1351. Inner shivering and heat, drooping eyes and vertigo, unquenchable thirst and shortness of breath afflicted you, you haughty city. But that was not enough. Black boils that sprouted like goose eggs in your armpits, jaws, and groin. Your speech became muddled, your gait staggering, but there were yet more pestilences to behold. Blood shooting from your lungs, blood in your excrement and urine. So did the plague afflict you when the dragon, the devil, was unleashed upon the earth. *Circulus vitiosus*; the terror unleashed madness, madness increased the terror. But did you pay heed? I see through walls, through walls of stone your slimy way of life, how you measure with crooked yardsticks and weigh with false scales. Woe unto thee, thou impenitent city, when I fetch thy soul for examination. Woe unto thee on the Day of Judgment when you shall be weighed on my scale and your debauchery shall be apparent. For evil still breeds in your alleyways, it still flies on dark wings and spreads its infected droppings among

your proud cloisters and rich men's houses, and its beak
will not leave you without sores . . ."

"That's enough now, Christoffer, come and have a beer
with us instead." Maria took hold of his cap with bells and
pulled his face to hers. "Stop! I said. You're horrible."

"I know. My friends call me the Plague." He guardedly
greeted Jonathan. "And who is this pale creature you've tak-
en pity on? He looks like he's been sitting with his nose in
a parchment scroll since the time of Magnus Ladulås. I'll
make a bet that his manliness is no more impressive than an
angle worm." Christoffer demonstrated with his little finger
in front of Jonathan's nose. "I know you have a good heart,
Maria, but one cannot constantly practice charity, sometimes one must divert oneself. If you will accompany me to
my humble room I shall make you the happiest woman in
Visby. No, don't thank me. The pleasure will be all mine."

"Who the hell is this?" said Jonathan with consternation,
as the color rose in his face. "Do you have anything against
my giving him a smack on the jaw?"

"Give him a smack on the jaw, he deserves it. How are
things with Mona and Olov?" Maria asked in a friendly
conversational tone, and Christoffer sat on her lap unself-
consciously and helped himself from her plate. He was not
very tall and with his overly long shirtsleeves and fool's cap
with bells he looked like a baby in Maria's arms.

He continued talking with half a lamb cutlet sticking
out of his mouth. Jonathan looked like the god of thunder
himself, but they ignored him.

"Mona is so happy with Henrik and that makes me a
little jealous. I don't get the love I deserve even from my
mother."

"You compensate in other areas, don't you?" Maria
laughed. "Anything new in town? Police officers are always
curious about what's going on."

Christoffer suddenly became serious.

"When the Black Death was raging they looked for scape-goats. It was the Jews' fault—it was said they poisoned wells. History repeats itself. Two restaurants had their windows broken this evening. As soon as it got dark a gang in black cowls came with cudgels and attacked restaurants and food stores owned by immigrants. They're out of their minds. The rumor says that the infection came from an immigrant who was found dead in Värsände and that the restaurants are buy-ing infected poultry from their home countries. There's an uproar in the alleys. I took a punch when I was passing by and asked what was going on, and even more punches when I got hold of a garden hose and sprayed water on them. I was being too kind. If it had been boiling oil there wouldn't have been as much fussing afterward."

"What are you saying? Did this really happen or only in your sick brain, Christoffer?" Maria took hold of his arm.

"I swear by both my balls and my mother's sacred em-broidered cross-stitch pillows that it's the truth. I was just talking with a newspaper reporter. He said they've received a stack of really sick letters to the editor the past few days. That is, nothing you'd want on the breakfast table if you want to eat in peace and quiet."

"What do they say?" Maria suddenly felt completely sober.

"That immigrants are making money under the table and buying their way ahead in line to get medicine and that the infection is going to go on as long as we allow them inside our borders. Plus proposals for measures of a bloodier type, a variety of medieval methods of torture."

"But that's terrible." Jonathan got up. "The risk is that more people will be injured and die in riots than from the disease itself. I can't just sit here and eat; I have to go see what's happening. But why don't you stay and ex-change memories?"

"Jonathan, wait, we have to pay." Maria considered herself invited to dinner and made a quick calculation, would the money in her wallet be enough? What got into him?

"Payment? A worldly matter for such a great duke as the Pale One. Maria, don't tell me you've become attached to this character. He looks so boring. Take me instead, or Olov, or enter a convent. Anything at all would be better than having to look at that maggot naked."

"I'll think about it." Maria summoned the waitress. Jonathan was already outside and by the time she had paid he was out of sight. Maria felt deeply worried by what Christoffer had said. Smoke was visible in the distance and the sound of sirens cut through the town. Maria glimpsed Jonathan far ahead and she had to run to catch up with him. One of the low buildings on Norra Kyrkogatan was completely on fire. The fire department was on the scene.

"What's going on?" Jonathan asked a man standing in the circle of onlookers.

"They're infected. Their child was at the soccer camp. The whole family is probably infected. Men in black cowls came and set fire to their house. I don't know where they went. When the police and fire department came they disappeared into the crowd. They said they were going to purify the area. You have to take matters in your own hands when the authorities don't act!"

"What are you saying?" Maria felt herself feeling really afraid. One of Emil's friends, Andrei, lived in the house.

"I'm a doctor, is there anything I can do?" Jonathan turned to one of the firemen.

"No, just keep out of the way so the vehicles can get through."

They finally caught a glimpse of the boy and his parents disappearing in an ambulance to the hospital. They had probably inhaled smoke.

"Well, what do we do now? This evening didn't turn out quite like I'd hoped." Jonathan put his arm around Maria and helped her past the agitated crowd. "It all feels like a bad dream. So unreal." They passed a store where all the windows were broken and the owner was trying to cover the gaping holes with cardboard. The street in front of the building was full of glass.

"Like a nightmare you just want to wake up from. Are people completely out of their minds? I mean, they could just as well have set fire to our house in Klinte."

"Yes, it's like a bad dream. Today alone I've talked with four doctors who were threatened because they couldn't prescribe Tamivir until the priority arrangements are ready and the pharmacies accept their prescriptions. Everyone in my family has called asking about medicine—I've never felt so liked! Everyone wants medicine. Damn it, I'm tired and mad! It would have felt good to thrash your buddy, by the way, but not really fair since he's so short."

"Forgive me, Jonathan. I haven't seen Christoffer in a long time and I was just happy to see him again."

"Were you ever, I mean . . . did you . . . ?"

"Been in a relationship with Christoffer?" Maria laughed out loud. "That's not possible. Christoffer doesn't have relationships, he loves all women fairly and exactly the same, and by that I mean all."

Maria was to catch a ride home with Hartman and he had promised to call her when he was ready to go. She and Jonathan wandered through the narrow streets up toward the main square looking at the destruction. Broken windows in a store that sold specialty foods from Italy and in a shop whose owner was from Iraq—Maria had been in there to buy olives not long ago. With a shiver she was reminded of Kristallnacht. The rain had stopped and the moon was shining brightly, reflected in the thousands of glass shards.

They talked about what they were seeing and what it might mean for the immediate future, before the conversation turned to the bird flu and Jonathan's work situation.

"One of the biggest problems right now is getting hold of personnel who are willing to work with those who are ill. Fewer and fewer people are coming to work. Although this morning something happened that was rather moving. A retired nurse in her nineties suddenly appeared in my office, reporting for duty. She had the Spanish flu as an infant and survived. I'm not afraid, she said. Evidently I'm not infected; I'm immune. And if I were to pick up a bug I'll be dying soon anyway. I can be with the children and talk with them. I'm not good for much more than that. But I'm not afraid of death and not afraid to answer their questions. I've done it before."

"Amazing! She has a mission to fulfill. There was something you wanted to talk about with me, Jonathan, and . . . well, you'll have to try to forgive Christoffer. He's into live-action role play and has a hard time separating that from reality. It more or less takes over when he's been at camp. He doesn't mean any harm."

"Apparently he has a complex about his earthworm. What an insult! Do you want to go get a drink somewhere?" Jonathan looked at his watch; it was just past eight. They decided on a nightcap and a saffron pancake at the Monk's Cellar. It was almost empty. People were probably afraid to go out. They chose a table for two close to the window facing Lilla Torggränd.

"There was something you wanted to tell me," said Maria, sipping her Calvados. The saffron pancake, served with whipped cream and mulberry jam, was not bad.

"Yes, there's something that struck me when I studied how the infection spread in the beginning. Everyone who was in the same taxi as the infected driver got sick. Every-

289

one except Reine Hammar. He also went home with Maria Berg and she died later. Once I'd realized that I couldn't keep from finding out why. There was a test tube with blood from Reine that had not yet been sent for analysis. It must have been left behind in the refrigerator. I asked the lab to analyze whether he had antibodies against the virus. Don't know why I thought that, because it seemed pretty far-fetched."

"But he did, right?" Maria held her glass, waiting for an answer.

"Yes, and I can't help wondering how that was possible."

"What do you think?" asked Maria, leaning forward to hear his reply. He kissed her quickly on the cheek and gave her a provocative smile as she looked at him with a serious frown.

"There are two alternatives: either he's had the disease or else he was already vaccinated when he was exposed."

"The strange thing is that the painting salesman also had antibodies," said Maria. "What do you think that means?"

Chapter 35

At 4:23 a.m. a hard thud on the steps woke Maria, followed by a series of similar bouncing sounds, although a little quieter. Hartman's cat. She tried to shoo it away, but it meowed insistently and stubbornly. Maria got hold of it in the darkness and carried it downstairs and closed the door. Then she fell into a superficial slumber where she was searching for Emil in a big building with endless corridors. The empty rooms echoed. He was nowhere to be found. At one point she caught a glimpse of him through a window, he waved, on his way to school . . . on his way to eternity. His smile made her cry. I'm going to be with Zebastian today.

When the alarm clock went off an hour later she had forgotten the cat. Quickly she threw her legs over the side of the bed so as not to fall back asleep, and stepped on something soft and damp. When she turned on the light she could see it was a dead seagull. The head was bitten off and its feathers were ruffled and bloody. Her scream woke Linda, who started crying, and Hartman came rushing up in just his pajamas to see what was going on.

"It must have been the cat, he was up here last night." Maria picked feathers from the bloody sole of her foot. She

291

vaguely recalled the recommendations of the past few weeks to contact the county veterinarian if dead birds were found.

Still in that unsettled mood, Maria arrived at the station at eight o'clock to question Hans Moberg—he too a strange bird who had been handled roughly by life, she thought when she saw his deplorable appearance.

Moberg was sitting on one side of the table with a court-appointed attorney, Maria and Hartman on the other side. His close-sitting eyes could barely tolerate the daylight. He obviously had difficulty keeping them open without tears running out. His clothes were dirty and wrinkled, and he smelled awful. Maria lowered the blind and nodded at Hartman to turn on the tape recorder. After a few introductory questions Maria intended to lead the conversation to the night of the murder but was interrupted.

"It's not illegal to sell medications on the Internet. Just pick up the phone and check! I'm clean. And if anyone says they've gotten sick from my immune-defense elixir, Teriak, they're lying. I make it myself and I know what's in it. Only organically grown nutrients: aloe vera, mint, red clover, cornflower, and marigold combined with black currant leaves in sesame oil. Can't get any more wholesome than that. If someone complained because it's too expensive it's because they don't understand how much time it takes to pick flowers and dry them. Can I go now? I feel so enclosed here; I suffer from claustrophobia. My doctor says that I can have heart palpitations from getting agitated like this and that it affects my blood pressure and my cortisol and cholesterol values negatively. I could die from a heart attack. Do you want to risk that?"

"It's not your sales activity we want to talk about, I think you realize that. To start with you were demonstrably driving under the influence yesterday. The breath test showed .334 grams of alcohol per 210 liters of breath, which corresponds to 3.6 per mille if we're going to talk health risks. But there's not much to discuss there either right now. The question I want to ask you is: How did you know Sandra Hägg?"

"I meet so many women, it's impossible for me to remember—"

"You must have read in the newspaper that she was murdered. That can hardly have escaped you. According to witnesses you were outside her door the night of the murder. Why were you there?"

"I don't know what you're talking about." Moby squirmed and blinked his eyes. "Can I get something to relax? I don't feel good, damn it. I can't concentrate. I feel sick and there's a whistling in my ears all the time, the sound comes and goes. This is just terrible. You don't think that I . . ." Hans Moberg stole a glance at his attorney to get support. But the attorney's face was blank.

"Let's put it like this," Hartman interjected. "You are on very, very thin ice. The only thing that can improve your situation is the truth."

"I don't remember much of anything. I was drunk off my ass when I went there. Yeah, I guess it doesn't matter if I say that," he said with a look at his lawyer. "One time or several, that doesn't really make any difference. All you can do is go to jail. I got an email that this woman wanted to see me. She must have found me on the Internet and wanted to know where I got my wares from. I said I would come and present my assortment. She said she had the key to the door on a cord on the inside and I should let myself in because she was sick with a migraine. I was so damned drunk. She was warm when I touched her. I don't know if she was asleep or if she was dead. There was a carafe of wine. I may have drunk that. Don't remember. I think I fell asleep alongside her and when I woke up I realized she wasn't alive. All of her furniture was smashed. I may have done it, but I don't remember." Moby perceived a cautious headshake from his attorney and fell silent.

"Did you kill Sandra Hägg?" Maria kept up the pressure.

Moby's answer was barely audible. He lowered his head and the scar on his bare head became visible. "I think I may have done it, but I don't remember. It's awful, but it just goes black. It's so horrible. I can't remember doing it, but how did it happen otherwise?"

"Did you see anyone else in the stairwell that evening?"

"When I arrived I saw two children under the stairs and I thought they must have run away from home. They had a big plastic bag of peppermint candy. I pretended not to see them. It was like they had a secret camp there, they had put up a sheet. Then there was an older man, I think he lived on the floor below, and a white-haired woman on the same floor. Don't tell me you found my wallet at the limestone quarry in Kappelshamn, too?" The attorney's face underwent a transformation from calm dissociation to outright dismay.

"Did you lose it there?" asked Hartman.

"It was stolen from my car. I have to get it back."

"What were you doing at the limestone quarry?"

"I'd arranged a date with a woman in the harbor area. I got out of the car for a short walk, but she wasn't there. I don't even know what her name is. I've only met her once."

"You've met her, but you don't know her name? That sounds a little peculiar. How did you meet?" Maria gave Hartman a look. She sensed that he was quite satisfied with the interrogation.

"She calls herself Cuddly Skåne Girl on the net. But I don't know what her real name is. You can check my computer and see what her IP number is."

"We've done that and we have a number and address. Is

there anything you want to add before we speak with her?"

"Tell her I miss her. There was something special about her. I mean if she has time to visit a poor man in his prison cell—it would be a good deed."

"Do you understand how serious this is? I get the feeling you don't really understand what this is about. Two people are dead and you were demonstrably in the vicinity when the murders happened. Did you kill them?" Hartman pulled out a chair and sat down right across from Hans Moberg.

"No, damn it, no." Hans Moberg dried the sweat from his face. Maria had been watching for some time how it collected and ran over his cheeks and nose. His shirt had large dark stains under the arms. He was shaking and twitching in his seat, and he was constantly wringing his hands and setting them on his lap.

"How much had you been drinking when you went to the limestone quarry?"

"No more than usual."

"How much is that?" asked Maria.

"A couple of beers and a quart of vodka maybe . . . I don't remember."

"How often do you drink so much that you get memory lapses?"

When Hans Moberg was led back under protest to the holding cell, they remained in the interview room. Maria opened the window and let in fresh air that smelled of the sea. Yesterday's rain had made its way slowly southward and a light fog concealed a blue sky. Next week would be sunny and warm, the meteorologists promised.

"What do you think, Tomas, is he guilty?"

"Presumably. But we have no motive other than pure madness and drunkenness. And the murder of Tobias seems planned. It doesn't tally with it happening unpremeditated. We'll have to speak with the district doctor so that Moberg gets help with his withdrawals. If we keep him, he should undergo a psychiatric examination. I questioned his buddy yesterday, Manfred Magnusson, nicknamed Mayonnaise. He told me that Hans Moberg checked into a mental hospital now and then for some unclear reason. He goes nuts, he said. He's the world's nicest buddy when he drinks moderately, but sometimes something takes over. Then he gets out of control."

"I know Mayonnaise from another context and I'm glad I didn't have to question him. What did the computer technician say about the email on Moberg's computer?" asked Maria.

"Sandra emailed Hans Moberg from her home computer and asked about his products. He answered her from Tofta campground. Then a reply email comes from Sandra. She tells him to come at once and to fish out the key from the mail slot because she has a migraine and can't get to the door."

"The key was on the floor in the hall with the piece of cord still attached and a bent paper clip. There was a little hole in the wood on the door right by the opening. I wondered about that when we saw the pictures. It would be possible of course to set the cord with the key there even from the outside. Purely theoretically, that is. He seems guilty. But I'd feel more confident if there was a comprehensible motive. Do you know whether IT has checked Elisabet Olsson's computer?"

"Cuddly Skåne Girl, is that what she calls herself on the Internet?" Hartman snorted and hid a smile behind his hand.

"What would you call yourself . . . Cuddly Martebo Boy? She ought to be here any moment now, I'll tell the receptionist to let us know when she arrives."

It's easy to acquire prejudices, even if you don't notice them until you're confronted with reality and must correct yourself. Cuddly Skåne Girl was wearing a navy blue suit and pumps and her red hair was cut short in a carefree style. Maria's image had been completely different. She'd imagined a round, giggly lady in a flowery dress and straw hat, with hobbies like knitting. Besides, her dialect indicated she was from Småland, not Skåne.

"You have to be careful with your identity on the Internet," she said. "You don't know what kind of nutcases are out there."

Maria offered coffee and Elisabet Olsson, Cuddly Skåne Girl, said yes to a cup, black with no sugar.

"I want you to tell us about your email contact with Hans Moberg, where and when you met or arranged a meeting."

Elisabet Olsson laughed and at that moment she was quite lovely. "Forgive me. I don't really know why I'm here."

"We want to ask you a few questions as a witness. You are not suspected of anything. How did you starting exchanging email with Hans Moberg?"

"I wanted to get some Tamiflu, my doctor refused to prescribe it even though I have asthma and I think I ought to be included in the risk group of people with heart and lung disease. I'd heard rumors that he had previously prescribed medicine to all the personnel in his brother's company. That really upset me. I Googled Tamiflu on the Internet and ended up on Doctor M's website. He shared my frustration and we became friends and more than that, you might say. We flirted a little and decided to meet in reality. At Tofta Campground—so there were other people around. It didn't feel that dangerous."

"What happened there?"

"He proved to be a fraud in many ways, but a charming one." Olsson recounted Moby's story of a deadly disease.

Oh yes, Maria nodded to herself. She knew the type.

"I told Finn, my brother, how Hans Moberg was dying from complications of his Strabismus; we had a good laugh."

"Finn?" Maria immediately thought of the security manager at Vigoris Health Center and her hunch proved to be correct.

"He's worked there since the beginning and presumably they can't manage without him. He's extremely meticulous and capable. His boss says that he has opportunities to advance to the head office in Montreal. I think he's very tempted by that. Although I would miss him. Who would service my computer if he was so far away?"

"Did you meet Hans Moberg on any later occasion?" Maria tried not to show how eager she was to get an answer to that question.

"No, I got an email that he was longing for me—it was barely legible, there were so many typos. I assumed he was drunk. I imagine he was trying to pick up ladies without much success, and happened to think of me when he didn't get any nibbles. No, I didn't reply to that. I don't think he's the man for me, if you know what I mean."

"Did you email him and ask him to meet you in the industrial harbor in Kappelshamn?" Maria asked the question, mostly to get it clearly on tape. She was fairly sure what the answer would be.

"No, why would I do that? Kappelshamn? Does Hans have anything to do with the murder up there? Is that why you're asking me about him? You know, I wondered when the police came yesterday to 'borrow' my computer for a couple of days."

"Does anyone other than your brother have access to your computer?"

"No."

"What about the password to your Hotmail address? Does anyone else know that?"

Chapter 36

Maria Wern glanced through her inbox. Most of it had to stay there without reply. The murder investigations had top priority. The articles by Tobias Westberg that Yrsa had faxed over that morning were about pharmaceutical companies. Maria skimmed through them and was especially struck by the reporting Tobias did from the city of Biaroza in Belarus. He had been there in the month of April and described the people and the surroundings in an engaging way. He clearly knew the language. While there he had interviewed a number of workers at the factory, including Sergei Bykov. It was the link that connected the three murders.

Maria rushed into Hartman's office with papers in hand, slamming them down on the desk in front of him so that the protocol he had just been reading flew across the floor.

"Check this out! There's a connection!"

With the help of an interpreter they reached Sergei's wife by phone. She confirmed that Tobias Westberg had met Sergei, but she could not recall that the journalist wanted anything in particular from him. They had gone to a bar and when Sergei came home he needed help getting into bed. It had been a pleasant evening and the vodka was flowing.

As far as she knew, Tobias and Sergei had mostly talked about everyday things. How far his salary went, compared to Sweden, the social safety net in Belarus, and future opportunities for the children. Sergei told Tobias about his work with research animals and Tobias asked about animal rights activists in Biaroza. But Sergei wasn't familiar with the concept. That was all she knew about the journalist's visit.

Maria summarized the last part of the article for Hartman. It was about the pharmaceutical companies' profits and was written in sharp terms. The more medications sold, the greater the profit. Tobias talked about speculation in fear. How the pharmaceutical industry uses politicians as obedient tools to draw attention to perceived threats that result in increased sales of precautionary medicine. The politician who promises the most medicine for the people wins.

In Belarus, a pharmaceutical company's campaign to sell bird flu vaccine had failed. The people didn't have enough money for drug purchases and the expected support from the outside world never materialized. Instead, a village was quarantined, the bird flu ran its course, and the drug manufacturer went bankrupt. The Demeter Group then bought up the supply of medicine and vaccine. For purely speculative purposes, Tobias thought. But it turned out to be a poor investment; the later outbreak of bird flu was a different type and the vaccine and medicine were ineffective.

Then he described how conditions had stiffened in the competition from companies on the open world market. Win or lose. Lower pay, longer work hours, shorter vacations, poorer employment conditions, shift work without extra compensation, tougher marketing methods. He suggested we ourselves are creating work conditions we don't approve of by buying shares in the companies that are most competitive, not in those that have the highest ethics. This was his final point.

"Do you still think it's so improbable that Sergei Bykov planted an infected pigeon with Ruben Nilsson?" asked Maria.

"I hope you're wrong, but maybe so. How do we proceed? How do we find evidence for such a thing?"

"I would like to see Sandra Hägg's apartment one more time before the barricade is taken down," said Maria. "It may be a waste of valuable time, but sometimes you have to slow down so your thoughts can catch up. I'll check with the technicians that it's okay, then I'll go there."

Maria Wern cut the barricade tape and opened the door to Sandra Hägg's apartment. The stuffy odor struck her as unexpectedly pungent. The landlord had asked permission to renovate the apartment and was eager for the family to pick up Sandra's belongings as soon as possible. Rental income was lost with every day that passed, and this was not a small amount of money. He called and discussed the matter with Hartman, and Hartman was willing to remove the barricade, but Maria wanted to take one last look. It was just a gut feeling.

She wasn't sure what she expected to find. The broken furniture was still scattered across the floor, where it had ended up after Moby went berserk. Maria opened the front of the beautiful old Stjärnsund wall clock. In the living room the blinds were pulled down. Maria opened them hoping the light would help her search. The apartment was in even worse chaos than she recalled. The glass panes on the showcase were broken and there were shards on the floor. A curtain was pulled down. The white flowers had withered in their vases. A couple shelves worth of books were scattered on the floor. The bowl of grapes and cherries would have to be thrown out.

Who were you waiting for, Sandra? Tobias, or perhaps Reine Hammar? It couldn't have been Hans Moberg. You wouldn't have taken such pains for a business meeting with him.

The massage bench was set up along one wall, a wide deluxe model with removable headrest and extra arm support on the sides. Alongside was a wrought-iron floor candelabra, with tea lights in a spiral loop. In the kitchen the table was set for two with plates, neatly folded napkins, and wine glasses. So inviting. Someone had put the casserole and baked potatoes in the refrigerator, and they were still there untouched. Were you going to celebrate something? Were you expecting a lover? The wine carafe was found next to your bed. Who was coming to see you, Sandra? You were dressed up. The whole apartment breathed celebration.

Maria stood in the doorway to the bedroom and looked at the destruction. The shattered mirror. The bureau drawer, whose contents were spread over the floor: tights, underwear, and chemises. She opened the closet and felt along the shelves. The technicians had already gone over everything minutely, but she still had a vague sense that something might have escaped them. The garments in the closet were few but carefully selected, mostly brand-name clothes. For work Sandra had her green uniform. Perhaps it was not necessary to have so many clothes for her free time. Maria stood on tiptoe to reach the topmost shelf and found a metal box with a red cross on it, a medicine chest. It was not locked, but the key was gone. She looked at the vials. There were cough-suppressant tablets, nose drops, Tylenol, aspirin, car sickness tablets, Band-Aids, bandages, a roll of tape, and an opened bottle of rubbing alcohol. No special medicine for migraine, as far as Maria could see.

Why was Sandra Hägg so eager to find out where Hans Moberg's supplies of medication came from? Why was it so important that he come to her home, even though she had a migraine? If she even *had* a migraine; no one could verify that. Did she even send the message herself? The computer was on and she had logged in. Hans Moberg's fingerprints were on the mouse and keyboard, but no messages had been deleted.

Maria browsed through the pile of papers next to Sandra's computer. Medical journal articles about infectious diseases, and a couple of articles about the anti-theft marking of the new passports that would soon be issued. One article, with the headline "You'll be your own key," detailed how one day fingerprints would be used instead of access cards.

Maria opened the door to the balcony and stepped outside. She took a few deep breaths of the sea air. From the balcony she could see the windmills on the edge of the cliff, the old yellow prison building with its wall, the harbor area, and, far to the south, the peak of Högklint as a sharp contrast to the gray-blue sea.

Her thoughts were occupied with the unreported break-in at Vigoris Health Center. Why did Sandra break into the clinic and what did she take with her in the plastic bag? Vaccine? Why, and for whom?

It wasn't until Sandra's neighbor Ingrid was right next to her that Maria noticed that she was not alone. The older woman's white hair was freshly washed and looked like a downy dandelion, ready to fly away if you blew on it.

"Hello! The weather's going to be nice." Ingrid Svensson shaded her eyes with her hand and leaned over the balcony railing. "I was thinking about something. Those children who were selling peppermint candies. Have you located them? You know, I think it's really irresponsible of parents to let children run around that late at night. In my day you ate dinner together at six o'clock and then it was time for the children to go to bed."

"No. It's been hard. We've tried to contact every third-grade teacher in Visby. But the schools are closed now and we haven't been able to reach them all. Some have gone on vacation. Did you find out something about them?"

"Yes, an acquaintance of Henriksson on the second floor—we play Bingo with him on Thursdays—says they go to the Solberg School. He's known their teacher since she was a little girl. Her name is Birgitta Lundström." Ingrid Svensson gave a satisfied smile.

Maria picked up her cell phone and tried Hartman. He would assign someone to call on her at once. It was high priority. For Hans Moberg, in particular, it was very important to find out whether the children had seen anyone else go down the stairs that fateful evening.

Still thinking about what Sandra might have taken from the clinic in the break-in, Maria returned to the apartment. The break-in had occurred at ten o'clock. By midnight she was dead. Maria stopped in the hall, as if she were Sandra just coming home with the plastic bag in her hand. Presumably she thought the break-in had been undetected. The cleaning lady did not think Sandra noticed her.

Why did she break a window at the clinic when she could just as easily have gone in through the outside door? She only needed to use her access card. The outside door was open until ten o'clock and from there she only needed to take the corridor over to the vaccination department, where the staff room was also located. It would have been simple for her to say that she left a magazine or her lunchbox behind if she was caught. As long as there wasn't another alarm system—one that Sandra knew about? Could that be the case?

Maria looked around the hall. She imagined that she was standing there with the plastic bag in her hand when she heard a sound on the stairs. Then she would have locked the door. Maria looked around for a place in the hall to hide the plastic bag. There was a drawer in the small dresser under the hall mirror. It was empty. It was too easy and too close to the door. She continued into the living room. Was Sandra afraid that someone might have followed her anyway? Perhaps the murderer was ringing the doorbell at that moment. Or maybe it wasn't that way at all. Maybe she was waiting for someone, someone to whom she intended to give a warm reception with wine and good food and perhaps a massage. Why else was the massage bench out? Maria went closer and removed the blankets and sheets and the buckwheat pillow that the technicians had cut open and emptied. If Sandra had quickly wanted to hide something before she opened the door, what would she have done? Maria felt the cushion around the massage bench. It was properly fastened, nailed and glued to the wooden frame. The head support could be pulled out, but there was nothing hidden in the holes from the wooden dowels that held it in place and the pillow itself was intact. Maria let her hands glide along the board to the arm support on the sides. Suddenly she felt a spot where it was possible to get her fingers between the cushion and the wooden structure. She got her bag and put on her latex gloves. There in the soft stuffing she felt something cool and cylindrical against her hand. She worked the arm support loose and continued to dig into the batting—soon she had a syringe in her hand. It was filled with a clear fluid and on the syringe was a text in Cyrillic letters.

It resembled the syringe used to give Maria her vaccination earlier in the week. She wished she had studied it more closely then instead of looking away. Maria took the syringe out of its plastic packaging and found that the needle could not be loosened.

Hans Moberg said that he tore apart the apartment, but did he cause all the damage himself? Perhaps it was this syringe someone was looking for. But why? What did it contain that was so dangerous?

Just then she heard steps on the stairwell and someone stopped at the door. Still playing the role of Sandra, Maria put the syringe back in the arm support and replaced it. A key was inserted in the lock of the outside door and adrenaline rushed through her body. Obviously. The person who murdered Sandra Hägg had a key to the apartment and then left a copy on the cord so that anyone could get it. No one would wonder how the murderer could open the door without breaking in.

The idea of Sandra lying in bed waiting for an unknown man to enter the apartment with a key fastened to a cord was completely absurd—especially once you'd taken a look at Hans Moberg.

Now the key was turning in the lock. In the middle of the room was a sofa; Maria crouched behind it. She heard the door being opened.

Chapter 37

With her face pressed to the floor Maria could see a pair of brown gym shoes moving across the parquet. Without making a sound, she tried to angle her head to see who it was but it was impossible. She heard a drawer being opened and closed again, and saw the shoes and a pair of denim-covered legs advancing into the room where she was cowering. Did the plant cover the space between the couch and the wall? She tried to control her breathing. Her heart was racing. If he went up to the bookshelves, she would be discovered. She should not have come here alone.

The sound of footsteps moved toward the kitchen. More drawers were pulled out and cupboard doors opened and shut again. She heard him swear. He turned on the radio. It was harder to hear where he was. Hard rock at high volume. If she screamed now it would barely be heard. It sounded like he was going into the bedroom. More drawers were pulled out and doors slammed. What was he looking for? She had to see who it was. Maria carefully moved into a crouching position and peeked out from behind the plant. At that moment, a sinewy hand picked up the fruit bowl on the table in front of her.

"What the hell!" Lennie staggered backward. "What the hell. I thought I was alone in here. You scared the shit out of me!"

"What are you doing here?"

"Getting my things before the vultures in Sandra's family get their claws on them. I've picked up my guitar strings and my metronome and music, and if you move I'll be able to get my electric guitar."

"So you still have a key to the apartment."

"Yeah, I watered the plants and brought in the mail for her when she was in Turkey with Jessika in May. She asked for it back, but it never happened, I wanted to keep it. Hoped in some sick way that she would take me back. We only had two keys, no spare."

"Who else might have a key?"

"Nobody. Can I check the one you have?" asked Lennie. "It's not new anyway. The metal in the newer ones isn't as yellow."

"And Sandra only had two keys, one of which you have and the one I got in with is the other. It was in her jacket pocket. Are you sure there were only two? Whose key was on the cord?" Maria weighed the key in her hand. "Has the lock been changed since the previous owner?"

"No. There was no reason."

When Maria arrived at Vigoris Health Center, accompanied by Tomas Hartman, the parking lot was full. After circling for ten minutes there was still no vacant spot. Cars were parked far out on the lawn facing every which way and bicycles and motorcycles left between them in an unorganized mess. On the drive there was a line and a crowd of people in the entryway. The mood was aggressive.

"There are no more appointments for vaccinations this

week. Please go home and schedule a time by phone or try your own health center. We cannot make any new appointments right now." The young nurse was trying to sound friendly and factual, but her voice was shaking slightly and her face was a bright shade of red.

"I don't intend to leave here until I've been vaccinated. I demand to get the help I've been promised. I've been paying taxes my whole life." A gray-haired man, skinny and muscular like a marathon runner, was holding firmly onto one of the pillars at the entry to the lobby. Maria could not help thinking of the tree-huggers who defended the elms in Kungsträdgården, or environmental activists who chain themselves to machinery to draw attention to important issues. "I'm not leaving."

Several others chimed in and the mood darkened, becoming increasingly threatening.

"I have heart disease and I should be first on the priority list according to the politicians. That list is worth no more than a handful of toilet paper. Who gets medicine? Just the people who have contacts and those who can pay. We should take matters into our own hands." The old lady was so agitated that she lost her breath and started hissing.

"Bring out the medicine, damn it!" the marathon runner shouted.

"Now let's calm down." The nurse looked like she was about to burst into tears. "If you don't disperse we're going to call the police."

"But people are afraid! Can I speak with your boss?" Yet another man stepped out of the crowd. He had a heavy red beard and a bald head. He wore his leather jacket unbuttoned with no shirt; around his neck was a sturdy silver chain. He forced his way up to the information counter, took hold of the nurse, and pulled her out onto the floor. "We're serious. Where's your boss?"

"The boss! The boss! The boss!" several people chanted in chorus. They clapped their hands in rhythm and stamped their feet. In a moment Viktoria Hammar was in the doorway.

"What's all this about?" If she was afraid, nothing in her posture revealed it; her voice was calm and well-articulated.

"Everyone is going to get medication and everyone is going to be vaccinated. If you follow the instructions you've been given it will proceed quickly and smoothly. At Vigoris we see paying clients. Those who are given a prescription by their doctors fill them at the pharmacy and are scheduled for vaccination at their respective health center. If you follow that procedure the work flows quickly and everyone gets help."

"The hell it does. There's no medicine at the pharmacy. They've run out, and there aren't any more appointments at the health centers. This is war, damn it! My friends are in the car. I want them vaccinated. Now!" The red-bearded man went up and stood in front of Viktoria at his full height. But she remained standing, apparently unmoved.

"It may be slow to start, but I promise that everyone will get help. Shipments of medicine are arriving daily and as soon as a priority arrangement has been agreed on by the county council, everyone will get medicine and vaccination in an orderly manner. Police and healthcare personnel and those who work in technical administration have already received vaccination. Soon the order for those in risk groups will be ready. It's not easy to decide who should have priority—whether individuals with cardiovascular diseases or cancer should have priority over those with neurological diseases.

"If you would please leave your names and telephone numbers at reception, we will contact you as soon as we have more appointments or cancellations. If you stay here in a crowd you risk getting infected."

Not without some admiration, Maria saw how Viktoria Hammar managed to calm the crowd and persuade them to leave the premises. She remained standing, her posture erect, until the marathon man finally sauntered out last of all, casting a hateful look that showed that he was not satisfied with how the situation had developed.

"Chickenshit Swedes. You obey orders even if your superiors ask you to eat your own shit. If this had happened where I'm from . . ." They heard no more before the door shut.

"And what can I help you with?" asked Viktoria in such an easy tone that Maria completely lost her power of speech.

"We would like to exchange a few words with your husband. Is Reine Hammar here?" asked Hartman.

"Yes, but he's very busy. As you just saw we have a workload that defies all calculations. I estimate he can see a patient every five minutes, and so the time you take up affects the patients. Is that clear?"

"We're investigating the murder of Sandra Hägg. As her employer I'd assume it's important to you to find out what happened to her."

Maria wanted to add that while she understood it was chaotic, a functioning legal system is even more important during a crisis.

"Where is Dr. Hammar?" Maria's stern tone surprised even herself, but Viktoria's emotional pressure was so obvious and so unpleasant that she couldn't control her irritation. An alternative would be for Reine to work an extra fifteen or thirty minutes in the service of humanity.

With a look of endless suffering Reine Hammar sat down in the armchair behind his desk and invited them to sit down. After a long bout of throat-clearing he turned away and coughed into his sleeve.

"Maximum fifteen minutes, I can't give you more than that."

"We'll try to be brief and we've chosen to meet you here and not at the station so as not to take up your time unnecessarily. Out of respect for your patients." Hartman's expression was unfathomable as he turned on the tape recorder and took down the necessary information. "We'd like to know where you were between ten o'clock and midnight on July 4."

"What do you mean? I'm sure you know I was in quarantine?"

"According to reports, you were away from the sanitarium that night. Your help was needed for an acute case, but you'd gone out. Where were you?"

"What is this? Is Jonathan Eriksson a hall monitor now? If that's the case, it's a matter between me and the disciplinary board, not the police."

"It is a police matter and I want you to answer my question: where were you?" Hartman leaned forward and Reine recoiled, clasped his hands behind his neck, and rocked in the chair.

"Then you have to tell me why you want to know." Reine cleared his throat and grunted several times. Maria was increasingly convinced that these were nervous tics.

"Sandra Hägg was murdered that night. You know that. And we want to know where you were."

"I needed to get a little air. I took a walk. That's not illegal, is it?" Reine stared at the wall behind them as if he could see there what had happened the night of the murder. He blinked as if he had something in his eye, took off his glasses, and rubbed his nose. A light redness spread over his face.

"Can anyone verify that? Did you see anyone?"

"Depends on what you mean by see. Well, in a way. Does anyone have to find out about this or can we keep it low-key . . . well, you know." He cleared his throat again.

"Who did you meet? If someone can give you an alibi it's in your own interest." Hartman's patience was about to run out. "If you're in a hurry to get back to your patients, it's best if you answer now."

"It was a nurse. We . . . were in her room in the building at the facility. Lena is her name. I don't remember what her last name is."

"We'll be checking that out. One more thing. You had antibodies to bird flu before the vaccine was distributed. Why is that?"

"What? Now I don't understand. It must be a mistake. And what do the police have to do with that? Test results are confidential. Where did you get that information?"

"Actually, test results are not confidential when the crime being investigated is punishable by two years of prison or more. This is about murder, Reine Hammar. The murder of three individuals, each with a connection to the vaccine against bird flu. What evidence was Sandra trying find? We're in the process of analyzing the contents of the syringe Sandra took with her from the clinic when she broke in. Would you like to tell us what this is all about?"

Reine Hammar shook his head. If his surprise was pretend, it was very skillfully done.

"I don't know what you're talking about!"

"We'll come back to this. One more thing before we go: do you have a key to Sandra Hägg's apartment?"

"No, absolutely not, and the only flu I've been vaccinated against is the usual variety. The whole clinic was vaccinated last November. I don't know what the hell antibodies you're talking about!"

Chapter 38

Reine Hammar pulled back the heavy satin drapes and took in the view of the city within the medieval boundary wall. The pointed black tower of Sankta Maria Cathedral was sticking up from the light fog and the ghostly outline of the cloister ruins was dimly visible in the darkness. He opened the bedroom window and let in the cool of the evening and the scent from the sea and the peonies and honeysuckle that trailed on the wall of the house. The house at Norderklint had cost 4.5 million kronor. A bargain, if life were assessed in money; a prison if a different measure were used. Was this all life had to offer?

He looked at the clock when he heard the key in the lock. It was quarter past eleven. We have to talk when I get home, Viktoria had said, and he felt the ground quaking below his feet. He hated her strength. Hated to be the first to look away when she asked a question and then waited for him with a mean smile playing on her lips, just a slight quiver, but very clear when you are looking for a sign of reconciliation. Once they had loved each other, the thought occurred to him. In a vanished time, so long ago, there had actually been warmth. They would sit drinking tea half the night in

315

the student corridor talking about life and death and the meaning of it all. They were convinced that love was everything; without love, life was meaningless and empty. You have to burn for someone or something. They were so young then. So full of lofty ideals and so certain of what was good and what was bad, who was a friend and who was an enemy. They made sarcastic remarks about the shortcomings and narrow-mindedness of their parents' generation. And now . . . What was left of their dreams? The last seven years they had not even once made love. A final clumsy attempt ended in awkward silence. Quickly they had gotten dressed, hurt and anxious. She had said nothing. For once she was unable to put things into words directed at him. It was so clear that the desire was not there—so frighteningly clear to them both.

"Reine, are you home?" Her voice sounded nasal and whiny, quite unlike the one she used at work.

He did not answer. It was part of their power struggle. He lingered by the window and let himself be carried away by the evening breeze out toward the sea. Resisted the unpleasant conversation that was coming. I'm disappointed, Reine, she would say and creep right next to him so that he could feel her breath against his face. At the same time she would play with the hair on his neck. It was not a caress but a violation and she knew it, knew that he hated it, that his mother used to pull the hair on his neck while she talked about how he ought to behave. He had mentioned it to her in an intimate moment when the contract between them still held. Contracts written in peacetime to apply in battle. She did not hesitate to exploit every advantage. He heard her hard heels clattering over the floor in the corridor. Now she was in the doorway to the bedroom.

"I'm disappointed, Reine." He turned aside so that she could not get at him. "How could you do that?"

"Do what?" he said stupidly. His pulse was pounding in his ears and his mouth was completely dry. She saw that he was nervous and he hated her for it. He tried to tense his muscles against the shaking that came from inside his body.

"Do what?" she mimicked. "Prescribe Tamiflu in exchange for sexual services."

"I don't know what you're talking about. There's no evidence." It surprised him that his voice could sound so steady. Maybe it was because the question came so unexpectedly. It was not what he thought she wanted to talk about.

"I have the prescription here. Do you want to see it?" The quiver at the corner of her mouth was there. For a moment he got the feeling she was going to cry. But her eyes were cold and unblinking. Just wishful thinking.

"It proves nothing that I prescribed Tamiflu to a woman. Even if she happens to be twenty-four and radiantly beautiful."

"Then why did you do it, Reine? Lechery? You know, I'm so damn tired of you. Do you understand the risk you expose us to? The clinic's reputation is at stake. This is the last time I cover for you. The last time, do you hear that? Men like you should be castrated. Finn saw you. Don't try to deny it. Don't lie to me. You're sick in the head, Reine, you need help. There is medication that dampens—"

"What do you intend to do with the prescription?" He reached for it. Viktoria turned away and tore it into little pieces. Evidently the hold she already had on him was enough. The prescription for morphine he sold for cash when he was just out of medical school. A single occurrence, a single crazy, wild action when he was in desperate need of money. He was her prisoner for life if he wanted to continue working as a doctor. Of course it was that bloodhound Finn, always on her leash, who had acquired the evidence. Who else? Perhaps they even had a relationship, the lapdog Finn and Viktoria. He snorted at the thought. It would be worth a fortune to see that. The mannequin Viktoria mounted by Security-Hitler. No, his imagination wasn't vivid enough. He couldn't even visualize it . . . Well, possibly with hand-cuffs and collar.

"Why are you smiling so stupidly . . . perhaps a thank you would be in order."

"Thank you." And just when he thought the danger was over, that she would leave him alone and crawl into her half of the bed with her back turned like a shield toward him, she asked the question.

"What did the police want?" He had expected it, but he was still not prepared.

"They asked if I was vaccinated against bird flu."

"Stop talking nonsense. What did they want?" She was stamping impatiently in her narrow, sharp shoes. Stamp, stamp, stamp, up and down she stretched her ankles. She'd had problems with low blood pressure in her athletic youth and the stamping was a holdover from that time.

"They wanted to know where I was the night Sandra was murdered."

Silence. She waited for him to continue, but he didn't intend to give her that. For a long time they looked each other up and down. She stared into his eyes until he became dizzy and his upper body started swaying. This did not escape her either.

"Did you love her?" Viktoria's face underwent a trans-formation. Her eyes narrowed and wrinkles appeared. Her mouth was pulled into a circle, a red sun with the wrinkles like black rays, and her neck sank down into her body. "Did you love her?"

"I love them all, everyone who's soft and friendly and warm, Viktoria. Everything you're not. What do you want with me? Can't I just have that morphine prescription back? Can't you just let me go?" He started to choke up, and he hated, hated, hated her because she could hear it.

"No. Where were you that night, Reine? Did it hurt that you couldn't have Sandra, that there was someone else she wanted instead?" The tip of Viktoria's sharp little tongue was playing at the corner of her mouth.

He did not answer her. Instead he turned his back to her and stared out into the blue-gray twilight.

"Finn saw you, Reine. He saw you standing below her window. She had set the table so nicely with candles and wine and even put on a dress, isn't that true? A white, low-cut dress she had put on for someone else. You wanted to know who it was, didn't you? Could you see them in your mind as they toasted each other and laughed and then made love in her soft bed? Did you go around the building? Did they pull the curtains . . . ?"

He suddenly turned around. "I hate you, Viktoria, do you know that? The sight of you disgusts me. And if you so much as breathe a word to the police I'm going to kill you, do you get that? I've got an alibi; they're not going to put me in jail, and you're going to disappear as suddenly as Tobias Westberg."

Chapter 39

S andra, my dear, I'm back. At midnight I'll be with you. You're the best friend I've ever had. Our friendship has meant more to me than I've ever dared to say. It hasn't always been easy, as you know. Lennie sometimes wanted me dead, and my wife hasn't been all that happy either about how close we've become. It's like we're having a love affair, the way we have to sneak off for our secret meetings, just to talk undisturbed. You once said that you felt guilty that you had to lie to meet me. It's been the price of our friendship. I didn't always mention our meetings either. I guess because they happened more often than might be considered appropriate. How often is it appropriate to see your best friend? Friendship between a man and a woman isn't always viewed forgivingly. There are times when I've wished you were a man. Don't misunderstand me. But it would have been simpler. Life is too short not to make the most of friendship and love where you find it. And who knows, if we had met at another time in our lives perhaps our story would have been different. We'll never know. I'm writing this to you because I probably won't have the courage to say it when we meet face-to-face.

As planned, I went to the city of Biaroza southwest of Minsk, where I met Sergei Bykov before. The story he told me during the spring, after we'd shared a bottle of vodka, seemed highly unlikely but when I heard that the bird flu came to the island through a pigeon and about his death I realized it must be true. His assignment was to plant an infected pigeon in a dovecote on Gotland. The pharmaceutical company was running at a loss and they were sitting on large stockpiles of Tamivir and vaccine that couldn't be sold. A powerful pandemic was needed to produce cash flow. Shareholders demand profit. I wasn't even sure I would come back alive and be able to report my figures and the taped conversations with Sergei's wife, but I did and the most valuable documents I managed to acquire are translated in the attached file. I want you to copy the text and make sure it reaches all the addresses on the list. I've hidden the paper copies and cassette tapes in the well out at the house, under a stone in the third row from the top. It's loose and can be easily removed.

It was just as you believed, Sandra, my friend, and much worse than we realized at first. Forgive me for not believing you when you said that your social security number came up on the display when you passed the scanner over your arm in the shopping center. It sounded so improbable. Completely sick. I understand the connections better now and I'll tell you when I see you at midnight. Have you been able to get what I asked you for? This will be the biggest scoop of my career and of course we'll share equally in whatever it may lead to. Time to uncork the champagne! I'll be seeing you soon. Someone's coming . . .

"We've managed to restore the information from Tobias Westberg's computer." The computer technician tried to hold back his smile but did not succeed, and his face became a strange grimace. "Or when I say 'we,' I mean the boys in Linköping. They had an expert from Norway who managed it." Maria could not keep from smiling.

"Where did you find it?"

"In the same dump for quicklime. They had never restored information from such a damaged hard drive before, but nothing was overwritten or reformatted, so miraculously enough it was possible to produce this text from the laptop. There were fragments of another computer in the dump but it was much too damaged, it fell apart completely. There was also corroded photo equipment."

Maria read through the printout one more time.

"If this is true it's a scandal the likes of which the world has never seen. He thinks that disease was deliberately planted on Gotland to sell medication? That thought did occur to me but I dismissed it because it seemed so unreasonable and crazy and fiendishly greedy. But I don't understand this part about the scanner and Sandra's social security number."

"We've done an analysis of the contents of the syringe you found in Sandra Hägg's apartment. It contained vaccine, but not only that. Listen carefully: you won't believe this is true. We've flown an expert here from Gothenburg and he's sure of what he's found. In the needle itself is a 0.4 mm chip. The inside diameter of the needle is 0.6 mm. When you get vaccinated"—the technician took hold of Maria's arm, aimed with an invisible syringe and pushed in the plunger—"the chip goes in under your skin with the fluid and remains there."

Maria felt her arm and her eyes opened wide. "I'm thinking about something—just a detail. When we got the preliminary autopsy report on Sandra Hägg, the medical examiner noted a small wound on her left arm, and the same thing where Sergei was concerned. A little tear a centimeter or two long on the left upper arm. Could they have had their chips removed? Just a thought."

Hartman came into the room where everyone had gathered for a joint run-through before the interviews with the management of Vigoris Health Center began. The police were already cordoning off the facility and securing evidence.

The expert from Gothenburg sat down at the podium. Anyone expecting a PowerPoint presentation was disappointed. He was of the old school and used a notebook and pen.

"This is not a new technology, actually, it's been around for fifty years in lift tickets and personal cards for entry to offices, anti-theft marking, or to identify goods in connection with transport and storage. The chip has a code and in another database, information is stored; for example, a social security number or other personal information. What is exceptional is that the components can be manufactured so much smaller than before, especially if what we call the tag doesn't have a separate power supply but is activated and emits information when energy is supplied from a reader. The reading distance on the chip we found in the syringe is up to three meters. It has a thin glass cover over its iron wires to prevent any biological effect on the unit. Thus it is completely feasible to install scanner arches in doorways, for example, and see who has passed room by room."

"At Vigoris Health Center they recently replaced every oak doorframe for cherry wood, even though it was new construction," Hartman recalled. "Could some kind of scanner arch have been installed then?"

"Possibly. An implanted chip has advantages compared to ordinary pass cards, where you can borrow someone else's card and identification is not equally certain. In time it will certainly be possible to produce chips just as small as this but with GPS function, and thereby be able to trace a person via satellite."

"But why? What is the purpose and why wasn't the staff informed about this?" asked Hartman.

"There would likely be a lot of attention from the media and the decision-making process would be long and uncertain. Perhaps they wanted to test-drive the system before investing too much money in it. The Demeter Group, which owns Vigoris Health Center, also owns companies that manufacture computer electronics. Through cross-fertilization you increase the possibilities of competing on the world market. In this case the pharmaceutical producer manufactures syringes that can implant chips under the skin. If this turns out to be a functional system, it could be sold to other countries where legislation allows marking of people. Perhaps you want to supply all immigrants with chips to verify their identity, or even have a GPS function to know where they are while awaiting asylum or citizenship. Imagine that everyone has to be 'vaccinated' in order to enter a country. I can see that would be an attractive solution in countries that have major problems with thefts or terrorism. If another attack occurs like the one on September 11, perhaps we'll be willing to resort to such an intervention, and then the product is already tested and ready for use. It's a competitive advantage if other companies were to manufacture something similar."

"Obviously they didn't want this to get out, so it's possible the order came from above—or at least there was silent approval of it. But who murdered them? It must have been someone with physical strength. Someone stronger than the victims or in any case stronger than Sandra, who was in good shape." Maria Wern looked at Ek, who was back on duty after his stay at the sanitarium.

That morning Ek had questioned the two children who were selling peppermint sticks on Signalgatan, and together with an artist they tried to recreate pictures of two individuals who passed them in the stairwell.

"They easily recognized Hans Moberg from a photo. But we also have another interesting face that the artist has produced. About half an hour before Moberg came, the children saw another man go up the stairs." It was not difficult to see who the drawing depicted. Before they made the raid on Vigoris Health Center, Hartman contacted the prosecutor.

Viktoria Hammar had been crying. Her big gray blue eyes were edged with red and her smeared lipstick made her look like a clown. When she spoke her voice was not the same. Maria found something redeeming in her finally showing weakness.

"I'm not saying a thing until my attorney arrives. It's pointless for you to ask any questions. I don't intend to answer."

"Then we want you to leave the room and follow Ek to the station so that we can speak undisturbed with your husband. Be my guest." Hartman held open the door.

Reine stared at Viktoria and his eyes were full of hatred. It could not be mistaken.

"I don't understand this. Why, Viktoria? Why did you lie to me about the vaccination and about Sandra's drug abuse? I didn't want to believe it at first . . ."

Viktoria stopped in the doorway. "You would be wise not to say anything until the attorney arrives, Reine."

"The hell I would. I'm innocent. Don't you get that it's over, Viktoria? I don't want to be involved. Watch carefully now." Reine passed Maria Wern and went to Viktoria's desk. There he logged onto the computer. "Password 'Pandemic.' You don't know whether to laugh or cry. Okay, check

325

the screen now. What do you see?" Reine pulled the optical reader over his left upper arm.

"Reine, stop it. I forbid you. You won't be able to count on support from the company if you do this, Reine. Stop, Reine." Viktoria rushed across the room but was stopped by Hartman.

"I'll accompany you out, we'll do the questioning at the station."

"I see a social security number. Is that yours, Reine?" Maria asked.

"Yes, and now we'll try it on you," he said. Maria recoiled. She had toyed with the idea but found it too far-fetched. When she saw her social security number on the screen she started to understand the scope of the experiment that was being conducted. "Viktoria is standing under a scanner arch right now. The doorway to every unit in the building reads who goes through, which is why Sandra forced a window to get in and out." Reine crossed the floor in a few quick steps. "Check now when I pull the reader over Viktoria's arm and nothing happens. Why? Because she didn't want to be monitored, and it's the same with Finn. I'm innocent; do you believe me now? I knew nothing about this until last night."

"It's not true. He's lying!" Viktoria screamed from the corridor as a uniformed officer appeared beside her.

Maria called Finn Olsson into the room while two police officers followed Reine to one of the waiting cars, to take him to the police station for further questioning. When Finn passed through the door there was no reading on the computer, nor when the scanner was directed at his arm. He stared at them with hostility but did not say anything.

"You sold your apartment on Signalgatan to Sandra Hägg and Lennie Hellström, is that correct?" Hartman's statement evidently came so unexpectedly that Finn did not have time to think before he answered. He simply nodded curtly while he followed Maria's work at the computer with concentration. "And you kept a key?" He nodded again.

"Where is it now?"

"I must have thrown it away, I don't know."

"The registry covers the entire government and everyone with key positions in society on the priority list of those who should get vaccines first. And those with the means to pay, they're marked with a chip too? What is your role in this, Finn Olsson? Who set up the registry?"

"I'll answer that when my lawyer gets here."

"Okay. There are traces of blood in your car. Can you explain that?"

"I'm not answering any questions until my lawyer is here."

Hartman's questions fell thick and fast. "Until quite recently you had a key to Sandra Hägg's apartment and you knew that your sister had email contact with Hans Moberg, a suitable victim who could take the blame for the murder. We think you emailed him and got him to go to the apartment after you killed Sandra."

"Prove it."

"I don't think that will be very hard. Take him to the car," said Hartman to the police officers who had entered the room. Maria was still standing as if bewitched at the computer, watching how her colleagues' social security numbers came up on the screen as they passed through the door.

On the front pages, images of infected birds like grotesque fighter planes ready to attack the civilian population of Gotland had been exchanged for close-ups of Finn Olsson and Viktoria Hammar. Accused of the murder and intention to murder Sergei Bykov, Sandra Hägg, and Tobias Westberg.

The news generated dismay throughout the island and the police spokesman submitted a report to the media every hour on the hour.

Later that evening, when Maria arrived to finally pick up her son from the sanitarium in Follingbo, she saw that Jonathan Eriksson was at his desk. She could only see the back of his head and she felt a shiver through her body. First she thought about slipping up and giving him a hug, but he was on the phone. She did not want to disturb him, so she stood quietly by the door and waited for him to finish so that she could talk with him. Say thanks and decide when they could meet again, if he wanted . . .

"I'm coming home soon, Nina. Have you made dinner? Sounds good . . . Malte has missed you . . . No, I'm not going to leave you, Nina. I promise to stay if you accept treatment . . . I promise. Yes, I promise. Malte needs both of us."

Maria did not wait for him to turn around. Silently she slipped away. If he wanted to start over with Nina there was nothing more to say. She didn't want him to see her like this, not when it felt like she was going to start crying. She only had herself to blame anyway, falling for a married guy. She just had to gather herself up and move on.

He must have caught a glimpse of her, because he called her name. But Maria walked faster and disappeared up the stairs.

"Maria!" Not now, Jonathan, maybe another time, she thought. "Maria!" She did not wait and his voice died away.

When she pressed Emil hard in her embrace she could not hold back the tears. He was healthy, and that was the important thing.

"Why are you crying, Mom?"

"Because I'm so happy."

"I get to go home today, too," said Nurse Agneta. "I get to go home and hug my kids."

Chapter 40

Like a boiling witch's brew the fog rolled in over the smooth cliffs; the outline of the mainland faded and disappeared from sight. The dark gray water, which turned into frothing white foam as it struck the pier and the stones, became peaceful under the blanket of clouds. Minister of Equality Mikaela Nilsson sat wrapped in a blanket on the terrace of her cottage on an island in the archipelago, where she'd asked to be left alone for a week. She was seeking solitude to grieve in peace, with no one taking her picture for the tabloids. Grief is a form of stress, and stress can express itself in many ways in your body. She was well aware of that. It could even manifest as a fever, according to a popular science magazine she'd read. She actually did feel a little tired and feverish. She had deliberately chosen not to take her cell phone along this week. No TV either, no newspapers, only radio to listen to music on P2. Perhaps it was a little foolhardy not to bring the cell phone, but she wanted to be undisturbed.

The last three days on Gotland she had kept watch at her mother's deathbed, and only an hour or so before the plane to the mainland took off did Angela quietly pass away after a long period of illness. Leukemia. Infection had set in. In consultation with the doctor, Mikaela had decided that her mother should not be treated and prolong her suffering.

Mikaela had traveled to Gotland with her mother, despite her weakened state, because Angela wanted to have a final wish fulfilled. She wanted to see an old love again.

Mikaela had driven her to see Ruben Nilsson in Klintehamn, and waited in the car after she led her mother to the outside door. "Now I'll manage on my own," Angela said so firmly that Mikaela had no choice but to obey. This was a sacred moment and something in Angela's eyes and posture showed that nothing that happened after this encounter would matter. She needed to experience the reconciliation in order to cross the threshold.

"I treated him so badly," she said when she turned around one last time and the wind from the sea took hold of her wavy white hair, lifting it up like a veil.

"What did Ruben mean to you?" Mikaela asked Angela before they left Klintehamn. According to rumors, he was an eccentric uncle she had never met because her father and his brother had a lifelong conflict. She would have liked to go in and meet him, but Angela refused.

"He was the life I never lived," she said, and then she fell asleep and slept the rest of the way out of pure exhaustion, with her head hanging loosely in the seatbelt.

Mikaela went into the kitchen to make coffee. She truly felt weak and strange, and she was cold, too. But it felt wrong to go lie down in the middle of the day. To keep herself awake she turned on the radio for the first time since coming to the island. She had wanted to refrain from taking in the outside world, instead trying to find herself and understand how life turned out as it did. Right now she felt abandoned and the perky voices on the radio gave her the illusion she was not nearly as lonely as she felt. Next March she would turn fifty. Many of her girlfriends had both children and grandchildren, but for Mikaela, life had no such thing in store. A few brief relationships and one longer one, a broken engagement, and many shattered hopes later she realized that love for another human being was too hard for her to manage. Perhaps it was because of her parents' love-hate relationship; their need for control bound them together for life. Or else perhaps, as the rapist maintained, it was because Mikaela had been abandoned so often while Angela went in and out of mental hospitals, leaving the girl at foster homes or with friends and neighbors. At that time, fathers did not stay at home with their children. Perhaps they were both true, or maybe they were only rationalizations. Perhaps she just needed an explanation for a life marked by abandoning rather than being abandoned. As a little girl, Mikaela kept Angela's photograph hidden under her pillow. My beautiful, beautiful angel mama. When you come back everything will be fine. Then there will be laughter and hugs and warmth again. But it didn't turn out that way.

"What did Ruben mean to you, Mother?"

"He was the life I didn't live, but I got you instead, my angel."

Mikaela poured a cup of coffee. She wrapped her feet in the blanket and pulled on the thick knit wool sweater she inherited from Angela, while she absentmindedly listened to the radio. It was about the bird flu, a monotonous harping that she was fed up with. She was about to change the station when a new voice broke in and spoke about the government administration. The female voice said that the majority of the Cabinet members had become ill with bird flu, probably due to the fact that someone on the airplane from Gotland had been infected, even though they had been careful to control the contacts members of the government had had. Mikaela reproached herself. She had not reported the visit with Ruben Nilsson in Klintehamn to them. It had been like a matter of honor to keep it secret . . . for Angela's sake.

"*Considering all the contacts members of the Cabinet have had in the past few days, we must view this situation very seriously. The infection is no longer limited to Gotland and we fear that there will be numerous cases in the days ahead. We therefore ask anyone with flu-like symptoms not to visit hospitals or health centers. Instead, county councils will set up bird flu information lines, and doctors will make house calls. There is no cause for alarm, however. We will take care of your calls in order.*"

Mikaela turned off the radio. She went into the bedroom and crept in under the blankets. The photograph of a young Angela was on the nightstand in a cheap wooden frame clad in black cloth. Mikaela stroked her finger over the frame draped in mourning and fell into a deep sleep.

About the Maria Wern series

Anna Jansson's crime series featuring Maria Wern—a complex and flawed woman with whom readers have come to know and love—are set on Gotland Island. While struggling with raising two children as a single mother and still mourning her husband's death, Maria manages to sustain her female perspective and approach to life in a harsh and male dominated environment.

The Maria Wern series has been turned into a successful TV series that has been broadcasted in Europe and in the U.S. during 2012. The Swedish actress Eva Röse portrays Detective Inspector Maria Wern.

About the Author

A nna Jansson was born on Gotland and grew up with storytelling. Everything she writes is pervaded with the intensity typical for fairy tales and her love for mythology provides a lot of inspiration. When she began to write her drive was to tell stories about people she met at the hospital, where she worked as nurse for many years. In a genre full of sudden, wicked death, Anna Jansson also manages to keep a discussion about present ethical problems concerning people's relation to life and death.

Anna Jansson is a master of tempo changes, from descriptive where the story needs it, to thrilling action when the investigation escalates or the relations between the characters are intensified. Anna Jansson finds a unique tone for each character.

Read the beginning of

KILLER'S ISLAND

BY

ANNA JANSSON

To be released by Stockholm Text in
January 2014

By simply tapping the keyboard he was able to watch, via satellite, the day-to-day lives of ordinary people; how they opened their front doors and took their dogs for walks or bumped into friends on street corners, as if things were ruled by chance—for these superstitious, dim-witted beings still believed in chance. His constant observation of them made him feel powerful. He registered their habits, began to predict where they'd be and who they'd meet. It had been child's play hacking into the Russian satellite that monitored the gas pipeline near Gotland. That its reception was so technically advanced came as a surprise. When weather conditions were favorable he could even watch their unsuspecting faces. This, perhaps, gave him more satisfaction than anything else.

Chapter 1

Friday, June 7, was an unusually hot day. Long into evening, the heat still lingered in the narrow alleys of Visby. A pale dusk lay over the creased surface of the sea, lighting up the dark bastions of the city walls and the monastery ruins hailing back to another, more powerful time. The silhouettes of the stepped gable houses that had been warehouses in Hanseatic times stood out eerily in the red-glowing evening light. In the distance someone was playing a wooden flute. A sad, medieval melody.

When Maria Wern started wandering home from Quay 5 at about nine o'clock, she immediately cursed her choice of shoes. Admittedly quite gorgeous, with sharp heels, pointy toes, and ankle-straps, they were nonetheless nearly impossible to walk in. The air was still clement. On the whole, she reflected, it had been a pleasant evening, apart from the last hour when Erika, as the situation warranted, had worked herself in a tizzy about a man. At such times she grew deaf and blind to anyone else. It was at that point that a fruity cocktail equipped with a straw and umbrella had landed on the table in front of Maria.

"Something for the lady, from that gentleman by the

door." There was a scarcely hidden, teasing quality in the waiter's smile.

Someone had weighed up the situation and was now opportunely moving in for the kill while she sat there, left to her own devices. Maria glanced up toward the door. The gentleman in question winked at her and carefully rotated his open palm in the air—like in a comedy movie. *Hey, it's me!* No, she wasn't quite as desperate as that.

"I think I've reached saturation point. Tell him thanks." Maria stood up and tried to make eye contact with Erika, now deep in conversation with her new acquisition. His name was Anders, he was a district medical officer in town and seemed unusually sympathetic. Was he married or a sociopath or a drug user or annoyingly perverse? There was usually something wrong with good-looking men who were apparently still available. When Erika invited him home, Maria couldn't help but feel a little tingle of anxiety. As a police officer, Erika knew one could run into crazies in a bar.

"Careful!" Her text message did not seem to get through. Although, when she thought about it, it occurred to her that *he* might be the one in need of a warning. Erika was usually more than capable of taking care of herself. "Erika, is your cell phone switched on?" Maria whispered as she stood up.

"Mother hen! You know I won't be calling you tonight." Erika laughed affectionately and gave her arm a squeeze. "Everything's totally cool, okay?"

"Exactly." Anders cut in. "Too cool if you ask me. I've got my daughter at home and my old mom babysitting. She'll be wanting a lift home at a respectable hour, so it'll just be a peck on the cheek at the door, I suppose. After that I'll be making my own way back through the dangerous streets of Visby."

They all paid for themselves, then walked out into the lukewarm night. There was a gusting southeasterly wind pushing them away from the edge of the quay. The street-lights reflected in the black water. Music and humming voices could be heard from the boats in the marina, but the main seafront was almost deserted. They separated at Donner's Place and Maria continued homewards down Hästgatan toward Klinten. Her feet were insanely sore. She tried walking barefoot, shoes in hand. Noticing the glimmer of glass and sharp bottle caps here and there, she was careful about where she put her feet. A taxi stopped and picked up a couple in party clothes. A taxi ride was not an option for Maria, whose finances were stressed. Anyway, she was almost home. She continued to Wallers Plats and then turned off down Södra Kyrkogatan toward the Cathedral, whose black steeple could already be glimpsed over the house roofs. She avoided the main square and headed for Ryska Gränd so she could take the long, steep Cathedral stairs up to Klinten as a workout—a punishment for being lazy and staying away from the gym all week.

Further down Ryska Gränd, Maria heard a call for help. A pubescent voice, just at the cusp of breaking. At first it seemed unreal: three hooded men standing around someone on the ground, kicking him. The lane was dark, but she could see some of the kicks hitting his head. The figure on the ground was a boy, no more than perhaps thirteen or fourteen—just a few years older than Maria's own son. Every kick catapulted his gaunt body off the ground. He was screaming.

"Stop that! Stop! Police!" Maria got out her police badge and tried to make her voice as strong and authoritative as possible, although she was trembling inside.

The three men looked up. They seemed to weigh her up, measure her with their eyes. If she could calm things down and make them respect her, she might just be able to resolve this without further violence. Purposefully she walked up to them. One against three. She dialed the emergency number on her cell phone. At best this would make them leave the scene, so she could save the boy. *Answer the phone!* She was placed on hold, an automated voice telling her the waiting time should not exceed three minutes. Three goddamn minutes! The tallest of the three men smiled scornfully at her as he unleashed another kick into the kid's stomach. The boy went completely silent, likely unconscious. One of the other men hit Maria hard, knocking her cell phone out of her hand and then crushing it under his steel-toed shoe. Maria bent down to see how things were with the kid. His face was been beaten to a bleeding pulp, his body was limp, and he was no longer shielding himself with his arms.

"Stop! You'll kill him!" Only then did the fear really hit her.

A tall man in his seventies wearing a cap and a light-colored overcoat appeared in the lane. Maria cried out for help but the man hurried by as if he were deaf and blind. His long overcoat flapped around his legs. He didn't even turn around. She saw the gray hair down his neck, hanging over his collar.

"Hello! Can you call the police! Help us! Call the police!" Her voice was still strong and authoritative.

The man disappeared. He was out of the game. Coward! Next time you'll be the one who needs help! You'll have to live with this for the rest of your life, Maria wanted to shout after him. He *must* help them, he *must* pick up the phone. Couldn't he see that? She filled up with impotent anger. The next few minutes would determine whether they came out of this situation alive.

"Don't come here poking your nose in this, fucking cop cunt!" The tall one aimed another kick at the boy. Maria didn't know where she got her strength but somehow she managed to shove him so that he lost his balance and fell. His kick missed the victim's head. One of them, shorter and fatter than the others, seemed to be drugged. His movements were floppy and his pupils tiny, like fly-specks. "Shit, Roy, maybe we should leave it and get out of here." The others weren't listening to him. The tall one resumed his attack on the defenseless boy on the ground. Maria screamed, called for help, clawed them, tugged at them, fought like a wild animal. They'd kill him if she didn't manage to stop them. That boy was not much bigger than her son, Emil. In her mind, he might as well *be* Emil. Maria gave it all she had. She punched and kicked and roared for help, then managed a direct hit in the tall one's groin, leaving him doubled up. At the same time she was kneed in the small of her back by one of the others. She fell to the ground, a hissing sound in her head. A hard fist slammed into her face. There was a taste of blood in her mouth. The pain had winded her. She crawled up again, took a kick in her back and lost her balance. Fell. Crawled to the boy on the ground and laid on top of him to protect his head, using her body as a shield. A powerful kick thundered into her side. Then another. She felt as if something inside her just exploded into smithereens. The pain was unbearable. She went into deep concentration, focusing on protecting the boy's head and also her own.

"Fucking cop cunt!" The tall one moved in close with a syringe in his hand. Maria saw him in the corner of her eye. The syringe was gleaming, filled with dark red blood.

"Please, I…. Don't. Don't. Ouww, oh God!"

He squatted down on her back. The others held on to her arms and legs. For a moment Maria thought that they were going to rape her, that they were only using the syringe as a threat. But it was far worse than that.

"Welcome to hell." The taunting voice cut into her. The needle pierced her trousers and skin, went in deep and grazed her femur. Maria tried to kick herself free. The needle glided out. Maybe it had snapped inside her flesh? She didn't know. He continued stabbing her with it. She had to try and mark him. She bit, scratched, clawed at his masked face. He spit at her. Right in her face. His eyes were overflowing with hatred. He stood up to kick her one more time.

Someone opened a window and a woman's voice called out.

"If you don't stop that racket I'll call the police!"

"Do it! Call the police!" Maria's voice did not carry. Another kick slammed into her, she convulsed and gasped for air. Her back was smashed. The pain was beyond endurance.

Another window opened.

"What's going on?"

"Help!" Maria's voice made a hollow, croaking sound.

One more kick swished into her. She tried to protect her head with her arm. Another kick. There was a cracking sound. The pain made her black out.

"Call an ambulance! Please…." Her voice was no more than a whisper, maybe just a thought. Everything went silent. The kicking stopped. Dark figures moved indistinctly round them, like a dance of witches. Steel-toed boots. The voices from the windows turned into echoes. A last kick cut clean through her whole body.

When Maria regained consciousness she only saw the staring eyes at first. Black human bodies with long legs and eyes. A quiet murmuring of perturbed and dismayed voices. Echoes, half-perceived words to cling onto in a sea of raging pain. She tried to make out the words but they remained indecipherable. The sound of an approaching ambulance accentuated everything. Someone touched her, tried to move her. The pain was indescribable.

A new face came up close to her. A man with an anxious gaze, though his words were calm. Clear. A kind voice. She wanted to cry.

"How are you? Where does it hurt?" The ambulance man was speaking to her.

"Is the boy alive?" He couldn't hear her. It was painful to breathe.

"Where does it hurt?"

She couldn't make herself understood. Her lips were swollen and she couldn't project her voice: each word felt like internal bleeding or a fractured neck. Her whole identity seemed to be in swaying motion, without any firm grip. The man's voice took command. Passively she let herself be moved. They were placed on stretchers and transferred to the waiting ambulances. She caught a glimpse of the boy's limp body. He simply had to pull through, had to survive, in spite of all the blows and kicks to his head. Where were his parents? Soon they'd find out. Maria felt a fit of weeping in her body, but without tears. Every time the car jolted, an excruciating pain coursed through her. The ambulance man was there, the one with the anxious eyes and calm voice. All the way on the bumpy road to the hospital he was there with her. He told her his name was Tobias. She held onto his name as if it were a mantra.

The fluorescent lights in the white room cut into her eyes. White-dressed figures flitted past like bright butterflies. They were hands and voices in a sea of pain. A doctor introduced himself but Maria couldn't fix his name in her mind. His face was round. He was sweating and his glasses had slipped down his nose; his lower jaw masticated as he spoke. He'd nicked himself on his chin with his razor. A tiny, bleeding cut. He seemed to be saying something about an X-ray. He asked a question, wanted an answer. But the pain engulfed her in darkness. The voices came and went in her wavering consciousness.

"The boy, is the boy all right?" Maria grabbed hold of a white coat. She had to know.

"Is he your son?"

Maria shook her head.

"He's in intensive care. The police want to talk to you later." The woman's voice was soft and calm. Do healthcare staff have to take an oral exam before they're offered a job? The quieter and calmer they sound, the more serious the situation. One can see it in their eyes. Only there does the truth leak out. At times of utter silence one knows death has showed up; death is beginning its struggle with life.

Maria was helped to crawl over into a bed. "They stabbed me with needles!"

"We'll take you for an X-ray in a minute." Two voices talking. No one heard her. The bed started rolling along.

"I could be infected. My blood." Fear cut through her body. "I could be infected!" Still they could not hear. The bed took off. The blinding lights along the girders flashed by overhead. White coats swished past, silent as shadows in a dream. Only the hushing of fans and the scraping and singing of the bed's wheels against the concrete floor could be heard. "I've been stabbed with a goddamn syringe!" Maria tried to make eye contact with the auxiliary just as he was greeting a passing colleague. "I may have been infected with HIV!"

About Stockholm Text

We come from Scandinavia. We are progressive, yet serious. We are innovative, yet with strong traditions. We represent quality. We bring the best literature of the region to the world.

With a long season of cold and darkness, reading and writing have always been genuine traditions. Conditions, made to foster literary excellence. A natural home for the Nobel Prize in literature. It is no surprise that Scandinavian literature is now getting a global audience. Girls in long stockings or with dragon tattoos have already made amazing characters. Stockholm Text is ready to bring you the next generation.

For more information about Stockholm Text, please watch The Stockholm Text Story on www.stockholmtext.com.

www.stockholmtext.com